About the Author

Sydney Buhrow is a first-time, teenage author who was born and raised in the Dallas Fort Worth area. She was raised in a family of book lovers who started her into writing in the first place. Now she is working on her bachelors in English while continuing to write new and thrilling stories.

On the Dark Side

Sydney Buhrow

On the Dark Side

Olympia Publishers
London

www.olympiapublishers.com
OLYMPIA PAPERBACK EDITION

Copyright © Sydney Buhrow 2023

The right of Sydney Buhrow to be identified as author of this work has been asserted in accordance with sections 77 and 78 of the Copyright, Designs and Patents Act 1988.

All Rights Reserved

No reproduction, copy or transmission of this publication may be made without written permission.
No paragraph of this publication may be reproduced, copied or transmitted save with the written permission of the publisher, or in accordance with the provisions of the Copyright Act 1956 (as amended).

Any person who commits any unauthorised act in relation to this publication may be liable to criminal prosecution and civil claims for damage.

A CIP catalogue record for this title is available from the British Library.

ISBN: 978-1-80074-635-0

This is a work of fiction.
Names, characters, places and incidents originate from the writer's imagination. Any resemblance to actual persons, living or dead, is purely coincidental.

First Published in 2023

**Olympia Publishers
Tallis House
2 Tallis Street
London
EC4Y 0AB**

Printed in Great Britain

Dedication

I dedicate this book to my family who has listened to me say I'm writing for five years without question and to those friends who listened day after day to a plot that seemed to never end. Thank you all. I couldn't have done it without you.

Chapter 1

Lena sat on her bed in the dark grey light from the moon. Her fingers were calloused from lacing her boots every night as she was now. She glanced at a mirror across the room to see the blonde roots bright against her black hair, something to fix.

She finished lacing her boots with a flourish and grabbed her leather jacket from a chair on her way out. Lena had just tugged it over her shoulders when she heard movement from the hall behind her. Without hesitation, she drew a knife from a concealed pocket. She held it behind her, out of the light of a nearby window.

"What are you doing, Lena?" came Timmy's drowsy voice. "You know Mom doesn't like you being up so soon."

"I have work, Timmy. Go back to sleep. I'll be back to wake you up for school," Lena prompted gently, re-concealing the blade in her pocket.

He nodded with a yawn and retreated back to his room, rubbing his brown eyes sleepily as his brown hair lay unbrushed in a mat atop his head.

Lena watched him go before heading downstairs. She peeked into Mary's room to make sure she was still asleep and crept silently out the door.

She didn't have a car so walked briskly in the warm wind of late August. Lena hated these walks, knowing what was at the end of them. Just the thought of who she was meeting made the memory surge to the surface. Lena remembered it well as she relived it every morning on the way there.

Lena was six and young. Her mother had just left out of nowhere, and Lena was at the end of the driveway, waving unknowingly after her mother. John came sprinting down the driveway. His dirty blond hair was a mess in his brown eyes as he yelled, "Where did she go? Lena, where's your mother?"

Lena pointed after the now distant car. "Mommy went in that car with that man."

"You don't move," he bellowed with an anger Lena didn't understand at the time. He pulled out his phone and dialed a number Lena didn't care to see. "Alpha, he got her. He fucking got her." He paused, waiting for the response, and replied in a quieter but ever more serious voice, "You do that. I'll be going after her. You better be there when I arrive." Lena sat down and began playing with her fingers as if they were people; John looked down angrily at her as she played. He hung up and lifted her harshly to her feet. "You'll meet me here tomorrow at six in the morning. You hear?"

"Yes, Daddy."

"Don't call me that. There are clothes in the left side of the bed in my nightstand for you. Wear those, you hear?"

"Yes, Dad."

"I'm Spider or John or Sir from now on. Do you understand me, girl?"

Lena nodded with wide eyes and felt herself being released before John ran to the garage, got in a car, and drove away.

Lena shivered at the memory; she could still feel the baggy clothes on her small frame and feel that naïve excitement while waiting for her father, the fear she had felt when he had pulled up, covered in blood, and got out with a battered Mary, her mother.

She shook away the memory and quickened her pace so as to not be late. Lena nodded to the undercover guards loitering by the entrance as she arrived.

They nodded to her and went back to scrounging through the trash and pretending to sleep as though they were some of the various homeless in DFW.

Lena sighed as she opened the door to the brightly lit lobby. In all reality, it was just a piece of the circle, but it was the main entry door, so they called it the lobby out of habit.

Beta happened to be walking through the lobby and walked almost casually over to her. Beta was a bit shorter than Lena. Her own black hair was natural and swinging in its normal ponytail. Her dark eyes displayed her maternal worry. "He's on his way, Sparrow. If you need me after, I'll be with Hound in the lab."

Lena nodded and watched her walk away. John filled her gaze in an instant and she stood at attention, as though he were a drill sergeant. He may as well have been for how he treated her.

He glowered down at her and asked in his deep, commanding tone, "Where's your brother?"

"He's at college in New York until Thanksgiving, sir," Lena responded. She tried to hold eye contact but couldn't bring herself to. His brown eyes were too hard.

As she had expected, his hand hit her cheek at a force strong enough to knock her to the ground. She waited there for a moment before standing up again, feeling the hand-shaped bruise starting the form.

"You are to bring your younger brothers here tomorrow."

"But sir, school starts today, and they—" Her words stopped as another blow came from the other side, knocking her down yet again. Lena gritted her teeth from the pain in her face but did her best to hide the pain as she stood.

"You will bring them here. I didn't ask you. Just bring them, you weak girl." He spat at her before walking away. Lena felt the spit roll down her cheek and quickly wiped it away and walked off to a nearby gym to spend the next hour or so before returning back home.

She practiced her knife-throwing most; she enjoyed it the most, and John hated it, making her love it all the more. He viewed it as a weak form that was easily defended against. Lena had been practicing solely to disprove that theory.

Lena still had fantasies about throwing the knife at John after everything he had done to her through the years. She knew it was unlikely to ever happen, but it was a reward worth working toward.

Sean walked in. His typically military-cut black hair was longer than normal. Lena was sure it would be cut soon, though it didn't matter. She turned away from him; she hated when her squadron members saw her hurt. Lena was the leader of Squadron Thirteen; it should have been her aiding with his wounds and not the other way around, or so she thought it should be.

Sean knew that she hated it but ignored it and turned her so he could see; his dark brown eyes appraised her bruises as his hand left her arm. "Lena, what are letting him do to you?"

"It's not like I get a choice."

"You could fight back."

"And be actually killed? No way. If the twins were safe with my mother and away from John? Sure, every day. Not like this though." Lena sighed and turned back to the poster that was now in shreds.

"How much time do you got left before you have to get

home?"

"About fifteen minutes," Lena replied, slightly surprised by how much he was speaking, being a typically quiet man.

"Let's see what Katie can do for those bruises."

"It won't help."

"Lena, come on." His normally calm voice had turned stern.

She didn't care. She was his leader, after all. "No, you go on. I'm going to finish up here then head back."

"You can't live this way. Always being beaten to a pulp."

"I know that, but there's not another option right now." Sean shrugged in apparent defeat and walked away. "Thank you for checking with me," Lena called after him.

He waved back in acknowledgement. Lena threw another round of knives before leaving to go home.

Chapter 2

Lena arrived before dawn at the house to make breakfast and change into her school uniform. She was just dishing out the food when Mary came out of her room. Lena didn't bother trying to hide the hand-shaped bruises as they covered her entire face.

"What happened this time? A drug deal gone wrong? An abusive boyfriend?" Mary asked in apparent disgust, wrinkling her nose so thoroughly that her orchid-blue eyes seemed nearly hidden. She swiftly turned away from her daughter, brown hair swinging in an unnaturally curly mass.

"You have no right to ask. When do you leave to go on another business trip with your boyfriend? Today? Tomorrow? When do you go?" Lena shot back at her in disdain. She hated her mother nearly as much as her father.

"Tomorrow."

"When were you going to tell the twins?"

"Tonight, after work."

"Tell us what?" Dillon asked as he walked around the corner from the stairs. Now both of the twins looked the same as ever; no longer was their hair in a mat but was neatly combed. Timmy's was in a smooth combover, and Dillon's in a less styled pile. Timmy had always been more meticulous and quieter while Dillon was loud and excitable; it showed clearly just in the way of their hair, which Lena found so endearing.

"Mom's leaving again. Business, right?" Lena pretended to ask for the sake of her brothers.

Mary looked faintly grateful as she nodded. "It may be a

couple weeks before I manage to get back home. My boss is very… persistent."

"I bet he is," Lena muttered under her breath before pointing to their food. "You'd better eat. Mary, get them to school today. I've got something to do before school."

"I love you, Lena," Mary said quickly, almost as though trying to catch Lena off guard.

Lena didn't respond but went to kiss the twins atop their heads. Both smiled thanks as they stuffed their mouths with the eggs.

She left quickly after grabbing her bag. Lena drove the short distance to the high school and pulled at the front door. It was still locked. She rolled her eyes and went to the side to get in through the gym, which, for some reason, never got properly locked.

Lena logged into the front desk and printed off her schedule to see where she needed to go for her locker. It was simple enough to find as the sophomores got the second bank of lockers. They didn't know the school yet, it being their first year at the school, and the placement of these lockers at the front of the school made it easier for the staff. No need to point students to the lockers if the students had to walk past them or, at least, that was the idea.

She dropped off her things and went to sit outside her favorite teacher's classroom. He was kind and didn't question her bruises and cuts. Everyone just assumed she had abusive parents and didn't ask about it.

Just as usual, Mr. Prit was one of the first people there. Lena shouldn't have known him as she did. It was by way of Maxwell, her eldest brother, that she had met him. His hair had greyed considerably from when she first met him three years prior, in

Max's sophomore year. His once neat brown hair was more than sprinkled with grey hair, something Lena knew she was partially at fault for. He sighed and rolled his eyes when he saw her there. "I had really hoped that this would've stopped happening, Lena."

"Not really, sir. You had a good summer?" Lena asked as she stood up.

"Well, the kids got to go to a summer camp, so the wife and I got some time without them. That was nice."

"Good to hear, sir."

"How's Maxwell? He enjoying NYU?"

"Very much, anything to get away from the… family."

Mr. Prit nodded. He seemed to believe, just as her classmates, that they were abused, as her face would demonstrate, and Lena never denied the story. It bought her an unnecessary explanation. All she would have to say was 'the family', and everyone just nodded and went on with life. They weren't completely wrong; her father was abusive, except not in the same sense that everyone else said it.

There was once that CPS was called to investigate after a particularly trying time. They had arrived at her house to talk to Mary, spoken with teachers and classmates, and interviewed each of the children. There was no sign of abuse from her mother or any other people near the children, so the case was dropped even as the signs of abuse continued. It was really the work of TNT that the case mysteriously disappeared, though it was never forgotten by the caseworker.

Lena went to the back of the classroom and began to zone out, trying to figure out how to get out of taking the twins to TNT without being murdered. So far, nothing had struck her. Lena was hoping that they would ask to stay at Caleb's house as they so often did, though it was only a fleeting thought. His mother took care of them and didn't mind if it was a school night or not, as they would go to sleep about the same time as normal. She had extra school uniforms for them already and cared for them without a second thought.

Lena jumped as the bell rang, and she looked up to see that the class was full. To her disdain, Makenzie and Trevor were there. They were the popular kids. Head cheerleader and the quarterback for their football team. Once, Lena had been friends with Makenzie. That ended rather abruptly after Lena started turning up with visible bruises and cuts along her arms and face.

Makenzie couldn't be seen with someone like that. Trevor didn't much care. He seemed more prone to look back at her than the others though. Most averted their eyes and pretended that she didn't exist. Lena didn't mind him so much. She only hated him because he was with Makenzie, who was determined to stop anyone from talking to her, as though they would anyway.

They stood for the pledges and sat quietly for the moment of silence as the school day began.

Mr. Prit started class immediately after this, so the class was still relatively quiet. "Hello, class. Hopefully, you had a great summer." He deliberately didn't look at Lena. "We are starting this term with a project. Don't start groaning. I have assigned y'all partners to work with. Before I announce them, no, you may not change nor switch.

"You will be making a poster about a topic you remember from geometry last year. No addition nor subtraction skills. Rubrics will be passed out after you have partners. Okay…"

Lena stopped paying attention then and gazed out the window again. She was sure her partner would sit next to her but at the edge of the seat, as always. Sure enough, someone came over and sat next to her.

He didn't sit at the edge of the seat though; when she didn't turn, he poked her shoulder. She yelped as a bruise had blossomed there from her fall with John. Trevor looked apologetic as he retracted his arm. His normally shaggy brown hair was still damp from a shower and slicked back. His light brown eyes seemed to speak his words even before he said them. "Sorry, you didn't turn or react. I didn't—"

"I realize that," Lena said, cutting him off. "Could you not poke me next time though?" It was colder than she had meant but didn't correct it.

"Sure. Now, do you want to do this tonight at your place or what?"

"Not my place. Never my place. If we are to work together, it'll be at your house. Tonight's fine."

"Okay," he restarted awkwardly. "I have football practice so do you want to wait here for me, or do you want me to pick you up at your place, or do you want to walk to my place?"

"I can wait for you. Give me your cell number," Lena said briskly as she pulled out paper.

"You could've at least asked."

Lena raised her eyebrow at him, and he rolled his eyes back but didn't back down. "Fine, can I have your number?"

"Sure," he replied as though he had just been praised. He listed it off, and Lena wrote it down. She wrote her own as well and tore it off for him.

"My number may change so don't be confused."

"You getting a new phone? What type?"

"I get a 'new' phone every couple weeks," Lena replied with air quotes.

"What's that mean?"

"I can't explain. My dad insists."

"Oh, I didn't think you had a dad." He looked confused, and Lena started internally cursing herself.

"I, well, I don't have a normal dad. He's more of a sergeant that gives me jobs rather than being a real dad."

"Like chores?"

"I guess," Lena muttered, trying to think of a way out of the conversation. Instead, she ended up staring out the window again.

"Lena. Lena, you're zoned out again," Trevor prompted as he snapped his fingers in front of her face.

"Huh, oh yeah, sorry. What do you want to do the project on?"

The rest of the class was filled with the mundane conversation over the project: what topic to cover, how to go about it, making an outline. Lena took the notes, looking bored as she waited for the bell.

Lena let out a sigh of relief when the bell rang. To make the end of class even better, she distinctly heard Trevor tell Makenzie, "She isn't as bad as you've always said, you know."

"You just met her. You don't know how bad she really is." Her golden-brown eyes were cold as she spoke of Lena. It didn't seem to matter that they had once been friends.

"Oh really, okay. I guess you're right."

Lena felt disappointment but left for her next class before she could dwell on it any longer, though any joy she had found had been quickly dashed.

Chapter 3

Lena went through her usual routine during the day, though she ended it with a call to Mary. "Hey, I'm going to a friends' after school. Can you get the twins?"

"No, I had to leave early. I'm already at the airport. Be at our house, not theirs. You hear me?" Mary demanded.

"Why the hell should I?"

"Because the twins aren't responsible enough to be on their own."

"I'll see if they can go to Caleb's place tonight," Lena replied, mirroring her mother's attitude. She knew they couldn't because of their play later, but Mary wouldn't know that.

"No, they are to stay home. You need to be there with them."

"How would you know if they were responsible enough?" Lena accused. She was right, but Lena didn't care. "Why'd you leave early?"

"Reasons."

"You have your date wrong for your doctor's appointment?"

"What? How?"

"You underestimate me. Go have fun with your boyfriend. If you come home carrying a baby in a couple of months, then I'll take the twins. You'll never even know where they went."

Mary hung up, and Lena let out a growl of fury at her mother. "Who was that?" Trevor had appeared behind her.

"My mother. Turns out we have to go to my place after all. At least, she won't be there."

"Okay, I'll text Ma. Come on, I'll lead you to the field."

"I can't. I'll meet you there. I need to go get my little

brothers." Lena sighed as she shut her locker a bit harder than she had intended. It rattled, and Trevor stepped back.

"Okay, I'll see you at the field then."

Lena nodded, and they parted ways. It wasn't a long walk to get to the middle school. Just a couple blocks off. She met them outside the doors and smiled lightly at them. "Come on, guys. We're going to football practice."

"Why?" Timmy asked quickly.

"Is it because of a boy?" Dillon added, looking excited.

"Not in that sense of the word but yes. He's my class partner and I have to wait for him." Lena rolled her eyes at them; they laughed.

Along the way back to the high school, they explained their day and how Caleb had gotten to go to a ski lodge over the summer. Lena smiled at them and listened to their enthusiastic explanation.

They took a seat near the end of the stands, farthest from the cheer practice. Both twins raptly watched the football practice as they aspired to be on the team one day. Lena sat at the back and did homework though she looked up periodically to tell the twins to be a bit quieter. They didn't quiet down much though they did look back and apologize before returning to their cheering.

A few players looked over at them occasionally as they huddled and laughed to their friends about the small boys. After she completed all the homework she had, bar the poster, Lena began watching the practice. Apparently, earlier in the practice, they had decided it was hot, so rolled up their shirts to right under their chest plate.

Each of them had red stomachs from being tackled but seemed happy enough. Lena watched as Trevor ran the ball for a touchdown and shook her head at the twins' loud cheering. She had long since stopped trying to quiet them, so when he turned, Lena wasn't too surprised.

He waved, and Lena allowed herself a small wave back, but the twins stood up, waving their entire arm. Lena put a hand on either of their shoulders and shoved them back into a sitting position. "You stay seated, you hear?"

"Fine," they replied, grumpily sinking into the bleachers.

Lena reseated herself and watched as the coach called the team over. They spoke for a brief moment before breaking. Trevor ran over to Makenzie along the sideline quickly, then jogged over to Lena and the twins.

Makenzie looked appalled and went to talk to Angelica, her best friend. They stormed off the field together; their ponytails swung in almost perfect time together as though from an old-time movie. Lena had to hold back from laughing at them.

Lena turned and watched Trevor jog up the stairs with a smirk on her lips. The twins jumped up and started raving about the plays. Trevor laughed, and Lena rolled her eyes at them. "Shut up, boys. He doesn't care. He knows what plays he did. What's up, Trevor?"

"Well, I needed to let y'all know that I'll be back in a couple minutes after I get out of these rags."

"Okay, we'll be sitting here," Lena told him with a shrug.

"Okay, uh, bye." He ran back down the bleachers and caught up with his friend Alex.

As he had promised, he was back in ten minutes.

Dillon led the way back to the car, Timmy chasing after him. Lena walked after them, Trevor beside her. They didn't speak as Trevor tossed his bag into the back of the convertible.

Lena drove them home, speaking quickly. "Boys, don't forget about your play tonight. Y'all start getting ready, and I'll make dinner. Oh, Mary can't come."

"Why not?" Timmy asked, leaning forward, so his head was between Lena and Trevor.

"Business trip?" Dillon asked.

"Yep, she didn't say when she'd be home," Lena replied calmly, turning swiftly into the driveway and into the garage.

The four entered as a group before the twins ran off, yelling goodbye to Trevor. Lena watched them go before heading into the kitchen on her right. Trevor sat at the counter, and Lena hummed away as she worked. Dinner was done before Trevor looked up from his texted conversation with Makenzie.

"Boys!" Lena yelled upstairs. They yelled something indistinctly, and Lena took the food to the dining room. The boys met them there, hair still dripping down their backs from their showers. They wolfed down their food and ran back upstairs.

Lena and Trevor worked on the project for nearly half an hour without speaking more than a couple of words. She only stood up when she happened to glance at the clock. "I have to go make a call. I'll be right back."

Trevor nodded, gluing down a paper.

Lena walked away into the office outside of Mary's room. She dialed up Maxwell and sat down.

"Hey, sis," Max answered quietly.

"He wants to take the twins, Max."

"When?"

"Tonight."

"You know your options. I'm sorry, but I can't help you from here."

"I know. I needed to hear it though," she said, a note of desperation entering her voice.

"I understand. I'm so sorry, Lena. I love you. Call me when you get home. I'll wait for you."

"Don't bother. I'll just call in the morning. Love you, too. Don't forget you still have college classes no matter why you're there."

"I'll wait."

"No, Max. Just sleep. I'll be fine."

Lena returned to the dining room to work more on the project. The twins eventually called downstairs for help, and the pair went upstairs where the twins were waiting, Trevor trailing behind.

Chapter 4

Lena tossed Trevor one of John's suits, which still hung in her mother's closet after they were done helping the twins find their costumes. "Go change in the bathroom. I'll be changing in my room."

Trevor started to protest before shutting his mouth and walking to the bathroom, deciding it wasn't worth the effort. Lena went to her bedroom upstairs and grabbed a dress. It was red and sparkled on the bodice. She found a length of black ribbon and tied it about her waist. Quickly, she slipped on some plain black heels that were masked by the sheer length of the dress.

Lena grabbed at some obsidian jewelry that Mary had given her as a bribe to stop her from telling the twins about her first abortion. She put on makeup more carefully than she had the rest of the ensemble, finally covering the dark bruises.

Her hair remained the same black mop it had been all day, and Lena rolled her eyes, going back into the bathroom. She brushed it out carefully and tied it into a black bun with a ruby comb she found in a drawer. The roots still shone through, but there was nothing to be done about that yet.

She walked out of her room to see Timmy trying to fix Trevor's tie at the top of the stairs. He had clearly come upstairs for help with it, though Timmy was hardly any better than he. Lena took the tie and tightened it calmly. "Come on, we're going to be late."

They went quickly downstairs and back out to the car. Lena

drove briskly, and, a few times, she glanced over to see Trevor holding onto the seat for stability. She rolled her eyes, but a smirk creased her lips.

Lena got the twins backstage just in time for the show, with much griping from the staff. She met Trevor at their seats, him sitting in what was supposed to be Mary's seat.

"So, when did they start here?" he asked, looking around at all of the suited men and bejeweled women.

"When they were about seven, the production needed some child actors for a show, so I got Mary to take them to auditions. They got the part and have been in ever since."

"They let them take the costumes?"

"Sometimes. This one is run by their friend's dad, so he doesn't mind so much."

"Oh," he replied simply.

They remained silent until intermission when they stood up to go get some food. Lena's phone rang. "I'll meet you at the seats," Lena told Trevor. Her voice was troubled, but he didn't want to ask. The last ten years of not talking to her still held its place.

"What, John?" He heard her say in the distance.

A long pause before she sounded pleading. "No, please. I just need time. No, you don't—" Another pause. "I'll be there." She looked over and saw Trevor listening. Her eyes widened a little, and she skittered away. Lena didn't return until the show had already resumed.

"Hey, sorry about—" Trevor started.

"Never speak of that conversation," Lena told him in a harsh whisper.

"Who's John?"

"I said don't."

"Boyfriend?"

"I said don't," Lena growled.

"Uncle?" Lena left. He went after her. "Who is he?"

"Will you drop it?"

"Who is he?"

"I said to drop it. You don't have the right to ask about it. You don't know me. You don't know my family. I asked you to drop it, and now I'm telling you to drop it. God damn it. We're going to go back in there as though nothing happened for the twins. God, just leave it be," Lena sputtered out, more emotional than Trevor had intended.

Trevor persisted. "Who is he?" Even he wasn't sure why he cared; it wasn't like they were friends. They were hardly even acquaintances.

"I will leave you here, boy."

"Why won't you just answer?"

"Because you don't deserve an answer. I haven't even told those boys out there let alone a boy I've spoken to once."

"Who?" His temper rose every time she said boy. "Why would it matter if they knew?"

"God damn it. That's my father. Is that what you wanted to hear? The man that left my family for the shithole? The man that left my mother for her to become a fucking whore? Is that what you wanted to hear?" Lena yelled at him.

"No."

"I didn't either," Lena said in a quiet voice, walking away.

They didn't speak until later that night when she showed him his room back home. His mother cleared it after Lena played a convincing role of Mary, telling her how Trevor had passed out on the couch while working. "You can stay in Max's room."

"I'm sorry."

"Don't bother."

She started upstairs, but Timmy stopped her by his room, down the hall from where Trevor was staying.

"Are you going out again tonight?" he asked softly, hoping that Trevor wouldn't hear. His eyes were big, too young even in seventh grade to understand why she was leaving.

"I have to, Timmy."

"Please don't go."

"I have to. I'll be home in the morning before you wake up."

"Dillon and I, we'll come after you."

"No, you won't, Tim. You know better. You'll stay here with Trevor. He'll protect you both tonight."

"Please don't go."

"I love you, Timmy. I'll see you when you wake up." Lena kissed the top of his head and walked upstairs.

Trevor walked into his room before Timmy could see that he had been listening.

Lena went and changed out of her dress and into her uniform for TNT. She stopped at her door and rested her head against it lightly, avoiding the bruised portions of her face. Lena didn't want to go. She knew her beating today would be worse than yesterday and any that week.

She left and silently closed her door. Lena slunk quietly downstairs, checking that all the doors were shut tight before she left. She called Hound outside the door, Trevor listening on the other side as he had exited his room after he had heard her close the front door.

"Hound, I need you to come by my house. The boys need someone here... thank you. I'll see you soon."

Chapter 5

Bianca arrived shortly, and Lena met her at the door. "Can we talk for a minute?" Bianca asked, gesturing inside.

"Of course," Lena replied quietly as she pushed open the door. Trevor dived out of the way but nearly knocked over a vase and made quite the racket. "Trevor, for heaven's sake. Go to bed."

He stood up, blushing and stammering, "Oh, I didn't see— Why are you—Who's your friend?" He rubbed the back of his neck in embarrassment.

"Hound, meet Trevor. He doesn't follow orders well."

"It's Holley," Bianca lied easily, reaching out to shake his hand.

He gratefully shook it, though he wouldn't meet either of their gazes. Her brown hair and black eyes were common features for many around his school. Even her heart-shaped face was a commonality, yet there was something about her that he couldn't quite place. He felt a tinge of familiarity from Bianca, as though he had seen her before, though he couldn't place it, so shook off the feeling.

"Go to bed, Trevor," Lena sneered angrily.

"No, I want to know what's happening," he retorted, still not meeting her gaze. Trevor couldn't say why he didn't just go.

"Doesn't follow anything," Lena muttered in frustration.

"Trevor, follow her orders. You don't want to endanger your family, do you?" Bianca asked sweetly.

"I won't go." He met her gaze, and Bianca smiled.

"I suppose I need to show you something right quick." She

pulled her gun and cocked it at him. "Go to bed, boy."

He jumped and fell backward, actually knocking over the vase with a crash. Lena pushed her gun down. "God damn it. Now we have to explain at least a little bit. You can't just do that to him."

"Why not? Just a little scare," she whined, uncocking the gun and hiding it away again.

Trevor started to say something but then closed his mouth again. He pointed between them and continued opening and closing his mouth.

Lena looked toward the twins' room, then at Hound. "Stay with the boys. We'll be back."

She nodded and walked away from them, going to grab a dustpan for the shattered glass. Trevor pointed at Bianca. "Holley isn't her real name, is it?"

"Let's go, Lynx."

"Lynx?" he called after her as she walked out the front door.

"Everyone has a code," Lena informed him as she got in her car.

He got in the passenger seat, asking, "What's yours?"

"Sparrow. I've always been Sparrow."

"Why?"

"John chose it."

"Oh, what about the twins?" He decided to ignore the mention of John again that night.

"They don't have one," Lena told him sharply, adding quietly, "And they never will, if I can do anything about it."

They were quiet upon arrival, and Lena put a finger to her lips, telling him to be silent. They exited the car and jogged around back. Lena smiled as he pointed to a sign warning of an electric fence.

"You afraid of a little danger?" Lena whispered.

"Never," Trevor replied, his voice cracking.

Lena's smile faded into a smirk at the break in his confidence. She knew the fence was never actually connected; the sign actually being more of a prop than anything else. Lena held up a loose section of fence, and he crawled under. She followed suit and led him to a back section of garden filled with delicate blue flowers.

Trevor was too fascinated by the flowers to notice Lena melting into the night. He looked up to speak to her and noticed that she was gone.

"Lena?" he whispered into the black gardens.

"Why do you care about my life, who I am, my family?" came her angered voice from behind him.

He turned but, again, she disappeared. "What do you mean? You're the one that brought me here."

"You ask questions. Why?"

Another quick turn. "Because you're interesting?" She didn't reply, and so he went on to say, "You're unlike the other girls. Can you come out?"

"No. Why didn't you just let me do the project and move on with your life?" her anguished whisper came from above him, and he looked up.

In the moonlight, he could see her figure sitting on a branch above. "Because that isn't how I earn my grades."

Lena gave up on getting the answers she wanted and hopped down in front of him. "You know the way to my house. I'll be back by morning."

He watched her go, bemused, and confused. "Goodnight to you, too." She was long gone.

Chapter 6

The drive was cold and short. It should've taken longer, but with the pain of death looming, her nerves sped the typical pace.

Beta stood outside with Alpha. Each was in their uniforms of leather jackets and bandanas. Beta had pulled back her hair as usual, but Alpha's flaming red hair made no attempt to be tamed. "Hound will stay at your house 'til morning. I'm sorry, Sparrow," he told her. His green eyes spoke the sorrow of his words.

It bothered Lena that they didn't take back the posts that were rightfully theirs, the leadership they were born and married into, but didn't voice it. After all, if this were their last talk, then there was no point in tainting it.

"I'd best go, thank you." Lena went past them without a goodbye and pushed open the doors.

She stood at attention in the lobby like area awaiting the looming footsteps. Eventually, they came with a slow click. Lena clasped her hands in front of her to contain the shaking. She felt the tears starting and held them back. She wouldn't cry tonight.

"Well, you're alone. No brothers for me?"

"No, sir. They're safe tonight."

"Unlike you. Follow me." He strode back the way he had come. Lena followed at a respectable distance and felt the fear absorb her.

That room had meant pain since she was very young. No one ever openly questioned it and took a long way around to avoid it during the night.

"Stand in the middle," John ordered.

Lena followed his directions as she always did. She vividly remembered the night she had refused. She hadn't awoken for two days after, and Mary nearly killed her upon arrival back home. She wouldn't do that again, not with Mary gone.

His fist hit her in the gut, hard enough to send her flying backward onto the ground. Lena grunted and felt tears sting her eyes and pushed them back. Not today, never again. She went back to the middle of the room, the new bruise throbbing and pulsing with every accelerated heartbeat.

"Brave tonight, are you?"

"Anything to keep the twins away from you," Lena snarled.

A punch hit the side of her head, and she crumpled. Lena spat out some blood but didn't cry.

An hour passed this way, John doing everything but kill her. Lena didn't cry even as she felt her nose snap and leg pop. It hurt more than usual and made her incapable of walking. Breathing was just as hard, but she fought not to show it.

John left saying, "I have a meeting during the day tomorrow. You best bring the twins tomorrow night."

"Never," Lena spat. He ignored her and left the room.

Beta ran in once he was gone and tried to pick her up. "Oh, honey."

"I can do it," Lena gasped as Beta tried to pick her up. "Move, please." Her vision was blurry, and she shook from the effort of standing.

"Alpha, get in here," Beta yelled into the hall.

"Sparrow," Alpha sighed as he took her other side.

"I'm fine."

"He didn't, uh, r—" Beta started.

"Never," Lena hissed. "He wouldn't go that far. I'm still his daughter, after all," she added.

They helped drag her to the ward where Aloe and Crow were already prepping a room.

"Sparrow," Katie nearly screamed. Her blue-green eyes were so expressive that it pained Lena more to see them hurting for her.

Aloe had helped so many times with her injuries that she had already tied back her blonde hair but never one of these nights, and never did it seem easier for those around her to help.

"I'm fine. You're all overreacting." Lena tried sitting down and cried out in pain.

"Yeah, overreacting," Crow muttered, brushing her own black hair from her eyes as she appraised Lena's wounds and centered in on one.

"Can you call Max?" Lena asked as Crow started on her leg, and Katie mopped up the blood pouring from her nose.

Beta went into the hall to dial him. She returned; Max sounded worried. "Lena, what happened? Are you okay?"

"I'm fine. I wanted to tell you that I kept the twins away from here."

Katie retorted, "Definitely not fine. I don't call any of this fine."

"Lena, what happened?"

Crow reported, "Broken nose, bruised leg, large abdominal bruises, broken rib, and cuts and lacerations everywhere."

Max sighed, "Lena, I don't want you there. Please, don't go back."

"He'll come for me, for sure, then. You know that. Remember when you tried running and what happened to me then?"

Lena could practically feel his wince through the phone. "I'm sorry."

"It isn't your fault that I look like Mary."

"Why do you insist on calling her Mary?"

"She's seeing another guy, Max. I think she's pregnant again."

"I'm sorry, Lena. I have to go. You know my mission here. I think that her first class starts soon."

"Call tonight."

"I will. Love you, sis."

"Love you too, Hawk."

Beta hung up the phone. "Why do you insist on trying to not tell him?"

"He worries," Lena reminded her.

"We all worry for you. You know that." Katie looked seriously at her. Her expression was more expressive than Lena would've liked.

"He doesn't worry as much if he doesn't know everything. It makes me feel better that way."

"Done," Crow whispered, finishing wrapping her ribs. The cuts on her arm had been roughly cleaned though they were less important.

"What time is it?" Lena asked, looking around.

"Nearly four," Alpha said, glancing at his watch.

"Fuck, I need a ride home."

"I'll take you," Beta said with a sigh.

They walked silently out to the garage, Lena on crutches, which she'd drop soon enough.

"Who's Trevor?" Beta asked quietly.

"Hound," Lena said exasperatedly, clearly she had been on call with her daughter.

"He's someone from school."

"And?"

"He's someone that needs to know what's happening here. If he doesn't, then he'll ask questions to the wrong people."

"Lynx now, is he?"

"John can't know."

"I wouldn't dream of it."

"He's annoying with how many questions he asks," Lena told her as they drove down the dimly lit street.

"That's how Michael was when we met. He asked about everything. I hated it. Luckily, I didn't have much to tell."

"Hopefully, he doesn't ask this morning."

"Well, we're here, so you better get to wishing."

"I'll get Hound for you."

"Thank you, Sparrow. I'll see you tonight."

"Bye, Beta."

Hound walked out the front door as Lena limped up. "Thank you, Hound."

Hound hugged her gently, releasing without question upon Lena's gasp and nodded. "Whenever you need me. That boy is calling for trouble."

"I have to tell him."

"I thought you might say that. I filled him in on a lot of things while you were gone. He won't be found by John though if I can help it. I'll try and erase him for you. It won't be easy though with your assignment and all."

"I don't deserve you."

She chuckled warily and waved goodbye.

Chapter 7

A fresh school uniform was sitting on the end of Trevor's bed when he awoke the next morning. A smell of waffles filled the air; he dressed quickly for the waffles.

He went into the kitchen to see Lena limping around the kitchen. "Are you okay?"

"Morning," she said in a quiet voice, not turning and definitely not answering the question. "Do you want a waffle?"

"Of course, I'm starving."

"Here you are." Lena set a waffle in front of him and didn't make eye contact as he saw her bruised and cut face, a bandage across the bridge of her nose.

"What the hell happened to you?"

"Language." Her phone rang, and Lena jumped at the chance to leave the conversation. "Hello?"

A lengthy pause ensued. "Thanks for letting me know. See you in four months, Mary."

She put down the phone and let out a muffled scream of frustration, which ended in a cough and a muffled cry. Lena picked up the phone again and dialed a new number. Trevor found it strange that she didn't care about him hearing the confidential conversations any more.

"Alpha, I need a favor. Yes, I'm fine. Please, just listen." A pause. "Yes, okay. I need someone to go find Mary and keep an eye on her. She is having Tulsi's baby. A girl. Also, I need someone to watch the twins around the clock now. Yes, I'll meet her. Thank you so much. I'll see you tonight... keep me updated."

Lena hung up, and Trevor thought better of asking about what had happened, yet still felt the need to fill the silence. "Can I ask you a question?"

"Shoot." A flicker of a smile played on her lips as though she had just told him a joke.

"Uh, why don't you get along with Makenzie?"

"Oh um, let's see. She thinks I abandoned her and that I wasn't a good friend. I honored her wishes and left her alone and she thought I was teasing her. Now she blames me for anything that goes wrong in her life." Her voice never rose as though it were a report for class. She looked like she had something else to say but stopped herself.

"What else?"

"It's not important."

"Then say it."

"You don't want to know."

"I think I should know."

"You should know by now. How you don't know baffles me," she said, still deflecting.

"Know what?"

"That she... no. Nope, not doing it."

"Tell me, Lena," Trevor pleaded.

"Fine, you asked, not me." She rose her hands as though in surrender, murmured a curse and dropped her arms. Her hand rested on her ribs as she spoke. "She's been cheating on you for the last two years or so with some kid from another district. They aren't very good at hiding it."

"What?" He looked confused both about her words and actions.

The twins ran in. "Food!" they yelled.

Lena grabbed some waffles and set them in front of them,

never extending her arms far.

"She's...wait. How?"

"I shouldn't have to lay this out for you." Lena started to explain, but her phone rang again. "One second."

Lena walked out of the room. "Raven, what's up?"

"I'm outside."

Lena hung up. She walked back out of the hall and to the front door. "Hello, Raven."

"Lena, I haven't seen you in forever!" She squealed. Her eyes were passive, which made Lena laugh.

"Come in. Trevor, get over here and meet my friend." He wandered over and shook her hand, obviously distracted.

Sam didn't look much more trustworthy than Lena ever did. Her long red hair was pulled back into a black baseball cap. She wore some ripped jeans and a black shirt. It was simple enough, but her green eyes were hard as stone, and her lips were in a forced smile that said, "One wrong move and I will literally kill you."

Trevor, reasonably, kept his distance. The twins, however, dragged her over to the counter, saying, "Do you want waffles?"

Sam looked perplexed by how passive they were in dealing with Lena's injuries. "Lena, may I speak to you for a second?"

"Of course. Boys, you finish eating. I'll be back in a second to send you on your way. Raven will take you to school today." Lena looked seriously at them, and they nodded and sat.

They heard Timmy and Dillon questioning, the still distracted Trevor all the way down the hall.

"What am I protecting them from?"

"John and anyone that may come from the Tunnel Snakes. I need help watching them and can't when I'm at school."

"Another thing—have they asked about your injuries?"

"They don't ask any more. They don't want the answer anyway. I'm sure they care, just don't want to know, just like Hawk doesn't. They know it's not the truth anyway. They're not idiots."

"Trevor knows?"

"He's being brought in silently. John won't ever know if I can help it. Hound is helping with that." She artfully avoided the question. Sam noticed but didn't mention it.

"That makes me feel a little bit better."

"Come on; I don't want them to be late."

The twins were listening to Trevor with rapt attention. He was surely telling them all of the secrets to getting on the football team in high school.

"Hey, boys. You've got to go. If you want, tonight you can stay at Caleb's house if it's okay with his mom," Lena informed them.

They nodded vigorously. "Thank you, Lena." Dillon hugged her goodbye while Timmy just waved as he ran to the car.

"Thank you, Raven. Call me if anything happens," Lena yelled after them, regretting it immediately, though tried not to show it.

"Nothing will happen. They'll be perfectly fine."

"Goodbye," Lena said with a faint smile.

Trevor finished his waffle as the door shut. "I'm going to break up with her."

"She can't know it was me," Lena replied, switching back to the conversation without hesitation.

"She won't."

"Yes, she will. Oh well, she can't do anything else to me. At least, nothing new…"

Trevor felt the tension in the room thicken and nodded.

"Yeah, um, you ready to go?"

"Can you drive?"

"Sure. Keys?"

Lena grabbed them from him as she picked up her school bag. "Let's go."

They didn't talk during the car ride, and Lena waited for Trevor to have entered the school before checking her bandages. Each bandage was a light pink, and Lena grimaced. It was going to be a long day.

Chapter 8

Lena sat at the back of class as usual and rolled her eyes as girls practically fell over Trevor. He sat next to her, and Lena ignored him for the majority of class, looking out the window.

"I'm ending it during passing period."

"Oh, fun. May I join?" Lena asked, trying to seem as though she hadn't been dozing off. She hadn't slept at all that night; while not an uncommon experience, it continued to be a nuisance.

"I thought you didn't want her to know you were a part of it?"

"I've changed my mind. I love seeing her uncomfortable."

Trevor shifted a little. He obviously still wasn't comfortable with the idea of being single for the first time in four years, nor was he comfortable with Lena's enjoyment of his breakup.

The bell rang, and Lena followed behind Trevor closely. She managed to hide in the crowd easily enough and listened as Trevor walked up to Makenzie.

"Babe, why didn't you answer any of my texts this morning?" she asked with a pout.

Lena chuckled as Trevor started. "I don't think this is working for us. I think we should see other people."

"What? Why?"

"Because you're a cheating bitch," Lena chipped in. Lena stood next to Trevor, and he put his arm around her shoulders. It made her ribs burn though she didn't show it, and he didn't move.

"Excuse me. Who are you to speak? Stay out of this,"

Makenzie threatened.

"Why? What are you going to do?"

"This is your fault, isn't it?" Makenzie accused her, venom practically dripping off her words. "And who are you to talk about cheating?"

"No, that's your fault," Trevor told her. "She just helped me see the light. Unlike you, we didn't go behind your back for years."

"Thanks?" Lena said, questioning his word choice. She didn't like how tight his arm had gotten, pressing into her ribs even more. "Let's get to class," Lena said through teeth gritted in pain.

"Okay, babe."

They left, and once they were out of sight, Lena slapped him. "Fuck you."

"Ow, what was that for?"

"Don't babe me and don't touch me," Lena warned him. She slipped up her sleeve and checked the stitches from a week prior though this was merely for his benefit; it was her ribs that needed attention. Spots of blood were at the surface and had stained her sleeve. "Ow, damn it."

He looked sorry and started to apologize.

"Lena! You look great!" came a sarcastic yell from down the hall.

"Allison, you're not dead! You haven't called. Why?"

"It was a surprise. Also, don't ever call me Allison. Like ever."

Lena chuckled and nodded. Allie held out her arms for a hug, and Lena shook her head. "Not today."

"Are you seriously that injured?"

"When am I not?"

"True that. Who's he?" Allie gestured to Trevor.

"Allie Hill, meet Trevor Stephens, the idiot that was assigned to help on the math assignment."

"Nice to meet you, idiot assigned to the math assignment. I'm cousin to this one." Trevor chuckled at the introduction and nodded to her, taking in her short black hair and Mexican ethnicity, clearly marked by her ever-tanned skin and a comment Trevor vaguely remembered from years before that Lena had made about her cousin.

"What's your next class, Delphina?" Allie asked in a quick revenge.

Lena shivered, and all humor left her at the mention of her real name. "Tech. Come on."

"Me too," Allie smirked.

They chatted calmly on the way to class, and all three sat in a row together behind the computers lined up upon the tables. The assignment was projected up on the board, and everyone was chatting loudly as they chose seats. Trevor and Lena got many looks as they sat together, and Lena glared at them all. Some were Trevor's friends, though he pretended not to notice.

She started quickly on the assignment, rolling her eyes at the simplicity of it. Write an essay in a specific format about your summer, nothing to actually do with technology. Lena finished quickly, making up some stuff about the summer. No one wanted to know about her real summer.

She submitted it a few minutes after class started and went on to her own project: finding who Makenzie was cheating with this time.

"Oh no, who are you stalking today?" Allie whispered.

"How can you stalk anyone without social media?" Trevor asked, glancing up.

"He doesn't know yet?" Allie asked, bemused.

"I do have social media. I'm actually friends with you and Makenzie."

"What? No, you're not," Trevor accused, looking between Lena and Allie.

"Yes, I am. Did you seriously not recognize Hound?"

"He met Hound? He's working his way in," Allie noted on the side.

"I thought she was just a recognizable person. Why?" He ignored Allie, choosing to focus on Lena instead. This must explain her familiarity, but there was a nagging in the back of his mind that there was more. It was a nagging that would remain for years.

"Because she is me. I am her. We are Kayla Brown."

"Wait, what?" Trevor sat back in his chair to take a moment and looked baffled.

"Yeah, anyway. Hunting time. Let's see what you've got on your secret account, Makenzie," Lena muttered to herself.

After a few moments of light stalking, Lena muttered to herself, "Oh, you are so dead, Monkey. So dead."

"Who is Monkey?" Allie asked.

Lena gestured to the kid on the screen. "That ass hat. I'll be back for lunch."

She shut down her computer quickly and put on a worried face, hurrying up to the teacher. "Coach, my brother just got injured during PE. My mom isn't home to go get him. May I get an office pass?"

"Of course, one second, Lena." She opened a drawer and wrote her a note. Lena left, and Allie smirked.

"How does she do that?" Trevor asked.

Allie finished her assignment and moved over a chair. "She

is just smooth as hell and this teacher isn't the brightest. Finish so I can get us out too."

Trevor finished faster with that motivation, and Allie walked up to the Coach. "Ma'am, I'm new here. May I get help finding my locker and next class from Trevor?"

"Of course…"

"Allie," she supplied

"Allie. Mr. Stephens, come up here, please." They were out within the minute.

Lena surpassed the office and left, heading for TNT. The gang was pretty subdued during the day. A few people nodded to her, and Lena stopped one. "Lion, you room with Monkey, right?"

"Yes, ma'am." He was in Squadron One with Beta and Alpha and knew about her predicament. Most of Squadron One was kind to her, unlike the majority of TNT. He, especially, was kind, helping her when Alpha and Beta were both out, though only out of obligation. Lena didn't mind even so.

"Do you know where he is?"

"I'm pretty sure he's still sleeping."

"Thank you, Lion."

"It's no problem, ma'am."

Lena ran off, hoping not to run into John anywhere. Sean was just leaving the barracks as she ran up. "Oh, hey, Bear."

"Sup, Sparrow?" He didn't smile much and was a pretty cool-tempered person, which continued to now, even as his eyes flicked yet again to more injuries with a shake of his head.

"Is Monkey still in there?"

"Yep, as is Mountain."

"Can you get that cat out?"

"I'll do my best. It'd be best if he never heard you call him a cat though."

"I know," Lena chuckled. Mountain Lion was a bad-tempered guy with red-brown hair. He was small but impressively good with knives.

"Mountain, get up, man."

"Fuck off."

Sean lifted him up with ease, and he snared loudly. "Get off me."

"Run along, Kitty," Lena said as he passed.

He glared at her, saying, "Run along, Birdie."

"I'd shut it if I were you," Sean warned, shoving him a little to get him to move.

"I'm going, bully."

"Oh, kitty got claws," Lena pestered him gently.

"I'm going. I'm going. No chill from either of you." He ran off to find some of his own squadron.

"Bye, Sparrow. I have to go meet Aloe. Don't kill my bunk mate in the room, please," Bear told her.

"Noted. See you later."

He left her alone with the yet sleeping boy.

"Wakey, wakey," Lena said as she prodded Monkey awake.

"Leave me alone," he grumbled.

"What were you doing dating someone from a different gang?"

"What?" He was suddenly wide awake and standing, long brown ponytail, monkey tail, more like, swinging from the back of his head. It gave him a skater kind of look, which wasn't uncommon around TNT, though more had the bodyguard build after the rigorous training provided by the various squadron leaders.

"You heard me. Break it off. You're lucky I didn't tell anyone for the last few years because I didn't care enough it find out it was you. Now you have to break it off."

"Says who?"

"Says me."

"You aren't even a Rank-One. You can't tell me anything."

"I'll duel you for it."

"You win; I break it off. I win; you don't tell anyone," Monkey said, rubbing any remaining sleep from his eyes.

Lena smirked. "Okay, let's go."

They left, walking alongside each other. They ran into a few people and, as was the rules, informed them of the duel. Each ran off to alert everyone, and so everyone knew by the time they reached the arena.

John stood at the podium, prepared to start the duel. Everyone settled, and Lena dropped her weapons at the entrance with Hound, who was smiling. "This'll be fun."

John's voice echoed over the speakers. "No weapons. No killing. No maiming. What are we dueling for?" He sounded bored and looked toward Monkey.

Lena replied loudly, "If I win, I become a Rank-One member. If I lose, then I lose all ranking and go down to five."

John looked excited at the prospect and nodded. "Then, with that exciting proposition, let us begin."

Monkey seemed perplexed by the large stakes that didn't rely hardly at all on him. They circled until he made the first move. She knocked him down with a simple sweep under his legs.

He was flailing and spluttering in a blind rage, and Lena cat-called, "You okay, Chimp? It looks like you fell from your tree."

He jumped up. He got his name from his ability to move quickly, but Lena got hers from her swift movement and knowledge. Monkey aimed for her gut, and Lena moved aside, slapping him on the ass as he passed. "You missed."

They continued this way for several minutes until he was done making the first move and being knocked on his face. As they had circled several times, Lena ran straight, and he spread his legs, ready to jump. She dived at the last second, bracing for the impact on her ribs. He froze, and Lena punched up hard. He crumpled into a fetal position, and everyone winced.

John looked outraged but nodded. He yelled, anger filling his voice. "Sparrow, you are promoted to Rank-One." He walked away.

Lena smiled and went to the hall to collect her things and get back to school. "That was fun."

"Nice reach there," Alpha congratulated her. "Though I must say, that hurt me just watching it."

"He won't be messing with anyone for a while now."

"Or having children," Aloe laughed. "Your wounds clean still?"

"Yes, Aloe. I'll let you check them again tonight but for now I need to get back to school."

"You go get straight A's," Aloe cheered playfully.

"Thanks, Mom."

It was a few nights later that Lena had another squadron meeting. It was held in the Squadron Thirteen room, which was, more precisely, a bedroom for them to pass out in and around after missions. For now, it was filled by the members of Thirteen.

Sara, or Badger, lay sprawled across the ratty, old couch. Her hair was spiking toward the floor as her head was off the couch, making her already spiky hair all the sharper. The one red streak toward the front was fading to pink yet again, something they'd fix tonight at the same time they fixed Lena's hair. It looked nice, though it was something no one would mention for their fear of her wrath and her electric blue eyes piercing into their soul.

Tyler perched upon the foot of the same couch. His own brown hair fell to his eyes in greasy wings, the same color as his eyes. He was about the only one that didn't fear Sara's wrath, making him a definite asset on the squadron.

Sean and Katie took to the head of the bed, leaning against one another in their unofficially dating way. Technically, they weren't supposed to date, yet Lena didn't mind, and it only improved their teamwork rather than diminishing it.

Lena had taken the foot of the bed, leaving the armchair empty as it was where Max had normally resided during these meetings when he wasn't away at NYU.

"Okay, y'all. We need to fix the training schedule. Classes have restarted for me," Lena told them, though they all knew already.

Sean scoffed at her reasoning. His reaction wasn't taken lightly by any of the members of Thirteen; he never reacted that way openly. It made Sara lift her head back onto the couch to look at him. "What was that about?" she asked, her words dripping with attitude.

"Oh, so we're all going to act like nothing is wrong. Fine," Sean snipped back. He turned back to Lena, speaking more to her than the rest. "Spider is beating her worse than two years back and more often too, or is that something we don't need to know about?"

Lena glared at him and didn't reply. Tyler spoke instead. "Is that true, Sparrow? Has it become that bad again?"

Her jaw tightened as she was forced into a reply. "Yes, it is. I have more pressing concerns, however—"

"What could possibly be more pressing?" Katie interjected. "Trevor, Lynx."

Sara and Tyler looked confused between one another. "Are we missing something? When did he become that? Isn't he...?"

"Lena has a boyfriend," Katie replied, not looking away from Lena as she spoke.

Lena turned red, though she didn't avert her gaze. She was the leader here, and she needed to get this under control. "That doesn't matter. What matters is John doesn't know that I've gotten this close to him."

"It's been years, Lena. This isn't safe. Hide him away or kill him," Tyler said with a shrug.

Everyone turned to stare at him. Sara kicked him from his seat on the couch. He yelled as he quickly caught himself. Katie was the one to actually speak, though. "You dumbass, that's her forever crush. She's not gonna kill him. If she intended to go through with the assignment, she would've by now."

Tyler didn't reply to that. Lena did instead. "He's not gonna die. He's going to join TNT. I need your help to do it though."

They planned his gradual integration as Katie fixed up her ribs once again. They continued to talk out scenarios as her hair was dyed. It took the rest of the night, meaning another sleepless night for Lena and another day of micro-naps, but it was worth it.

Chapter 9

A few weeks passed; Lena met Trevor's friends and relaxed a little as her ribs and other wounds healed. John's beatings had been less after his initial anger. He was away on vacation for a week, which actually meant that he was off at some mafia making deals and having affairs.

Trevor managed to get her to agree to go on a date at some point to be determined. For now, they were spending time together with Lena showing him how to handle guns and knives. He was fully emersed in TNT living. He had met all of Squadron Thirteen as they stopped by the house and convinced his mom that they were studying, so he could hang out nearly every night after school.

Lena had shown him to a hidden room behind the mirror in the main hall of her house. It was outfitted as a practice room. Dummies and targets and weapons littered the floor. The walls were fully soundproof and made it fairly easy to hide from the twins.

Today, they were working on knife throwing, and Lena had let slip about an assignment during a conversation.

"What assignment?" Trevor asked quickly.

"Come here, let me show you the symbol I just got back from Monarch yesterday."

"Lena, what assignment?"

Her cheeks reddened, and she shook her head, eyes down. "It's not important. Come look. I got your gun and blades engraved yesterday as well."

"Lena." He moved closer to look but wasn't giving up. She set the things down and twirled her own knife in her hand.

"You see knives are—"

"Tell me."

"No."

"Why not?" he asked sharply.

"Because it was to kill you. Damn it, Trevor." Lena dropped her knife and picked it up clumsily. Her mind wasn't so sharp around him any more. Her eyes focused on his body rather than conversation, leading to slips like this.

"Wait, what?" He backed up and looked apprehensively toward the knife in her hand.

"I got it a week ago. You would've already been dead if I intended to kill you."

"Why me?"

"John said it was because he harbored a grudge on your dad. It's actually because he knows we're getting close. He's testing my loyalty."

"Is that why you got the gash on your arm three days ago?" He no longer looked so scared, but worried.

"I'm not worried. He gets angry but… he gets over it," Lena said, dodging the question.

"Why haven't you killed me?"

"It's not that easy. I can't just kill you. I would have to make it look like someone else did it, have a cover story, make sure your parents didn't know where you went, wipe cameras nearby; it's a lot of work."

"You sound experienced."

"Can we please just move on from that?" she grumbled, not admitting anything.

Trevor nodded, inwardly telling himself that some things

should stay secrets. "Knife throwing, huh?"

"Yep, watch me."

They worked without knives for a long time before Lena let him try with a knife.

"If you drop a knife, don't try and catch it. I can catch it due to experience and a lot of pain. Don't you try it on your first day."

He nodded, and they started working on it for a while longer. Lena occasionally had to yell, "Don't get sloppy," or "Don't do that," or "What the actual hell are you doing?" as their session continued. They both laughed and messed around but only when he wasn't holding any knives after he nearly sliced her leg.

They took a break after an hour of hard work. "Hey, when can I actually meet Alpha and Beta?"

"Tonight? I can give them a call right quick. We need to discuss some things anyway," Lena yawned, pulling out her phone and standing up.

He nodded. "Where are you going?"

"This room has absolutely no cell service, so we have to go out there."

"Should we clean up?"

"Nah, it's fine." Lena stretched then went to the door. Trevor shut the door as Lena dialed up Hound.

"Hey, Hound. You guys open for dinner?" A long pause ensued with some loud yelling on the other side. "Great, I'll see you soon. Yes, I love you, too. Bye. No, really, I've got to go. Hound, just let me leave. You can rant when you get here. Bye."

Lena shook her head and headed for the kitchen to start some dinner. "Hey, can you tell the boys to start wrapping up their game?"

"Sure. I'll be back."

Lena started up dinner while Trevor informed the boys that they were having company. The bell rang as he was on his way back.

"That was quick," Trevor said, walking into the kitchen as Lena wiped her hands on a hand towel.

"I've got it." She went through the archway that led directly to the front door. "Hey, guys. Come on in. I hope you like macaroni and cheese."

The three of them entered, and Lena hugged each of them. Her arm got tangled on Avery's unnaturally curled hair. The woman chuckled as she untangled it for Lena. Avery remarked quietly on it as it got caught on her jacket too. The one identical to the ones her daughter and husband wore too.

Alpha's red hair was frizzy and going every which way. He hadn't seemed to try and tame it as he typically did at TNT to keep up with appearances.

Bianca looked very much like her mother on this day in particular. Her hair was up, but her eyes had the same happy glow that lit up the room.

Trevor moved into the hall, and everyone moved forward to introduce themselves. "Hello, I'm Trevor." He waved casually.

"I'm Avery. You probably know me as Beta. Lena and her formalities." Avery cupped his hand in hers and smiled. "It's great to finally meet you."

"I'm Alpha. It can stay that way," Michael told him with a serious look.

"Michael!" Avery elbowed him hard in the chest. To Trevor, it seemed to be painful, but he had learned in the ensuing weeks this was just how they picked on each other at TNT. "He's just joking. You may call him Michael. Isn't that right, honey?"

He nodded; his face didn't show that he would ever let Trevor call him Michael.

"Nice to see you again, Lynx. How's life?" Bianca asked, fist-bumping him to lessen the tension emanating from her father.

"Just fine. Thanks for asking, Hound."

Michael took him by the arm. "I need to speak to you for a second."

Trevor looked nervous as Michael pulled him away. Lena gave him a nod and an encouraging smile that may have looked more teasing than anything else.

Bianca pulled Lena back into the kitchen while Avery went to go say hello to the twins.

"He's your assignment. You can't get this close to him."

"I'm not doing that assignment."

"Do you realize how much danger that puts you in?"

"Don't try to make me feel bad, please. I know you hid that family in Maine on your assignment. You can't peg me with this as well. I won't be made to feel bad by my best friend."

"I don't want to make you feel bad; I just want to make you realize the consequences."

"And the other option is he dies," Lena whispered angrily.

"I'm worried for you. You pushed it by not bringing the twins then forcing him to promote you. Now, you're openly disobeying orders."

"He doesn't have the right to give orders and I'm tired of taking them. I'm tired of dealing with my family's problems."

Their conversation was cut short by Michael and Trevor coming back into the room. Trevor was pale, but he had stopped sweating. Michael was in the middle of saying, "Never mind, you may call me Michael, anyway."

"Thanks?" Trevor said, a bit of nervous laughter tied in on the end.

"Did you guys even say 'hello'?" Lena asked, looking between them, hand on hip.

"Hey."

"Hello."

Chapter 10

Trevor came over every night for the rest of the week to work on his aim with a knife. He was pretty good at consistently hitting the kneecap but not the chest. Lena didn't mind too much as she didn't want him worrying about killing a man just yet.

It was Friday, and Lena had stepped out of the concealed room while Trevor took a bathroom break. Her phone rang, and Max's face covered her screen.

"Well, this was unexpected. What's up?" Lena asked, smiling. She hadn't gotten to talk to Maxwell in over a week.

"Can you fly up tonight?"

"Why?"

"There were complications with my assignment."

"Why is this a running theme in the family?" she groaned, already thinking through logistics.

Trevor appeared around the corner. "What is?"

Lena held up one finger and listened to Max say, "Please, I need your help. I heard Lynx. Bring him if need be. Please, I can't do it on my own."

"We'll be there. I'll get Raven to watch the boys. Listen for more info. I'll have either Beta or Hound send it along."

"Thank you, love you."

"Love you, too. Don't do anything rash." Lena hung up and grabbed Trevor's arm. "You need to call your mom. Tell her that you're with Alex or something. Then call Alex and let him know, call Rob just in case. He'll be able to make a better cover story in case Alex falls through."

"Why would Robert be able to do that?"

"He's Wolf. He was in charge of watching me," Lena informed Trevor as she pulled open the secret passage again. "That scar across his face was from John. I need to make a call really quick. Pack up as many sheathed knives as you can and my gun with some extra bullets in that bag on the wall. You can make those calls when I finish."

Lena left quickly. She ran upstairs, dialing Beta along the way. "Hey, Beta. Can you prep the jet?"

"Why the jet?"

Lena's voice was muffled as she had a ponytail holder between her lips as she pulled her hair up roughly. "Max needs me in New York. Can you do it?"

"I'll see what I can do."

Lena's voice cleared again as the ponytail went up. "I need it now. I'm packing a small bag before I head over. Please make sure John doesn't know. I'm bringing Lynx."

"Will do. Bye." Avery hung up before Lena could speak any more, surely to make some calls of her own.

Lena grabbed some extra clothes from her closet while her phone was ringing on another call.

"Sparrow?"

"Raven, I need you to watch the boys. Are you open?"

"I guess I am now. When?"

"Literally right now. I've got to go. Thank you. Bye." Lena reached over and hung up the phone quickly. She had thrown a first aid pack into the small backpack along with a blouse and skirt that seemed necessary, despite the fact that she hated skirts, and they weren't very functional.

"Trevor! Please, call your mother before I do!"

"Working on it!"

Lena ran downstairs to the twins' room, where they were fully engrossed in Halo.

"Boys, I've got to go. Raven is going to watch you tonight," Lena panted.

"Why?" Timmy asked absentmindedly, not looking up from the console.

"Max needs me to help him with some stuff in New York."

That got the game paused. "Can we come?"

"Max only had enough room for two. No, I'm not taking only one of you. You be nice to Raven. I'll be back home late tonight."

"You're gone almost as much as Mom is," Dillon muttered.

"Excuse you?" Lena turned away from the door, back toward the boys.

"We never see you any more," Timmy complained.

"I am doing my best. I'm trying. Max needs me, and I can't leave him on this," Lena told them, crouching down in the door.

"You're always with Trevor now," Dillon reminded her.

"That's different. I'll be around more after this, okay? I'm sorry."

They nodded and went back to the game, which was the best Lena could hope for.

Trevor was down the hall with the gun bag slung over his shoulder. "Ready?"

"Yep, here." Lena handed him her small bag to put in the larger bag.

"You make the calls?"

"All but Rob. I didn't know how to handle that one."

"Okay, I'll call in the car." They passed Raven on their way out and, she nodded to them.

Lena drove fast, causing Trevor to clutch the door as the

phone rang. "Sup, Birdie?" came the voice of Robert.

"Seriously? I thought we were over that, Pup. Anyway, later tonight if you get a call from Alex or Trevor's mom, I need you to cover. We're heading to New York, and his mom can't know."

"It's never easy with you, is it? And okay."

Trevor watched her joking with Rob and felt a slight tinge of jealousy. He turned away to hide what he could and heard the phone shut off.

"I don't know what is going to be waiting at the strip. Be prepared to run. Don't try and fight. I'll protect you. You get to the plane. Understand?"

"Yes."

"What's up?"

"Nothing."

"Can you answer with more than one word?"

"Yes."

"Prove it."

"Why?"

Lena sighed and sped around a corner. The car screeched to a halt, and Lena slowly turned it off. "Let me go first. Stay behind me. If I tell you to run, you run."

"And if you're hurt?"

"Then you leave. Don't stay. I'll be fine, but you won't."

"I won't do it."

"You will go. Now, follow me." They got out of the car, Lena waving Trevor to come around the car to her.

Lena fell silent as she pulled out a hidden gun. She checked the corner and ran to a nearby storage container. Trevor followed on her heels. She motioned for him to go to the jet. A round of gunfire hit their barricade as Lena grabbed his arm. Trevor tripped, but Lena managed to maintain her grip on his arm before it hit him.

"Stay here," she whispered.

He nodded, heart beating out of his neck. Trevor no longer had the brief flash of bravery that had struck him as he ran through empty space. Now, he was nearly paralyzed with fear and awe. This was an action movie playing out in real-time to Trevor. It seemed cooler in the movies, with explosions and gunshots happening without fear, but Lena seemed straight out of Hollywood. She hadn't even flinched at the shot and was shooting over the container just like one of those characters as he regained his wits.

"Go!" Lena yelled. He stumbled and ran blindly toward the large jet, the gun bag hitting the backs of his knees with every step he took.

He heard more gunshots and a splattering. Trevor forced himself to keep going. It would be worse if he didn't run. Once he reached the plane's stairs, he turned. Lena was limping and stumbling. Her leg had been hit by a stray bullet, and she was out of bullets.

Despite everything, she was going as fast as she could and yelling, "Go! You idiot, get on the plane!"

She made it just as some more bullets hit the stairs. Sean closed the doors. "What did I tell you about getting shot?"

Sean picked her up and put her in a seat. "Thanks, Bear," she grunted, starting to get woozy from the adrenaline.

"Aloe, get yourself out here!" Sean called into the back.

"Badger, you get us off the ground before he hits a tire," Katie said at the front. "I'm coming, Bear. Be patient."

Sean grabbed a first aid kit from the wall as the jet started moving forward. Katie took the kit, and Trevor nodded to them. "Hello."

"Why are y'all here?" Lena groaned.

"Beta sent us along to prep the plane. Guess she wanted us to help you," Sean told her, ruffling her hair.

"Hawk only needed me."

"This is about Hawk?" Tyler asked, looking up with interest.

"His assignment is struggling," Lena informed them.

"Done." Katie sat back and nodded. She continued, "Well, we can sit with the plane if that's really necessary."

"He'll want to see you." Lena grimaced as she moved the leg. They'd have to fix it again when they weren't on a moving jet.

"I thought so," Sean said, helping Katie up and into his lap in a different seat.

"Did anyone call Hawk?" Lena asked.

"We didn't know, so no." Trevor nodded with Bear's logic.

Lena limped up front to get flight information from Sara to text to Max before coming back, watching as Katie sat with Sean, their hands entwined.

"I'm going to sleep," Lena told them as she crawled to a secluded chair. Soon she was snoring, and Trevor decided to sit across from Sean and Katie. They chatted for a little while before Trevor went to sit by Lena.

She was completely asleep, and he put his arm around her shoulders carefully. Lena shifted, and he went to take his arm away, but she grabbed his arm. Trevor jumped and let his arm go limp. They sat this way until Sara called that she was starting the descent.

Trevor moved back to the front and went through the weapons carefully as Squadron Thirteen chatted happily.

"Hey, can I see one of those?" Sean asked, motioning to the knife he had pulled out.

"Uh, sure, here." Trevor handed the knife to him, and Katie shook her head.

"She's not even the favorite and still gets all of the best toys." Katie chuckled and took the knife gently from Sean.

"I don't understand how John can stand to give her new gear yet still torture her and shoot her," Tyler growled.

"Was that him?" Trevor asked, pulling them away from the knife.

"Back there? Oh yeah. There's no doubt," Katie assured him.

"How do you know?"

"Because it was his bullet in her leg."

"You recognize it?" Trevor looked horrified at the mere concept.

"I've pulled a lot of shit out of her leg and plenty of those bullet casings."

"We're landing!" Sara yelled as they felt a sudden jolt.

Not long after, the door was pulled open, and a tall man with dark brown hair walked in. He had kind eyes and a scarred face.

"Max!" Katie jumped up to hug him happily.

"Nice to see you too, Aloe. Where's Lena?" He acknowledged Trevor with a curt nod.

"I'll wake her," Tyler volunteered. He groaned as he stood and walked to the back of the plane.

"Thanks, Bull." Max walked a few steps over to shake Trevor's hand since his plan to see Lena had been cut short. "I've heard a lot about you. You ready to meet my assignment?"

"I think so."

"Good. Once my sister gets up here, we're going."

Chapter 11

Max whistled at a passing cab, putting out a hand, and it screeched to a stop. Lena yawned and said quietly, "I need to change."

"Uh, take us to the university, north side," Max said, thinking of the nearest place to change that wasn't the apartment.

They rode silently, the cabby glancing back every so often at Lena in her blood-stained clothes nervously. It wasn't often that they went on vacations, so Lena watched as the tall buildings idled past in the flow of traffic. Each thing was as bright as the sun or as dark as night. Lena silently pondered which one was Mr. Stern's office.

"We're here," the cabby told them at the end of their ride. Max lagged behind to pay him while Lena and Trevor grabbed the bag from the trunk.

"There's a girl's bathroom over there." Max pointed to a nearby café on campus, and Lena left with the smaller bag from earlier that evening.

Max and Trevor chatted politely as they waited. Each had some reservations about the other, having only heard stories of each other with few run-throughs at school plays or parent nights.

Lena returned in her skirt and blouse, looking grumpy. "Skirt?" Max asked, looking Lena up and down.

"It's typically more inviting than the uniform." Lena shrugged, but Max knew she was going to hold a grudge whether it was his fault or not.

They walked across campus, Max gesturing vaguely at

buildings as they passed. Lena had thought about coming to school here before she had the rude awakening related to the twins. Both were a full five and a half years younger than she was, meaning that they wouldn't have protection if she left.

Lena sighed and turned her attention back to Max as he said, "And this is my apartment complex. I'm on the first floor."

"She isn't going to attack us upon entry, is she?" Trevor asked, worry hidden somewhere deep inside his words, or at least he thought it was deep.

"No," Max muttered, not looking at them. He seemed embarrassed and unlocked the door quickly, making sure they were inside before locking the door tightly.

There was some muffled banging coming from a room near the end of the hall that must've been Max's room.

"Max, you sit down. I'll go get her," Lena told him. He nodded and swallowed stiffly.

Lena rolled her eyes, snatching a knife from the bag on her way over to the door, murmuring, "Idiot."

She tapped lightly on the door. The banging stopped, and a nervous voice said, "Hello?"

"Hey, Alyse. It's Lena, Max's sister. May I come in?"
"No."
"I can't help you from out here."
"I don't have another option, do I?"
"Not really."
"Fine."

Lena entered slowly to see Alyse tied tightly to a chair. Her hair was a frazzled mess of red across her face as she had clearly tried to escape. Her green eyes were wide with fear at her appearance. "Max!" Lena yelled in frustration. She walked over and quickly cut each rope. "Don't run."

Alyse winced at each slice, nodding vigorously. "I won't."

"I'm sorry this happened to you. Max should've explained before all of this."

Alyse nodded in agreement, her eyes not leaving the knife. Lena saw and slipped the knife into the waist of her skirt calmly. "I'll have a nice chat with my brother when all of this is explained."

"Thank you."

"He's a good man."

"I know, this though." Alyse sighed and shook her head as she looked at the loose straps, rubbing her wrists to get rid of the rope burns.

"Come on, let us explain." Lena led her out and sat her down on the couch. "Max, sit your ass down."

Max gulped and hurriedly sat back down. Trevor rose up to shake Alyse's hand. "I'm Trevor. Sometimes known as Lena's assignment or Lynx."

"You're not—you know what. Fine, just fine," Lena muttered to herself as she sat down on the couch beside Alyse.

Max chuckled, and Lena shot him a look that made him stop suddenly. Alyse laughed, and Lena let a small smirk cross her lips.

"Anyway, explaining?" Alyse said questioningly.

"Max, you best start," Lena told him. "I'm going to call Thirteen really quick and let them know we're alive."

Alyse looked confused, and Trevor said calmly, "Just let them explain." Lena left for a few seconds to call Katie, who picked up on the first ring.

"We're safe."

"Good. We're in the middle of an intense game of BS. I've got to go."

"Bye." Lena hung up, rolling her eyes with a chuckle.

She walked back in to hear Max saying, "Yeah, so Dad is a lot more powerful than anyone you've ever had the pleasure of meeting."

"Also, he's John, not Dad," Lena reminded him. Max pursed his lips and nodded.

"So, why couldn't you have just said no?" Alyse asked innocently.

Lena let out a bitter laugh. "He doesn't take no as an answer."

"What would happen? He can't actually hurt you... can he?"

Lena sighed. "Just a few hours ago he put a bullet in my leg. He also does this." Lena rubbed on her arm, wincing as the makeup disappeared, slowly revealing the scars, new and old.

Alyse recoiled and looked appalled before leaning forward for a closer look. Max looked away with a small snarl. Trevor seemed pained and turned away too. Alyse traced the small white lines with her finger in a fascinated horror.

Lena put a hand back over her arm. "Anyway, this is what we have dealt with, so no wasn't an answer."

Max turned back, the snarl of anger still apparent on his lips.

"So, you were supposed to kill me?" Alyse asked quietly.

"Not exactly," Max said, happy for the distraction. "I was supposed to ruin your life along with your father's. My whole job was to ruin your studies and plummet his business all because your dad did a lawsuit against my dad and won."

"So why is he against you?" Alyse asked, looking at Trevor.

Lena cleared her throat and said stiffly, "Because he believes that I've grown close to Trevor and wants me to prove my worth by killing him."

"Oh," Alyse whispered.

"But here I am," Trevor said, trying to lighten the dark mood.

Alyse rolled her eyes as Lena looked at Max. "Can I speak to you? In private," she asked her brother quietly.

"Of course," he said, worry reappearing rapidly. "We'll be just a moment."

Lena dragged Max to the other room, and they could hear quite clearly as she yelled at him.

Alyse looked at Trevor as he looked at the door of where Lena and Maxwell disappeared. "Do you love her?"

"What? No, of course not. What would give you that idea?" Trevor retorted immediately, attention fully on Alyse.

"Just... nothing. I'm sure you'll know soon enough."

Max and Lena returned shortly, and Max was a bright shade of red. "What were you guys talking about?" Lena asked, a wide smile across her face as Max glared at her the way any sibling would.

"Nothing," they said together.

Lena looked between them curiously but let it be. "Let's discuss how we're going to protect both of you and avoid John."

They talked intensely for over an hour before Lena snapped, "I've had to do it before. There's no point avoiding it. He'll kill her if we don't."

"I don't want you killing anyone if we can avoid it," Max told her sharply.

"Max, I don't want her nor Trevor to die because we couldn't make the hard decision," Lena said, clenching her fist tightly.

"You shouldn't have to do this."

"None of this would've happened if I had been brave enough to do it years ago."

"What was that?"

"Nothing."

"Lena," Max called, anger starting to boil over.

Alyse looked between them, and Trevor was still out of it from Alyse's comment while Max and Lena were out of the room.

"Years ago, Bianca agreed to help me kill John. I lost my nerve at the last second. I should've just done it. We wouldn't have any of these problems if I would've just done it."

"We won't do it," Max announced finally.

Lena's jaw stiffened. "If you'd prefer not to know, then I won't tell you."

"Lena, please. Just don't. We can hide her for a while at the house," Max reminded her, voice lower and more dangerous.

"I won't risk their lives any more. I'll only take so many more beatings because you won't let me do this."

"Don't go back."

Lena got up and left. She unlocked the door and slammed it behind her. They could hear the thump against the wall that signaled that she was right outside the door.

"I'll go talk to her," Alyse said calmly, squeezing Max's hand as she stood up.

Max took a deep breath and looked at Trevor. "What's your opinion?"

"What—oh. I don't want her to do it any more then you but if it means she's safe again then we should do it."

"Why were you so spaced out?"

Trevor looked sheepish as he answered, "Are there any good date locations around here?"

"Excuse—never mind. Central Park, I swear if you hurt her…"

"I won't."

"I'll drop you off. I need to work on packing this place up.

I'll get some boxes then head back here," Max told him with a small grimace.

"Thank you, Max."

"I never expected her to date a jock."

Trevor chuckled and shook his head. "We're not dating."

"Yet."

Lena and Alyse wandered back in; Lena's eyes were red and puffy. "I'm going to go get her cleaned up."

"Alyse," Trevor called, waving her over.

"You go wait in the bathroom," Alyse told Lena, pointing sternly.

Lena left, and Trevor whispered, "Can you get her ready for a date in the park?"

"Yes, of course." Alyse was smiling shyly, and they heard her whisper as she walked away, "Did I go to class today? Was that yesterday? What time even is it? Is it the same year?"

Max shifted uncomfortably. "You good?" Trevor asked, peering at him.

"Yeah, it's just—" He let out a huff and continued. "I like Alyse I just… what's going to happen after this?"

"Well, she agreed to come to Texas, and she hasn't run away screaming, so I think it's going well for now."

Max shrugged and let out a long sigh. "It's been a long night."

"Need help getting started with unpacking drawers?"

"Please." Max groaned as he stood up.

Lena and Alyse emerged from the bathroom after what felt like forever. Max and Trevor were in the kitchen wrapping the glasses and cups in paper towels and napkins that Max swore he didn't buy.

"Are we ready to go?" Lena asked, a small smile on her face.

Trevor glanced up from wrapping the last of Max's two dinner plates. "Yeah, uh, Max?" Trevor pulled his eyes away from the heavily makeup-ladened Lena to get Max's attention.

"Yep, let's go. Alyse, we're here for the night packing. I'll call the squad and get them over here," Max told Lena simply.

"I doubt they would like you calling them 'the squad'," Lena pointed out.

"Sara would skin me alive," Max agreed. "Anyway, I'm going to drop them off and get boxes. If a group of people barge in, then don't freak out. The blonde girl will protect you."

"Thanks?" Alyse said nervously.

Max shrugged, and Lena hugged Alyse goodbye as they left. Alyse seemed still in the exchange, but she let it happen which was more progress than Max had hoped for.

Max dropped them off at the edge of the park before wandering off to find a box store.

Trevor laid out a blanket he had borrowed from Max. They sat down on it quietly and looked up at the sparse trees. It was chilly outside, and Lena ended up nestled in the crook of Trevor's arm.

"I have something for you," Trevor said slowly.

"Really?" Lena sat up and looked at him expectantly through the exhaustion evident on her face.

He laughed nervously and pulled out a small, flat box from his pocket. He popped it open to reveal a small bracelet with two charms on it: a sparrow and a tree.

"Thank you, Trevor," Lena said, staring at the silver glinting in the streetlights. "I actually have something for you. Damn, where did I put it?"

Lena grabbed the bag and searched through it for a second, blushing all the while. She let out a small gasp and sighed as she found the small box.

"What is it?" he asked quickly.

"Why don't you open it?"

A titanium and silver ring glinted against the black plush cushion. "Why do I recognize this?" Trevor put it on one of his fingers and smiled as it fit.

"My brothers each have one. I actually have one, but it doesn't fit well, and I can't get it fitted but occasionally I wear it on a necklace."

"Really?"

"Yeah, anyway, we should probably go so we can get home tonight."

Trevor nodded and smiled. "Thank you for the ring."

"Thank you for the bracelet."

They called Max to come get them and met him at the edge where he had dropped them off about an hour earlier.

Chapter 12

Lena touched down with everyone just to be greeted by Avery rushing up to the plane. She looked stressed and refused to speak to everyone at once. "Sparrow, a word, please."

Lena limped over to her after handing the bag back to Trevor. "What's up?"

"John needs you immediately. You should take Trevor home then go."

"You got Max a flight home?"

"Yes, he and Alyse will arrive tomorrow with all of their things," Avery assured her.

"Thank you," Lena muttered calmly, walking away.

Lena gathered Trevor quietly, waving goodbye to the others and moving toward the car. She didn't speak for a while, not until Trevor spoke anyway.

"What happened?"

"I don't know. Something bad. Watch for word."

"I will," Trevor assured her. He squeezed her hand in his.

Lena pulled it away slowly; she felt herself inwardly trying to get rid of links that could hurt her. She pulled to the side of the road to let Trevor out by his house.

"I'm sorry. I'll contact you later."

"I'll wait for it." He left and watched her pull away.

Lena wiped a tear away from her eye and sniffed. She shook her head and took a deep breath to calm herself. She sang quietly for comfort as though she were singing the twins to sleep again.

Silence filled the car as she pulled up to TNT. Slowly,

carefully, she left the car and went to the lobby as she always did. John was already there, pacing back and forth, back and forth.

"No twins I see. Shame, though it's not of importance. When is Maxwell coming back?" He didn't seem concerned any longer about the events at the air strip.

"Soon," Lena replied in an even tone.

"Where's your mother? I haven't seen her about of late." Lena's heart skipped a beat. She knew that he had followed Mary but never had admitted it openly. "She is away with her boyfriend. She's pregnant."

"Never mind, it is unimportant to what you are to do. You are going to die."

"Excuse me, sir?" Lena felt her pulse quicken, and her voice quivered.

"Not literally, you stupid girl. You are needed for things outside of school. I need you to stage your death. To the outside world, you are no more."

Lena nodded. "Yes, sir." She held back her tears. There would be no changing his mind. "And my assignment?"

"Shall be transferred to Monkey at the soonest time."

Lena bit her tongue. Monkey would complete the mission without a minute's thought.

"Run along now. I expect it to be done at the soonest time," John chuckled, though the situation had no humor.

"Yes, sir," Lena replied shortly. She walked at a brisk pace until she was out of sight. She began to run and searched, tears blurring her vision, for anyone that could help her.

Eventually, she found Bianca and snagged her by the arm. She dragged her to Beta's office and collapsed in a sobbing pile. Bianca held Lena as she cried and gently petted her hair.

The door opened, and the calm chatter from Beta and Alpha

stopped.

Alarmed, Beta whispered, "What happened?" She and Alpha sat and hugged Lena in apparent fear.

Lena finally pulled herself together just enough so she could explain what had happened. "John, he... he wants me to fake my death, and he's transferring my assignment."

They all fell silent; each had their own thought though Lena knew they followed the same plot. John had gone insane. No one knew exactly what he wanted, but gosh dang it, he was going to get it.

Trevor entered his house to a cannon blast from his mother.

"Where have you been? Are you hurt? Who were you with? What were you doing? We were so worried!" Ana yelled at him, running down the hall and grabbing him into a tight hug.

"I've been out with friends."

"No, you haven't. Alex and Robert are terrible liars. Where were you?"

"I was out with Lena. She had some family matters that she needed me to help with."

"Why didn't you call and tell us?"

"I couldn't; we were outside of cell range and really busy. I'm sorry, Mom."

"You're grounded from your car for two weeks. Do you understand me?"

"Yes, ma'am."

"And you're not allowed to go anywhere afterschool without express permission from your father or I."

"Yes, ma'am."

"Okay, go freshen up. You smell like a park."

Trevor kissed her cheek and ran upstairs to his room. His mind raced with thoughts of the horrors that could be happening to Lena at that very second, too much so to be upset about the punishment levied.

He looked around to see the piles of clothes and towels that covered the floor and began picking them up. The work helped him keep his mind off any thoughts of Lena. It took a long time, and, eventually, he sat down on his bed and looked around to see if there was anything else to put in the bag of trash by the door.

His eyes flicked toward the desk, where there was most likely to be more cleaning to do. A paper caught his eye, which he didn't remember stacking in the corner with his schoolwork. He stood up with a groan and grabbed the paper.

Meet me with the twins in the garden. Thank Raven for me, please.

-Sparrow

He nodded and looked toward the door. There was no way Ana would let him go out after that New York stunt. Trevor looked toward the window, which was unlocked. How he hadn't noticed her come in, he wasn't sure, but it was beside the point.

Trevor pulled it open and ran back to the door; he locked it calmly. He moved back to the window and climbed out, standing on the small roof outside of it so he could close the window.

Trevor managed to get down after a minute's inward debating. He eventually decided to jump and successfully didn't break his legs.

He went around the back and grabbed the bike that he knew hadn't been touched since the previous summer. It was wet from the sprinkler system, but he disregarded it. Trevor thanked his father inwardly for the all-rubber, no inflation tires, which prevented the dusty bike from having a flat.

Trevor knew from experience that the ride to Lena's house wasn't far, but it felt like forever. He dropped the bike at the front door and knocked. Raven answered the door with a tight face.

"That took longer than I anticipated," Raven said calmly as she allowed him in.

"I need to take the twins and one of the cars," Trevor told her quickly.

"Don't hurt her car."

"What do you mean? Isn't it just the normal car?"

"Lena has that one. The only one left is the Camaro that John left the family."

"Oh." There was a moment where he was in too much shock to reply before remembering that Lena was rich, and he had to go. "Okay, where are the twins?"

"I'll get them," Raven sighed.

The twins appeared a moment later and were rushed to the car by Raven.

"I never got your name I don't think," Trevor said as he was tossed the keys.

"Oh, you did. It's Samantha. Anyway, no dents or scratches."

"Okay, thank you. Oh, Lena says thank you, as well."

"See you soon, Lynx," she replied slyly.

They pulled out quickly, and Trevor drove them to the gardens in silence. Neither of the twins spoke from anticipation and could probably feel Trevor's stress washing off him in waves.

Trevor led them around back, but the twins ran ahead, obviously already knowing the way. They were hugging Lena as Trevor slipped under the fence. He couldn't see her eyes in the pitch blackness.

"What's happened?" Trevor asked, trying to hide his fear.

"I am going to be going away for a while," Lena told them.

"What do you mean?" Timmy asked quickly before Trevor could.

"I... you are going to find a body in my room when you arrive home. I have to disappear for a while. I will still be around and leave you notes. I just won't see you," Lena explained quietly.

"Excuse me?" Trevor said loudly.

"Trevor, can I speak to you in private?" It was apparent from her voice now that she had been crying.

"Sure."

They walked a little way off. "I'm sorry."

"Me, too."

"Please, watch the twins for me. I have to stay at TNT from now on. I'll do my best to keep an eye on them, but I won't be under the same roof."

"Why are you doing this?" He reached for her hand but got only the air where it had just been.

"I have to. Please, will you?"

"Of course, I will do that, no matter what."

"I have to go. Protect yourself."

Lena pecked him on the cheek and kissed the twins on top of their heads and disappeared.

Trevor stood frozen for a few moments before motioning them back toward the fence.

"Will she come back?" Dillon asked quietly.

"Of course, she will. It probably won't be soon though. You'll be fine. I'll visit you both."

"Trevor, I'm scared," Timmy told him in a muffled voice.

"Me too. I'll be there with you though."

Trevor brought them to the house. Raven was still there; she was just putting down the phone and said calmly, "The police are on their way."

"Thank you, Raven. I have to go."

"Goodbye, Trevor."

"Goodbye."

Chapter 13

A year came and went, and it was now Christmas break of Trevor's junior year. The letters still came, breaks becoming greater as the detailed assignments became longer and harder. He had yet to see her again. All he could see now was the funeral columns covered in blue orchids and pictures of Lena illuminated by candle's' flickering light when he thought of her.

Trevor visited the twins almost every day, Mary becoming more and more used to his visits. Her newest daughter had been born and named Sierra Foster, keeping with her children's names rather than Sierra's father's name, as she had intended until Maxwell intervened. The girl had blonde hair and blue eyes, characteristic of her mother and sister. Sierra liked Trevor and sat quietly in his arms whenever he visited. He, meanwhile, enjoyed watching her, imagining that this was how Lena looked as a baby as well.

Both twins loved their new babysitter and spoke in secret to Trevor about Lena's visits. She had come to see them three times, and each new time hurt him a little more. He hadn't moved into the new school year easily. Friends tried to keep him cheerful, but he missed seeing Lena, which they didn't understand.

He missed her too much to avoid ending each letter with 'When can I see you again? Please let it be soon.'

He already knew the response and wished it would change. Many nights he tried to catch Lena placing a new letter on his desk, but each night he would stay waiting, and no letter would come, or he'd fall asleep in the meantime, bound to have a headache and a new letter come morning. Once, he swore he felt her hand on his in the dead of night, another time her lips on his head. Each time was brief; she was like a blown candle's warmth that he was trying to grasp with frozen hands.

Trevor decided that night to sit on his small bit of roof outside his window. He lay down and looked up at the moon, not moving for hours, how he had many times that year. It was cold, but he ignored it, telling himself that the three pairs of pants and four shirts were enough in the middle of winter.

When the moon was at the highest point and clouds were covering the moon, threatening another snowstorm, it happened.

"A nice night, am I right? Just right for camping, I thought, well, if it doesn't snow. I may just go camping unless I find something better to do." Lena sat farther up the roof, shielded by darkness, but her silhouette was still visible.

"Lena, where… how?" Trevor crawled toward her, spinning around at once.

Lena moved back, footsteps silent as a ghost. "I don't want to be seen. It's gotten worse over the last year. I wouldn't want to tarnish your image of me."

Even from his spot on the roof, Trevor imagined he could see her bright blue eyes facing the roof in disappointment. "I can close my eyes if you'd like. I won't open even one." He clamped his eyes shut. He could hear her small giggle carry to him in the wind. "Why'd you choose tonight?" The desperation was too plain in his voice, but he couldn't help it.

Her voice appeared right next to him. "You seemed to be losing hope. I never wanted that. You must know that this is the hardest year I've ever had. I can't stay away, but I have to."

"Why? Why do you do this to us both?"

"Because I need to be able to think clearly. I don't know if

I'll be able to now that I'm actually here. I don't know if I can leave again." His closed eyes creased with worry, then nearly opened before firmly shutting again.

"Then don't."

"I have to. I'm so close to that goal from a year ago in New York. I'll come home after. I'll come home." Trevor heard her voice crack and reached for her. His hand met empty yet warm air.

"Promise me you'll be safe."

A dry laugh came from his other side. "You say that so seriously."

"Can you at least lay with me for a while? Just 'til I fall asleep. I don't want to see you go."

"I wouldn't go, anyway."

Her confidence in the small sentence made him happy. He lay back to the roof, and he felt her slide into his arms. She began singing quietly, the lullaby she had sung so long ago. He smiled at the memories of the safe times. He opened his eyes slightly in her hair. The blonde hair was engulfing his vision as her sweet scent filled his nose. It was blonde again, a change that must have happened through the year. Trevor tried to stay awake, but, eventually, her sweet voice lulled him into a doze.

He awoke on the roof alone and cold the next morning. Trevor went to go inside and felt something heavy in one of his pockets. He tugged his phone out and wrinkled his nose in confusion; he didn't remember bringing it out.

He opened it, and his camera role was open. There were no pictures but a few videos. He played the first one, and Lena's lullaby emerged. Trevor opened each one consecutively; they were each unique and beautiful in their own way. The last one was different from the black screen of the rest.

The video was full of small bits of his life after she had left, the few truly happy memories he had experienced. Her voice was edited over the flips as he watched clips of the twins and Sierra and his parents across the screen. "You definitely know these people. They work and love and feel pain and achieve for you. Don't let me down. I'll come home someday soon, and I expect to hear more stories. Until then... I love you. I'm sorry I couldn't tell you in person. I don't think I could've left if I did. Anyway, I think you being able to listen to it over and over will make you feel better. I won't say goodbye but... see you soon. You won't hear from me for a while, but I'm safe. I love you. Thank you for everything. Oh, and tell the twins that I miss them. See you soon."

The video ended, and Trevor smiled. "Thank you, Lena."

He climbed down from the roof and began getting dressed for another dull day.

"Morning," Lauren called as he came down the stairs. Her hair was a brown frizzy mess this morning that blocked her caramel eyes, making Trevor wonder how she could even see her coffee.

"Morning, how's Brit?"

Brittany was her girlfriend, though no one actually called her Brittany, only Brit.

"She's fine, though she has to take an extra shift tonight."

Trevor nodded and moved to the kitchen, Lauren following him. Ana had left a note on the counter, and Trevor picked it up before Lauren could. "Work called. Someone was out sick and asked her to fill in."

Lauren perched herself on the counter and looked sideways at Trevor. "What happened?"

"What do you mean?"

"You're happier."

"Am I?"

"Did you get over that Lena girl? She's been dead for over a year. You don't seriously believe she's still alive, do you?"

"Lauren, I am not over her. I never will be. I loved – love – her. That's not something you just get over."

"You didn't answer the second question."

"And I'm not going to."

"Why, because you finally realized that she's gone, or you have proof that she's not?"

"I'll be late if I don't go."

"Late for what?" Lauren called after him as he grabbed his keys off the table. She didn't follow him outside immediately, allowing him to approach his car in peace.

Trevor hopped in the driver's seat and sighed, "Hurry, Lena."

"I'm trying. I need your help." She was standing outside of his window.

Trevor jumped and hit his head on the roof of the car. "God damn it, Lena."

She had covered her face with excessive makeup, and her hair was a dark brown. Lena was wearing a mail uniform, and had a package under her arm and was extending a clipboard to him. "Sir, my name is Kayla. Do you want your package?"

Her face was stern, and her eyes flicked toward the front door where Lauren had just emerged. "Um, yeah, of course."

"Sign here." Lena gave him the board, which he signed quickly. She handed him the package and nodded. "Have a great day, sir."

"Thanks, you too." Trevor pulled out and headed in the direction of Lena's house. He ripped open the package once he was a few streets away. Inside was a neatly wrapped gift, which he had to open as well. A card fell out first, and he pulled off the envelope. Inside read:

Happy Birthday

I do hope you've accepted my invitation to celebrate your seventeenth at my secret garden. If so, then I will see you soon.

Best regards,

Kayla Brown

A gift came out next, and Trevor found a green bandanna, gun belt, and a pin that depicted a lynx head in silver. He smiled and tucked the gift away again before setting off to the garden.

Lena walked around the corner and took off her wig. She was tired of hiding and being the social outcast. Her jobs were important but not as much as the rest of high school.

She missed the simple things she used to enjoy, such as driving in the view of cameras, going to a restaurant through the front door, or even using a public bathroom for usual things rather than changing identities.

Lena had one more job to do before she could go meet Trevor; sighing, she slipped into the alley behind her old home. Her hands were calloused from climbing to her old room, but Lena didn't mind. She knew everything that happened there, even met her baby sister a time or two. Lena didn't go for her new family; she went for the memories and reminders that she wasn't truly dead.

Every once in a while, she had thoughts of what a difference it would really make if she were to die. No one would know, but Lena couldn't convince herself of this. Lena was stuck in a deep depression, lessened only by the occasional visits to her brothers or Trevor.

Lena pulled open her window and stepped into her dusty room; it made her shiver. It was cold and grey in that room. It was strange to see it this way as compared to the immaculate cleanliness of times before.

Lena pulled open her satchel bag and grabbed the five gifts, one for each member of her family. Slowly, she set them down and turned back to the window. The door began to creak open, and Lena leapt through the window before they could see more than a flash of blonde hair.

She had misjudged her landing, and her ankle twisted as she landed. Lena held back the scream as she had many times before. She limped to the fence and leapt over, hoping beyond hope that Mary hadn't seen her and taken her gift first. Lena headed for the gardens early and sat nursing her ankle for some minutes before Trevor appeared.

"Lena," he sighed in relief. He ran to her and scooped her up before she could protest. She whimpered quietly, and he set her down. Lena bent over and looked down at her ankle in pain.

"Ow," she moaned and closed her eyes against that renewed pain. "Less forceful next time, please."

"Information, now." He sat down on a rock and propped her up.

"There's too much to tell you today. Though you need to be more cautious in the next couple days." Lena straightened back up and looked him straight in the eyes.

He waited before remembering that she had been gone for over a year, and so there was no way she was joking. "What's happening?" He really just wanted to look at her as he hadn't the night before, though they didn't have the luxury of time.

"You were passed onto Monkey a year ago, and he only just finished his previous assignments. I'll make sure you're safe. I promise. Also, I've risen a hidden rebellion against John. That will take place in the next week."

Trevor looked confused and opened his mouth a few times before anything came out. "Then, why come back now?"

"I don't know how it will go," she replied softly. Her eyes went to the orchids. They were filled with good memories.

She was fifteen, and it was the twins' birthday. They had never been to her private garden. They both looked fondly on the flowers and seemed to work harder to achieve creating something as pretty as her flowers, each developing new skills to show her.

Lena was seventeen, and she watched Trevor from the trees as he looked around in wonder. She reappeared, and he had found, at least, what she thought was peace in her presence.

"Lena, you never fully explained the reasoning behind your father's vengeance, the story."

"That's because I don't know the whole story. He's secretive, the little I know is from my briefing."

Trevor stared at her as she shifted uncomfortably. Her eyes flicked up and met his briefly before they went back down. "Lena, are you okay?"

"Yes." She didn't look up as she twisted her gold bandanna between her fingers.

"What happened?" Trevor tried to meet her eyes, but she wouldn't look at him any more. "Lena, you have to talk to me."

"Why? Confiding just makes it harder."

"What harder?" It was harsher than Trevor had meant out of frustration.

"When I have to go. When you realize that I can't re-enter society. We've been pretending that'll work, but it can't unless you leave society behind too. I'm not worth that. I'm not worth the pain I'm putting you through." Lena turned fully away from

Trevor and sighed. "After you're safe and John is long gone, then I'll go too. You'll take care of the twins just like you promised along with Max."

Lena stood up and went to her bag, starting to pull something out. Trevor spoke as she fished about in her bag. "I'll go with you. I'm an adult. Mary's been leaving on longer trips. We could take all three with us, and she'd never know."

Lena stopped moving and shook her head, "No, Trevor. You don't understand. This isn't a place you can come with me to."

She turned around and handed him a small bundle and began to limp off.

"Lena, don't go."

"Happy birthday, Trevor." She walked away into the shadows and away down the path. He let her go, knowing he couldn't stop her even with a twisted ankle.

The gun glinted in the flickering sunlight, shining through the canopy. Knives were set around it, and a note was on top.

If one tree falls in the ashes and another grows beneath it does anyone know?

Even if the one beneath is important? If that tree dies, will anyone know?

I believe not, the animals that took refuge there they will notice

Will the others?

Do they know, or care, that beneath the ashes something used To be beautiful?

Does anyone know?

Trevor looked after Lena. She was long gone. He picked up the gift and left the note with his answer upon the ground.

Everyone knows now.

Chapter 14

Lena slept fitfully that night, waking to see Trevor's scrawled note each time her eyes unwittingly opened. After the third time waking up, she decided it was time to find Monkey.

He had received his reassignment the previous day. She had set Sean to tail him, bringing her information of his plans to find Trevor today. She couldn't kill him now without John knowing.

Her only option was going to Trevor again. Lena got up and dressed after only three hours of rest. She went to his house and knocked on the door.

Ana opened the door, with curly hair freshly done and with a precise makeup look. She saw a college talent scout on the other side with a large clipboard full of carefully composed pamphlets, large brown braid, and a badge showing that her name was Diana Rosenburg.

"Hello, you must be Mrs. Ana Stephens, am I right?" Lena asked in a falsely cheery voice, taking her hand firmly in a handshake.

Ana withdrew her hand carefully. "Uh, yes. I'm sorry I didn't catch your name?"

"Oh, I'm so sorry about that. My name is Diana Rosenburg. I'm a talent scout," Lena replied briskly. "I was at your son's last football game, and I was wondering if you had time to talk about his college prospects?"

Lena could see Ana was confused. She had recognized something about Lena but couldn't quite place her. Lena was betting on that to hold.

"Um, Trevor! Chris!" Ana called behind her. "Oh, you can come in. I don't really know how much time... school, y' know?" she muttered vaguely at Lena, trying to regain the composure she had lost to Lena's fast tone and unexpected appearance.

"Don't worry about that. I've already called the school; they said he needn't come in today," Lena told her calmly, stepping in behind her. She had actually had Bianca hack their system before leaving, leaving him an excused absence on account of a college tour.

Ana seemed to accept this as she led Lena into their home. Chris emerged from a side room, eyes landing upon Lena. She moved forward to shake his hand. "Hello, sir. My name is Diana Rosenburg."

"I'm Chris." Lena, of course, recognized him with his black hair and brown eyes. She had seen him at various events, through the years though couldn't give it away.

Trevor appeared on the stairs. "Who?"

Lena turned and was quick to introduce herself yet again before he had the opportunity to speak. His eyes already showed recognition.

"I'm sorry to have startled you. I was hoping to discuss college prospects with you today."

He nodded, and Lena proceeded to act as a tour guide of how college sports would work for a talented young man such as Trevor for the following two hours. All of the twins' lectures on sports and Tyler's complaints about his own debut into college sports had paid off, allowing for her to ramble with little issue on the topic.

"I was actually wondering if I could take your son out to lunch and the practice field to get a more in depth feel of what his skills are and what I can pitch to colleges," Lena finished, hoping her speech had inspired trust in the parents or at least bored them into wanting her to leave no matter the request.

Ana and Chris looked between each other to debate before they agreed, asking that he be back by dinner. Lena agreed, thanked them, and awaited Trevor as he grabbed his football gear.

Once they were finally alone in the car, Trevor asked for an explanation. "Monkey was going to the school. He's coming, Trevor. I warned you. I said I'd keep you safe."

"But coming to my house?"

"What choice did I have?" Lena asked irritably as she pulled out.

"Call?"

"Trevor, I'm trying to save you here. We can figure something else out at lunch if you care so much."

Trevor nodded, watching her drive through the back roads. "Can I just say that I didn't realize you knew so much about college football?"

"I picked up a lot from the men in my life and the rest from bullshitting people," Lena replied with a quick grin.

"Well, count me in for college football."

"You plan to go to college?" Lena asked, genuinely confused. Trevor heard concern in her voice as well, creating concern of his own.

"Well, yeah. Why wouldn't I?"

"TNT and college don't mix well."

"Max did it."

"It was an assignment," Lena reminded him.

"Oh, I forgot about that." The disappointment was evident in his voice. Lena didn't know what to say to help him. She had always known college wasn't an option even though she had dreamed for a time that it could be.

They spent the afternoon talking before Lena took him home. "Keep your weapons handy and your window locked. I'll be around to protect you, but you should be ready too."

"What will you do?"

"End this."

"Lena?"

"You should go. Your parents are expecting you," Lena told him, not meeting his gaze. Her own was strong and defiant, not one he was used to. It lacked remorse; it was deadly.

"I love you."

"I love you too. Stay alive, okay?"

Trevor kissed her in response before leaving to grab his things and head to dinner.

Chapter 15

Lena found Monkey prowling that night outside Trevor's house. Monkey only saw her when she spoke.

"Leave."

"Look who's alive, after all. You can't protect him, ghost," he spat at her with as much contempt as he could muster.

"Watch me."

"What are you gonna do? Kill me?"

"If necessary," Lena agreed. She allowed her knife to glint in the moonlight from her side where it had been concealed a moment before. She knew John would find out, yet she saw no other choice. Monkey was known for completing his assignments.

He shifted his footing uncomfortably as he weighed his options. "So, either I leave and get killed by Spider, or I stay and fight you. At least I stand a chance here."

He rushed her with a knife of his own. No longer was it sparring for rank as it had been before. It was fighting to kill. Monkey fought for life; Lena fought for love. Each stayed quiet, knowing the sight of a neighbor would mean the end of them both.

Lena landed the first slash across his calf, knocking out one leg. He stumbled, and Lena lunged again. It didn't land. Instead, her ankle gave way under her weight, forcing her into an unintentional roll. Back and forth it went until Lena's knife left her hand, landing with a thump in Monkey's chest. The shock left him no time to cry out before he died.

She dragged him to her car before it was too late to slip away without the bloodstains becoming permanent. The grass had absorbed the blood like it was nothing so far, but it wouldn't last. She put him into the car before going back and setting a small stack of letters on Trevor's windowsill. She gave the window a sharp tap before jumping back to the ground and leaving, ever careful of her ankle.

He glanced around, finding the letters but no Lena. A bloody thumbprint marked one of the current day, making him do a double-take. He considered for a moment before realizing he was in too deep to back out now, no matter what that meant. It read:

He's gone, don't worry.

The following letters each had a date, which held no meaning for him. He opened the most current of them first.

7.14.16

The second worst day of my life.

Max left that day, and so did my best protector. I think John planned it that way; the twins didn't even get to see him off. I didn't go to work that night. He came and found me. He nearly killed me that night. That was three days before school started. I almost lost all hope that night; I felt it happening. Thank you for helping me.

-Lena Foster

Trevor didn't remember what he had done for her on that day but smiled that he had unknowingly helped. Next in the pile was dated 2013.

8.29.13

The day I realized.

I was sitting on the bleachers of the gym in seventh grade. You were playing flag football with your buddies. You didn't realize that I was there, nor that I had begun to like you. It hurt that Makenzie liked you too. A competition I couldn't win had begun. I didn't win. You asked her out that same day. I stayed back and avoided you both. I didn't try for your attention in the small ways that I had been doing for weeks without realizing it. I never got over you. I got my assignment that night.

I made excuses but never even thought of completing it. You were part of the reason that I have come to school the way I have. I don't regret it. Thank you for my strength.

-Lena Foster

It startled him to hear it had been so long. He remembered her saying she had only gotten the assignment a year ago. Another lie for his sake. He found he didn't mind, though. What he didn't like was that she went through so much pain for his sake. Was it worth his life? He wasn't sure.

He started to put away the letters with his others before he noticed one last envelope stuck to the back of the first one he had read. It was dated 2016, though it had a current note to it too.

1.1.16

I completed your file this day.

I knew everything John could ever know to ruin you and your family. I refused to give it to him. I got new information on him. No one knows but us. He is a Tunnel Snake.

They are the rivals of TNT. They took Mary and corrupted John. He does everything for them. Jackson speaks to John, and his brother impregnated Mary. Sierra is the link they needed. Protect her.

Your file isn't yours now; it's his. It's under your mattress for when the time is right. You can know everything. If you want your papers, I have them. Find me.

-Lena Foster

He decided he needed to sleep before he would delve into

the papers laying beneath him. It proved difficult, knowing they were there. It was the pea that kept him uncomfortable no matter how many mattresses he piled his mind with.

Around two that morning, he gave up and reached under his mattress, fingers closing on the file. The first pages were general details and an image. He saw a little of Lena in John's features, though many of his qualities were in his sons instead: the jaw, nose, eyes.

The description said he had a sister who was mysteriously unnamed, though Trevor couldn't see why. It also held the details of his own four children and ex-wife. He was in his mid-fifties. He was trained as a doctor. Trevor hadn't known that.

Trevor read every detail of his crimes, the public ones anyway. This folder held enough evidence to put him on death row, yet it rested in the hands of Trevor. It wasn't enough to have him just put away. It had to power to do the same to Lena. She was involved too heavily, a strategy surely employed by John. He was smart, no doubt.

Trevor fell asleep reading the pages, woken abruptly by his alarm a few short hours later. Briefly, Trevor forgot the papers, the letters. He got ready for school quickly, ignoring the pages roughly thrown in a drawer, having to head out before he could fully reconcile their importance.

School was long and dull compared to the papers at home. The classes passed too slowly as he awaited meeting Lena. Eventually, he could leave and did so, forgetting football to the dismay of his coach and the real talent scout.

It was Mackenzie who drew him back to high school life, cornering him at his locker as he hurried about, trying to escape.

"I haven't seen you at the parties or games lately."

"Been busy of late," Trevor tried to brush past her. She

caught his arm.

"Hey, I've missed you. You've been spending a lot of time alone lately. Ever since she died... you've been distant." Her hand slithered onto his chest.

"Oh, stop. You've moved on. I've moved on. Get over it," Trevor grumbled, pulling away with a shiver of revulsion. "I've got places to be."

Chapter 16

Trevor threw his bag in the backseat of his car before trailing around the building. He didn't know the first place to search, so aimlessly wandered before remembering her tendency to dwell in dark places. He picked up the pace and went to the trail behind the school leading into the woods, hoping he had guessed correctly.

He saw a glint of light off her hair and turned the corner to find her sitting on a log, clutching a manila folder.

Trevor smiled and walked over to her. He gently tapped her shoulder, and she immediately handed him the folder. "Come on, Lena. Let's go see the boys. I think they've waited long enough."

Lena turned around, confused. "Don't you want to know first?"

"It can wait."

"No, you should turn to page six."

"It can wait."

"Please, just turn to the page."

Trevor rolled his eyes though his heart was beating wildly.

The title read: Birth Parents. His eyes flicked over the phone numbers, addresses, and extra information. Trevor's eyes finally rested on the pictures of his parents. "How long?"

"Four years. They're lovely people." Lena had tears of guilt in her eyes as she turned away. "I'm sorry. I didn't know you… I didn't know how..."

Lena broke down completely from lack of sleep, stress, and guilt. Trevor sat down, still studying the picture and put his arm around her. She threw it off, yelling, "No, you shouldn't be calm! I've met your parents and you haven't. You were my assignment, not them! They could've been in danger yet you're calm! No, you should be yelling."

Lena slumped back onto the log, crying into her hands. She ran her fingers through her hair to help herself calm down. "You should meet them. They're looking forward to meeting you. Alexy's always wanted to meet the twins as well."

"Wait, do they know you're alive?"

"I never died to them."

"Okay, how are you going to introduce me?" He tore his eyes away from the folder. There was pain from her lying to him, remaining alive to them, and more, yet Lena answered as truthfully as possible.

"As a friend, I guess. As their son?"

"What about as your boyfriend?"

"I would be pleased to do so. We must be careful though; John can still be dangerous." Her cries quieted at the prospect and at the ever-present danger.

"You're mine. I've only waited forever."

"Hey, I had to watch you with Makenzie."

"Want to know an embarrassing hobby of mine?" he offered as a distraction to them both.

"This should be good," Lena giggled, accepting his hand to help her up as she wiped at her tears with the other.

"When I was younger… I would come up with thrilling stories of why you came to school so battered and hurt. I had hundreds of conspiracies not nearly as thrilling as real life." Lena laughed, and he nodded, blushing. "Who knew that you'd be the one telling me the true story?"

"Fate did," Lena told him simply. He nodded and watched

as she pulled out her phone and dialed a number.

"Hey, oh yes. I'm sorry, I've been meaning to call. We're going to be ready to meet tonight. You pick the place. It better be nice. Dinner will be on me. Text me the location. We'll meet you in two hours. Okay, yes. See you soon."

Lena hung up and huffed, rolling her eyes animatedly. "Is she talkative?" he asked, suddenly finding himself nervous.

"Very much so. She loves to talk. You probably had a calmer life being with Ana and Chris than you ever would've with Alexy and Quincy." Lena shook her head, a smile parting her lips ever so slightly. Trevor got the door, and Lena nodded to him in gratitude.

He went around the car to drive. "Where to?"

"My home."

"Okay, I forgot to ask. How is John taking this mission?"

"He doesn't know. Not yet anyway. Right now, he thinks I'm in Africa. I only have a week at the most before he'll know."

"Does that mean you'll disappear again in a week?"

Lena turned to the window and began singing the lullaby from the roof. It filled the car, and Trevor felt it sting him. They pulled up, and Lena got out first, going around the back.

"Lena, the front door."

"Mary's home. She won't be leaving for a long time now."

"And why not? She's left before."

"I left her a little present."

"What present?"

"I made a fake claim to CPS for her. I can't have the twins left alone."

"You're still going? But what about us now?"

"I can't... I can explain more tonight after dinner. Now go tell Mary you're taking the twins to a fancy dinner. I need to go get some things."

He nodded slowly and went back around to the front door while Lena headed around back. She scaled the wall as she had so many times and popped the latch. The window was pulled tight and was harder to open, yet Lena managed to get it open. Finally, she saw why it was so hard to open: nails. She had one foot inside the window when she saw the camera. Lena threw a knife through the lens and felt her pulse accelerating.

There was now proof of her existence. She grabbed what she had come for from the closet and ran back out. Her fingers nimbly shoved her through the window, catching herself in a roll to avoid her ankle this time around.

Lena threw the things in the car and hopped around to the twins' window, her ankle flaring with renewed pain. She stopped just short of the window and saw their outlines shadow on their curtains. She reached her arm out and gave it a sharp tap.

Dillon thrust open the curtains and window and looked around. "Lena?"

"Clear?"

He nodded, and Lena emerged from against the wall. "There was a camera in my room. It's gone now, but it caught me."

Dillon looked back toward Timmy and did a quick hand motion. They had created a language that was a mix of ASL and random motions that they taught Lena, which they called Twin Effect. It was rather useful for quick, silent communication and Dillon turned back to her. "Timmy can get it. Where we going?"

Lena disappeared as their door opened, and Dillon pulled the window closed, muttering about wind.

Mary appeared and looked suspicious. "Trevor's here. Dress nice, he's taking you both to dinner." She took another sweeping glance of the room before leaving.

Dillon left the curtains as he and Timmy began getting dressed while Lena hurried back to the car. The question had been left hanging, but it didn't matter anymore.

She got on another call once in the car. "Hey, Alyse. Yes, it's me. We're having a family dinner tonight in about an hour and a half now. I sent Max the location. You should come. See you soon, Alyse. Yeah, I missed you too, bye."

She looked at the house she loved; the flowers out front were wilted, and the grass was turning yellow in the cold, though it didn't matter. It was beautiful due to the memories it once held. Lena turned away from the house and jumped as yet another call came in.

"Hound."

"Sparrow, there's been a problem."

"How so?"

"John tracked you."

"No."

"Yes."

Lena remained quiet and shook her head. "Push the plan forward then. I'm busy now. I'll send you the details."

The line went dead, and Lena formed into a ball. Her blonde hair covered her face. Lena didn't flinch as the door opened nor moved as Trevor and the twins spoke.

They seemed worried but Lena didn't care much at the moment. She didn't move for any of their words. Memories swelled and flexed their strength over her mind.

She was eight. John stood over her. "Pain will be our best teacher. Always has been. Look at how far you've come."

Lena shuddered and tried stepping away just to have him grab her wrist. "But I don't want to."

"You will do as you are told. Emotions are weak; we will get rid of those, don't worry. Sooner the better."

Lena tried to pull out of the memory, but it held tight and continued ever onward.

Her mind was too young to comprehend what that meant for her future. No matter how much she had learned, that wasn't something that she could learn.

"I don't like…" Lena gasped, trying to get her arm back.

"Of course, you don't like it. It's what I like that matters. That's all that matters to you now." He stepped further forward, and Lena could feel the heat of his breath that was about to bark out an order.

This time Lena managed to withdraw from the memory. She sat up and took a shaky breath. They hadn't moved, and Lena looked scared. "Go to your house." Her breath was fast, but the words were strong and steady.

Trevor started the car, and they went on their way without question. The silence threatened to break Lena as her mind wondered. She distracted herself for a few moments by sending Bianca the information she had promised. Once they had pulled up, Lena grabbed her bag and ran inside, escaping the silence completely.

Trevor brought the twins in before hurrying upstairs. He knocked lightly on the bathroom door, which Lena was hiding in. "Um… Kayla, are you okay?"

There was no response, but he heard her throw up into the toilet. He tried to get in, but the door was locked. He knew she didn't want him to see her that way, so he went to his room to change, despite wishing to comfort her.

He was trying to tighten his tie when he heard his door open squeakily.

Chapter 17

Her eyes were stony as she glided over to him and took the tie from his hand. Her fingers were cold as she undid the tie and readjusted it. Trevor looked down at her mournfully. She looked stunning in her off-white dress. It faded into a burnt black lace at the bottom as though flames had once danced on the seam that swished around her knees. There were no sleeves, though she had a shawl around her shoulders, covering scars more effectively than the near-permanent makeup on her arms ever could.

"You look beautiful tonight."

"Thank you." Her voice was stiff when she answered. She pulled the tie and adjusted how it was laying a final time.

Lena's eyes still hadn't looked up. "Lena, what happened?" he asked gently.

"Something that you needn't know tonight." Lena left Trevor as he followed quickly on her heels. She was determined not to care. His door was open, and Lena riffled through a drawer for some paper. Lena checked the time as she pulled the paper out. "I have half an hour before we go. I have half an hour to write my story."

Trevor didn't like how that sounded as she started writing, scribbling, on the paper. Each was carefully folded, sealed, and stacked. Trevor tried for a while to read over her shoulder, but that only made her lean farther over the paper, slowing her down. He finally resorted to flopping down on the bed, that was until a letter hit him in the face.

He sat up quickly and opened the unsealed letter. He sighed

and thought about what it could say, then realized that it didn't matter what it could say, just what it did. He wanted to know her life no matter what pain it had.

8.1.13

A poem

I despise you. In every way, I despise you. You may not cause pain, but you help it. I love you. In every way, I love you. You may not cause hope, but you fuel it.

I hate you. In every way, I hate you. You may not cause hurt, but you help it.

I adore you. In every way, I adore you. You may not cause inspiration, but you fuel it.

I loathe you. In every way, I loathe you. You may not cause abuse, but you help it.

I like you. In every way, I like you. You may not cause joy, but you fuel it.

I tolerate you. In every way, I tolerate you. You may not cause grief, but you help it. I enjoy you. In every way, I enjoy you. You may not cause laughter, but you fuel it.

I wrote this the day I realized, the day you asked out Makenzie. It holds true. I do love, adore, like, and enjoy you. I also despise, hate, loathe and tolerate the effects of the first list. I don't like how much you mean to me, but I do love that you brought me into your life. Thank you.

-Lena Foster

She didn't look back to see Trevor's melancholy stare, but he did see that she had stopped writing. Lena straightened up and wiped her eyes from the wetness that lingered there.

Trevor looked down at the poem and noticed how the ink had smeared from the wet paper. It was hard to see why this was happening. He stood up and turned her chair around. The wheels squeaked a little as he pulled her out of the chair. He dug his nose into her hair as he felt her tears wetting his shirt.

Lena clung to him, and Trevor rubbed her back, still unsure of the causes of the tears. All he knew was that she was grieving a loss, and he was afraid that it was the loss of him.

Lena broke the hug first and looked at the clock. "Go change your shirt while I clean up. I'll meet you downstairs in just a moment." Her voice caught a little, but she shrugged off his hand when he tried to comfort her. Trevor turned to leave and heard her whisper, "I'm sorry."

He wanted to turn. He wanted to tell her that everything was going to be okay, that he would protect her. He refused to show that he had heard her, that he had heard her moment of weakness.

Trevor did indeed go to put on a new shirt, but he dialed someone along the way. "What happened?"

Bianca sounded confused. "What?"

"What happened to her, Hound?"

"I can't tell you."

Trevor took in an angry breath. "Hound, tell me."

"I can't."

"Why? Because you don't know or because you're afraid?"

"John knows that she's here," Bianca sighed as she relented, knowing he wouldn't give up. Trevor could tell from her tone that she had wanted to tell someone and that this was a relief.

"I want to come."

"Of course, you want to come. You don't always get what you want. He will kill you. That's not what she wants."

"Do you even know what she's planned?"

"Of course, I know the plan." Bianca seemed confident and bold in her assuring.

"And what she's planned for herself?"

"For herself?"

"She's going to run. She wants it over. All of it."

"No, she's just worried. It's not every night that your father is murdered, right?" Bianca chuckled nervously.

"You're a terrible liar."

"No, you just don't want to believe me." Something still sounded false in her tone, but Trevor couldn't tell if it was just his imagination or not. He didn't know her well enough to know if she was lying, and he wanted to believe her. He made himself believe.

"I'll see you." Trevor hung up. Pain welled in him, not only because of his sudden doubt, but he was about to meet his birth parents. He sat down on his bed, holding his tie. A gentle knock came at the door.

"Trevor?" Lena's voice came at the door.

"Come in."

She entered, and he stood up. Her eyes looked at his for the first time that night. Again, she came over and took the tie from his hands. She fixed it calmly, a small smile playing on her tired face. "You must learn to do this yourself."

"Why? You can be here to do it. It doesn't have to change." Trevor held her gaze, but she stepped back.

"We need to go before we're late." She turned back toward the door. Trevor caught her arm and swung her back around.

"Please, don't do it."

"Do what?" Lena's voice had a false cheeriness to it that made him wince. "Come on, Alexy has been waiting far too long for this meeting. Quincy would be upset if he thought we ditched him, especially since I said I am paying." Lena took his hand and guided him out the door. "Timmy, Dillon, we must go. Thank you, Ana."

Lena hugged Ana tightly before leaving and pulling the twins back out to the car. "She seems happy," Ana remarked, returning to the kitchen as Trevor headed after her. "Do I know her?"

He hugged his mother before leaving. "Bye, Mom. I'll see you later, okay?" He ignored her question, hoping she would too.

"Bye, honey. Tell the twins that they're welcome to come visit any time they like. I miss having little boys around here."

Trevor left the kitchen but glanced back toward his mother as he left. Something felt off, yet he knew he'd come back. He had to come to get his gun belt from upstairs after all.

He walked out the door and felt as though a weight had dropped onto his shoulders. He wasn't sure if it was because of Lena or if it was due to the worry he had for their future or the quick approach of his past.

Chapter 18

Alyse and Max were waiting outside when they pulled up. Max got Lena's door, and Lena went to the valet service and handed them the keys. Alyse pulled her into a hug the moment she got back.

"You should've called, visited, anything."

"Max should've told you. How are you enjoying Texas?"

"It's great. Though Maxwell should still let me join TNT."

"He will, very soon." Lena smiled and led them to the doors of an expensive restaurant she had been to a few times before with mafia leaders. "Reservation, Foster."

"Of course, Ms. Foster. Right this way." The man recognized her from previous visits and ushered her to the waiter. The waiter then led them to a private room.

Alyse looked around thoughtfully. "This would be a nice place to work. I bet they pay well." She twirled, looking at the hall they were passing through, her golden dress fluttering out around her.

The waiter led them into the private room, taking drink orders immediately as though under threat of death. Lena supposed that he may very well have been from his manager based on the reverential treatment she was always given.

The group chattered a bit, eventually landing on the topic of Trevor's friends, which each agreed he needed new ones after a few stories were shared amongst the group. It was fun, and Lena enjoyed watching, though she didn't join in. Trevor noticed and squeezed her hand. "You all right?"

Lena nodded and looked toward the door. Alexy and Quincy were there. Trevor froze while Lena went to greet them. She hugged them both, and they returned the favor.

Lena went back to the table and took Trevor's hand. He clamped his hand upon hers and stood up. His parents stiffened slightly and looked at him, their eyes devouring him. He focused first on his mother, then on his father. His eyes began flicking between the two, unsure of who to focus on more.

Lena tried to fall back, but Trevor gripped her hand tighter. "Okay then. Alexy, Quincy, this is my boyfriend and your son. Trevor, this is your father, Quincy, and your mother, Alexy."

Alexy rocked on her heels, making her short, dark-brown hair swing, clearly wanting to hug her son. Lena whispered to him his mother's wishes. He shook his head, but Lena pulled him forward. Trevor awkwardly held out his arm, and his parents jumped on the opportunity. His mom's light brown eyes, Trevor's eyes, clouded with tears. His father enveloped him in his deeply tanned arms, his own shaggy brown hair just as unmanageable as Trevor's was.

Lena slipped away, not just from the group but from the room. No one seemed to notice as they were all focused on Trevor and his family. She went to the front desk and smiled at the manager. "Please, put the bill on my usual card and if anyone asks where I went or is searching for me, make sure you think of something good. I'll pay extra tip if you do well." He nodded, and Lena left, going out the front door.

"Bianca, did he buy your bluff?" Lena asked as she walked to a woman in a floppy hat.

"Of course. Are you sure?"

"Yes. You'll help me, right?"

"Yes, I don't like it, but yes. I hate to see you suffer." Bianca took her hand and led her to a black limo at the beginning of the row of cars. "We have to change quickly if there's any chance of this working."

"Max is keeping them there. He doesn't know the whole plan, but he does know about John." Lena got in quickly and grabbed the bag Bianca had sitting on the seat and began changing. Bianca locked the door and pulled off her fur coat to reveal her uniform.

"Smart planning," Lena said as she threw on her pants.

"I thought so."

"Are you ready?"

"Of course." Bianca seemed reluctant yet determined, nevertheless.

"Did you already poison John?"

"Yes, where to?"

"We'll do it at my house. That's where my bad luck needs to remain."

Chapter 19

Four years had passed now. Lena was sitting, blank-eyed, outside her one-story house. She sat here every day, awaiting her fiancé's return. Lena hated his return but waited anyway, wispy brown hair drifting into her eyes in the late autumn breeze. Her contacts bothered her less now. No longer did they sting to put in, changing her eyes from blue to brown.

Lena remembered her brothers' every detail, although she hadn't seen them in years, not since that dinner. It was such a happy memory, which she wished wouldn't fade. Her mind loved creating fake memories of them, of Trevor too.

He remained perfect in her mind. She hadn't finished writing her life for Trevor, so she wrote most days and nights. She now had a plastic tub worth of letters hidden away under her mattress. It was a nervous tick to write her memories. She didn't know how many letters were repeated nor how many were fake. All she knew was that they were there.

A car pulled up, and Lena twisted her fake silver ring on her finger as Jeff Cox stepped from his car. He was a round man that refused to diet. Jeff was in his mid-thirties next to Lena's twenty-two. She had spun him a web of lies, telling him that she was conservative, wouldn't use her first kiss till marriage and even refused to sleep in the same room. He never cared, not enough to let her leave the house anyway. He was just proud to have secured such a pretty fiancé, even if she was a bit mental.

Lena was contained to the property and never even thought of leaving. All he needed her for was to make food, clean the house, and bring him beer. His excuse was that it was his parents that wanted him to marry a good girl such as her and that he couldn't have her stolen away by some other man, which would surely happen if Lena left the house. She didn't mind, though, not any more.

Lena hurried to the car to grab the groceries he had bought after work, one of the few chores he was openly willing to complete without too much complaint.

Jeff left to sit in front of the television with his case of beer. Her thin arms struggled to carry many bags; he had told her that her workout should be with bags and that her diet should contain only healthy food.

Lena had agreed and hoped this meant well. She had realized quickly that Jeff didn't buy much healthy food, nor did he think of it as an important grocery to be gotten every week. He did notice, however, if she ate any of his food, going red with fury whenever she did.

"What would you like, dear?" Lena called to the living room. Her voice was a forced octave higher, which made her vocal cords strain and crack.

"Spaghetti, a few servings." He didn't even thank her. Lena didn't care; she couldn't have chosen a better person to base her new life around.

Her mind wandered to their first meeting while she cooked.

He was no charmer but was a bit stocky with his floppy black hair and dark eyes. Lena knew she couldn't choose someone she would normally like; she had to make a new person, someone no one would want to find.

"Hello, I'm Diana Wincock."

"Jeff Cox. Why are you at a bar?"

"Burn off bad memories or meet a guy like you."

They went out a few more times, and he proposed quickly. Lena regretted saying yes, but she knew there wasn't an option. She needed to remain hidden somehow.

He had planned the whole wedding. It was to take place in the daytime just the following day. Following tradition, Jeff would leave after eating to go to his bachelor's party, though it was no different from any other evening, while Lena sat outside and waited again, although she knew he wouldn't return until dawn at the soonest. Nevertheless, Lena would wait and be awake on the porch when he stumbled home.

Trevor sat in front of his computer at TNT. He had begun living here after he had finished high school. Avery and Michael had retaken their positions of power after John's death; neither minded him sitting in his fruitless search, only mentioning for him to eat or shower.

Everyone seemed convinced of Lena's death this time. Only one person seemed to avoid the topic entirely: Bianca. He had tried getting information but failed as she held the same case as the others yet wouldn't meet his eyes.

He tracked every woman who could have anything to do with Lena over the years. He had narrowed it down to two women: Elena Adman and Diana Wincock. He visited every event he could for Elena but never saw the glint of blue eyes from her. Diana was more elusive, though. Trevor had resorted now to tracking her fiancé. Finding out she had one was a chore, but Jeff had made a post about his engagement to her.

Jeff didn't seem the type that Lena would go for, but he was determined to hunt every possible case. He found him at a bar that night with his buddies. Trevor refused to get close; instead, he sat with a full beer in one hand and watched. What he watched appalled him. Jeff left with some brown-haired girl for quite some time before returning.

Trevor wrinkled his nose before passing the laughing men and going to the girl who had just returned. Trevor tapped her shoulder, and she turned around. "Makenzie?"

"Trevor? Long time no see."

"Yeah, how have you been?"

"Like you care. Why are you here?" She seemed tired in her skimpy clothes and big eyelashes. "You here for sugar?"

"I need information about that man." Trevor gestured to Jeff and his buddies. Makenzie looked and rolled her eyes, stopping her flirtatious movements as, clearly, he wasn't here for the same reasons as Jeff and his posse.

"Unsatisfied, about to marry a girl at the Chinese garden around the corner; I think he said that it was tomorrow. That's it." Makenzie pursed her lips, looking Trevor up and down. "You've had better days."

"So have you. Thanks for the information. I need to go."

"That's it? No 'let's get together for coffee some time'?"

"Nope, bye, Makenzie." Trevor disappeared and left the bar, his drink untouched upon the bar. It was black outside, but he walked down the street to a men's fashion store.

"We're closed." A surly man behind the counter announced loudly to him.

"I need a tux for tomorrow. Please will you help me?"

"Depends."

"I'll pay a hundred dollars extra."

"Two hundred, and you've got a deal."

"You got a black one?"

The man walked to a rack of tuxes and handed one to Trevor. "Should fit. Go try it on." Trevor hurried and tried on the tux. It fit well enough, so he went and paid for it and left the man counting his takings.

Trevor went back to TNT to sleep, and when he woke, it was already bright out. He showered and changed before heading for the restaurant where it was to be held. It was starting when he arrived, so he took a seat in the back.

Someone inexperienced started playing the bells, hitting as many wrong notes as right ones as the door opened which further added to the already sad scene. Lena stepped out in an ill-fitting, stained, second-hand wedding dress.

Trevor focused on her eyes and saw that they were glazed with tears as she looked down at her fake white roses. A flash of blue passed on her eye before it was covered again by the contact. He gasped, and she looked at him. Her eyes widened with fear before she faced her flowers again. Trevor watched her with concern; this wasn't the girl that had left four years ago. There was a change that he couldn't identify yet.

He looked up toward Jeff and saw no hint of a smile, just a blank face. Trevor was anxious for his part in the ceremony to come; it took what felt like forever before it came.

"Please, speak now or forever hold your peace." The preacher looked around, and his eyes landed on the now standing Trevor. "Your objection?"

"That man has already committed adultery, and I love the bride." Trevor pointed at Jeff, and his eyes shifted first to Lena, then to the disappointed groom's father, who had stood up and was berating Jeff. Lena had tears freely running down her face now as she ran out of the restaurant to the sounds of muttering guests.

Trevor followed, unsure after so long of what to say. Lena wasn't down the street as Trevor had expected but just outside the door.

"Won't Jeff find you here?"

"He doesn't care; he was only doing it for his parents," she told him, her voice much quieter than he thought he remembered it being.

Trevor walked around her and saw tears trailing down her face. She shocked him; Lena pulled him into a hug. Trevor relaxed and returned the favor. "I've missed you."

"I've missed you more." Then, in a sudden rush, she broke the hug saying, "I have to go."

"No, never again." Trevor held her tighter, though felt the change beneath his arms and released her a moment later.

"Yes, it's unsafe. He'll find me. He'll find you. He'll know I didn't do it. He'll fulfill his promise. I have to go." Anxiety took her over completely in a way Trevor hadn't seen.

Trevor wasn't sure what to do. All of the worry she had pent up for years seemed to be bursting from her. It scared him.

"Who, Lena?"

"Him. The man on the other side. He contacted me when I was gone."

"A name, who?"

"Him. They have created bonds. They are near; they can't know." Lena looked around as if one would appear. Her state had worsened more than he had ever imagined.

"Lena, let's go to my car. I'll take you home."

"Not yet, I have some where to go first." Lena seemed a bit more lucid in that moment.

"Okay, can you direct me?"

Lena nodded vigorously and followed him to the car. She

pointed down the streets, and they arrived at her small house. Trevor pulled into the house driveway, and Lena hopped out. Trevor followed quickly, looking at the rundown neighborhood as he passed by. Trevor ducked in and found the house perfectly clean.

Lena was in her room, piling the letters into a bin she had pulled from her closet. Trevor watched her with her letters and went over after the initial shock had subsided; he pulled out an armful of letters.

Trevor looked at one and saw that it was the same one as he had gotten on the first night. He put it in with the rest and helped carry the box out to the car. Lena tried to help, but she was much too frail. Trevor took it from her and heaved it up. "How much did you write?"

"Every day for hours. Writing fills time while I wait. Jeff buys me paper. He doesn't mind buying me paper."

"Wait for what?"

"I used to wait for Jeff, but I don't know any more. I guess I was waiting for you." Her brown eyes landed on his. Trevor felt a pang of longing at her words and pain as he saw a new vacancy in the back of her eyes that he wasn't sure if he could fill.

Lena got in the passenger seat while Trevor closed the trunk on the letters. His mind seemed foggy with the unexpected changes in her. She was still matter of fact, but little else was as he remembered.

"Off to TNT."

"What will I tell them?" Lena's true voice came out a little more than he had seen thus far.

"Here, call Hound and tell her you're coming."

Trevor handed her his phone, and she looked at it. She just moved it a bit for a few minutes before opening to call Bianca.

"The controls are new."

Trevor looked over at her and took the phone. He dialed Bianca. Trevor handed it back to Lena, and she put it up to her ear.

"Trevor, I'm busy." Her words were sharp, yet the tone was light-hearted.

"You aren't busy enough."

"Do… I know you?"

"Thanks, really thank you. It's Diana, no. No, it's Lena." Lena tried for sarcasm, but it just sounded sad.

"Lena! Why do you have Trevor's phone?"

"I'm with him. I'm coming to TNT now. Please get them together."

"Of course. It's good to hear from you, Lena."

"You too."

The line went dead, and Lena handed the phone back to Trevor. He smiled and took her hand. She jumped a little but didn't pull it away.

"Don't leave me when we arrive," she told him, quiet again though seemingly from nerves this time.

"I won't. We're here. You ready?"

"No."

"Great."

Lena glared at him, and he laughed, "Don't get mad at me. You're the one that ran away and got engaged and nearly married, remember?"

She seemed to shrink into herself at the mention. He winced and apologized though she didn't seem to hear him.

Chapter 20

A few people stopped to stare at first; others just walked on. More people seemed to be recognizing her the farther they walked, and whispers broke out behind them. Trevor had given her an old uniform jacket to wear to avoid everyone's attention though it didn't seem to matter as her white skirt continued to draw unwanted eyes in the halls of TNT.

Lena nodded to those which she recognized, and Trevor beckoned to those of Squadron Thirteen that they passed. Each showed shock but didn't speak about it. Trevor sent Sara to go find Tyler before he went off to dinner while Sean and Katie fell into step beside them.

"They are under my command for now. I'll formally return Thirteen to you once your strength is back," Trevor whispered.

Lena nodded, part of her normal confidence seeming to return, though she didn't meet anyone's eyes. Lena knocked lightly on Beta's office door to hear Bianca saying, "Max, sit your ass down. You go and sit, now." There was a thump as he sat. There were some quiet footfalls as she walked to the door.

Trevor entered first, then Lena. There were some gasps, and Alyse shrieked gleefully. Lena started at the sight of not just Max but the twins as well. They must have joined despite her wishes. She remembered laying it out to Bianca before she left, but she couldn't blame her for forgetting things after four years. It didn't matter now. Instead, Lena looked at her brothers' hungrily, searching them for changes. The twins were both taller, broader, and had more chiseled faces. Maxwell had shorter hair and more age lines.

Alyse sat on the arm of his chair. She was smiling and seemed as cheerful as ever. Her hair was longer and fell gracefully across her forehead. Her face, too, was lined, but her eyes were the same as ever.

Avery and Michael had more grey in their hair but not as much as Mary had had when Lena left. Mary wasn't there, but Sierra was. Sierra was being held back by Avery's arms. She had blue eyes and blonde hair just like Lena remembered. She wiggled in Avery's grasp and didn't seem particularly pleased that she wasn't being released based on her angry mutters.

Lena last turned to Bianca, whose black hair had been cut shorter than before. Her laugh lines were all dwarfed by the premature wrinkling across her forehead. It seemed as though she had not been so carefree since Lena left.

Lena stumbled toward Max, and he caught her quietly. He held her tightly so tight that she gasped in pain. He loosened his grip just enough for her to breathe more freely but didn't let her go. His nose was pressed into her hair as the twins ran up and joined them.

Alyse moved from the arm of the chair to watch with everyone else from a distance. Lena sobbed quietly, and Max loosened his grip to let Sierra wriggle into the knot of people. Lena held her sister tightly; Sierra giggling as she played with Lena's hair.

New arms wrapped around them. They stood in a big hug for what felt like forever. Eventually, they parted, and Lena stood back from them.

Max spoke first, a crisp fear lining his voice, "How... how did you disappear?"

"I ran. Also, I found a really crappy guy to date." Lena

nodded as though that explained it all. "I didn't want to come back. I didn't want to say your names again. I still have to go. You're not safe. I've got to go. You're not safe."

Lena tried to leave, but Sean blocked the door. Lena whispered to Sierra, who was still hiding in her arms, and Sierra ran over to Max.

"What danger were you running from?" Avery asked, looking confused as she moved closer to Lena.

Lena jumped back as if she were a scared animal. "Him, the man on the other side of the phone."

"She won't say his name," Trevor informed them over the end of her sentence. Avery nodded, her eyebrows furrowing in the middle.

"I can't stay. Please, just let me protect you," Lena begged.

"How, Lena? How will you leaving help any of us?" Trevor pleaded for her answer as she backed up.

"I'll fight him. I need to go. I have a home I can rest in. I have a place I can stay to regain strength. Please, just let me go." Lena looked desperately between the crowds. There were too many people for her to handle. She felt trapped under their expectations.

"Only if you'll let us come," Max told her. Lena nodded silently to herself.

"We'll all go. Crow can watch things here. I would've chosen someone else, but, well, she isn't an option," Beta announced, looking directly at Lena, implications hiding beneath her words that Lena was too tired to figure out.

"Where will we go?" Michael asked, looking at Lena.

"I have cottages; I bought them before leaving. I stayed there for three years before I met Jeff. He was a strange man, no manners. He was quite a terrible human being." Lena's inward thoughts seemed uncontained and wondering, making her receive worried glances from around the room. No longer did her speech have a refined calculation to it.

"Why did you stay with him for so long?" Trevor asked, his mind hating him for asking. Fear overrode his thoughts; he knew she couldn't love him, but it made him wonder more.

"I knew I could never love him. I would never forget what we had, and I would never be reminded of it either. Also, I wouldn't be expected to go out, be found. Also... I don't remember." Her brows furrowed in thought, yet nothing seemed to come of it as she didn't speak.

Lena refused to tell them details from her exile, only answering with cryptic answers and meandering off into some memory. Her eyes glowed happily with seeing them, but she didn't seem completely with it as they talked, occasionally panicking that she was with them.

Too soon, a bell ran for the start of dinner, and Lena looked up, confused. "Dinner," Bianca said shortly, opening the door.

"But... I don't eat dinner with everyone else. I am to wait in the kitchen until my day is done," Lena reminded them calmly, mind flashing to memories of Jeff.

Everyone looked worried again as they saw how convinced she was of this sad fate. Trevor led her along with everyone out the door, saying, "You can eat with everyone else just like you used to. Anything you want to eat."

"I don't know what I want to eat. I only eat fruit and vegetables. That's my food. That's what I eat." Lena tried to think of the last time she had eaten something she actually liked. She couldn't remember when it had been. Her eyes welled up with tears, and Lena started trying to remember the trivial things of her previous life.

"What happened? You can tell me," Trevor assured her, pausing on their way to dinner, waving everyone else forward.

"I don't remember any of it. I don't remember my birthday or address or number or food. I don't even know if the dates on my letters are real. I don't—" Lena tried remembering all of the little things from school and felt her mind burning from strain. "I don't remember my teacher's names either. I don't remember any of it."

Trevor pulled her into a hug to comfort her. She relaxed in his arms as he told her calmly, "Your birthday is November twenty-first. You no longer have an address, nor do you have a number. You can find out the rest later. You'll be fine. Come on, let's get some food in you."

"I didn't even know that I turned twenty-two."

Trevor led her to the dining hall with everyone else. Food lined the table, but Lena didn't seem to want to take any of it.

"Come on, you need to eat," Trevor prompted.

"Why?" Lena asked, looking around at everything, even as her stomach growled.

"To regain strength, so you can fight."

Lena nodded slowly and grabbed an apple. She ate it faster than Trevor had expected, and he loaded a plate with steak and mashed potatoes for her. She dug in as everyone watched her. They all ate more slowly and laughed as she scraped her plate of the last bits.

"Not too much. We don't need you throwing up, do we? One last thing. Here." Trevor handed her a brownie.

Lena held it and sighed. "I haven't had sweets in so long. Not even before I left. Mary's lemon bars kind of ruined it for me." She took a bite anyway. Her eyes lit up, and she smiled.

Lena went back with Trevor to his room after dinner, and he

pulled out some of her old clothes that he had kept for this day.

"They may be a bit big, but you'll fit them again soon enough."

Lena nodded and went to the bathroom to change. She came back out in her pajamas and sat on the bed. "Can we just talk for a little while?"

"About what?" Trevor climbed on the bed and sat across from her.

"Nothing sad. Funny things we missed?"

"Well, you first."

"I learned that I like goats."

"Goats?"

"Yes, they are nice and funny. I helped this lady nearby cure a baby goat with a broken leg. It was so cute when it left."

"Well, I searched for you, right? I met this old lady Delanie, who I visit every Tuesday. She's very kind and tells me about her kids all the time."

"She sounds kind."

They stayed up half the night telling stories until Lena passed out. Trevor tucked her in and kissed her forehead gently. He walked to his armchair silently and fell asleep to the sound of Lena's gentle breathing.

Both of them had a calm, dreamless sleep, neither wanting to leave the room.

Chapter 21

"What did you tell Mary? She must be worried for the twins and Sierra; what about school?" Lena pestered Max early the next morning.

"Trevor didn't tell you? No. Of course not. Mary deserted after you left. I have custody of all three of them."

"Really? That's great. Much easier to deal with. When's your wedding?"

"Delayed for now. We'll wait until the threat is gone," Max replied, trying to keep up with her quick topic changes. It was disturbing how much she had changed, yet he took comfort in her return, nevertheless.

"It shouldn't be delayed. I'm sorry. What type of wedding?"

"Small, preferably in the snow. Alyse only wants close friends and our family. Her father disowned her last year when she turned down the company in New York."

"Then we can have the ceremony at my home. It's January now, so we may even have snow."

"I'll talk to Alyse about it. Anyway, how much room do we have? We have—" He counted on his fingers the number. "— fourteen people, as long as no one else tags along."

"Well, I have eight small cottages. No electricity or anything, completely off-grid. There's a school about twenty miles out that the twins and Sierra could go to. Sierra next fall."

Max listened calmly, noticed the small things Lena would remember and hung on. School, especially, was a sticking point, brought up often and for long times. She could recall that Sierra wasn't yet in school and that the twins were freshmen, though not know where she was.

Avery came into the small room they had been speaking in. "I sent everyone to go bring their possessions and clothes to the cars along with as much nonperishable food."

"No electronics except for the cars. We'll have one emergency phone there."

"Do you mean the old cars?"

"Of course." Lena smiled, and Avery grimaced.

"I hate those cars," Beta remarked quietly.

"Lena, what about food after our stock runs out?" Max looked at her expectantly.

"There's a grocery store by the school. Other than that, we'll get everything we need from the garden, which I'll need to expand. Beta, can you grab enough cash to cover the year with fourteen of us?"

Beta rolled her head around, calculating the numbers as she left.

Max stood, and Lena followed suit. "I'd best go pack some clothes of my own," Max said, realizing that suddenly.

"I'll go to the convenience store with Trevor to grab some things. What of people's families?"

"By people's you mean Trevor's, right? He has time to go visit them before we leave. I think Beta said lunch time."

They went in opposite directions, both off to complete their own tasks. Lena entered Trevor's room silently and sat on the edge of the bed in front of where he was sleeping. She shook her head and went to shower and change before waking him. Lena found hair bleach when she was looking for clothes, presumably from a disguise.

She redid her hair happily, even though she had already

showered. Lena found an old pair of jeans along with a large flannel in a cabinet to wear. Each was too large for her, but a belt that was in the back of a cabinet made the jeans fit better, and the shirt was fine as it was. Lena exited slowly and sat again on the edge of the bed. Instead of prodding him awake, she went about trying to find her old army boots, singing as she went.

He opened one eye blearily and groaned. Lena turned. "Good morning."

He jumped and said, "Oh, you're here. I thought it was a dream."

"I'm very much here. I need you to get dressed, but first, where are my boots?"

He stood, stretching with a yawn, and walked to a cabinet she hadn't yet searched. "Here you are. I'll be just a minute."

He went to the bathroom after grabbing a stack of clothes, turning back to make sure she was still there as he went. The door closed behind him, and Lena heard the shower start and finish as she laced her boots. The string felt natural in her fingers, and she nodded. At least her foot size hadn't changed.

"So, where are we going?" Trevor asked as he opened the door. He was drying his hair with a towel; his jeans were spotted with water while his shirt sat folded on the counter.

"We need to go visit all of your parents. Also, I need to get some stuff at a store before we go." Her voice remained quiet, though the false high pitch was gone.

"You're coming to see my parents? They all know you're dead." Trevor hung up the towel, and Lena went over to help him button up the shirt.

"Yes, I'm sure. You're going to be gone for who knows how long. They deserve to know why you won't be picking up your phone. Speaking of which, you should call Ana and let her know we're coming." Lena pecked him on the lips and went to grab his phone from the side table.

"You're happy today."

"Well, I'm unmarried, I'm around my people, and I get to go scare people. All my favorite things to do in one day," Lena joked with a little strain. Trevor could tell that she was struggling to be back and that leaving was going to help her relax more than being around him was.

"I'll call on our way out," Trevor told her, calmly wrapping his arm around her shoulders.

Lena shivered at his touch and sighed, "I've missed being here. It's strange wanting to go so badly now."

"Well, we'll be together every step of the way now. Come on, we best go, so they don't get mad."

"Who?" Lena asked, walking a little faster.

"Hound or Beta."

Lena thought for a few seconds before murmuring, "That is their name, isn't it?"

Trevor got Lena's door and walked around to his own, pulling out his phone. "Hey, Ma. Yeah, I know. Hey, we're coming over like now. You'll understand when we arrive. I'll see you in a bit."

Lena looked out the window, recognizing all of the places as they drove, small memories from each popping into her head. "Ana will be worried."

"Chris won't be. He trusts me by now."

"I hope they don't faint."

Trevor chuckled lightly, "You remember this place?"

Lena looked back to the side and saw his house as they pulled up. "It's so cute. I always loved this place."

"Come on, time to scare my first set of parents," Trevor told her, parking the car.

"This should be fun. Who do I start as? Diana or myself?"

"Doesn't matter."

"You're no fun."

He unlocked the door and walked in. "Mom! Dad! We're home!"

"We? Who's we?" Ana appeared at the doorway to the kitchen.

"Lena. I'm Lena," she told her as she moved forward to hug Ana.

"Lena? But you're..." She didn't finish the statement. Ana didn't seem to know how to as Lena's very real arms wrapped around her. Ana returned the hug, but they broke apart quickly.

"Trevor, you best not be saying she's back again..." Chris stopped walking as he saw Lena.

She walked up to him as well and gave him a hug, which he didn't return; rather, he just stood there looking down at the young woman.

"You may want to come sit," Trevor called over to them. Lena nodded and went to go make coffee and tea. "Lena, I don't think—"

"Just because I was trapped in a house for years doesn't mean I'm broken, just impaired. I can most definitely make tea and coffee," Lena interrupted calmly, raising an eyebrow.

Ana laughed nervously as Lena went into the kitchen. Both she and Chris were watching Lena as Trevor explained some of the necessary details of her death and their leaving.

Lena came back into the room, hands carrying drinks for each of them. She set the drinks in front of the appropriate person to be untouched and unseen for the rest of the conversation.

Lena interrupted, forgetting Trevor was speaking. "You

should also know that I didn't want to leave. I just needed to protect my family and now yours. The danger I ran from isn't yet gone and now is after your son as well, meaning I have to hide him too. I'm so sorry."

"Where will you be?" Chris leaned forward, his shirt brushing the cup.

"Off the grid. We should be able to send letters from time to time but no calls. It'll be quite some time before we manage to come home," Trevor replied.

"Can you protect him?" Chris asked carefully, looking to Lena.

"Of course. I can't tell you how for other reasons, but he'll be safe," she promised.

"Were you the reason he didn't go to college? Why he was depressed? Why he was always on that damn laptop?" Ana yelled finally. Her anger and confusion seemed directed at Lena, though Trevor knew it was out of love.

"Mom, seriously?" Trevor looked furious.

"I'm sorry. I truly am. I'll let you say goodbye." Lena left the room, quickly trying to distance herself.

She pondered by the stairs, glancing up. After a few moments delay, she finally decided to go up.

Lena decided on the off chance to check Trevor's room for her forgotten things. She went to the small desk where she had written years previously. Lena sat and looked at the small gap between the desk and dresser. Her fingers went to the seam and grabbed at the papers there.

Everything was there. The calendars and a few sheets of paper. A few calendars had ripped but all together well-preserved from where she had stashed them during her first death. Trevor hadn't known that during the time which he slept, waiting for a letter, she had been there; Lena had written on calendars all the dates and events she could remember and sometimes on ones she couldn't.

She took her pile of papers and walked back downstairs. Trevor was waiting there, looking around. He looked drained.

"What did you find?"

"Somethings that I left behind," Lena replied. Trevor looked confused on what that could possibly be but left it be.

She looked back down the hall to where Ana and Chris still sat at the small table, steaming cups sitting in front of them. Trevor took her hand and pulled her outside. "They'll be fine."

Trevor tried to cheer her up by trying to get the papers from her as they walked to the car. She laughed and turned away from him, hugging the papers to her chest. "No, you can't have them."

Trevor tried to snatch one, but Lena turned. Her mood shifted to that of protection. She no longer wished to joke and held the papers all the tighter. Trevor noticed and stopped his attempts; instead, he opened her door.

He went around the car once she was in, Trevor quickly dialing Alexy and Quincy. "Hey, Mom. I'm coming over. Yes, I'll see you soon. We won't be long. Bye, Mom."

"How'd the rest of that dinner go?" Lena's voice had now become timid and scared of the reaction coming.

Trevor hesitated before sighing, "Stressful, very stressful. I learned a lot. Why did you have to leave then?"

"It was the only time that you wouldn't come after me."

"You knew it was going to happen before that, didn't you?"

Lena nodded as they drove along the freeway. "It's a funny thing. I knew that he'd find out. I knew that I'd never make it to the end of the week, let alone the end of the school year. I had hoped for a week; I didn't even last three days. I never wanted to lie to you. I also didn't want you killed. I chose the option with the least pain, one I thought would last. Why'd you come back after me? Why couldn't you just make yourself believe I was gone?"

"Because that's not who I am. I couldn't bear the thought of you being with someone else. I wouldn't rest till I saw your rotting corpse."

"I knew you'd come get me. I had my doubts, of course, but I knew that you'd come in my heart. I still love you."

"I love you too, Lena." Trevor took her hand once again.

They sat in silence the rest of the way to their next destination. Trevor would periodically kiss the back of her hand, and she would smile and continue to look blankly out the window clutching her papers.

The car pulled up to their destination within a few minutes of the call. Trevor walked around to her door to get it again.

"What do I say?" Lena asked quietly, accepting his help from the car. She turned to set down her papers then back to him.

"That's up to you."

"Thanks, really. What would I ever do without you?"

"Try and marry so you would never forget me." An awkward silence filled the air. Lena looked toward the ground. "I'm sorry. I shouldn't have said that. It was stupid," Trevor said guiltily.

"I understand. Don't apologize, please. It just makes it worse. Let's just get this over with. I don't wish to linger."

Trevor nodded. He retook her limp hand. Lena kept pace with him as he looked sideways at her. "You can't blame yourself."

"A debate for another time." Trevor heard the sadness in her voice. He squeezed Lena's hand before ringing the doorbell.

"Trevor, why—" Alexy stumbled back and almost fell over,

but Lena got to her before she hit the floor. Lena winced at the strain on her weak muscles but set her back on her feet.

"Quincy!" Alexy called once Lena had gone back to Trevor. She stepped behind him and clutched his arm. He wrapped it around her shoulder. Lena edged into Trevor for protection, which he didn't understand.

Trevor held her through explaining to his parents how she was alive, briefly why she had left, and a summary of why they had to go. Alexy broke into tears while Quincy looked worried.

"How will we know if you were hurt?" Quincy pulled Alexy back from them. Neither one of the couple seemed to want to invite them in.

"We would inform you of heightened danger. We'll send you an address and number in case something suspicious happens. You should send anything out of the ordinary. The same number will contact you if anything were to happen," Lena spoke quickly, her grip loosening on Trevor a little bit.

"Be safe, both of you," Alexy whispered.

Lena nodded and backed up. Trevor followed shortly after her. "Are you almost ready?" Trevor replied.

"As I can be. First, the store than back to TNT. Let's be quick."

"Of course, I'll drive this time. There's only one I can go to."

"Go ahead."

Chapter 22

Everyone was packed and ready by noon. The twins had bidden farewell to their friends; Max and Alyse had worked together to get her fired, which proved harder than expected, and Bianca had gotten everyone's new identity papers printed.

"Papers for everyone. Find your stack please. Everyone gets a new name. There is a list of everyone else's names in your stack," Bianca called as they moved toward the table in the middle of the locked gym.

Everyone read off their name and seemed confused by the end of it. They each looked to one another, trying to recall each name. It didn't matter when they were together as no one would be around to question it; they were only for outsiders.

"I'll be driving the pickup with the majority of the luggage," Michael announced. "Max, Sean, come help me." They nodded and grabbed armloads of luggage to help take to the truck.

"Girls are with me," Lena called. "Let's make you actually match those papers, shall we?"

The girls all followed Lena while the boys helped Michael load the car.

Lena put the girls in one room to start bleaching or dying their hair. She started by bleaching some of their hair, then adding dye until Bianca, Katie, Alyse, and Sierra were each brunette. Avery kept black hair while Lena joined her, clearly upset to already change away from the blonde she had missed. Sara, to her own immense displeasure, went blonde, moaning and groaning the whole while.

She cut their hair to match right after, and each left once they fit the character they had been assigned. Lena had to next go fetch all of the men to change their appearance as well.

Trevor, Max, and Tyler got or kept black hair while Michael got to remain a redhead. Everyone else either remained or became a brunette. Lena cut each of their hair to the appropriate length, which none of them seemed happy about. The men with changed hair color seemed the most uncomfortable, but no one complained openly, and definitely not to Lena, who seemed almost normal with the given task.

They decided to stay the night and leave at dawn the next morning. Lena and Trevor returned to their room, both reeking of hair dye. Trevor retook his chair before remembering something suddenly. He rushed over to a dresser and opened a top drawer.

He pulled out a neatly wrapped gift and handed it to Lena. She smiled and looked at him. "You didn't have to."

"Just open it."

"Remember the bracelet? I still have it." She set the box in her lap and pulled at a chain around her neck. He watched as she pulled out a necklace, holding all of the charms from before. It was simple and easy enough to hide beneath clothing.

"Just open the gift already," Trevor told her, smiling all the while. He was happy she hadn't gotten rid of all her past when she left.

Lena nodded and pulled off the bow on top before unwrapping the present. She opened the top and found a ring. Lena looked up at Trevor, mouth open in surprise.

"This isn't a proposal, at least not yet. This is a promise ring that one day I will make a vow to forever be yours, and, more important, that you'll promise never to run from me again."

Lena nodded and he slipped the simple silver ring with a blue sapphire in the shape of a heart onto her finger. She kissed him gently, and he smiled as they broke apart.

"I think that was the correct finger."

"I know it was the correct question," Lena replied. Her eyes were blue again, as the contacts had been thrown out nearly immediately upon her return, and she seemed happy again.

"Thank you. So, you agree?"

"Would I let you put the ring on my finger just to tell you no?"

He chuckled, and Lena laid back down. Trevor went back to his chair, and Lena shook her head. "You can lay in the bed. Nothing more."

Trevor looked happily surprised as he stood back up. He first sat on the edge of the bed, and when Lena didn't back down, he curled up under the covers as she put her head down on his chest.

The car trip lasted for nine hours, and the three old cars groaned with the distance and weight. Lena led the procession in an old, wagon-looking van. She had five people squeezed into the vehicle while Bianca's muscle car carried five. Trundling along right behind her, Michael's old pickup truck lagged with four people and the majority of the luggage in the box.

Lena, about an hour away from their destination, pulled over to the side, along with the rest of the party. "Electronics have to be destroyed here and now. We have one satellite phone in my car for emergencies. Bury the pieces in the ditch," Lena called. She dropped her phone on the asphalt and stomped on it. The others followed suit and buried the pieces, none too pleased.

They piled back into the cars and drove the final hour into their camp, passing the town that Lena had told them about previously.

"Welcome home, everyone. The last building is the gym and dining hall next to it is the garden. I will assign cottages before you grab your things." Lena began pointing at places, and people slowly left the group.

Michael, Avery, and Bianca were to be in the first cabin on the left. Lena and Trevor were the first on the right. Dillon, Timmy, and Sierra shared the second on the left. Sara and Tyler shared with Sean and Katie next to the kid's cottage. Max and Alyse, meanwhile, took the one next to Lena and Trevor. The last open one, beside Max and Alyse, was to be for storage and extra gear.

Lena left the rest to unpack while she went to check on the garden. Everything was just as she remembered, though with a few more weeds in the paths. The cottages were in a sort of oval with a large campfire in the center. The garden behind the dining hall was out of control.

She sighed and went to pluck off the dead leaves and rotten fruit. Her mind wandered as she looked back toward the large orchard behind everything else.

After she had been there for a few minutes, Trevor knelt beside her and began helping to pluck off the obviously dead leaves. "What are you thinking about?"

"I forgot the letters at home."

"No, you didn't. Of course, we would bring them. I put them in a drawer in our cottage."

Lena turned to him. "How did you know that I wanted them?"

"I know you. I knew that you'd want to have them. Now, how much can I do to help get this garden in order?" He looked around as Lena shuddered at the look of it. She had forgotten how intuitive he could be but was happy for it.

"Just continue what you're doing. I missed being here. It's so peaceful here. I never had to do more than I wished to, nor any less."

She looked back out into the distance and smiled. Lena took his hand and pulled him up to the front of the dining hall. Her stride was more confident here, and she seemed calmer.

Her fingers worked the latch on the door, and it swung open. Lights flicked on as she walked by the tables toward a back room.

"I thought you said there wasn't electricity," Trevor said, looking around.

"I have solar panels. I can make candles as well. The generator lasts for about a week without any sun, but I suppose that was just for me." She seemed to go off mentally for a moment but returned faster than she had been of late. "Now, come on. I want to show you the gym." Lena pulled him along to a back door.

She pushed it open, and he found himself in a padded room. This one was at least ten times as large as the one hidden behind the mirror at her house. It had a full weight room, sparring rings, and targets.

"Come over here. There's something else to show you."

"This isn't it?" He found himself grinning as she dragged him about.

"No. Why would it ever be just that?"

She lifted a bag on the ground to reveal a small bomb she had left. Lena disarmed it quickly, muttering, "Just in case." She put the bag back and pulled back a pad on the wall to reveal a real bomb shelter. Inside was also any other weapons and supplies any army would need.

"How long did it take to build this?"

"I worked on it during the last couple of years of John's life and through my deaths. I haven't worked on building for over a year, but this is enough for now."

"Damn right it is."

Lena blushed but nodded. She had every right to be proud.

Chapter 23

The first week was the hardest for everyone. People would wake up in the middle of the night for a snack and not find a kitchen or would look for a light switch that wasn't there.

Lena adjusted the fastest as she had lived there for three years previously and off and on before that. She had other problems instead. They hadn't packed much food as there hadn't been enough room with fourteen people's stuff. The garden wasn't putting out as it was winter and buying too much food at the local store would draw attention.

Lena's muscles were weak, and many mornings Trevor would wake up without Lena. She would be working in the gym, trying to find her strength. Lena's techniques were still perfect, so the knives would hit the target perfectly when she had enough strength to make it fly straight. The bullets would hit the center when she could keep her hand steady enough to hold the gun up.

The twins returned to school after a couple of days, Michael shown as their legal father with their fake identities. After about two weeks, people began wondering how they were going to clean their clothes.

Lena laughed, "The same place we get our water. Lynx, come on; I'll show you how to clean clothes."

Before she had left, she had finished up on a plumbing system for the cottages but didn't have the money for a washer or drier for her clothes, nor did she have the electricity to run those machines. She and Trevor took all of the clothes down to the river behind the orchard. It ran directly through the forest and made a soothing, rushing noise.

They took a few trips to get all the clothes down to the river, walking past the large water filtration system that supplied all of their water. There was a large tub that Lena filled from a spigot on the side of the tank.

She and Trevor washed the clothes while chatting and discussing nearing occasions.

"We should start collecting firewood. I'm sure we'll want to cook more outside as the weather grows warmer," Lena told him, breaking the calm silence.

"You've gained strength."

"Indeed, I have. Soon, I'll need to go buy some goats and chickens and cows and maybe even a horse. I have a pretty nice pasture behind our cabin that they can stay in. I started collecting materials for a barn, but I don't have any of the necessary wood or framing but that shouldn't be too hard now."

"When should we start?"

"After you all go home for a while. You need to see your family. Assure them that I haven't killed you."

"What? You would come home with us, wouldn't you?"

"No, this is my home. I have things to do here, especially if we have animals." Lena involuntarily reverted momentarily to the timid, quiet voice she had used with Jeff. It was much less common here, yet not gone.

"A debate for another time?" Trevor watched as she hung the last pair of pants and nodded.

"I have sparring with Avery." Lena wiped her forehead and jogged off to the gym, leaving Trevor to deal with the few remaining clothes.

"You're going to overwhelm yourself working like this," Avery commented as she finished stretching.

Lena began their typical circling while saying, "We'll have to pause lessons during the heat of the summer. We have to build a barn and that'll take up most of our time."

Avery landed a jab that made Lena gag; however, as she tripped, Lena took Avery down too. "You need to change your routine. More running and less sparring. Your arms are out pacing your legs," Beta told Lena sternly. She helped Lena to her feet, dusting herself off calmly.

"They will gain strength as we get wood. We have to walk far in order to find the driest wood."

They worked until dinner. Lena, who had taken over the distribution of food, went to the storage to grab some fruit, which had been a substantial part of their meals for the last week.

"I'm tired of apples and pears and oranges and fruit," Sara complained, biting into the apple grumpily.

"You'll be able to eat other food when you all go back to visit TNT in a few weeks. If you bring other canned goods back, then maybe we can eat some other food too," Lena told her, passing out food to the others. "We'll be building a barn soon as well. We need to get some goats, chickens, cows, and maybe a horse."

"How will that work with school?" Dillon asked, apple juice spraying across the table.

"You'll stay in school if that's what you're asking. You'll help with it after school and full-time during break. After school is out, that's when you'll all head back to the city. We have to start wood collection tomorrow. We'll start scouting, tying string on dry, dead trees for now. Through the rest of the week, we'll cut them down and stack them in storage."

They finished the meal in calm silence. Everyone drifted off to bed quietly while Lena went back toward the gym. Her fingers were rough and calloused from work with the knives, guns, and bows in the gym. She was able to perform her typical stunts with knives and guns with confidence. Her arms were now filling with strength that Lena thought she had lost forever.

Trevor watched from the door for a while before heading to bed himself. It made him happy that she was coming back to her normal self, no longer so afraid and weak though still not one hundred percent. He just wished she would allow herself more rest.

Their routines became fluid through spring. On Monday, they would mark firewood, Tuesday Lena would go get supplies for the barn from town, Wednesday and Thursday they would cut wood and build, and Friday everyone would chip in to do laundry or pluck fruit from the garden or orchard. Weekends they left open except for doing some more building or finishing chores they hadn't gotten to during the week.

Nothing exciting came from Crow's reports except for another bout of homesickness. Lena and Michael went to buy the animals when spring break rolled around. They came away with eight chickens, three cows, and two goats. Lena had gone out later to find a horse since the field needed plowing that she couldn't do on her own, not for the numbers she was now feeding.

The wheat she hadn't harvested before had died, and the next generation of wheat had sprung up in its place. It wasn't a large harvest, as only a small amount had made it through the winter. Lena harvested the little bit that was left and fed it to the animals while Michael went out to barter for a large sum of hay.

They put together different shifts to allow for more sleep on specific days as the heat was taxing to everyone. All together, they had bonded and worked as a team better than ever before.

Lena regained the rest of her strength while Sierra grew and grew. She couldn't do much with her tiny arms or weak legs but did lift everyone's spirits. She would run around laughing as she fetched water or tools that they had forgotten. Everyone agreed that country life was better for her to grow up in than a city due to the physical limitations of the city.

It was officially summer before they knew it. Lena was sad to do it but knew they all needed to visit the city to catch up on things or, in Alyse's case, plan a wedding.

Trevor wanted to stay behind with Lena, but she convinced him to go visit his family in the end. She personally didn't want to go back; Lena liked the wilderness and peace that the forest brought.

"I'll come back as soon as I can," Trevor promised on the day that they were leaving.

"I'll wait then. Bring me something from the city. I'll miss you," Lena sighed. They kissed, and she pushed him to the car. Tears slipped down her face as she hugged her siblings. They were all gone within ten minutes, Lena waving until they were out of sight.

Lena walked into the silent village of cabins. She walked through, listening to the eerie whistle of the wind blowing between the cottages. Lena walked to the small stable that they had managed to build beneath the large frame of the barn. They hadn't yet made doors, but at least the animals had a shaded area to sleep and eat. It was too quiet for her now.

"Missy, here, pretty pony," Lena called to the back of one of the stalls. Missy trotted up, her golden-brown mane swishing back and forth. She put her mussel into Lena's hands, searching for an apple or sugar. "Not today, pretty pony. You want to go out and run?"

Lena rubbed her large neck for a while, feeling the powerful muscles ripple under her brown and white coat. Eventually, she released her to run about in the pasture, surely annoying the grazing cows.

Lena watched for a few minutes before moving along to the garden. She felt more efficient, but the slightest noise gave her chills. A few times, she thought she heard the crunch of dead grass from the forest or crunch of gravel underfoot but convinced herself it was just a trick of her mind. The rustle of branches now startled her, the galloping of Missy made her jump, and the crackling of old leaves under the cows' hooves made her stumble.

Lena hardly slept any more, paranoia messing with her at all hours of the day and night.

Her skin was dark from the constant sun, and her hair had returned to blonde in the sun's rays. Lena had reverted to writing letters in her spare time again. She could better remember the dates and events due to the calendars recovered from Trevor's house. She had even worked to sort the previous letters, stacking duplicates, though she couldn't bring herself to throw them away.

She had stopped writing for a while as it worried Trevor, though, in the silence, she reverted back to what she knew. The memories filled time for her. The memories were her friends.

One night, two weeks after everyone had left, Lena was eating in the dining hall when the door creaked open. She turned and saw a dark figure standing at the door. "I didn't hear the car."

Lena walked over, cautious. It was unlike Trevor to just stand there silently. As she neared the man, Lena saw the dark hair, strong frame, green eyes; this was not Trevor.

Lena pulled out a knife and threw it effortlessly. He barely managed to dodge the knife. His laugh echoed through the room. The deep tone resonated in her bones, making her shiver but not back down. "Silly girl, you can't hit me."

"That's a bet, Jackson."

Lena threw another knife and ran toward him. It was probably a stupid move, she acknowledged, but it was the only one she could think of. He grabbed for her, and a bullet went through his outreached hand. Lena jumped over his doubled figure and kicked his keeled over form with her shoe. He staggered forward but didn't fall.

"Stupid little girl," he cried out to the room.

"I figure I'm pretty smart for keeping away from you for so long. John did teach me a few things, whether he wished to or not." Lena just kept talking, trying to come up with a plan. No one was coming to help as their only phone was in the gym, and her closest friend was nine hours away anyway. "How'd you find me, Jackson?"

"Cameras placed around the town. You aren't that hard to recognize. The eyes give you away. You did well for a while there, girl."

"You do realize that my name isn't girl, right?" Lena watched as he stalked forward; she stepped back, watching his jerky movements with a careful eye. He was keeping his injured side behind him as though that would help. "I thought you weren't supposed to show weakness. That's what John said every time he beat me, anyway."

Lena lunged to the side, grazing her knife across his chest. A long red line appeared on his chest, clearly visible through his ripped shirt. "You bitch!"

"Oh no, honey. I'm just someone you don't like. There's a difference between enemy and bitch." Lena followed his circle and sighed, "You are giving me quite a mess to clean up. Do you think you could bleed less for me? That would be a big help."

Lena and Jackson lunged back and forth for a while before Jackson was truly wounded. Lena had gotten a few scrapes here and there, but Jackson was pouring with blood. "Delphina, stop now!"

"You used the wrong name!" Anger swelled in her. Her knife sunk into the soft tissue of his throat. Lena pulled it out, anger fading as fear took over her.

Lena collapsed on a nearby bench, rocking back and forth. Her vision blurred with tears as she listened to the gurgling of blood coming from his throat. Her sobs reached the door, and footsteps came running down the path. She threw her last knife toward the door as she put her head down.

This wasn't her first kill, yet it felt significant. It didn't even last long. Years' worth of running and fear just for it to end in two minutes. The tears were there because the fear hadn't disappeared with the man's life as Lena had hoped it would.

A grunt issued from the door as the person skidded to a stop. "Really, Lena?" Her sob only grew when she heard his familiar voice. He ran over and knelt in front of her. "Lena, are you all right? Did he hurt you?"

Lena didn't reply, so Trevor wrapped her in his arms and carried her outside, ignoring the cuts on her arms and torso that stained his shirt.

"Is there anyone else?" Lena whispered hoarsely. She pulled her head off of his shoulder to look at him.

"Avery and Michael should be here soon. They were unloading the car. Everyone else decided to leave tomorrow." Trevor kissed her forehead gently as he sat down on the bed of their cottage.

Footsteps started to pass the cottage, and Trevor pulled his arms out from under Lena to run outside. Lena heard their voices but not the words. She could only see the replay of Jackson's dying face in front of her; then, it faded to be John's face, back and forth until they were interchangeable. Avery knelt in front of her, and Lena made an extreme effort to see her, to ignore the faces.

"Lena, are you there?" Her voice was low yet calming. Her face was just as always, with her deep brown eyes and flowing black hair. It was comforting to see.

Lena wrapped her arms around Avery. She didn't protest; instead, she returned the hug. Lena had always thought of Avery as the mother she should've had, needed to have. This moment increased that feeling. Lena fell asleep in her arms, twitching in her sleep.

Avery sang quiet, sweet melodies into Lena's ear to help calm her; her voice wasn't as sweet as Lena's but coaxing, nevertheless. Michael returned during her song and smiled. "It's been so long since I last heard you sing."

"I don't like singing," Avery whispered. "Help with these bandages, would you?"

"You should," Lena replied drowsily, reopening her eyes and leaning away from Avery.

"Why is that?" Avery asked, turning to Lena.

"Then we could sing duets."

They all laughed sad little laughs, and Lena fell asleep again. Her head fell onto the bed, sliding off the edge toward the floor. Michael snagged a first aid kit and helped wrap the worst of the cuts. It was quick work and mostly on her forearms, aside from a scrape on her cheek.

Avery waved Trevor to the bed while she and Michael went to deal with the body after it was done. He readily agreed and made his way around Avery to the bed. Trevor sat on the opposite edge before crawling under the covers. He pulled them back from under her to place them over her. She snuggled up to him and placed her head on his chest.

Trevor pulled the chain out from around her neck and examined the charms, a small smile playing on his lips. A new charm had been added that he hadn't noticed before. A small, sealed envelope was hooked on. He ran his finger over it before adding a new one of his own. A small flying sparrow now flew on her neck. It was a beautifully engraved charm that he had always imagined when he called her name. It fit right in the center, an old yet new symbol.

Chapter 24

Everyone had returned by dinner the next night. They were all filled in on what happened, clearly at a time when Lena wasn't around and warned not to talk about the previous night. Lena hated it; it made her feel fragile and weak again.

She left dinner early in disgust, heading for Missy's stable. "Missy, here, pretty pony!" Lena saw that she wasn't in her stable and moved around back to the field, where Lena spotted Missy running. She whistled loudly, and Missy galloped over, flipping her mane and nickering. "Hey, pretty pony. Ready for a ride?"

Lena climbed up on the fence then leapt onto Missy's back, holding her mane tightly in one hand. She laughed as Missy took off at full gallop. She loved riding Missy around. On the second lap around the field, Lena leaned most of her weight off Missy to grab a fallen leaf. It was tricky as she had no saddle, but Lena kept hold of her mane and successfully picked up the fallen leaf.

She had fallen many times perfecting this stunt, but Lena was never satisfied. Lena swung down again and again until her hand slipped, and she fell in the dust.

"Let's go back, Missy," Lena called after her horse. She whistled, and Missy ran back over, proudly flipping her mane. "Yes, you dropped me. Good job. Let's go to bed."

Lena led her back over to the stables and into her stall. She spent some time brushing through her now knotted mane. Lena found she still didn't want to go back, yet she couldn't hide back here forever. Missy nuzzled Lena before she left.

"I love you too. Goodnight." Lena gave her an apple before

leaving for the night. "I'll be back in the morning."

She went out to lead the other animals back to the barn for the night. The goats were cooperative, unlike the cows, who were enjoying grazing still.

Lena swung the makeshift door the twins had created that day closed to keep them in until morning.

Lena decided to try and talk to Trevor as she felt bad for leaving so suddenly during dinner, but when she arrived, he was already asleep. She backed out and went to go practice. The gym typically stayed bright due to Lena's late-night practicing. Her gymnastic skills were back in full, and she had been practicing being able to smoothly catch and fire a gun within seconds. Tonight, however, she was determined to work on archery.

"Lower your shoulder, Lena," Dillon called as he walked in. He went over and adjusted her form. "Lower here, strong here. Relax, breath, and release." The arrow hit its mark perfectly, and Lena smiled as she lowered the bow.

"Thank you, Dillon."

"They don't call me Archer for nothing," he joked, though it felt forced rather than the light and casual way they had always spoken.

"What are you doing up?" She eyed him, caution lingering in her.

"I could ask you the same."

Things had never fully healed between them after Lena returned from her second death. He blamed her for causing the rift in their family. Dillon, unlike Timmy, held a grudge.

"Are you still mad?" Lena asked carefully.

"How could I not be?"

"Because I was trying to protect you from that man last night. He could've easily cut right through us three years ago."

"Then I would've died happily." His eyes looked like John's in that moment.

Tears well in her eyes as she looked at him. She walked past him, jaw set. As she reached the door, she turned around. "I don't know what else I can do. At least let me fix this while I still have the strength to fight for this family," Lena growled at him.

Lena left him there, bow still in hand. He ran after her to apologize. She was gone. Dillon cursed under his breath as he looked around in the darkness. It was at times like these that he wondered if it were Timmy or Lena who could hide better. Ever since joining TNT, both seemed elusive, and not just because each were proficient at hiding.

Dillon sat at the steps leading up to his cottage for a long time, waiting for Lena to return. He didn't realize he had fallen asleep until the sun came over the roof of a nearby cottage and blinded him. He staggered to his feet and went over to Lena's cottage to see if she was there.

He let himself in quietly and glanced cautiously into the bedroom. Trevor was snoring on the bed. Dillon went to breakfast quickly to see if she was there. When he didn't find Lena in the dining hall, he grabbed an apple and walked out to check other locations.

Lena wasn't in the pasture with Missy nor the barn. He checked the orchard quickly, and when she wasn't there, he regressed to the garden.

He walked through the rows of tall tomato plants, cucumbers, peas, strawberries, and other assorted fruits or vegetables, which were full of baby veggies or flowers wilting away. Dillon stopped as he spotted a large puddle drying into the soil. He knelt down. It was blood.

A trail through the grass led into the trees. Dillon wanted to run down it but felt that would be reckless, that he should tell the others before disappearing. This was a critical difference between him and his elder sister. Dillon was safe to a fault; Lena was not. He ran back into the village, searching for the nearest person.

Max was the most easily accessible as he was walking toward the garden.

"Lena's been taken," Dillon cried at him, a panic over-taking most of his senses like they had upon finding her gone after that dinner so many years ago.

"Calm down, what do you mean she's been taken?" Max had heard many of these warnings before and was now quite calm in dealing with many situations in this manner, especially when it came to Lena.

"There was blood in the garden and there was a path leading back to the forest and I haven't seen her anywhere else," Dillon explained quickly; he had also grown used to the situations; although due to his youth, he was more prone to overreact in his fifteen years of age.

"Go tell everyone. If I'm not back in an hour, then come after me. I'll see you later," Max called as he took off to the barn to grab Missy.

Lena woke up in a dark room. It was easily bigger than the cottage, judging by the sound her breathing made in the silence. She tried to see, though there was no light coming from anywhere in the room, not even from below a door. Her head pounded, and she tried to touch the spot on her head where she felt she had been hit.

Ropes ground against each other and rubbed her skin, startling her as she had been much too focused on the darkness to feel their weight and rough fibers. She shut her eyes tightly as to avoid trying to rely on them.

Her fingers were too short to reach the knot. She thought for a second, trying to ignore the loud throbbing in her ears. Lena crouched on her feet and worked her arms painfully under them, so they were in front of her legs, yet they still caught on the chain on her ankles. She sat cross-legged, working the rope with her teeth, bending around the chains.

Lena felt it loosen and twisted her wrists back and forth, trying to loosen it more. They gave way a little more, and she managed to slip her arms free. Her freed fingers reached for the ankle cuffs and found a small keyhole.

She smiled as she reached for the hem of her shorts. Lena unzipped the small compartment, and she pulled out a small version of her typical knife to pick the lock. The first cuff popped off and the second did just as easily.

Lena decided to take a walk around her surroundings. She counted her steps carefully as she walked around the sides of the room. It took nearly two-hundred steps along the wall she had been chained to and only a hundred along the opposite wall.

A small scuffle came from the opposite side of the room, and Lena made her way toward the sound. Her knife prodded something soft, and Lena reached out. A blanket had been placed upon the floor. Another scuffle, Lena turned to the sound. This time the soft thing made a gulping sound.

"Who are you?" Lena snarled at the person.

"Lena?" The voice was masculine yet unfamiliar.

"Who are you?" Lena asked again slowly.

"I'm Robert from high school."

This was not Rob. Lena knew it wasn't yet still asked the question she'd ask any member in a dark room. "What's your code?"

"Code?"

"Who are you?"

"I told you, I'm Robert." He sounded anxious this time.

"He wouldn't be stupid enough to not know his code. Answer my question or I'll cut your throat."

"I can't tell you my name."

"And why would that be?"

"They'd kill me." He sounded younger, though; based on the height of his throat, he couldn't be younger than junior high age.

"Then give me a good enough reason not to kill you instead."

"They have my little sister, Annie. They sent me to knock you out and bind you in here." The voice had enough fear to be plausible.

"Then why are you in here?"

"To drop off the blanket. I swear that was it." His voice was getting faint now as he seemed to not be breathing with her knife at his throat. She lessened the pressure slightly.

"So... you're my guard then?"

"Obviously."

"Don't get snarky," Lena warned, moving the blade back to his throat for a momentary reminder.

"Sorry."

"You need my knife?"

"I'm afraid so," he sighed. Relief was in his voice, which Lena could understand.

"I don't really like you. Here, for your sister's sake." She twisted the knife around and placed it in his hand.

"Just like that?"

"Don't expect me to do it again."

"Do you have another?"

"Not if you want your sister to remain alive."

"No other knives, right. I'll bring dinner in an hour."

"Do these lights ever turn on?"

"There are no lights in here to turn on."

"Great."

"We never spoke."

"Under what circumstances would we ever have the opportunity to speak in the first place?" Lena said smoothly. Rolling her eyes, Lena thought of the fact that there would be no opportunity for anyone to find out anyway.

"I placed the blanket next to you, then walked out."

"No problem."

"Bye."

"See you in an hour."

He left in a hurry with the knife. Lena rolled her eyes again. She continued her patrolling. Her fingers slipped along the top of the wall. There were very short ceilings.

Her fingers hit a grate about halfway around the room from her chains. A light breeze hit her fingers, and Lena nodded. She reached down to her shorts once more and pulled out a knife from the identical pocket on the other side of her pants.

Lena pried the grate away from the wall. It clattered to the ground but, as the door didn't open, Lena figured it was just the guard from before. There wasn't a large opening, but Lena figured it would be enough for her to fit through. Her frame was still small, despite the continuous workouts and improved diet.

Lena knew it was too high for her to jump, but if she gained just a few inches, she'd make it. She edged back around the room and grabbed the blanket.

It gave her the height she needed, but it was still hard to get a good grip on the smooth metal. She took a few shots at it before finally managing to wiggle into the grate.

Lena made a few wrong turns before managing to find the grate over the hall outside of her cell. She pushed it off after making sure it was clear. It clanged to the floor, and Lena popped her head down.

"Hello."

"How'd you... never mind."

"Which way do I go to get to Annie's room?"

"Straight two halls then two rights and a left. She has frizzy hair and is about six." His frazzled blonde hair fell into his blue eyes as he spoke, clearly genuine in his need to save his sister, which was enough for Lena to trust his directions.

"Okay, bye. I'll see you in two hours on the west side."

Lena pulled her head back up, and the guard put the grate up over the hole. She had to stop three times on the way to Annie's room when guards passed in the halls below her. Lena made it there pretty easily, negating the fact of being slightly claustrophobic. She spotted Annie's hair from the vent and looked at the young girl.

"Annie, wake up, honey," Lena whispered from the vent. The young girl shifted and sat up, rubbing her eyes. Her door clicked open, and Lena wiggled back in the vent to avoid any possibility of being seen through the grate.

"Emily, where have you been?" Annie bolted forward and hugged the guard.

"Mason sent me. I was told to give you these. He also wanted me to tell you that no one else will be coming this way tonight. Okay, baby girl?"

"Okay!" Annie squealed happily, dancing around the room in the large jacket that was clearly a guards' uniform.

Emily left, and Annie continued dancing around the room in the jacket.

Lena pushed open the grate and saw Annie turn. "Hey, Annie. I think you have my clothes," Lena said calmly as she landed on her feet.

Annie seemed unsurprised somehow by Lena's appearance and stuck out her bottom lip as she handed Lena the clothes. Lena pulled on the clothes quickly over her clothes and knelt in front of Annie.

"I need you to follow me in the vents, okay?"

"Okay."

"I'll boost you up. Crawl backward so I can get up okay?"

"Okay, stranger lady," Annie replied, bounding over to stand under the vent with her arms over her head like she was ready to have her shirt taken off.

"Be very quiet, Annie."

Annie held one finger to her lips innocently. Lena smiled and nodded. She lifted Annie into the vent and watched as the small girl easily wriggled back in the vent. Lena jumped and hoisted herself into the vent with some difficulty.

Lena crawled along until she found a clear hall that Lena was confident in escaping from. She exited first and helped Annie out.

Lena pulled out her knife and checked around corners, holding Annie's hand calmly. It took them an hour to escape unnoticed, and Lena was carrying Annie by the time they got out of the building to keep their noise level down.

She ran through the low, dense trees until she could find the river and gauge her location in accordance with the building. Mason appeared only a few moments after Lena had found a west exit to watch.

"Come with me," Lena whispered, moving Annie to Mason's shoulder. "I don't live to far from here I don't think."

"How can I repay you?" Mason looked so earnest, even as

his hair fell in his eyes.

"Just give me back my knife and let me know if you see anyone." Lena shook her head slowly as she started her way back into the forest.

Mason gave her the blade. They traded holding Annie periodically when the other's arms got too tired to support her. Lena started a quiet conversation to fill the awkward silence.

"Tell me something about yourself, Mason."

"Well, I used to live with a mafia. My dad and his girlfriend ran it. Mom died when I was young after my twin sister committed suicide. I also have an older sister, though she ran away with her boyfriend, now fiancé, after that. Now I live with my girlfriend and her little sister and aunt."

"What you're really saying is you have a lot of women in your life," Lena commented, watching him out of the corner of her eye.

Mason chuckled, "Yeah, I suppose so. Anyway, what about you? Why did they want you and not anyone else?"

"Let's just say I'd take your life any day."

"Oh, come on. I told you my whole life story there. Give me something to work with here."

"Okay then. I have one older and two younger twin brothers and a half sister, though we'll get to that. My mother was kidnapped when I was six and rescued by my father. He was a gang leader and had me tortured. My mother is a whore who slept around with your boss and had my baby sister. Then, six years ago, my dad made me fake my death."

Lena thought for a second before continuing, "He was an asshole, so I had him poisoned while I faked my death again for the people that knew I was actually alive, including my boyfriend, family, and gang leaders. Um, I hid where I'm taking you for three years before returning to society to marry some random asshole off the street. My boyfriend came and saved me from that before reintroducing me to my family.

"Next, we all had to move to the country so we could avoid your boss' brother, who found us anyway. Killed him a few days back. One of my brothers hates me, which made a nice distraction for you to catch me in."

Mason's eyes were wide with surprise before he pulled Lena to the side suddenly. "I see someone." He whispered incredulously, "He's riding a horse. Who rides horses any more?"

"Don't judge my Missy." Lena clicked her tongue at Missy, who trotted over, ignoring Max's yells and tugs. Lena came out from behind the trees they had been walking behind and patted Missy's nose.

"Lena, you're here!" Max cried excitedly.

Lena laughed, "Miss me much?"

"Where were you? We looked everywhere."

"I got captured and escaped with Mason and Annie here."

Annie had woken up and evidently listened to the last bit of the conversation as she asked, "What about Emily?"

"She's fine, Ann. She's a smart girl," Mason replied calmly.

"Why was she there?" Lena asked, rubbing Missy's side gently.

"Debt. She's out in about a month," Mason told her.

"Good, let's go home then. Max, get off my horse."

Max slid off and boosted Lena up. Mason handed Annie up when Lena motioned for her.

Annie played cowgirl the whole way back, making them laugh and play along. Missy seemed annoyed, but Lena promised to give her an extra apple, and she seemed to relax.

All was well until Lena made it back to the cottage where Trevor was sitting on the bed, staring at the opposite wall blankly.

Chapter 25

Trevor didn't look at her as she entered. Lena sat beside him and put her hand on his shoulder. He jerked it away.

"You promised wouldn't leave again." His voice was angry and quiet.

"I was taken. I didn't want to go." Lena didn't blame him for his anger; she just wished he could be a bit more sympathetic. She felt an unnatural coldness coming from him.

"I can't trust you not to disappear."

"What do you mean?" Lena took his chin and forced him to turn and face her.

"I can't do this, Lena, not any more. Not like this." Something had finally broken behind his eyes. Her fake deaths didn't but a brief disappearance and, finally, it snapped.

Lena tasted tears before she felt them. "Keep your ring then."

Lena took off her ring and set it on a dresser as she walked out. She wasn't sure where she was going but kept walking. Lena found a blade the most comforting thing in that moment. Each time it thudded against the mat they used as a target, tears came pouring down her face.

Each blade seemed to hurt her more. Her necklace jingled with each movement, making her more upset and forming more anger until she ripped it from her neck, charms going in every direction.

No one came that night. Lena continued to throw each knife over and over. She didn't notice as the sun came up and started to droop again. She hardly even noticed the dullness of the blades or the searing of her muscles or the foam that now covered the floor from the mat. Lena didn't care about anything but the lack of a ring on her finger, Trevor sitting in their cottage, and the glint of charms on the floor.

Her eyes were red but dry when Avery walked in. Avery didn't notice her agony although she couldn't help but notice the various debris. It wasn't until she had asked enough questions without responses to make her walk around Lena, finally seeing her face and reason enough for the anguish of the room.

She tried to find out what had happened, why she wouldn't reply, but Lena wasn't willing to reply to anything. Eventually, Avery was just holding her in her arms. Lena felt no inclination to reply or to return the hug, only to return to her knives that were protruding from the wall.

Beta ended up leaving her but only returned with more people whom Lena didn't want to see. Max tried to speak to her. Timmy held her hand comfortingly while Dillon stood awkwardly at the door, wanting to console her but fearful of what may happen.

Lena ignored them and turned around, walking past Dillon without a word. She didn't stop to get food in the dining hall but went to sit by the fire they had set the night before, or, at least, she thought it was that one. It very well could have been new for all Lena knew. She wanted to watch it go out, but daylight came before the flames disappeared.

She stood, the green phantom light blocking part of her vision as she returned to the gym to grab a bow and quiver before returning outside. Lena headed for the orchard and shot down leaves that fell from the trees. Each arrow caught a leaf, and Lena didn't bother to empty them until they no longer flew due to the weight of the leaves up and down the shaft.

No one attempted to stop her but watched from the garden. Lena didn't look at them, though she knew they were watching to see what she was going to do. They wanted to know what she was doing, but no one was willing to ask any more.

She sang the lullaby as she always did. It no longer had the typical singsong, happy tone but was sad to listen to. The whistle of arrows and the muted whispering of nearly everyone from camp only added to the near silence of the camp. Lena only turned when a new set of footsteps approached the group.

Her eyes met Trevor's and she turned away immediately, tears forming again as she headed toward the forest, leaving the bow on the ground where she had been standing. She could hear the cool running of water and headed toward it.

The rocky bank was uncomfortable, rough and wet, but Lena laid back despite that. She didn't know she was falling asleep until it was too late. It wasn't planned, but she hadn't slept in days; she needed it.

When she woke, Lena was in a warm bed with her head on someone's lap. She turned, hoping it was Trevor, hoping it was a dream. Max was lying there in a light doze.

He started awake when he felt her move. "It's good to see you awake. How do you feel?"

"Like crap."

"Why? What happened?"

"Ask him. Get him to tell you," Lena told him, unwilling to say anything else. She leaned forward, off his legs.

Max nodded and swung his legs out of bed to go. Max felt bad leaving her in such a state yet felt he had no option. He looked back at her quickly, saw her pull out paper for another letter, and felt a twinge of some unknown emotion. He left to find

Trevor, unsure what to expect. It took only a few minutes for him to find Trevor in the orchard, gathering the fallen apples before they began to rot outside of their composter.

"What did you do to my sister?" Max yelled at him, not caring that half the camp had turned to watch his angry descent.

"I didn't do anything," Trevor replied, voice quiet, knowing it wasn't true.

"Then why isn't she wearing her ring? Did you think I wouldn't notice? She isn't willing to speak, Trevor. That isn't caused by nothing." Max shoved Trevor, causing him to drop the apples. Trevor didn't try to stop him.

Mason, standing by the garden, moved forward to step in, but Michael held him back. His eyes didn't leave Trevor, waiting for his reply, although he couldn't hear it from where he stood.

"She couldn't keep one promise. One simple promise," Trevor replied calmly, quietly.

"What promise?" Anger still roared in his ears, but curiosity stopped him from shoving Trevor again.

"She promised not to leave. She left, and I can't deal with that any more."

"You broke up with her because she was fucking kidnapped? You caused her to become a practical mute because she was kidnapped? Now we can't defend her from these people coming back because of you? We just got her back, god damn it! I want to hear her happy for once," Max yelled, punching Trevor in the chest, leaving him in the dust.

This time, Michael and Mason did rush forward to stop Max from killing Trevor. Avery stepped past them as they dragged Max backwards to speak to Trevor.

"That girl has gone through enough without having to deal with you, too. Go home and don't come back. Pack your things and don't leave anything else. You've caused enough damage," she spat at him.

"I'm not leaving."

"She only wants her loved ones here."

The words hit Trevor nearly as hard as any of Max's punches. He hated it too much; the order was too much. "Come with me."

"Why would I do that?"

Trevor could feel everyone's eyes on him, but he didn't back down or drop eye contact. "Do it, Beta."

"No."

"Beta, it wasn't a question," he told her, seeing Lena out of the corner of his eye and feeling a pang as she pointedly didn't look at him. He brushed off his clothes and walked toward his cottage when he was sure Beta was following. Avery did follow but with enough distance to silently voice her distrust.

They entered the cottage, and Trevor sat down at the small desk they had placed there. He pulled open a drawer and pulled out a letter, which Avery disregarded initially as just another one of Lena's letters.

"I didn't have an option either. Whoever took her is blackmailing me. They planted a letter they knew only I'd find. They let her go so easily. They wanted to speak to me."

"You have to tell her." Avery looked again at the letter and now noticed the different handwriting, understanding how he'd mistake it for Lena's. Trevor covered the words before she had a chance to read them.

"I can't. They can't know that I told anyone."

"She's more deadly now than ever."

"I know that," he sighed, putting his head down in a look of submission.

"She was throwing knives the other day, Trevor. She wasn't shredding just that pad; she was shredding her heart. If you don't fix this soon, there won't be anything to fix. They clearly wanted her this way for a reason."

"Better she's alive," Trevor reminded her.

"Read her letters, Lynx. They tell her story. Even if not all of them happened, they tell of her emotions." Avery grimaced and looked again at the letter she couldn't read. She wanted to know what could possibly scare him into submission.

"Okay, I will."

It took days for him to read them all. They had been moved from the cottage with Lena to the one he shared now with the supplies and extra equipment as every other cottage was full of people or filled with people that would kill him. He read all of the letters, whether they were unique or duplicated. By the end, he understood why Beta had him read them.

10.18.17

Maybe my last day.

I am not sorry. I want it to be over. The twins would be fine after a while. Trevor would be devastated but, eventually, forget all about me. Beta, Alpha, and Hound would get rid of me like an unwelcome reminder of John. No one would truly remember me because I'm already dead. What good is a living dead girl?

-Lena

4.29.20

Another day to round out my life.

I sold my animals so I could rejoin society. No one would even know I was here. They wouldn't know I died here either. Maybe that's best. If I go outside to snow, I'll die here. If I go outside to rain, I'll stay. If I go outside to light and sun, I'll go. I don't know which one to wish for.

-Lena

6.23.22

My real last day.

I'm sorry, Trevor. I release you of your original promise. Tell the twins or Max or anyone. Please just don't come for me. I always knew I wouldn't live my whole life. That's the thing. I always thought I'd die because of John, and I suppose I am, but not in the same way. Water runs faster than blood. I like the sound of that, but I hope it's not true. I hope that blood will run faster today.

-Lena

Trevor looked at the calendar hanging up on his wall. He hadn't yet crossed out June 23, 2022. He dropped the letter and ran out the door.

He searched the riverbank quickly, running along the bank toward the waterfall they had found. It was filled with jagged rocks and a powerful current that could pull the fastest swimmer under.

Trevor sped up, trying to get there before anything happened. Lena saw him just as she started leaning back. Her face registered fear but determination. Trevor sprinted and looked over the edge before backing up and taking a running start over the edge.

The water hit him like cold knives. His arms could hardly hold him above the water's surface to look for her. Her head barely breached the surface before being sucked under once again.

Trevor went under and grabbed wildly at her arm. He caught hold and began dragging them to the shore. It felt like forever, but he managed to pull her to safety.

Lena wasn't breathing when he got her on shore. He felt tears and water rolling off his face as he started CPR. Over and over again. Time seemed to slow until she gasped and coughed. He rolled her to the side so that water could escape her lungs, relief filling him. Lena stopped coughing eventually but didn't face him. She shook violently from cold despite the heat of the day, and Trevor helped her lean up, trying to hold her so she could warm up.

She pulled away, moving closer to the falls. Neither of them spoke. Her normally bright eyes were dull; Trevor blamed himself, which he knew was wrong as it was the letter's fault, but he couldn't help it.

"Lena, I'm sorry," he managed to force out.

"That's what you're supposed to say. You're supposed to say how you're sorry, then leave. I suppose it's true."

"It's not, though. I didn't have a choice either." He pulled the wet letter he had shown Avery. Trevor handed it to her.

She set it down without a second glance. "I never told you to break up with me."

"It's not from you. This is from them."

She picked it back up and carefully pulled it out of the envelope, trying not to tear the wet paper. The ink had run a bit though it was just legible.

8.18.22

My request:

Now that I have your attention, you're going to break up with Delphina when she returns. We will know. We know your location, and we'll know if it happens. Don't tell anybody. There will be consequences if you do. Welcome to the dark side, Trevor, or should I say Lynx?

-Tulsi

Lena didn't look up as she glared at it. "He failed at my

handwriting: how dare he?"

"Really, that's what you care about?"

"It's better than thinking about everything else." Lena looked back at him sadly. "Sometimes, I wish I would've gone before I met you, but, other times, I know that I wouldn't have because I had nothing to die for."

Lena shakily stood up to start up the slope ahead of Trevor. Once, he had to catch her, and he lifted her in his arms. "Just let me carry you."

She didn't say anything but leaned against his chest. Trevor gave a small smile down at her and brought her up to camp and sat with her at the dwindling fire.

"I believe this is still yours." Trevor pulled the ring out from the chain around his neck. Lena nodded and helped him take it off the chain, no smile yet appearing. She returned it to her finger and fell asleep in his lap.

At dinner that night, Trevor explained what had happened, and, though there were still some hard feelings, they all forgave him. No one mentioned Lena's attempted suicide, though each noticed the change in her demeanor. They saw how she now slumped more in her seat, spoke more carefully again. While the return to careful speech should have been a welcomed return, this measured way of talking was different.

They didn't speak much at dinner, and Trevor returned to their cottage with Lena for bed, though he knew he wouldn't sleep in the same bed. They were still harboring the feelings of the last few days, despite the new knowledge.

"I wanted to tell you something," Trevor said as he grabbed a blanket from their dresser to sleep with.

"What is it?" Lena asked. She was already in bed and rolled to face him.

"I shouldn't have made you promise never to leave me. I love you. Just please, never try to… never do that again," Trevor pleaded.

"I never will, not again. I love you and I shouldn't have done it today. Never break up with me again. Next time, I may succeed if I'm pushed too far."

"I promise I won't. Goodnight, Lena."

"Goodnight, Trevor."

Chapter 26

Weeks passed by, and Mason ended up going home with Annie. He had left behind his uniform and maps, along with the plans he and Lena had worked on. They had set up patrols as one of their precautions for camp. Tulsi's threat loomed over them, yet no attacks came.

All of the precautions were made at camp, and plans were being finalized between Lena and Beta. They had agreed to bring Sierra with them; better they have her so as not to worry or leave anyone behind to protect her. Alpha had taken the uniform Mason had brought and the uniform Lena had been wearing to the city for TNT to duplicate and to pick up provisions at the same time as he took Mason and Annie to a train station that would deposit them home.

Max let off an alert on the day of their infiltration while Lena was double-checking their bags. "Sparrow, we need you!"

Lena exited the gym once she had zipped the gun bags to see Max standing over a bruised man.

"Who is he?" Lena asked, nodding toward him.

"Spy. We found him wandering the woods," Max explained simply, stepping back to let her through. "Must've been the one the letter talked about."

Her frame had expanded slightly with added muscles, but her eyes were sunken back, giving her an intimidating look. "What's your name?" Her voice was low, cold, and unlike her.

The man faced her but tightened his lips. Lena knelt in front of him and waited, patient as ever. When the silence became too unbearable, he spoke. "Noah."

"Good, you speak. Now, what have you told your bosses, Noah?"

He blew at the black hair that had fallen into his face, eyes facing his bound hands without speaking. Lena sighed and pulled out a knife; she slid it down his cheek, neck, chest until, finally, she sawed at the bonds while saying, "If you tell us what we need to know, we can get you out of here to where you need to go. You have to be useful though if you want to be released."

The bonds broke. Noah rubbed his wrists, thinking over her offer and unspoken threat. "They know you're coming."

"Tonight?" Lena asked, tone remaining reserved.

"No, just that you're coming. They've added guards."

"How many?"

"Twenty or more."

"Improved inside?"

"No unguarded halls."

"Why were you there?"

He hesitated before replying. "They took my mom."

She nodded and stood up. "You're going to get us in, Noah."

He hesitantly stood up, eyeing Maxwell warily. Noah followed Lena into the dining hall where the rest of the camp had been eating but now were watching the door, waiting for an explanation.

Michael was chewing on a chunk of bread as he called, "Who's he?"

"This is Noah. He's a spy and is going to get us in. They've increased security."

Everyone nodded, going back to the meal. Max and Lena sat with Noah, eating as they talked over the plan. Trevor walked over and silently joined them.

"We have uniforms," Max informed him. "Male and female for everyone, but we need to get Doe in."

"Who?"

"See the little girl." Trevor pointed over Noah's shoulder at Sierra, who was picking grumpily at her food while Katie whispered to her, surely something about growing up into a big, strong girl.

"Vents. If you managed to get through them, she can," Noah said with a shrug.

Lena hadn't noticed that other conversations had ended and that they were all actively listening until Bianca yelled, "I'll go with Doe. We can start freeing people."

Lena nodded. "Noah, you'll go soon. We'll move before nightfall. They won't expect us to move before nightfall. Don't let us get caught."

"I won't risk my life for you if it comes down to it. I want you to know that," he told her firmly.

Trevor clenched his jaw angrily but didn't speak. Lena smiled tightly. "I wouldn't expect you to. I expect you to fight for us so your mother will go free. Otherwise, Hound over there may... forget to open the cell or slip when cutting her bonds. You never know."

He nodded warily and stood up. Everyone watched as he glanced around and skittered nervously toward the door as though he expected them to stop him. When no one moved, he pushed open the door and left in a rush.

"What now? Do we trust him?" Trevor asked, looking from person to person briefly before his gaze rested finally on Lena. He didn't like her undisguised threat. It wasn't something he had ever seen her do, yet he found it less disturbing than he had expected.

"We don't have an option. We've prepared for this. Go shower and pack. We won't be staying the night here whether we get out or not. Anything you don't bring with you to the mission goes in the car. Someone come help me pack the gym, please," Lena called out to the silent people.

"I'll help," Dillon volunteered. It would be the first time they had been truly alone since her abduction, and both felt apprehensive, but she nodded.

They all began clearing dinner, and Katie went with Sierra to do the dishes and begin packing the kitchen. Lena and Dillon went into the back room and began their own work.

"Begin packing the knives. I need to go empty the punching bag so we can load it with weapons," Lena called across the room as he made his way toward the main cabinet.

"Are you sure you don't want me to get it?" Dillon asked.

"I've got it," she replied stiffly.

They worked in silence for a while before Dillon worked up the nerve to speak again. "I don't hate you, Lena. I've heard the rumors around camp. You don't need to prove that you're protecting me. I was stupid for being so rude and ignoring you. I love you."

Lena sighed as she began to wrap up the bullets they weren't bringing on their mission in a protective cloth. "I knew there was going to be backlash when I returned to society. I thought of you and your brothers and Sierra and everyone daily. I may have forgotten dates and times and everything else, but I knew you. I jumped, thinking I was saving you all from more pain. Clearly, I was wrong."

Dillon stayed silent for a while, thinking of what to say next. "I missed you when you were dead. I knew Trevor hoped that you were still alive, and I hoped for a while too. I avoided him for a while to try to ignore that piece of me. I realized eventually that I could never be as happy as I was when you were alive. It hurt to admit. I always missed you, though. I knew that."

Lena stopped what she was doing and walked over to him and wrapped him in a big hug. She felt his arms wrap around her, and she smiled.

"I missed being your big sister."

"Well, you feel a bit small right now."

"Oh, shut up, Dillon. It's not my fault that you grew while I was gone," Lena laughed. He nodded, and they broke apart, tension lifted, to return to work on the last of the packing. Everything fit in the bag as nearly everything collapsed to be small or was being brought to their mission.

Lena left him to bring the bag to the cars and went to check the other cottages to make sure everything was out. They had done well, and Lena only had to pull out one forgotten item from under one of the beds.

They were ready a full hour before nightfall, and though it was still hot, Lena insisted they wear normal clothes over their fake uniforms. They had packed all their weapons into beach bags with colorful towels. All together, they looked like they were going to the beach or, at least, a deeper part of the river in case any other spies lingered in the tress.

Everyone was chatting happily, it seemed, though each was thinking hard to formulate sentences that matched their code. They had carefully learned and practiced for weeks to perfect it.

Each focused hard and learned how to use it yet still make what seemed like a happy group. The only one that didn't understand how to decode it or use it was Sierra, who listened as though they were facts.

Lena didn't participate in many conversations though would

correct them to ensure reliability in information. Trevor moved up and linked his hand in hers.

"Please be careful," she whispered, not bothering to try formulating the code for her message.

"We will both be safe after this. I promise." He replied, also ignoring the code.

"I don't want to lose you again."

"You won't. Now just don't leave me."

"I don't intend to. Don't be reckless."

"Same goes for you."

Lena nodded and came up behind a tree and stopped. "We've arrived. Unpack quickly and load up."

Through the trees, they could see the large grey building that they planned to infiltrate. They managed to unpack within five minutes and were hiding behind a large patch of trees to talk.

Lena looked from person to person, seeing their worried expressions. It had been years since they had tried a mission of this magnitude with such few people. "Stay calm inside. Trust one another and work together. We've prepared for this. If you're in trouble, then use the earpieces. Good luck."

They nodded and parted ways, Michael walking with Lena to their post. He watched her nervous glances over her shoulder and put a hand on her arm comfortingly. "They'll be fine. We've planned for this."

"I wouldn't let them come if they weren't ready."

"We best get to work then."

Lena agreed with a small nod before slipping into the cover of some trees and running along the perimeter. She shot a guard quickly, and they ran into the building before anyone else could come after them. Alarms were already blaring through the whole facility.

She and Michael waded through opponents that seemed to multiply as they went, and they were slowly backed into a room she recognized briefly before the guards threw the door shut. Complete darkness engulfed them. Lena touched her earpiece in a call to the others.

"Yes?" It was a short reply from Avery, followed by heavy breathing and a gunshot.

"We're trapped in my old cell."

"Have you tried the grate?" Avery asked, a loud bang temporarily cutting off their connection.

"There's no way that Alpha would fit through it."

"True, Bull and I will work our way there."

"See you soon."

Lena began walking around the room carefully how she had before, picking her way toward the grate despite what she had told Beta.

"Sparrow? Sparrow, where'd you go?" Michael called through the darkness; his voice had an added measure of fear that Lena didn't think he was capable of.

"I'm by the grate. Come to my voice. Just follow that," Lena told him; she continued to speak until she heard him fumbling in the darkness.

She grabbed his arm and pulled him to the wall.

"Why are we here? I thought you said we were waiting."

"They're on the other side of the complex. Might as well try and get out on our own if we can."

"I can't get through that."

"I know that. Boost me up and I'll go through how I did last time and open the door."

"Okay, just hurry. I don't like the dark."

"I will." He lifted her up, and she pulled off the grate. Lena wiggled through the vents as quickly as she could and dropped into the hall.

She pulled her gun quickly enough to shoot one guard but had to kick another down while yet another came up behind her. Lena stomped on the one's foot to loosen his grip.

She managed to kill both of the immediate guards and shot the door handle rather than attempt to unlock it during their temporary break.

Alpha came out of the room running and panting from fear.

"Shh, Alpha," Lena said soothingly, checking their surroundings. "Calm down. It's okay."

He shook his head quickly, still shaking.

"Okay, Alpha. Wait outside with the clothes. I'll get someone to you."

"See you soon, Sparrow." He ran out the nearest exit, punching a guard so hard he fell backwards, unconscious.

Lena touched her earpiece again to contact Beta. "Beta, Alpha had to go out. Send Bull to him by the clothes, and I'll come meet you. Meet halfway."

"See you soon," was all Beta said in reply.

The earpiece returned to the white noise they had all been listening to before. She moved down the hall toward where Beta had been originally positioned and had to start using knives halfway as she didn't have time to reload her gun.

Beta didn't seem to have moved very far when Lena caught up, but she saw why almost immediately. She had an opponent on each side, and it was all she could do to stay alive.

Lena planted a knife in one man's forehead while kicking the nearest one into the wall, making him fall unconscious to the ground. Beta managed to finish the other two just as their earpiece crackled back to life.

"We need help. Hawk was shot and needs to get out," Trevor called worriedly.

"We're two corridors off from you. We'll be there," Beta replied, panting heavily as she straightened up.

Lena looked determined and scared as she ran toward where Trevor and Max lay stranded.

Beta fell behind and yelled after her, "Sparrow, I need to go to the twins. They don't have any protection."

"Just go!" Lena screamed, not turning away from her goal. Even in the brief time it took to run to Max and Trevor, Katie called in that Sara was out of ammunition and that they were heading back out.

So far, only three groups hadn't sent out a distress call; Timothy and Dillon had help on the way, whether it was needed or not, and Lena had to put trust into Sean to protect Alyse as well as Bianca to protect Sierra.

Lena reached Max and Trevor, looking as though she had been murdered with blood covering the front of her uniform. Trevor was trying to help Max keep pressure on his wound, though he kept having to release the wound to shoot at guards that came their way. He was so distracted, and Max was so dazed that neither noticed that she wasn't a guard until after he shot.

Lena hit the floor as quickly as possible, but the bullet still grazed her cheek, sure to add yet another scar the numerous ones on her face already. She hissed in pain but rushed forward anyway with little more than a glare thrown toward Trevor.

"Oh my god, I'm sorry," he gasped, returning his blood-soaked hands to Max's leg.

"I would've done the same. I'm angrier you let this happen to my brother." She stepped over a body and pulled a roll of gauze from her pocket. "Where'd your gauze go?"

"Fell out while I was running," Trevor explained.

Lena moved his hands away from the wound to examine it. "You're lucky it went straight through."

Her mind momentarily flashed to her experience with a bullet that hadn't come out. She remembered long needles and alcohol that had burned for hours.

"Lena!" Trevor yelled as a guard that had dodged his knife lunged forward, pulling her violently from her brief flashback.

Lena pulled a knife from her belt as she jumped to her feet, barely managing to hit him in the throat before he got to her with his own weapon as he apparently lacked a gun. His body landed across Max's other leg, causing him to jolt in pain.

She, too, winced as she heard his yelp and helped Trevor move the suffocating man off of Max. Lena quickly wrapped the wound the best she could and grabbed a belt off of a nearby body to use as a tourniquet. It slowed the visible flow of blood, but Lena knew he'd need to see Katie as soon as possible.

"Get him out to Aloe now," she told Trevor quickly. Lena moved as to leave, but Trevor caught her arm. He applied a short length of gauze to her cheek, using some tape to adhere it over the, not serious yet gushing, wound.

"Don't do anything dangerous."

"So, do nothing? Get Hawk outside. I'll be outside as soon as I can. Don't worry about me." Lena ran before he could stop her. She could hear Max's murmured complaint and smiled briefly, knowing he would be fine if he could still complain.

Lena heard the earpiece fizzle to life again, hearing a deep, panicked cry of "They're here," before going to white noise once more.

She paused, trying to learn her location, before running off in the direction of Sean and Alyse, the only group left in the building with a man that could've made the cry. Lena sprinted with all of her remaining energy, attempting to keep calm as their plans crumpled around her. There were too many. They were too poorly manned. She should have known. Lena didn't have the time to dwell.

Sean was in hand-to-hand combat with two disarmed guards and seemed to have injured his dominant arm at some point as he was leading with his left and was trying to keep them to the one side. Alyse wasn't much better as she fought another opponent behind Sean that was too strong for her. Luckily for Alyse, she had speed, unlike her attacker.

Lena hoped Alyse could hold her own for a little bit longer and rushed in to help Sean. She took out one opponent, giving him the chance to finally knock out the other. He nodded to her as he moved over to help Alyse finish her battle.

The battle ended quickly, and the silence was all-consuming after the noise that had filled the hall before. Alyse broke the silence with a whispered, "Thank you, Sparrow."

Lena gently rubbed her curled back, feeling her shaking from fatigue. "It's okay, Phoenix. Just calm down now. You're safe now."

"No, this isn't okay, Sparrow," Alyse gasped; Lena only then realized that the shaking was from tears, not fatigue. "These people have families too. I just, we just, ended that."

"They made their decision when they decided to work for them. Anyway, these people are already thought to be dead by their families. You saved them from a life of pain. Go to Hawk by the clothes. He needs you," Lena told her, trying to keep her voice still. She hoped what she told Alyse was true but wasn't sure; no one could be sure.

Alyse left more willingly than Lena had hoped; she had

hoped she'd at least acknowledge what she had said as true, but she hadn't. She and Sean just walked away, Sean taking the lead.

Their plan was crumbling before her eyes, and nothing could be done now. Pulling out would mean letting them go but continuing would be fatal.

"Sierra fell," the earpiece reported. "Sprained her ankle. Taking her out now."

Lena growled in frustration but plowed further on. In her distraction, she quite literally ran into Timmy, Dillon, and Avery. All of them stumbled and Lena managed to right herself and Timmy while Avery and Dillon hardly avoided collapse.

"Sparrow, we were looking for you," Timmy informed her as he released her arm.

"Good to see you're all unhurt. How many weapons do you have left?" Lena asked, looking between them.

Avery shook her head, Dillon glanced sadly at his empty quiver, and Timmy pulled his last knife.

"We didn't know there were this many," Avery explained, as though she owed Lena something.

Lena nodded, turning away the knife that Timmy had offered her. "Go join the others. You may need that knife. I'll come join you shortly."

"We can't leave you," Dillon protested, stepping forward. Lena saw her own defiance in his gaze. It scared her. He should have never had to wear that look.

"You can, and you will. Go now. Don't you dare hesitate. I'll come soon; I promise." Lena hugged each of them and watched as Avery ushered the boys away before turning her gaze toward the center of the complex.

Chapter 27

Trevor looked over their small crowd of people that had reformed in the trees. "Lena's alone in there. We can't leave her."

"Why not? She left us," Tyler pointed out slyly, sharpening one of their last remaining knives on a stone he had found, though it didn't seem to be doing anything.

Half of the crowd turned to attack him while the other half nodded in solemn agreement. "Because she left to protect us, dumbass. She cares about our safety, but we can't let her sacrifice herself," Max growled from his spot propped against a tree.

"How many are injured?" Avery called over them. Max and Sean looked at each other, rolling their eyes as they raised their hands along with Sierra.

"Okay, we'll split resources," Michael announced, demanding their attention. "We have to be diligent with the use of our weapons. Play to your strengths. Trevor, get to the grid and shut it down. Panther, get to Sparrow by any means necessary. Aloe, you'll stay with Bear, Hawk, and Doe. Bull and Archer, get up high and pluck them off. Badger, do something to distract them. Hound and Beta, knife play. Phoenix, we'll set traps around the battle before entering ourselves."

Everyone nodded, splitting supplies based on talents and positions. Bullets were taken by Tyler and Sara while knives went to Bianca and Avery. Dillon took the extra store of arrows. Neither Trevor nor Timmy took anything but a blade each, and Alyse with Michael took anything remaining.

Trevor set off around the outside of the building to find the power grid before he followed the rest inside to find Lena.

Lena entered the room with her head held high and voice defiant. "You wanted me alone. You proved that; now what?"

The man in the middle of the room laughed. His features were similar to Jackson, though he had a rounder face and seemed to be shorter than his brother was. Tulsi stepped forward, a smirk curling his lips. "Well, killing you would be fun, but that wouldn't do my brother any justice, would it?"

Lena rolled her eyes as she watched him shaking his head. "You won't do that, so what will you do?"

"I have a task for you. Joey, bring out my girl."

A man with black hair and equally dark eyes moved out of the room, and Lena tensed. Half of her wished he was referring to Sierra so she'd know if she was truly hurt or not, but she knew that would be worse. Best Sierra was away from their torment.

To her relief and horror, they brought out a sobbing girl much too old to be Sierra. She looked about eighteen, and she had dark almond hair that fell to her mid-chest and bright green eyes.

"Meet my niece, Reet. Reet, say hello."

Reet looked up, and her eyes were red as tears flowed quickly down her face, which was bruised and scarred, distorting the innate beauty Reet must have had.

"Hello, Lena." She spoke with such a calm and flat tone that Lena wouldn't have known she was crying if she hadn't seen the girl.

"Hello, Reet," Lena replied, stopping the quiver in her voice as to match the girl's calm tone.

"Now that you're acquainted, you'll line her face some more."

"And why would I do that?" Lena sneered, looking at Reet with a mournful eye.

"Because I have your family." His eyes betrayed no lie, yet something made Lena look to Reet in confirmation. The girl's eyes had flicked up, and her face registered a brief surprise before they returned to Lena with a knowing look.

Lena looked back to Tulsi with a smirk. "No, you don't."

"How would you know?" Tulsi's eyes betrayed his misgivings.

"Because they're surrounding us. Now, Bull!" Lena screamed, hoping she was right as she lunged at Reet, knocking both to the ground.

The bullet zoomed past her and hit Tulsi in the shoulder as he had moved just before contact. Joey had thrown himself away from any coming bullets, giving Lena the time to cut the bonds on Reet's wrists and pull them to cover.

"Would you have done it?" Reet asked, fear making her eyes wide.

"Of course not. We're practically related. I care for my family."

"Welcome to the family?"

"Thanks. Now get to the door. I have to try and kill him. Sound good?"

Reet agreed by running for the door. Timmy caught her, and both disappeared into the darkness, though Lena could still hear Reet's terrified shriek echoing through the halls.

A few seconds later, the rest of the lights went out. Lena could've jumped with happiness but instead touched her earpiece. "Beta, I need vision."

"I see you. I'm coming." The piece once more went silent, but the footsteps of Beta could be heard faintly beneath the sound of battle. Beta pressed the glasses into Lena's palm.

Lena quickly put them on, and the darkness of before glowed with infrared light. She identified her people quickly by the glowing red metal in their ears. She quickly turned her attention back to Beta. "Do you have any weapons for me?"

"Handful of knives. Who's the girl?"

"Jackson's tortured daughter, Reet."

"I'll go tell Panther." Beta ran off, her glowing figure slowly disappearing into the darkness after Tim and Reet.

The lights flickered on, then back off again, and Trevor came onto the piece. "I'm fighting for control of the lights out here. I need them gone. I'm working with limited control."

"I'll deal with it," Lena told him before rushing off.

"Thank you, Sparrow." His strained voice seemed more relaxed, relieved. Lena knew that he must have been worrying, unable to see what she had become in her brief time alone.

The lights flicked on for longer the next time, and Lena caught sight of Tulsi fighting Michael, whose night vision glasses wrapped all the way around his head so not to see any of the darkness which caused him so much panic.

Lena saw a slightly glowing door handle in the distance and ran off. She threw the unlocked door open and saw a man working furiously on a computer. He leapt to his feet when he saw her, but it was clear that he was no fighter as Lena knocked him out with one well-placed punch to the face.

He crumpled, and Lena threw off the glasses to undo the man's work for Trevor.

"Thanks, dear," Trevor called over the earpiece. "I'm coming in now."

"No, make the lights flash. Don't let them get their bearings." Lena put on her glasses once more just as the lights began to flash.

"Done. I'm coming to help."

Lena could see the lights heating and cooling as she exited the small room. She paused to watch the guards stumbling around in the strobe lights. Others tried to continue their attacks, only to lunge and misjudge their target.

Michael still was fighting Tulsi, Avery against Joey, and Sara against Andrew, another henchman she had been warned about. Alyse had already been around that area, Lena saw, as tripwires were rigged everywhere. There were so many that Lena had to watch her step, a difficult process without heat on the wires to warn her of their presence.

Bianca was nowhere to be seen, and Lena couldn't find any trace of her either. "Hound, report."

"With Reet," she replied immediately.

Lena left the conversation there and looked around, trying to account for the rest of their party. Dillon and Tyler could be seen upstairs, and slightly glowing arrows and flaming hot bullets could be seen flying through the air.

Timmy was clearly busy running about, but Lena managed to pause him. "Where's everyone else?"

"Doe, Hawk, and Bear are injured outside with Aloe," he replied, running off.

Lena returned to the battle, going to aid Avery, who was losing ground to Joey. The three main opponents seemed to have adapted to the lights and were pressing harder than ever.

Joey didn't see Lena coming, so he took a long, deep gash across his left eye down his nose and finishing across his right cheek. Avery backed off to help the others while Lena took her fight.

Joey spat blood and grinned wickedly. "You need to learn

your place, girl."

"Or you need to learn yours," Lena countered. Lena leapt over his low lunge, barely avoiding slipping in a pool of blood upon landing. She turned around and nearly stabbed him in the back quite literally, but he managed to roll away. Her gun contained a few stolen bullets she had snagged earlier, and one went straight through his shoulder.

Someone appeared behind her, and Lena glanced his way to see Trevor. "He's yours now, Lynx."

Trevor nodded and began dueling with Joey. Lena began to go to Sara's aid, but Sara spotted her and shook her head, nodding toward Michael.

His arm was wounded and could only use the other arm. Lena ran forward, yelling, "Get out of the way!"

Michael turned but too late. The scream left Lena as the bullet flew through the lower part of Michael's abdomen. She jumped straight over him onto Tulsi's shoulder and felt herself break his neck before she knew what was happening.

Lena ran to Alpha and applied all the pressure she possibly could to his gun wound, but blood still seeped through her clenched fingers.

Michael was gasping and put his hands over hers. She could barely see him through the glasses and through the tears. Lena yelled out in her anguish; nothing coherent left her. Trevor was panting as he ran over at her cry.

"Fix the lights!" Lena screamed at him, watching with horror as the blood continued through.

Trevor ran off immediately, though he hadn't seen the source of her anguish. Lena struggled to remove her jacket in the still strobing lights, seeing everything as though it were taken one picture at a time as her glasses had flown off when she had leapt at Tulsi.

The jacket came off at the same moment as the lights came on completely. The jacket soaked up as much blood as would be expected of a leather jacket but, when tied around his waist, stopped the most significant bleeding from continuing.

Lena touched her earpiece quickly and spoke as calmly as possible over the sobs that racked her whole body. "Aloe, Alpha's been shot. Get here now."

"I'm coming." Her hurried voice came through muffled as though she were already running.

Other voices that weren't fighting came over the airwaves with questions Lena couldn't answer. She instead was watching as Michael's face grew steadily paler and his fist began to loosen. Katie arrived within seconds and worked to wrap the wound, telling Lena to keep him awake. Her face showed more fear than Lena wanted to see, but she didn't ask because she didn't want to know how dire his fate was.

Lena noticed that the others were staring, having finished the battle as Katie worked. Avery and Bianca stood nearby, horror-stricken, though unable to remove their gaze from Michael. Katie left Lena to watch him and keep him awake while she called Crow to get the jet to them.

Avery and Bianca edged over, tears cutting through the blood that had splattered across their faces over the last hour, making their tears run red. They knelt beside him, Avery taking his hand, which he gripped weakly. His eyes fluttered beneath the lids, and Avery yelled at him as though it would change anything.

Katie came back, taking charge in the crisis. "Phoenix, Bull, and Badger, go get the cars and drive them back up here. You'll take everyone back home. Alpha, Beta, Hound, and I will be in the jet with Crow."

Everyone nodded, and Alyse, with Sara and Tyler, left to head back to camp. Trevor held Lena in his arms, trying to soothe her. She rubbed Michael's hand, feeling the gentle pulsing of his blood beneath her fingers. It was slow but steady for now.

"I could've stopped it. I could've been where he is now. He doesn't deserve this." Lena sobbed into Trevor's shoulder, continuing to rub Michael's palm.

Trevor shushed her calmly, staring at Michael over her shoulder. "No, this isn't your fault. We decided to come back for you. Don't blame yourself."

"If I would've left, married Jeff. If I would've run again. If I would've just died on the shore like I was supposed to. If I would've jumped in front of that bullet. None of us would be here if I had just died like John wanted me to. He was right all along," Lena sobbed.

"Never say that, Sparrow. It's not true. I would've never let you die. I love you. Don't ever say you should be dead." Trevor clutched her tighter to his chest, and Lena could feel his tears falling silently on her shoulder now. She wasn't sure who he cried for: her or Michael.

Lena turned to watch Michael again. She watched as his nose flared and relaxed, chest rose and fell, waiting to see if each would be the last. Eventually, car tires could be heard outside, and she was forced to leave Michael. Trevor deposited her in a car, promising to return once Michael was safely in the jet.

She watched as they loaded Michael and Avery into the back of the truck, which had been hastily unloaded upon the ground and driven to the main road where the jet was to land. Timmy and Tyler could be seen helping to get Sierra and Max to the cars. Max was placed with her while Sean stayed in the car with Sierra, having walked there himself.

Neither spoke of what they were thinking about. Lena only raised her head when she saw dust flying in the distance as the jet took off and the truck approached once more. Trevor didn't come immediately but instead helped to repack the truck, grabbing three extra shirts along the way.

He was the only one that came to her car; the rest were left to pack into the other cars. They lead the procession home, silent as could be. Only when they were halfway home did the questions she should've been asking after the battle come to her.

"Where did Joey and Andrew go?" Her voice was small and hoarse from the crying and lack of speech.

"Andrew was killed during the battle, and Joey escaped at some point," Max told her. He gently rubbed her back. Lena looked back out the window to the eastward bound road. She had managed to kill one of her greatest threats but created a new one in the process. This was one she had no knowledge about and knew wouldn't go down without a fight.

Chapter 28

Lena sat beside Michael's bed for a week, waiting for him to move or speak. It was slow at first, the waiting, but she got used to it. Avery or Bianca typically waited with her, but they both had gone to sleep early tonight.

She, at first, thought it was just a figment of her imagination, but his arm moved again. Lena slid off her chair to the floor next to him, watching for his eyes to open, which they eventually did. He winced first at the light, but slowly he adjusted.

"Michael, are you awake?" Lena asked gently, taking his hand in her own.

He nodded, opening his lips to speak but only a dry rasp left them. Lena grabbed the cup of water on the bed stand. She helped him drink by raising his head and placing the cup to his lips. He drank greedily, but Lena removed the cup.

"Not too much now. We don't need you to throw it up again," Lena told him as she placed the cup back on the bed stand.

"Thank you," he rasped; he reached up and touched his throat but felt the muscles pull along with the stitches.

"Careful, Alpha. I should go get Beta and Hound. They've been waiting for you to wake up."

Lena stood to go, but Alpha caught her arm. "Wait." He tried to sit up but couldn't manage it.

"Careful, Alpha. You have to be very careful. You have a lot of stitches." Lena sat again.

"Why can't I feel my legs?" he whispered, trying his best to speak loud enough to hear.

"They were paralyzed by the bullet," Lena murmured, dropping her eyes in shame. "It grazed your spine. We're lucky it wasn't worse. We had to take you to a real hospital, bribe some people. You know the drill."

"Thank you, Sparrow," he said after a shocked minute of silence.

"This shouldn't have happened."

"You saved me, Sparrow. I have nothing to complain about," Michael assured her.

"I didn't save anyone. It shouldn't have come to this."

"I want to ask you something." Michael's voice increased slightly in volume, and he seemed more awake the more he spoke. "Would you like to run TNT?"

"Wait, run? As in be Beta?"

"Well, if I'm paralyzed then I can't run it, and while it's Avery's position, she can't do it alone. She'll have already thought about this too."

"Wouldn't it go to Hound?" Lena was clearly grasping for anything to deflect from the prospect. She couldn't understand how he could speak so calmly and so immediately, yet he did.

Michael nodded slowly but said, "She doesn't want the job. Your mother was supposed to take TNT anyway; you're a rightful leader."

Lena's eyes widened slightly, but she shook her head. "Then it would be Hawks."

"He wants a family."

"I want a family too."

"Sparrow, you know you'd do better than Hawk would. You know that he'd take the position but wouldn't want it. You and Lynx would run it well."

Lena's head buzzed with the idea of leading; of course, she

had thought about it but never believed it would happen. She stood up and looked in his direction, though not truly seeing him.

"I'm going to go get everyone else. They deserve a say in this."

"Okay, be quick."

"I will." Lena left, unsure what to make of the proposition. She first went to retrieve Beta and Hound, so they could go to Alpha first before going to retrieve Max, Alyse, and Trevor.

They came in to see Avery hurrying around her husband, checking his bandages, though he insisted he was fine. Hound sat in the chair Lena typically occupied, smiling and laughing as she watched her father moving about, even if it was just his arms.

"Sparrow, you're back," Michael exclaimed, using her reappearance as an excuse to turn the attention away from himself.

"Good to see you moving, Alpha," Max said, coming in from around Lena.

"You, too. Last I saw you, you looked worse than I do," Michael replied with a lighthearted laugh. Everyone chuckled at his joke, knowing it was far from true. Max now walked with a cane, which he hated, but could do away with it in a week or so once his leg had healed completely.

"Very funny, Alpha. Now, why are we all huddled in here?" he asked, leaning against the wall opposite the door. "Shouldn't this be family time?"

Avery sat in the seat where Bianca had been while her daughter moved to the arm of the chair instead. Everyone's eyes were trained on Michael, which seemed to make him uncomfortable, but he hid it well. Years of leading did that to a person.

"Well," he sighed. "As I am now paralyzed, we must decide

who is going to take over TNT since I'm no longer fit to lead."

"I thought I was taking over?" Bianca said, confused by the prospect of not taking TNT.

"You don't have to if you don't want it. Your mother was third in line behind Mary and Maria, so the line would've gone to Max and Lena here," Michael informed her.

"So... I don't have to become Beta?" Bianca looked mystified yet excited at the idea.

"We would like the line to go to Lena as we believe she would lead TNT without a second thought, but we need both you, Bianca and Max, to willingly step down and for Lena and Trevor to accept," Avery told them as though she knew of this plan all along.

Bianca spoke immediately. "I'll pass it along."

Both of her parents rolled their eyes and looked to Alyse and Max. They looked between each other, and Alyse nodded. Max hesitated a moment, then looked back to Beta. "We'll pass it along."

Lena looked at Trevor, excitement filling her. He took a long breath and turned to Alpha and Beta. "We'll accept the post."

Everyone chuckled, and Lena hugged Trevor.

"We'll announce the change of posts as soon as Alpha is well enough to sit up," Avery told them, looking slightly disappointed about giving up TNT.

Lena and Avery left the rest to go discuss how the transfer would work. They talked for a bit in her office before they began making important phone calls to other gangs, mafias, mobs, and various dangerously important allies.

"You and Trevor should remain here, though that will be completely up to you. Alpha, Hound, and I would also like to remain but that too will be up to you," Avery told her between phone calls.

"Of course, you can remain here. We'll give you all the time you need to get Hound a place of her own and to make arrangements at your own estate to make it comfortable for Alpha."

"You'll need to make a power play at the very beginning of your leadership so other gangs don't think you're weak and step in. Change squadrons or uniforms or something, so they know how you'll run things."

Lena nodded, biting her cheek. "I'll retest everyone for skills and ranking. I think I may want to return the old uniforms too."

"Make sure to talk to the current squadron leaders about it before you make any changes. I'll begin arranging meetings with the other mafia bosses around town. You make sure to get a good cover name and profile for you and Lynx. You don't ever give out your real name if you can avoid it."

"Thank you, Beta."

"I'm not Beta. You're Beta. I'm Tiger again and Alpha is Eagle." Avery smiled and laughed wistfully at the return of her old name. Lena stood and left her to make more phone calls. "Wait, Beta, before you go," Avery called.

"Yes?"

"You can't change Squadrons Forty through Forty-five."

"Why's that?"

"I'll explain later. Just trust me about them."

Lena nodded and left. She had, of course, heard of those squadrons, but, as she thought about it, she had never seen them anywhere. Lena called all of the squadron leaders to meet in a large conference room that was typically used as a large dining hall for important guests.

Forty or so people showed up over the next half hour,

including Max, who was to take Squadron Thirteen, and Trevor. Each leader sat with friends and had their own touch of arrogance about them. Lena looked around, and, sure enough, she could see the six leaders that Beta had told her to leave sitting stiff-backed in a corner. No one neared them, and those that looked their way looked quickly away as though in fear. Lena edged over to speak to them before she called everyone to order.

"I need to talk to you six after the meeting is over," Lena told them.

The oldest one there was no more than thirty-five though had so many worry lines that he could pass for fifty. He was the first to speak. "Yes, ma'am. I assume you have a new assignment for us?"

"Assignment? No, I need to have a word with you six." Lena watched as they all met each other's gazes and exchanged a silent nod. They all seemed very close, bonded in a way Lena didn't understand.

"Very well," one of the girls there said as though there were a question if they would remain or not. The bags under her eyes revealed that she hadn't slept in days. Lena somewhat doubted that she was going to sleep too.

Lena moved away, more confused than ever about the tight group, though determined to figure it out. She returned to the head of the table and called them all to attention. "Thank you all for coming on such short notice."

"Not like you gave us a choice," Dolphin said from the front.

"Thank you for your opinion, Dolphin. We are here to discuss the reformulation of squadrons. If you would like to retain your post as a squadron leader, I would advise holding your tongue."

"You can't do that. Only Alpha and Beta can create or

disband squadrons or their leaders," he reminded her, unphased. He was a senior member, getting his name from his greying hair even at the young age of twenty when he first joined and for his ability to learn quickly. That didn't make him much of one to defer to power however, as he saw anyone younger than him as below him, something Lena had learned long ago.

"Another good point. Lynx and I are officially taking over TNT at the next assembly meeting," Lena announced.

Murmurs swept the room. The six in the back glanced at each other and nodded slightly. When the noise didn't subside on its own, the eldest that had first addressed her calmly spoke over the crowd. "That's quite enough chatter."

Everyone turned to look at who had spoken and fell silent upon his command. The man nodded to Lena and leaned back once more in his seat. Lena became still more curious about the odd group but forced the matter to the back of her mind.

"I mean to return the glory of TNT from before my father. I intend to retest skills and assign squadrons accordingly. I need your input on how testing should work. Don't forget that you will be tested too."

"Skill ranking based on a scale of one to ten. Hour long tests for each test. The best of the best rank the skills," Crow proposed from her seat at the front.

"That's all well and good but what about favoritism?" Alligator, a fairly new leader of Squadron Forty-two, asked from her seat with the other intimidating leaders.

"A panel of three then," Lena replied, seeing that no one else had the nerve to reply. Every time one of them spoke, the air seemed to leave everyone as though they were a ghost everyone could see.

"Ten tests over two days," Trevor told them.

"Marksmanship, throwing, trapping, tracking, tech, leadership, archery, nursing, strength, and stealth."

"And how will we redivide squadrons then?" Salamander, a small girl with scars like gills, asked from behind Dolphin.

"Each person will be assessed on the same platform. No one is allowed to have a member of a higher rank than oneself in their squadron. Five ranks with one as the top. Each squadron will have between four and fifteen people. Each squadron must have someone with each specialized skill. Each person can account for no more than three skills for their squadron. Each squadron will have a range of three ranks in their squadron. A leader must be rank three or higher. Be warned, you can be ranked down from what you are now, so risk losing your squadron. Ranks will be determined on skill points," Lena announced in what seemed to be one breath.

Trevor assessed their confused faces and rephrased her rules quickly. "Rank Four and Five can't lead. No less than four people per squadron. Each squadron will have at least one of each skill. You'll have three tiers of ranks at or below you in your squadron."

Everyone nodded, some visibly sighing in relief from Trevor's explanation. Lena rolled her eyes but continued anyway. "You'll get a calendar with your squadron's trial times and when you will be judging, if you get to judge at all. It will have any extra information too. You may go."

Everyone nodded and began to file out. The six remained in their corner, watching everyone leave. When everyone had gone, they took seats near the head of the table where Lena and Trevor were now sitting. Each had a calm yet domineering air about them.

"You wished to speak to us?" the man asked, yet again taking the lead in the conversation.

"What are your names?" Lena asked, looking between them.

The girl from earlier pointed around them. "Raptor from Forty. Vulture from Forty-one. I'm Alligator from Forty-two. Hyena Forty-three. Doberman Forty-four. Crocodile Forty-five."

Each gave a polite nod when they were named. Lena nodded, taking note of their predator names. Raptor seemed to be in charge as he was the eldest, but Vulture looked to be making the calls. He seemed to not be so lined as the others, though still had streaks of grey through his brown hair, which only accented the light specks in his light brown eyes, intelligent eyes. Alligator was seemingly the most vocal of the group as she was the youngest though that didn't say much as none of them were particularly old in years.

"I need to know why Tiger won't let me change your squadrons," Lena told them bluntly.

Doberman sighed and looked to Vulture as though for permission before speaking. "You will become leader soon so you both should know what we do as we will be important to the running of TNT, but we do prefer to remain somewhat of a secret around TNT."

"That's understood," Trevor acknowledged, leaning forward with interest. Lena pulled him back into his chair as she saw all of them shifting uncomfortably with his interest.

"Please, continue," Lena prodded.

Raptor took over this time, not looking to Vulture at all. The power dynamic of the group seemed off-balance, though Lena ignored it just as Raptor was. "We do TNT's dirty work. The things gangs are known for so everyone else can do the good deeds of the gang. You go out and attack the bad guys while we are the bad guys."

"What do you mean?" Lena looked between them and waited for an answer to come from any of them.

Crocodile sat forward, her long face not giving away any emotions she may or may not be feeling. "We get the money to fund your assignments. We kill for the money, sell the drugs, kidnap the kids, and so on. We make sure you stay safe by putting ourselves in danger."

"Right now, we complete jobs for TNT and for some mafia around town that Alpha has allied with," Vulture told them. "Well, Eagle, sorry. We go where we're told to go and do what we're told to do. We stay away from the rest of TNT as much as possible as to avoid the rumors. Most think they know what we do, but we neither confirm nor deny any of it. You give us a place to live and a job to do, and in return, we protect you and stay out of the way."

Lena nodded, now beginning to understand why so many avoided them. She also began to understand why they demanded so much respect from the other leaders. It also explained why in her lifetime she had never learned about them, why they had been hardly more than a footnote beyond TNT legend. "Do you enjoy your work?"

"No." All of them answered at once before Raptor explained, "Our first and only rule is that you may not enjoy your work. We have, unlike the other squadron leaders, full control over who enters and exits our squadrons. We tell you only when we need a new member or need to remove a member. Enjoyment would make us no better than Jackson or your father."

Lena felt some surprise at that explanation and at the fact that they knew of Jackson. Vulture seemed to pick up on her surprise and chuckled coldly. "He was one of us once, you know? For nearly two years, he was in my squadron. That was back before your mother got kidnapped. We removed him soon after, before he went insane and made you fake your death. Yes, we know of your little disappearance and why. It's our job to know everything about everyone. We're the ones that watched your 'death' the first and second time. We gave you the space you needed to disappear properly. You see, Beta, that's our job. We make everyone comfortable by making them uncomfortable."

Lena shivered and nodded. "You'll still be expected to be tested like everyone else just to have a full skill assessment in my private folders, but I'll allow you all to continue as usual. I do ask, though, that I get a more in-depth explanation of what you do at a later time."

Raptor shook his head. "We'll be tested by you alone, and you may have your folders, but you needn't know any more than what we told you today. By you knowing only so much, your conscience may stay clear. I'll come by and pick up our assignments personally when you need us."

They all stood; Lena and Trevor stood as well.

"It was nice to meet you both officially. We'll talk again," Raptor told them, giving them each a polite nod. Each leader nodded to them then left in their small pack.

Lena felt no more sure of their presence than she had before. Instead, she felt lacking as a leader, belittled in some way, which seemed wrong, as they had spoken with no level of defiance or superiority. Rather it was the looks between them, deciding whether to answer. Those looks told her of their equality to her, if not superiority. Lena decided not to take it personally, leaving it up to time on whether it mattered or not.

Chapter 29

Squadron One was tested first and then Two and so one down the list. It took ten hours per person, but Lena managed to ensure multiple people were tested at each skill at the same time to speed along the process. It took thirty judges every day and was very time consuming but, slowly, they got through. After two weeks, they managed to make it through the first thirty-nine squadrons.

Lena brought in all six of the remaining squadrons at once, and she scored them. It made the process last longer, but Lena also cut down the testing time for each skill. Each person was ranked on the same scale as the others, but, unlike in other squadrons where people would score very high in one category and low in others, each person scored extremely high in two or three categories and still moderately high in all the rest.

Every member in the six squadrons was ranked as a Rank-One or Rank-Two member; those in Rank-Two were just barely so, and none scored below a five in any skill. Lena was very impressed and made sure to congratulate Raptor on their training skills.

He gave her a morose look. "I cannot accept anything positive about our work. In another squadron, I would be proud, but here it is a matter of life and death. I do thank you, though, for not bringing in other judges to see us work."

Lena nodded. "I believe I can understand that. You should take some pride in how you've taught your members to be respectful in their work, though. Many with the influence you have would wield it as to create fear. I'm glad you taught them to understand their importance and yet know their place."

"Thank you, ma'am. I'll make sure to tell them of your praise."

"I appreciate it."

Lena moved away to collect the scorecards from the table where they had been laid. She stayed up all that night with Trevor, calculating the ranks of all the members. They had agreed on a percentage of skill to determine ranking. Above seventy-five points would be Rank-One, sixty-five to seventy-four would be Two, fifty to sixty-four would be Three, thirty-five to forty-nine would be Four, and anything less would be Rank-Five.

Lena was happy to see that of their two-hundred and fifty or so members tested, only seventeen were Rank-Five, and that was only due to their lack of training. Only about forty of TNT reached Rank-One under their new ranking process. Most were from the six 'secret' squadrons as Lena had taken to calling them or from the original Squadron One or Thirteen. Of course, there were some outliers from low squadrons that Lena was shocked to see rank highly.

She called a meeting the next morning with all of the squadron leaders. Only two had to be replaced, and the new leaders had been called in early to be told of their promotion and were sitting awkwardly in the middle as the senior leaders walked in. Lena nodded to the secret six as they took their seats at a separate table she had placed aside for them with their member's files already stacked in the middle.

Lena yawned but took a swig of coffee and called their meeting to order. "You may notice we have two new squadron leaders, Octopus and Camel. Congratulations to you both." There was some polite applause from around the table, and both were clapped on the back by the people sitting next to them.

"Okay, I'm now going to ask that you sit according to ranking. It was on the card you all received this morning when you were called here. Rank-Ones, please take the first four chairs up here. Rank-Three please take the last fifteen chairs. Rank-Two please take the middle twenty," Lena told them and paused, waiting for them all to be reseated.

Slowly, the conversation died away once more, and faces returned to her. She took another drink of coffee and continued on. "I have already pulled my squadron members. For this, everyone will get five to six total members in their squadrons. You must negotiate with the other leaders if you'd like more or less than that number. Don't forget, you must, one way or another, have a specialized person in each squadron. Rank-One, you'll get all of the first-class members now to debate among yourselves for. Rank-Three, you get all of the fifth-class members now as well. Rank-Two, you must wait for a couple minutes."

Lena plopped the piles of folders in front of the necessary groups and went to talk to the secret six while they debated among themselves. "You six may change around anything you like in your squadrons if you wish to change anything. If not, then you may go, but I do ask you to leave the folders here for me."

"We will stay," Raptor told her. He was flipping lazily through the folders of his squadron. "We don't want to draw attention by leaving now, do we?"

Lena smiled and nodded. "I suppose not."

Raptor reminded her of the old curators or librarians in books that knew more than they would let on. He seemed much too responsible for his age. The grey hair only emphasized the point.

Vulture began laughing with Alligator as he pointed to

something in one of the folders. Each leader took the folder in turn and chuckled at the information before returning it to Vulture. Their laughter and jokes set Lena at ease, reminding her that they were still people.

She returned to the larger group and set Rank-One and Two to debate on their Rank-Two members, reminding the Rank-One leaders that they had to leave room for at least one Rank-Three member. They each nodded, Crow making a joke as an aside. When they finished with that, Lena gave everyone the Rank-Three folders. That took the longest as everyone at the table had to take at least one.

Rank-Four went quickly between Two and Three as Two had already filled most of their squadrons, and Three had taken their free time to decide among themselves who they would take. Lena found that the leaders had stopped forming the cliques she had seen earlier that morning and had bonded more among themselves due to the debates.

"Everyone needs to come up and give me your squadron folders. I will check over them all. Some changes may be made where I see fit but largely, they should remain the same. Official squadrons will be announced at the assembly later this week. Also, squadron numbers will be reassigned based on overall skill in each squadron."

Laughter came from around the room as everyone turned to the Rank-Three members that had thrown up their hands in defeat. Some jokes were told among the Rank-One leaders, who were debating who would be the lowest among them, and a couple of arrogant Rank-Two leaders joined in, placing bets amongst them on whose skill levels would be the highest in the end.

Bundles of folders were handed down to her, which she filed

together, then turned back to everyone. "Okay, guys. Don't go making promises to new members at dinner. I'll make sure to get you all lists before the ceremony. Let's go eat, shall we?"

Everyone nodded vigorously and stood up, filing out in a mob that filled the hall. Lena followed behind the rest by a couple of minutes as she had to take her cart full of folders down to her new office, which Avery had temporarily emptied while she worked to empty her own office for Lena.

She went to dinner and ate with Trevor at a table further away from where the rest of the leaders were sitting.

"How'd it go?"

"Fine, we've got another long night ahead of us. Everyone got sorted, so that's something."

"Why don't we take the night off?"

"Can't, we need to get the squadrons renumbered and all of the members sorted properly. Eagle will be ready for the ceremony any day now," Lena reminded him, shoving a spoonful of corn into her mouth.

"You haven't taken a night off in weeks. Come on, just one night," he pleaded.

Avery came up suddenly, and Trevor rolled his eyes as Lena turned away from him. "What's up, Beta?"

"It's Tiger. I've got you a meeting with another leader tonight. Alpha, you should get dressed up for this one too. We'll need to leave in an hour."

Lena nodded and got up, ignoring the fact that she hadn't eaten anything but the spoonful of corn. "We'll meet you at the cars."

Avery nodded and went to get changed. Lena took both her plate and Trevor's to clean them off.

"Just one night," he muttered. "Please, just one."

They left to go get changed and ready for the third meeting that week. Each one was more important than the last, yet Lena was struggling to remain awake through them the more they went to.

Trevor was becoming more distant as they plowed into the work of Beta and Alpha, which made Lena nervous. She wanted to take the day off and spend it with him as he wished to but couldn't bring herself to do it. There was just too much to get done.

Lena noticed as they walked away from the cafeteria that they weren't alone; Raptor was following them.

"Raptor? What is it?" she asked, turning.

"I'll meet you at our room," Trevor told her.

Lena squeezed his hand and nodded. "I'll be there shortly."

"We need new assignments."

"I don't have any for you right now," Lena told him, looking after Trevor with a worried eye.

"You always have more assignments for us. Talk to Tiger about it. I'm sure she had something for us. You best talk to him, Beta," Raptor informed her, taking note of her worry with an impassive glance.

"I will. I'll talk to Tiger tonight about it. Stop by my office in the morning and I'll let you know."

"I'll come by in the afternoon. Get some sleep tonight. You look tired," he reported in such a casual manner that it made Lena feel as though he said it often. She realized that he probably did say it often to his own squadron as sleepless nights of work went by for them too.

Chapter 30

The crowd was dim compared to the spotlight Lena was standing in. Michael and Bianca were to her right, while Avery and Max stood to her left. Trevor wasn't on stage with her. Avery had told them both that Lena needed to be inducted into her position alone until her control, and their relationship, were secure.

Lena knew he disliked the idea and wished to be inducted as well, but that wasn't allowed, or so Avery insisted. She sought him out in the crowd, trying to find him among the dim figures. His outline was better lit as he stood in the front. Lena flashed him a smile, and he waved, attempting a smile as joyous as hers. It didn't work, but Lena knew he was still proud.

The ceremony started quickly; Avery spoke for the majority in her own spotlight. Lena would've liked to say she remembered every word, but she couldn't. Her head felt fuzzy, and her sight slowly blurred as the hours passed. It all collapsed when Avery knelt, the final portion of the ceremony. Everyone else followed her lead; Michael bent his head as he couldn't kneel, but the idea wasn't lost on her.

Lena felt her breath catch, not at the sight of everyone knelling for her but for a sudden burn in her ribs. She stumbled backwards, sight diminishing rapidly now. Max caught her before she fell back, and Lena felt where he touched burn with heat.

Her ribs burned with waves of fire that felt as though she were submerged in lava. Her thoughts were slow to catch up with the pain. Lena pulled his head down, feeling another wave coming. "Poison."

Max lifted her and caught Katie's gaze in the distance. She and Trevor broke through the crowd that parted ways for them. Both caught up fairly quickly, though Lena only felt them slipping farther away.

She held her ribs, and the pain was becoming too much to handle. In the distance, Avery could be heard trying to calm the crowd. Either she was successful, or Lena couldn't hear over the pain.

Max's arms were replaced with the cold sheets of a hospital bed. Her hand was engulfed by what she assumed to be Trevor's hand, which she clutched tightly, though his touch burned.

Katie began sticking in needles, and various sensors were placed on her skin. Lena held in a scream of pain, focusing instead upon remaining awake against the wishes of the poison and adrenaline flooding her system.

She couldn't hear Trevor's cries, nor could she hear him yelling. Her eyes were forced closed as she held in yet another scream that left her as a whimper. Only when Trevor's hand was forced out of her own did she open her eyes again.

Max had lifted Trevor against a wall, choking him. Lena couldn't hear what he was yelling but knew he blamed Trevor. She wanted to yell for Max to stop but couldn't make the words leave her lips. Another scream came before she could stop it; Katie yelled something at Max, causing him to drop Trevor.

Trevor's hand returned to her own while the hands of Katie and Max worked to determine what was happening. She squeezed his hand, but she felt her will to remain awake slipping away. She saw him yell something at her, but she couldn't make out what he said as she fell unconscious.

"She shouldn't be in pain now," Katie told them as she sat down at the end of the bed. She seemed out of breath from the frantic rush to slow whatever was happening.

Max nodded and looked over at his sister. "Who did this?"

"I don't know," Trevor murmured, continuing to hold her hand as he sat on the edge of the bed, ignoring the bruises which were forming on his throat.

"How don't you know? Hasn't she talked to you about anyone suspicious or something?" Max asked, glaring at Trevor.

"No, we haven't had time to just talk in a while," Trevor told Max defensively.

"Bullshit. She's been talking to me. You've had all of the time in the world."

"Oh yeah, and what had she been telling you then?"

"That you're more distant now. You're becoming different in a bad way," Max shot angrily.

Katie pursed her lips as though she wanted to defuse the situation to prevent another argument but didn't speak. Trevor didn't either. He just hung his head in shame, staring at her hand in his.

"What's happening with you?" Katie prodded, hoping for anything that could be useful.

"I don't know."

A voice from the door became annoyed. "Like hell you don't know. You're just scared and jealous."

Everyone looked over at Raptor, who was leaning in the doorway. He moved further into the room now and looked at Lena with an appraising eye.

"What do I have to be jealous or scared of?" Trevor asked. His voice sounded angry, though they could tell part of him wanted to know.

"You're jealous of her new position and her new bond with me," Raptor told him, looking at him impassively. "You're scared of losing her. You know she doesn't leave those that she loves. She protects those that she loves. You're scared because she's trained for this her whole life while you haven't. You never wanted this."

Katie eyed Raptor cautiously but nodded. "She's not stupid though, Lynx. She knows she can't protect you forever. She knows you're not ready."

"I know that," Trevor agreed; he hated to admit it but had no choice.

"Then show her that you trust her to do what's right," Max growled.

"You have to show her you still love her. You may believe that keeping distance is what she needs right now, or you may believe she's making distance, but that isn't true. You have to show her that you haven't given up, that you're ready," Raptor told him, speaking as though from experience.

Trevor nodded, turning back to look at Lena. She seemed carefree in her painless sleep. He knew it was temporary at best, but there was nothing to be done in that moment to fix the rift between them.

"Come on, Aloe. We need to go help at the ceremony. Let's go find who did this," Max told her.

Katie offered Trevor a meek smile before she left. Max looked at Raptor but didn't say anything to him. The man nodded and stood up from his leaning position in the door. "Lynx, you should stay with her. I'll sort out what I can."

Trevor nodded and heard him leave. The tears he had been holding in broke from him. He didn't want to believe what they said was true but knew it was. He wanted to believe that he was doing the best he could, but that wasn't true. Trevor couldn't remember the last time it had been just the two of them. Not just being alone in a room, but when they weren't running. He should've made her take a break, taken her somewhere to get away for a few hours.

New York, he realized. Not one time since going to New York had they been carefree, even for a moment. He began in that time, holding her hand in the silent room, to understand why she hadn't fought Avery to get him inducted to his position at the same time. By being Beta alone, it gave her total control for once.

For a time, he thought that, naively, she was only his. She had never been, never would be, purely his. Lena was her brothers'; Lena was her sister's; Lena was her friends'; Lena was TNT's; and, most of all, Lena belonged to anyone that leaned on her. She was his love and his responsibility but not his possession.

He fell asleep, dwelling on all of his unfulfilled responsibilities. Trevor only jerked awake when Lena's hand was pulled away from his as Lena woke up. She was clutching her chest as he opened his eyes.

"How do you feel?" he asked, repressing a yawn.

"Pain... get Aloe," she forced out, eyes watering.

He didn't want to leave her, but as there was no one else, he ran for her.

Katie was in a neighboring hall, deep in conversation with Sean. They seemed to be thoroughly entrenched in the conversation, but he ignored it.

"Aloe!"

"Hey, Lynx, can this wait a bit? I'm busy," Katie told him without even looking toward him. Sean rolled his eyes, looking toward Trevor, seeming about to speak.

"No, Beta's awake. She needs you," he panted, itching to return to Lena's side.

"She's – right. Let's go," Katie stammered. She seemed completely unprepared for the sudden change in conversation but followed, nevertheless.

"We'll continue this later, then?" Sean yelled after her, clearly annoyed.

"Oh, shut up, Bear," she called back, rounding the corner after Trevor.

Lena was curled into a tight ball and unintentionally resisted all of Katie's attempts to unlock her arms.

"Go get more people," Katie ordered, trying to pry open Lena's fingers as Lena shrieked in pain.

Trevor got Dillon, Timmy, and Max from a nearby hall, where they had evidently been waiting for word. Max had calmed enough from the previous night's argument to help without question. Each grabbed an arm or leg and pried her from the ball she had formed. Each held her down and attempted to ignore her screams.

Pain lined everyone's faces as doctors came rushing in and out, taking blood samples and asking her questions and watching her reactions. No one told the guys what they were thinking, but whatever it was, they didn't like it. Lena remained awake through the whole ordeal and did her best to control the screams or convulsions and answer questions.

Her hand held tightly to Trevor's even as he could feel how disconnected she was from them. Crow spoke to everyone, and it was as though the Earth had fallen silent as they listened. "A new poison. We have only a few records of it. It's from Tunnel Snakes, their creation. They have the antidote too."

"What does it do?" Dillon asked, hoping with the rest that

the future wasn't as bleak as it appeared.

"Short version: death," Crow replied, voice clipped. "Seems to be low dose to prolong the process."

Lena's eyes fixed upon Crow, and she clearly wanted to speak but only coughed, then was racked with another round of convulsions. She pulled her arm from Trevor's slackened grip and wiped her mouth.

"There's no way we can get it. Get me up," Lena groaned, shuttering as she tried to sit up.

"We can't get you up, let alone to your feet in this state."

"Then get me a sedative!" Lena yelled, ripping her arm from Max's grip and sitting up. She felt as though her ribs might break in the process but managed to remain sitting, even as another convulsion hit.

Katie grabbed a needle from the tray of antibiotics they had brought in and shot it into her arm. Lena winced but slowly felt the medicine take hold. Her legs felt numb and her head fuzzy, but Lena ignored it.

"Get me up." Everyone shook their head, and Lena growled in anger. "Boys, let go of my legs. If no one else will get me up, then I will do it myself."

"This isn't wise, Beta," Crow told her, backing up.

"I don't care if it's wise or not. Aloe, get these things out of me."

"Where are we going?" Max asked, nodding to the twins to let go of her, which they reluctantly agreed to.

"We're going to make Lynx Alpha, aren't we? If I'm going to die, let's at least do one thing right," Lena told them, swinging her legs out of the bed. Trevor helped her up, sharing a questioning look with Max.

Max and the twins both left before the rest so as to alert the rest of TNT to the impromptu meeting. They left shortly after, heading straight for the stage. Trevor held her up as her legs shook, but she quickly took over for her own.

Raptor was the first to arrive and made his way over respectfully. "You have recovered then?"

"If it appears so to you, then that's all I need to know," Lena replied, offering a small smile, which was not returned.

"How long then?"

"Not sure. Months, weeks, days, hours? They didn't tell me," she replied. Lena moved away from Raptor and over to the doors where Avery and Michael had just entered.

"You're okay! Thank God," Avery cried, hugging Lena too tightly. Lena pushed her away, feeling a burning rush from her ribs over her entire body, but she remained standing, though only barely.

Katie immediately was at her side. "What's happened? Are you okay?"

"I'm fine. If I make it through the ceremony, someone else can do the assignments; I'm sure. Get me a microphone, will you?" Lena asked, deflecting quickly from her pain. Lena followed Katie over to the microphones, and Avery walked over to Max, who had just returned.

"What's happened? I haven't heard."

"She's dying. She's naming Lynx Alpha, so TNT will pass to someone she trusts. There's an antidote though. She doesn't want to get it," Max told her, throat closing as he spoke. His eyes welled up, watching Lena from a distance getting a small microphone clipped to her jacket. Somehow, she was smiling and laughing with Katie and Trevor, who was refusing to leave her side.

"How long do we have?" Avery asked, watching Lena too

now.

"Days. I asked Crow. She said we have days." Max covered his mouth and took a deep, rattling breath before speaking again. "I can't lose her again. I've lost her twice. Please, not again. Not again, Avery."

Avery pulled him into a tight hug as his sobs broke from him. Lena turned from where she was trying to cheer up Katie to see Max crying on Avery's shoulder. She moved through the small crowd that had formed by now and took Max from Avery. She disregarded the pain in her chest to hold him.

"How are you so calm?" he asked, voice muffled against her shoulder.

"I accepted death long ago. I have to be strong, but I need you to be strong too. Hawk, please, I need you to be strong for the twins and for Lynx. I'll be your protector and everyone else's until my last breath, but I need you to be theirs too after I'm gone. Promise me, Hawk." Lena held him at arms-length, tears glazing her eyes too.

"I promise, but who will protect me when you're gone, Beta? I don't know what to do."

"My spirit will be here. Now, it's time to put on a show so dry up those tears. We'll have time to cry later," Lena told him. He nodded, cursing his pondering on how much time that would be, and dried his tears.

Trevor, who had seemed unable to locate her during their heartfelt bonding, wandered over, putting his arm carefully around her. "Are you ready for this?"

Lena smiled and nodded. She took a deep breath and walked back to her post in the middle of the stage where she had fallen just a few hours before. Everyone fell silent, and the last stragglers filed in quietly.

"Welcome, everyone. You may be seated now, and I apologize for the abrupt ending of last night's ceremony. Let's finish what we started and get on with the ceremony, naming Lynx as official Alpha."

There was a small ripple of applause that quickly died out. The ceremony took half the time it had taken for Avery to perform as Lena sped through half of the formalities. Trevor rose from the kneel as Alpha and Lena gave him a brief kiss before he left. Oohs and aahs left the crowd with a smattering of giggles and applause.

Lena turned back to the crowd, which fell silent at her gaze. "Will Hawk please come to the stage to officially be named Gamma?"

Mutters ripples out from the crowd. Older members looked to one another for confirmation of what they had heard while younger members attempted to convince the elder members to explain. Only the oldest members remembered the last Gamma in TNT, and others had only heard rumors.

Many of the stories had inklings of the truth behind them, though never the full truth. The last Gamma had been during the time of her grandparents but only briefly. His name was Elephant before being named Gamma. It was for three months at the end of her grandmother's pregnancy with Mary and Maria, her twin sister. He had tried to make a new faction of TNT, which would be a sort of money generator. Not the good kind either. Rather, he created a home for pimps and drug smugglers, infamously shut down by her grandfather with the use of Squadrons Forty through Forty-five, though they were performing many of the same deeds more discretely and still remained a secret, surely doing so even as Lena began the naming ceremony of Gamma.

Lena stopped the chatter with a quick cough. "I'm sure you

all have questions about the position, which I shall answer. Gamma is not a proper leader but a guard. If a leader is to fall, they will temporarily take the position or, if both are to fall, they will become the new Alpha or Beta."

Lena took even less time with Max than she did with Trevor as no one remembered the ceremony for the last Gamma, so it mattered not whether it was proper or not.

"Thank you, Gamma," Lena said, ending Max's naming.

"Thank you, Beta," he whispered so only she could hear the sorrow in his voice.

"Now the fun part. Everyone knows they have been tested and reassigned squadrons. Alpha will begin making those announcements. If all squadron leaders would join us on stage and anyone not a leader, please leave the stage," Lena announced.

Trevor moved back to the stage and took the mic off her jacket and put it on his own. "Thank you, Beta. We have sorted everyone based on skill and ranking number. Each squadron leader is at or above Rank-Three. Each also has three rank levels and at least one of each skill. I will call members to come greet your leader on stage, then please return to your meeting room unless your leader tells you otherwise. We will start at Forty-five and work our way down."

It took three hours to complete the sorting, and most squadrons left, but the secret squadrons opted to remain through the entire ceremony. Raptor watched them all go and followed shortly after.

Max, Lena, Trevor, and Dillon all walked together to their meeting room. Lena was careful to avoid her condition, which she had felt worsen during the ceremony but refused to tell them.

"Why isn't Alyse with us? She's the correct rank," Max asked, feeling slightly annoyed.

"You would've only focused on her safety, and you know it. Anyway, she's with Crow. She'll be perfectly happy," Lena replied sharply. "You got a big promotion tonight, be happy."

"I'm not." The mood fell back to the bleak silence Lena had been hoping to avoid.

Lena felt a strong jab in her ribs that made her stumble, and vision went blurred once again.

"Beta!" Trevor caught her arm quickly, and she swayed a bit on the spot.

"I'm fine. I'm just a bit dizzy. I nearly forgot. What did I do with it?" Lena fumbled in her pocket, hardly noticing their looks of worry. Lena pulled out a small box and pressed it into Trevor's palm. "Open it when I'm gone, okay?"

"What do you mean?" His words became frantic, eyes wide with the fear of actually losing her.

"Promise me, god damn it," Lena told him, words slightly slurred and leaning more heavily on Trevor.

"I promise."

"Don't cry, please. Don't cry." Lena fainted into his arms, head slumping forward.

"Is she?" Dillon cried, staring in horror at his sister.

"No, she's still breathing. Get Crow!" Max yelled, panic descending upon him suddenly. Dillon ran across the hall to where Squadron Two was having their meeting.

"You can't leave yet, Lena," Trevor cried softly. "We have an entire life ahead of us. I'm sorry I haven't been the best I could be. I'm sorry I did everything I did. Don't go."

He slowly sank to the ground with her in his arms and felt as her pulse quickened to a frighteningly high rate, then a startlingly low rate, all within the time Dillon was gone. Reet and another girl who seemed to be strolling away from their meetings came upon them.

Reet's eyes widened and stammered. "What? How? She was—no. How?"

The girl quickly assessed the situation and pulled Reet away and into a nearby meeting room, ignoring the angered voices of that squadron. Something happened there, and she and Crow appeared again simultaneously.

"Alpha, back off. You'll suffocate her that way," the girl ordered.

"Correct, Otter," Crow said approvingly. "Get a pillow."

Dillon ran into their meeting room and to one of the side rooms, where there was a bed that he pulled a pillow from. Crow took it from him and quickly shoved it under her head.

"Should we get her away from so many people, Mandy?" Otter asked.

Max, looking for any distraction, cried, "Your name is Mandy? I've known you since I was ten and didn't know that."

"Is that important now?"

"Ah, no. Everyone out. If you're not a doctor, then you keep people away from this piece of the hall, understand?" Max commanded, taking control of the situation to the best of his ability.

"I'll go get Aloe," Dillon told them, eyes locked on Lena still.

Everyone nodded and moved away from where Lena lay unconscious.

A Rank-Three with platinum-blonde hair and blue eyes suddenly appeared, seeming to have taken a different, longer route to get to their room. "Where's Beta?"

"What's your name?" Max asked, trying to keep the attention away from Trevor as much as possible.

"Lizard. What's it to you?" He was new to TNT as well as to the squadron, evidently, as the girl that was standing next to him started shaking her head violently.

"I'm your leader. You need to respect that; now, what's your skill?"

"Hiding, searching, and sniping. What are yours, sir?" he sneered. Max was now shaking with rage and wondering whether Lena would be mad if he smacked the shit out of the boy, but he decided to respect her decision and answer the boy.

"Strength, shooting, and tracking. What's your name?" Max nodded toward the girl and lightened his tone.

"Pidgin. I have stealth, marksmanship, and trapping," she replied softly. Her hair was black and her eyes a light brown.

"Good. Okay, who are we missing?" Trevor asked, drawing the attention back away from Max as he dried his eyes of the tears that hadn't stopped.

"Otter over there is healing and knife throwing," Pidgin replied quickly.

Katie was just returning with Dillon and heard Trevor's next command. "Beta doesn't want us to save her life, but she doesn't get an option now. We're going to Tunnel Snakes tonight."

"Be careful all of you," Katie told them. "Alpha and Gamma, if either of you die, then I will bring you back just to personally kill you again. I'll go get Otter for you now."

"Thank you, Aloe," they both replied, sad smiles playing on their lips.

"I'll keep her alive long enough for y'all to save her," she promised before going to Crow and Otter.

Chapter 31

Lena woke again before they arrived back at TNT. "Katie, where's Trevor?" Her voice was slow and measured as to keep the pain out of her voice, but Katie knew anyway.

"He'll be back soon." Her voice, too, was even and measured, but tears filled her eyes.

"That bastard left. Can I at least see my sister?"

"Of course. Crow, would you—"

"I'm already going," Crow replied, using the same tone that Katie had.

"I miss being around you," Lena told Katie as Katie sat on the side of her bed. "You didn't deserve what happened to your parents."

"Neither did you. There's nothing to be done now. I ran just as my mother told me. I ran and made a new life." Tears dripped off her cheek, and Lena smiled.

"That's good, though. You met Sean that way. I wish I had that. I don't even know where my mother is, and I killed my own father. I'm about to make my death go from two to three times, and I hate it. I don't want to cause this pain," Lena told her; she didn't hide her fate from herself any more but accepted it, feeling the now-familiar loss.

"It can't be three times. I won't let it be three times. Stay strong."

"I'm tired of being strong, Katie. For once I want to be weak; I haven't had a break in being strong since I was six years old. Two decades worth of strength, Katie. I don't want it any more."

"Of course, I have always seen that. Your brothers need you, though. Please, at least to say a proper goodbye."

"They need to learn not to need me. It's time Trevor move on like he should've ten years ago. Saying goodbye will just extend their pain. Please, just no more."

The door opened, and Sierra ran in. She knelt beside her older sister, surprise registering across her face. "What happened?"

"It doesn't matter. We can just talk for a little bit now. Just stay here," Lena said, taking her sister's hand.

She nodded, sucking in her lips to avoid the inevitable tears from falling. "Do you remember visiting me when I was a baby?"

"Of course, you would run straight to the twins' room if you even thought the window had opened. You didn't ever want me to leave, so I'd give you a gift to distract you." Lena laughed, setting aside the burning she felt go through her chest. She was still so young, yet another young soul forced to grow up much too fast due to a harsh world.

"Mary could never figure out where they came from. It made her mad," Sierra laughed. Her smile faded away. "It stopped working."

"Just as everything would fail in time. I missed you. I figured you were better off, though."

"Do you still believe that?" Sierra asked, slightly scared for the answer.

Lena hesitated before replying. "Yes, I do. I believe that if you hadn't had me back in your life you would've had a normal childhood. You would've been in school. Trevor could've loved another; our brothers could've learned to depend on each other and not me. I still wish it would've worked. Max would've been married and the twins in college. You would have a mother."

Tears trailed down both of their faces. Lena grasped Sierra's hand tighter for a moment as the tears reached her chest like molten lava. Sierra gasped in pain and pulled herself free of Lena's hand as Lena's eyes fell and her hand went limp.

"Katie!" Sierra yelled to the bathroom where Katie was washing her hands. The water turned off quickly, and the door flew open with a small spray of water from Katie's hands.

"Lena, stay with me. Don't you dare leave me. Talk to me, Lena. Sing or do something," Katie said frantically as she reached for more painkillers.

Lena's eyes rolled back farther in her head, but a faint lullaby came from her, comforting Katie ever so slightly.

Max and Trevor were forced to their knees by a henchman. The burly man seemed dull of mind though his tattooed arms did all the speaking truly necessary for him. His shaved head added to the mixture, though it was thrown off by his too small, dark eyes. Joey stood in front of the pair, a wide smirk stretching his lips.

"Did you really think that barging in here would work after all of the times you've done it before?" Joey accused, a smile on his face too.

Trevor spat at his feet, and the man smacked him across the back of the head, yelling angrily, "Show some respect!"

"He is right; I'm prepared to call your precious Lena right now to bargain with her, so you'd best remain silent. Cole, gag them to ensure their silence, would you?"

Cole nodded and shoved a cloth in each of their mouths, carefully avoiding being bit by either. Joey pulled out Max's phone from his back pocket and snickered, "Cute photo."

Max tried to pull his wrist through the rope bonds around his wrists. Joey just tutted his tongue as he moved the phone to his ear, wagging his finger at Max, which just further enraged him.

Lena's voice could be heard even though the phone was pressed hard against his ear. "Kayla Brown speaking." She sounded strong and confident like always, though Max and Trevor knew her condition must have deteriorated further in the passing hours.

"Where's Lena?" Joey asked calmly.

"Hey, Joey," Lena replied.

"Lena, you sound better already. Isn't that swell?"

"Shut the fuck up, asshole. What do you want?"

"Well, I have your eldest brother and boyfriend-fiancé person, whatever he is now, sitting in front of me."

"No, you don't, they're here." There was a short conversation on the other side that ended with an exasperated huff from Lena.

"What do you want for them?"

"You."

"Deal. When are we meeting?"

"Your house in, say what time, an hour, sound good?"

"Fine. Bye."

"Bye, love." He hung up with a smirk. "Looks like I get the girl again."

Trevor was desperate to get out of his bonds and go find the members of the rest of his party that had been taken too, so he could go to Lena. He felt it odd to long for the rude little boy, new girl, Otter, and Dillon in that moment, but it was all he could do.

Cole, on the other hand, knew his orders and loaded them into a moving truck that was to be driven to her house. Lena, meanwhile, was sitting on that curb, half-conscious and waiting.

Trevor tried desperately throughout the ride to get out from his bonds or at least get rid of the gag that made breathing in the stifling, moving truck near impossible. He only got relief when Cole opened the back of the truck and dumped them onto the road, filling his lungs with fresh air at least.

Lena was already standing by the truck, grey in complexion and wobbling in the uncommon heat of autumn. She locked eyes with both, one at a time, before saying, "You will both obey any deal I make. I don't care what it entails. This is your punishment for disobeying me. Tell everyone I love them."

She moved past them as though nothing had happened, gently brushing by Max's shoulder, which was disregarded, and went to Joey. "I'll go with you willingly for these two, but what do I need to do for everyone else's freedom?"

"Make me an offer," Joey said, rolling casually back on his heels.

"My forces won't come to save me."

"I kinda want to keep your boyfriend, too."

"No, he's off the table. My offer is fair. Take the offer."

"You'll obey my every order."

"Fine, let's go." Lena wobbled and doubted that she'd have the strength to disobey an order anyway.

Joey smiled even more broadly. "Kiss me back then." Joey kissed her, and, as disgusted as she was, Lena did as she was told.

"Are we done here?" Lena asked when he finally backed off.

"You'll refer to me as 'love' from now on, but otherwise, yes, my dear. Get in the truck," Joey ordered.

Lena wiped her lips and got into the van, keeping herself from glancing back at the horrified men that were still bound and gagged. Joey, on the other hand, went back over to them. "You best hold the deal, or she'll be dead before either of you can say goodbye."

Max held Trevor's wrist as Joey sauntered away. Both were shaking with rage, but Max had learned to control it better than Trevor ever had; at least, he could hold it in the face of danger. They slowly worked to untie each other, back-to-back in order to access the ropes, and, gradually, they calmed down to be able to have a conversation as they rubbed the rope burn off their wrists.

"There's already a car on the way. They'll save her," Max told Trevor, sitting on the curb in front of his childhood home with his head in his hands.

"How do you know?" Trevor asked, surprise mounting in his voice as he heard the confidence in Max's.

"Lena dropped a piece of paper on the ground when she brushed my shoulder. Cars are already at their base with our squadron, and they managed to get the antidote. They're now waiting to rescue her."

"She'll be shot before they even reach the base," Trevor pointed out, slumping over in a sign of defeat.

A female voice behind them spoke carefully, causing both to jump. "That is one fact I ensured would never happen. My daughter deserves better than that."

"Mary?" Max turned around suddenly and toppled over the edge of the curb he had been reclining on for the last several minutes.

"I'm saving my daughter, Maxwell, nothing more." Mary said it as though she weren't speaking to one of her sons in that moment as well. It seemed to sting Max.

"How are you saving her?" Trevor asked stiffly, taking the attention away from him for a moment.

"A quick explosion."

"A fucking explosion? No one can survive that," Max told her, getting to his feet in fury.

"Of course, she can. It's Lena, and she defies the odds," Mary told him, confidence oozing off her demeanor.

"Well, we best go if there is to be an explosion either way," Trevor reminded Max. Mary nodded and moved away as though her job was over. They made no move to stop her from leaving, although it felt so sudden for her to have appeared just to disappear again. It was unsettling, especially for Maxwell, as he felt a strange level of indifference toward his mother leaving, leaving him with an uncomfortable knot of guilt.

Max nodded in agreement and walked backwards a few steps before flipping around, so he could rejoin Trevor properly. They had been running toward TNT for a few minutes before a car came to a screeching halt beside them.

"Get in the car," Bianca yelled through the window.

"I think you just destroyed the brakes," Trevor commented casually as he climbed into the car.

"Do you want to discuss my driving, or would you like to go save Lena?" Bianca hissed angrily.

"Save Lena," Trevor replied shortly, tone slightly apologetic.

"How'd you know we were here?" Max asked as the car rumbled back to life.

"Lena gave me a rough time in which you'd be heading this way."

"But how—?"

"Don't question this," Bianca told him.

She carefully monitored their speed, careful to not go too fast or slow while they were still at risk of seeing cops. Trevor, meanwhile, used his phone to find any way to slow Lena's van.

Max was beginning to clean his gun fully for the third time just as they left city limits. Trevor cried at the same time, "Floor it! I managed to stop them by short circuiting an old lamppost, sent such a jolt that it fell over and is blocking the road."

Chapter 32

The car came to an abrupt halt. Lena felt her seatbelt digging into her chest as she heard the lamppost burst with the sound of breaking glass. Her chest felt that same pain, though it wasn't at the point of blacking out, which she was grateful for. The medicine Mary had given her did seem to be working to a point, more than Lena had believed it would, anyway. Lena now just had to hope that Trevor and Max had decided to not go with Bianca, even though it was a piece of Mary's plan.

Lena hadn't wanted to involve anyone she didn't have to, though Mary insisted that Bianca be included within the plan. She had been working for months to find Lena, years actually. Ever since she had gotten Lena's Christmas present, she had aimed to find who had given it to her.

She had found Lena only recently and placed a spy, the rude boy within her squadron, in TNT to keep tabs. The boy was how she had learned of Lena's illness in the end. Even as Lena knew her mother had good intentions for watching her, Lena hated taking orders from her. She hated taking any orders.

That's why, when the lamppost fell, and Joey looked at her as though it was her fault and ordered her to go move it, Lena was defiant. "I'm not strong enough to move a lamppost. Who do you think I am? Hulk?"

"Then how did it fall? Did you do it?"

"I've literally been sitting here under your constant supervision. How would I have made that post fall, my love?"

Joey's jaw tightened as he accepted what she had said. "Fine, go move it anyway."

Cole sneered at her as well, mocking her in that he didn't have to go, although careful not to push it. Even if she was their prisoner, Joey would make him help her if he were too obvious.

"How the hell?" Lena grumbled as she exited the car. She wandered around and around the post, taking notice of the fried wiring within the post itself with mild interest.

Finally, she decided to try and move it to the side of the road, pain and all. She pushed as hard as she could and, slowly, thanks only to the gravity helping to pull it in the correct direction on the slope, she moved the post far enough for the car to pass.

In the distance, as she moved toward the car, she spotted a car, something they hadn't seen for their entire journey.

Joey left the car, followed by Cole, and pulled out a gun. Lena rolled her eyes. "Why now? What have I done, my love?" She sneered the last phrase, but he grinned anyway.

"Nothing, just thought about why I'm even bringing you all the way to base. I'm going to kill you, anyway."

Lena smiled, a little insanity briefly touching her as she stepped toward the gun until the barrel was pressed against her forehead. She whispered at that point, "Oh, but you're just a boy. Have you ever killed anyone? You've been in a few battles but to actually watch their last breath?"

His eyes flickered to look at Cole, who looked confused and back to her, unprepared to answer the question they all knew the answer to.

"Well, there's always a first," Lena told him. She took a step back and gently guided the barrel to face Cole, who swallowed hard.

"You don't have to do this. She's manipulating you," he said in a panic, disbelief making him a bit more frantic than before, although freezing him.

"If you're not willing to do it, then why am I still here? Why would you kidnap me if not for my advice, my love?" Lena whispered in his ear.

Joey pulled the trigger. The fear hadn't left his eyes, but a new sense of power had joined it as Cole slumped to the ground. "There."

"Good. Now it's my turn," Lena replied, and, before he could react, she reached up and snapped his neck. His body hit the ground at the same time as the car exploded.

Lena heard the blast, then only ringing, and felt only pain as the searing heat inside and outside of her body became too much to bear. The second car holding a piece of her family came to a screeching halt just outside of the ring of fire surrounding the van. She saw the figures running toward her, but she felt as though she were made of lead.

A pair of arms from one of the people scooped her up. It felt gentle and familiar, though she couldn't make out the face. "Trevor?"

"Yes, Lena?" came the soothing voice she knew so well, though he seemed to be whispering beneath the ringing and the roar.

"I can't see you. Why can't I see your face?"

"You're going to be okay," Max told her from the front seat as she was placed in the back. She felt a cloth being tied around the top of her head. She only then realized that she was bleeding.

"You'll see me soon," Trevor promised. "I'm right here."

His hands slid into hers. She squeezed them tightly and closed her eyes, allowing herself to relax a little as the adrenaline began to slow and the heat outside of her body abated. Trevor's hands began to move away, and she gripped them tighter.

"I'm just going around the car. I'll be right back."

He was true to his word, and, as he sat, Lena leaned herself down into his lap, comforted by the warmth of his skin. "Am I cut out for this job, Trevor?"

"Yes," he assured her.

"You don't sound convinced." She dug her cheek further into his leg as she spoke.

"I am convinced. You are strong, confident, and a born leader. You deserve it more than any other." He looked down to see if she believed him, only to see that she had fallen asleep.

"That was nice to say," Bianca giggled from the driver's seat.

"It's true," Trevor replied defensively, having momentarily forgotten she was there.

"We never said it wasn't," Max reminded him quietly. "You know as well as I do that she needs assurance from loved ones."

The car trip back was fairly quiet, with a few jokes about the nearly dead brake pads as they squealed. Lena awoke just as they re-entered the city at one particularly loud squeal from the brakes.

"Oww, my head," she moaned, sitting up a little and wiping her eyes.

"How are you feeling?" Max asked, turning around.

"Fine but for this splitting headache, and my body having been thrown by an explosion," Lena told him, rolling her eyes. She regretted it as it sent her world spinning, making her blink hard and gag from nausea.

"You're right. Dumb question."

"Oh," Lena said excitedly, remembering something. "Can I plan your wedding?"

Max chuckled, "That's up to Alyse."

"Aww, but I've always wanted to plan a wedding," Lena

grumbled, laying down across Trevor's lap again.

"Well, you may just have to wait 'til Trevor here decides to pop the question," Max replied happily, turning back to the road.

"That'll take forever though," Lena complained. She turned back to face Trevor and announced, "I can see again."

"I can tell." Trevor nodded, starting to laugh.

"Don't laugh at me. I haven't been able to talk for days," she said dramatically.

They all nodded, knowing it to be true, but rather than discuss the recent events, Trevor continued joking with her. "I think you should calm down a bit."

"No, I shouldn't. If I talk about other things, then I don't have to think about the fact that my mother tried to have me killed. Also, then I don't have to think about a gun being pressed against my forehead or coercing someone into killing someone else before killing them. I also don't have to think about how much I have to get done upon returning. Oh, look at that, we're back," Lena told them cheerily.

Bianca came around to her door, saying, "Welcome home, Beta."

"When will the others be back?" she asked, the medicine she had taken before she left seemed to be kicking in. It had been awhile since taking it, yet the euphoric effects seemed to be manifesting.

Bianca helped Lena from the car and heaved one of her arms over her shoulder. "In five to ten minutes. They had to deal with the car and bodies and such, which doesn't take too long but well… you understand. Now no more scaring us, okay?"

"Yeah, it wasn't my intention. I'm gonna go work out in the gym, but first, I need to find Alyse. I need to ask her something important." She ran off yelling, "Phoenix! Phoenix, where are you?"

Bianca backed up while laughing, "She's going to be a great leader, won't she?"

"The best," Max replied as he watched Trevor go running after her.

They could hear his voice yelling as he went. "Beta! Beta, you have a head injury!"

"He'll be okay, too."

"You're not nervous about her planning your wedding?" Bianca asked, giggling as she watched Lena go running by again in search of a new hall to search.

"No. Well, a little bit. I snagged her antibiotics from the road, she must've shoved them in a pocket just in case. Read through the side effects. Hysteria was there."

"How long does she take it?"

"It says a month. Once daily."

"It's gonna be a fun month then," Bianca sighed. She began walking toward the doors.

"You gonna go take away her weapons?" he called.

"Yep. You gonna change the brake pads?" she replied, turning around while still going to the door.

"Why not?"

"Well, your fiancé may be being attacked by your sister, so there's that."

"She can hold her own. Anyway, Alpha's there to hold her back."

They both laughed and parted ways.

Lena managed to track down Alyse on her third lap around TNT. Alyse had to hold her steady in order for Lena to remain standing. She wanted to hear what Lena wanted but instead listened to her giggling for a while before Trevor arrived, panting and about to collapse himself.

"What happened?" Alyse asked, looking between them.

"She got her meds," Trevor panted, leaning on his knees for support.

"I need to ask you a question," Lena giggled, moving off Alyse to support herself on the wall.

"Shoot."

"Can I please plan your wedding? Please?" Lena begged, hiccupping a little as her laughter subsided.

"No," Alyse told her flatly.

"Please, I've always wanted to plan a wedding."

"Plan your own," Alyse told her, clearly tired from worrying about Max and the rest.

"I can't, though. He hasn't asked, and I can't plan it until he asks. Right now, that doesn't seem to be happening," Lena said, stumbling on her words as she spoke.

Alyse shot Trevor a look and rolled her eyes. "Seriously? Trevor, can I talk to you for a moment?"

He nodded, glancing at Lena, who seemed to have checked out of the conversation entirely as she seemed to be falling asleep again. They moved down the hall to talk.

"Yes, Phoenix?"

"Do you love that girl?"

"Of course, I do."

"Then why haven't you asked her to marry you yet? It's not like you're getting younger. She needs more than a promise of a promise, otherwise known as a ring. Don't leave her waiting like an asshole. I'd love for her to help with my wedding, but not because she's waiting for her own," Alyse told him in an angry whisper.

"I don't know how to do it."

"Find somewhere pretty and get down on one knee." Alyse seemed to spit the words at him before walking back down the hall to Lena. "Of course, you can help with the wedding."

"Really? Yay! Have you figured out a date yet?"

"Not yet. We had one set but then you came back home."

"Oh, I'm sorry. I'm really sorry, Alyse. I didn't mean to do that." She began to cry, and Alyse hugged her as she glared at Trevor.

"Oh honey, you didn't know," Alyse said before mouthing at Trevor, "You owe me so much." He nodded and backed away, still listening to Alyse. "Come on. Let's get you to the ward to get that head stitched up."

Chapter 33

Two weeks of smiling and laughing pursued Lena. TNT seemed to have new life and be more light-hearted. Everyone got the unofficial task of watching after Lena and keeping her out of trouble while her medicine was in effect. A group of Rank-Five kids insisted on following Lena everywhere. They were a good group of kids and seemed to adore Lena.

Trevor had been running around trying to run TNT in Lena's mental absence and work on planning his proposal. He had his work cut out for him as, when he left Lena's side for too long, she would begin searching for him in the same manner that she had searched for Alyse in previous weeks, a flock of young children hot on her heels.

This display had caused many disturbances as Trevor became caught up in various activities over the last two weeks, though no one complained. Many just seemed glad to have her there and have some source of joy, no matter where it came from. Those who were less pleased attempted to stay out of the way, though with little success, as Lena tended to appear just about everywhere.

Lena hadn't stopped entirely in her duties, though many were cut out so as to avoid a multi-gang war as they realized that TNT was under misguided leadership. Instead, Lena was given gymnastic and stealth classes to teach. Her gymnastics classes consisted of her teaching rolls and dives as well as climbing techniques that often left her in fits of laughter, though she was still tough on her students, expecting mastery of each technique by the end of the class. Her stealth classes were less serious and were made up of students attempting to show her how to be stealthy rather than the other way around. It was a trial by error in how both to be stealthy and how to teach.

During one memorable class, however, Lena had turned off all the lights and ran around playing Marco Polo. She had been abnormally good at the game as her students ran into each other, yelling, "Marco!" at the top of their lungs, which Lena would return just as loudly. At the end of class, her students gave up and turned on the lights to find her hanging upside-down from the ceiling, her face bright red from blood.

"Stealth isn't about being fair and truthful. You must cheat. I've been up here for the majority of class, yet no one knew," she called down to them, surprisingly calm.

No one was quite sure how she managed to mount the eighteen-foot flat walls, thus leading to a more interesting gymnastics class the next day. That class had doubled in size as her other students had come as well. The result of this lesson was that, when Trevor walked in, he found the class empty. He had searched for a few minutes before looking up in annoyance to find thirty people hanging like bats from the ceiling. Lena giggled and waved. "Hey, honey."

The hardest part of the day was when the drugs wore off, and she returned to her serious and pained self. While he was searching for his phone one day, he had opened some drawers in their room to find more letters. He hadn't thought she needed to write down her memories any more.

That night, he brought up the existence of them to her when they were getting ready for bed. Lena was already lying in bed, a heating pack on her head to relieve the headaches that came when the medicine left.

"Lena, what are these?" He had opened the drawer and held them up to where she could see them.

"You weren't supposed to see those," she groaned, sitting up. Lena seemed suddenly more awake, yet Trevor saw these weren't the same type of letters as before.

"Why didn't you want me to see these?" he asked softly, sitting beside her on the bed. She coughed and took the handful of letters.

She shuffled the letters for a moment before deciding on one. She pulled it from the stack, hands shaking slightly as she did. Lena coughed and groaned from the pain but handed it to him again wordlessly.

He opened it and began to read:

11.14.2009

Attempt eighteen.

I tried again today. Maxwell found me again. He threatened to tell John. He wouldn't. We both knew it. It would be a worse fate than death. He knows better.

-Lena

"Are these all…" Trevor didn't finish his sentence. He just looked at Lena, and the letters still clutched in her hand, his thoughts on the drawer still full of letters just an arms-length away.

She nodded, not meeting his eyes. "I stopped. I should show you something, though."

Lena got to her feet slowly. She never stood up off her meds but determined this was too important to wait.

He allowed himself to be led through TNT, fairly sure he knew where they were going, only to be brought to a door he had never opened. Lena heaved a sigh before opening the door. She never brought people here.

Inside was a small garden scape. There were trees and succulents and flowers everywhere. It wasn't what Trevor had expected to see. "What is this place? It's beautiful."

Lena offered a small, sad smile with a nod. "It was meant to be. You wouldn't know…"

Trevor felt an odd sense of mourning from her that contrasted so thoroughly with their surroundings. She weaved through to the back, where an artificial stream cut through between the only two trees in the garden were planted. It was thin and weak, edging around a tiny, new sapling.

She crouched down beside the baby tree and gently touched a leaf on the only branch the tree possessed.

"What is this place?" He asked again, hoping to get an answer as he knelt beside her, careful not to step on any of the delicate plants.

"Every time that I attempted to… you know… die, I came here. It helped me calm down and think, I guess. That tree," she pointed across the stream to the maple that arched above everything else, "was the first one I ever planted. Max convinced Avery to make this space a long time ago. He's the only one that I've ever brought in here."

"The waterfall then," he said, pointing to the sapling.

"I don't want to any more. I thought it would be a nice beginning and end. A full circle conclusion."

"I'd prefer to not have a place like this, anyway. How many…"

"I don't know. I don't want to know. It's really easy to try when you're constantly surrounded by weapons and fresh pain."

"Those letters."

"I needed to see them. I want to burn them. They're not me any more," Lena told him with a wince.

"I've been planning for a while, but now is the best time I could possibly think of." Trevor pulled the ring box from his pocket and opened it to show her the diamond on a silver band.

"Of course, you'd have it with you," she chuckled, eyes only half open with the pain that often woke her in the night. "Yes, Trevor."

He kissed her gently, knowing that any more and she'd have to pull away. Trevor was careful with her, knowing her boundaries since she had been poisoned. It was for this reason that he was unsurprised when she pulled away. He slipped the ring onto her finger.

She gazed at it quietly, leaning on his shoulder as they sat in her garden. They didn't talk for a long while before Trevor decided to speak. "So, what is it like during the day?"

She sighed in happy exasperation, "I won't be able to smile for a month. I'm so tired during the day but lord is it fun."

Trevor laughed, making Lena laugh too. They sat for a long while, just laughing at her daily life before they both drifted to sleep. It was the first time in weeks that she had slept soundly, without waking to the pain.

Only when the morning light appeared over her maple did she awake with a fire in her chest. Lena shook him awake, tears in her eyes as she did. "Trevor, medicine."

He awoke quickly as he had become accustomed to tending to her in the night. "Just stay put. I'll come right back."

He left quickly, leaving her lying in the garden. Her chest felt like fire and, with every breath, Lena felt it spread. Trevor was back within a minute, clearly having run through the building in both ways.

He started to hand her pills, but she took the bottle, reading it for the first time, though the pain was building still, feeling worse than ever before. Lena threw the bottle against the wall where the glass shattered, scattering pills in every direction. Trevor watched in shock, unsure of why she would do such a thing.

"Those weren't medicine. They were meant to make me go insane," Lena told him, voice catching. "My own mother won't stop at anything, will she?"

"If those aren't your medicine, then what is?" Trevor asked, mind reeling. How had he not checked? How had Katie not checked? He had checked everything else in TNT but for the most important thing.

"Tunnel Snakes," Lena hissed through her teeth, pain surging up more than it had in weeks. "They have it."

"We'll get it, Lena. I'll send Squadron Two. They can do it, I'm sure. You stay here. I'll send Max and Alyse here. I have to go," he told her, already standing as though to go.

Lena caught his hand. "Wait, thank you." She pulled herself to her feet and hugged him, trying to ignore her ribs.

He held her for a moment, fear ripping through him. "I love you, Lena."

"I love you, too, Trevor." Lena kissed him before she released him. He glanced back at her before he ran to the door. The door slammed behind him, leaving Lena in the silence of her past mistakes.

She slowly stumbled to sit beside the door, waiting for Max and Alyse as tears streamed down her face. Lena faded in and out of consciousness as she waited. Her vision slowly blurred, and she finally passed out. It was dark again when she awoke, though she was still alone.

Her entire body convulsed in pain and hunger as she lay there. This was supposed to be the best day of her life thus far.

Her family was safe, and she was promised to the man of her dreams. Her mother had, yet again, managed to ruin it for her.

For the rest of the night, Lena managed to remain awake, staring through hazy eyes at the metal door. As daylight came yet again, Lena could no longer sit there idly waiting for help to come. With excruciating pain, she pulled herself to her feet, doubling over almost immediately as the fire grew in her bones.

She managed to pull open the door and collapse into the hall. A scream pierced the air. Lena attempted to run toward the sound, only managing to get to her feet, only to fall again. "D-don't hurt them!" she tried to yell, only managing a sound above a whimper.

A more panicked yell returned from down the hall. "No! Go back! Beta, go back!"

It was Trevor, and all she wished to do was help him. She needed a gun, but all of her weapons had been seized due to the medicine. Lena pulled herself around, tears drenching her face as she did so, and pulled herself to a supply closet just feet away. It may as well have been miles for the pain that continued to rip her inside out. She had to go through most of the drawers before she found some knives, not her goal, but at least it was something. She looked, absent-mindedly, to the emblem engraved on the knives and almost dropped them.

She had unknowingly dragged herself to her father's old chambers. Lena felt the fear shoot through her, though she had no choice but to use what she had. Lena dragged herself back to the hall, attempting once more to get to her feet. She heard footsteps coming and took a deep breath before scrambling up toward the rafters, pain feeling like bullets with every movement, though there was no choice but to move.

The man walked right beneath her, clearly not from TNT. Lena fell onto his back and stabbed him in the chest. He yelled in shock but fell and was still within seconds. She searched his jacket for a moment before finding an earpiece he must've taken from a member of TNT.

She put it in her ear and heard it crackle with dead air. She felt relief wash over her with the sound. "Who hasn't been captured?" she asked, her voice full of pain.

About twenty relieved voices came over the airway, none of which Lena recognized. "Who here is tech?"

Only one male voice replied that he was. Lena nodded; that's all she needed. "Get to a control center and get ready to turn off the lights. Everyone else, who is in the gymnastics class?"

About five voices replied. "Good. Choose a wavelength and stay there. Find two of three other people and stay with them. Contact me when you find them."

The lines went silent. Lena sat on the floor by her attacker, heart beating wildly as she waited. No one came down the hall, and she could no longer hear Trevor. It hurt to know he was so close, but she couldn't help him.

The line came back on as a member reported in. "I've got two people, Beta."

"What skills?"

"Offensive and healing."

"Teach them to climb."

She gave each group the same instructions and, slowly, they trickled back onto her frequency. "Turn off the lights."

They went out immediately, and some shocked screams could be heard echoing through the building.

"Find your way to a supply closet and get what you need to fight. Lights will come back on in exactly five minutes. Good luck, everyone."

There were murmurs wishing her well as the groups signed

off. Only one remained on the frequency with her. "Beta?"

"Yes?"

"What're you going to do?"

"I'm coming to you."

"How, ma'am?"

"Do you know your location?"

"Sector 8 and corridor 5."

"I'll be there shortly."

Lena stumbled her way through corridors, hopping into the rafters when she heard footsteps or voices until she reached the center that the man was at. "Hello?" she whispered.

"Beta?"

"It's me. What's your name?"

"Stallion, ma'am."

"What are your skills?"

"Tech, strength, and stealth."

"Good, how long until the lights come back?"

"Thirty seconds."

"Can you make them flash?"

"Yes, ma'am."

"Good. Do it now."

"Yes, ma'am."

He set them to a slow strobe, enough to get your bearings, then immediately lose them again as the lights shut off.

"Are you ready to go?"

"To where?" His voice had a slight tremor, and Lena felt for the man. He looked like he could've been one of her brothers, though he was larger and seemingly stronger somehow.

"Where everyone is," she replied. The pain now was a burn beyond anything she had felt before; she allowed it to fuel her.

"Ma'am, I'm a Rank-Five."

"That's quite all right. This is just another practice. Are you good at deception, Stallion?"

"Yes, ma'am. I can do that."

"Come along then."

She reached for the door and nearly collapsed. "Ma'am?"

"I'm fine. Whatever you do, keep moving. Leave me if you must."

"Beta?"

He nodded, fear evident on his face. The earpiece crackled back to life.

"I'm here."

"What do we do?"

"Make your way to the cafeteria."

There was a hesitation before another voice came on. "But that's where they're all at."

"I know. Let's go. I'll meet you all there. Be safe. Don't get caught."

Voices confirmed their movements, and this time they didn't leave her frequency. Lena moved out to the hall, leading Stallion as she went. She leapt up into the rafters, but she missed one as her ribs suddenly burned as they hadn't before. She dangled for a moment before pulling herself up by her other arm. Stallion watched in amazement, surprised at how nimble she was.

"How did you do that, ma'am?" he asked, staring up at her as the lights continued to strobe around them.

"I got my name for a reason, Stallion. Give me an arm. I'll pull you up."

"I'm too heavy, ma'am," he told her, taking a step back.

"You underestimate me. Jump and grab my hand. I'll help you."

It took two attempts, but they successfully got him up. Lena was panting from the effort but nodded to him. "We need to move quickly. Let's go."

It took several minutes to get there. When they arrived, they could already hear the sound of havoc as the other groups snagged other captured members from the invaders. There were screams from inside the cafeteria from unseen people.

She spoke into her ear again. "Get people out and to safety. I'll see you on the other side."

A few people replied, but many replied by sending people fleeing through the cafeteria doors.

"Go, Stallion. Don't get hurt. I have your back."

"Thank you, ma'am."

He dropped to the floor and ran into the battle already waging just beyond the doors.

Lena watched for a moment before throwing a knife into a man who went charging after her new friend. She moved into the room on foot after she had appraised the situation in the brief moments of light. Lena ran out of knives quickly, and soon after, she felt herself collapse, unsure of why her vision had disappeared.

Chapter 34

Lena woke up in a hospital bed, lights bright above her. Her head was bandaged, and her chest throbbed, though no longer from an internal fire. She tried to speak, but that didn't seem to work. A hand closed on hers, making her jump.

"Don't touch the brace, Lena," Trevor told her soothingly. "Don't try speaking either. That will just hurt more. You got pretty busted up during that battle."

She cocked her head; Lena didn't recall any battle. Trevor seemed to see her confusion and called for Aloe. "I don't think she can remember the battle."

"She got hit over the head. Probably got a concussion. It'll probably come back over the next couple hours," she called from the hall as she came in. Katie turned to her and asked, "What's the last thing you remember?"

Lena held up her hand with the diamond ring on it. Trevor sighed in relief. Katie squealed excitedly, "How did I not notice? Oh my god, that's amazing!"

Lena groaned from the high-pitched sound emanating from her friend. She clutched at her chest, rubbing at a sore spot on the side.

"You've got a couple bruises on your ribs from after you passed out. I managed to get free pretty quickly and got to you, but some people accidently tripped over you," Trevor explained, taking her hand away from the area. "We got the real medicine. You're going to be fine. The other meds apparently still stalled the drug in your system, which is why you didn't die. You should be better in a week, according to Aloe."

Lena nodded, regretting it immediately. She pointed to the brace as she looked at Katie through the bottom of her eyes.

"Today's the last day," Katie replied.

Lena recoiled at the word day. She looked to Trevor for an explanation. "You've been here for three days, Lena," he told her softly.

She began to tap in Morse code on his hand, wanting to know more. He stopped her, and she glared at him before turning to Katie for further explanation. Katie just laughed. Lena became annoyed by both and refused to look at either of them, instead deciding to stare at the ceiling.

Trevor gently rubbed her hand; Lena snatched it away, not caring about being petty. He rolled his eyes. "Don't be that way. Come on. Hawk and Phoenix want to see you. I'm going to go get them and make sure they come this time."

Lena didn't look at him, feeling a little bad when he left. She'd apologize later. A few minutes after he was gone, Max and Alyse appeared in her doorway with Trevor just behind them.

"How's the baby sister?"

Lena pointed at the neck brace then held up her hand to show them the ring. Alyse rushed forward and took her hand, examining the ring. "It's so pretty. Finally, he asked. Did you see, Maxwell? Oh, sorry, Hawk. I'm terrible about—"

"I saw, dear. It's beautiful, Beta. Congratulations," he interrupted swiftly.

They caught her up on current events and what she couldn't remember from the battle. Lena was allowed by Max to tap out questions that he would promptly answer for her after the extended silence that filled the room during her taps. Once night had fallen, Max and Alyse had to leave, promising to return the following day. Lena was disappointed and lay there silently, waiting for Trevor to return again as he had left to get them dinner when her brother was still there to keep her company.

Trevor was back a minute or so later. "You have fun?"

Lena gave a thumbs up. He smiled, shaking his head. Trevor set down the trays of food on the bedside table for them. "Guess what? We can take off your brace as long as you promise not to sit up or touch your neck. You'll be able to talk and eat."

She gave another thumbs up in response. Trevor leaned forward and unclasped the brace. He gently pulled it out from under her, setting it beside the bed. Lena had to stop herself from reaching up to rub the sore skin on her neck. She coughed a bit and groaned in a rough voice, "That was awful."

"I can only imagine," Trevor chuckled.

"I got a run down by Hawk and Phoenix, but what happened to me during the battle?" Her voice was hoarse and quiet but just loud enough to be understood. He grimaced, though was thankful it wasn't worse; he thought her dead at the battle, but she didn't need to know that.

Trevor shook his head, handing her a piece of bread to nibble on. "You yelled something at some large man. He cut my bonds along with most of Squadron Two. He ordered everyone to leave the battle. Almost punched me when I didn't. He wants to talk to you by the way."

"He was following instructions. You can let him in. He's a good man," Lena replied, voice becoming a bit stronger.

"He can visit in the morning. Right now, you need to eat then get some sleep."

"I've been sleeping," she reminded him, taking a bite of her bread. "Can we talk about what happened before my induction?"

Trevor, who had stood up to go to the bathroom, sat down

again. He put his face in his hands. "I don't know what happened."

"But you do. I'm not holding it against you. I don't want it to happen again." She turned to face him, rolling onto her side though her ribs groaned and smarted under her weight.

"I was afraid. You're so protective. I didn't want to be protected any longer. I didn't want to question you…" He sighed and looked up, meeting her eyes.

"I understand that," she replied. "Do you want to know why I didn't want to give you the post immediately?"

Trevor nodded. His eyes were pleading. Lena took his hand. "I've never had something that was mine and only mine. I wanted to understand TNT better before I gave up some control. It's dangerous to lead alone, but I needed respect from the members before allowing a man to take some of that power. They are more willing to follow a man. It's just how the system works," Lena explained.

Trevor nodded. "That makes sense. Max said you were looking to protect me and enjoy something that was yours, too."

"I need to focus on gaining respect for a while before I begin planning our wedding. Crap, I still need to help Alyse with hers, too. Oh, I'm sorry for being such a pain in the ass for the last couple weeks."

"It's fine. Do you want anything else?" He gestured to the tray.

"No, thank you."

He nodded. "Get some rest. I'll be back in a couple of minutes."

Lena flashed him a small smile and rolled back onto her back. He kissed her forehead, then went to the door and turned off the lights before leaving.

Lena lay awake while he was gone, contemplating her mother. It made no sense. There was no reason to kill her unless she wanted Sierra back, although even Lena dying wouldn't get her Sierra since they had left the public, and legal, eye. Lena hated that she had willingly given up her daughter only to try and get her back by killing her other daughter. She wasn't sure what Mary would try next, but she'd be ready this time.

Lena didn't remember much from the battle, but bits had come back, like what her mother had done with the medicine. It was a low point, even for her. Lena was still thinking about it as Trevor returned.

He walked in to see her staring at the ceiling and sighed. "Are you going to sleep tonight?"

Lena jumped but relaxed again upon realizing it was him. "I guess. I just don't know why Mary would go through such lengths to kill me. I'm her daughter."

"We could always look in her file," Trevor suggested, sitting down again beside her.

"We have a file on her?"

"Well, yeah, TNT was supposed to pass to her, remember? Of course, there's a folder. I'll grab it in the morning. For now, you need to sleep."

Lena nodded a little and curled up, facing Trevor. He leaned back in his own chair and waited for her to fall asleep. He closed his own eyes a few moments later, only to be jolted awake by a loud crash. Lena jumped awake too, but Trevor turned to her. "Keep your head down. I'll check it out."

"Be careful," she whispered, heart beating wildly against her bruised ribs.

Trevor left quickly, ducking into the hall. There he saw a red-haired woman that he hadn't seen in nearly a decade. She was fighting off two men who were attempting to get her into a hold so they could move her elsewhere.

"Hey! Release her!" he called over the ruckus. He jogged over as the men backed off. "Raven, where have you been? We thought you were gone. We didn't even put you in a new squadron."

"Lynx? What're you doing here? What about Spider?" She seemed genuinely concerned. The two men chuckled, clearly senior members.

"Men, go away," he snarled. "I can protect Beta."

They left quietly, having been shunned. Samantha looked after them, somewhat surprised that they listened to him.

"So, Avery's injured?" she asked in a subdued voice, looking about in case anyone was nearby to overhear the names: there were not.

"No."

"Then why—?"

"Lena's injured."

She hesitated. "But you said Beta."

"Lena is Beta. I am Alpha."

"How?" Her face seemed genuinely perplexed, as though nothing could have changed in her absence.

"Michael is partially paralyzed."

"What?" She looked horrified and blinked a few times to clear her head. "How did that happen?"

"It isn't a short story. I'll fill you in once you explain what happened to you."

"I was following orders."

"Who's orders?"

"Sparrow's orders."

"What were they?"

Samantha shrugged. "I was to integrate into a mafia nearby. They took a while to trust me. Now, I'm fully integrated and have some authority."

"Why would she order that?"

"Ask her. I was just following orders."

Trevor shook his head and put his hand on the knob to Lena's room. "Do you want the long or short version?" he asked, referring to the story he promised her.

"Short, I can get more details later."

"From the top then. After we met with you, we went to New York, as you know. We picked up Phoenix who was Hawk's, now Gamma's, assignment. She's now his fiancé. Spider made Lena fake her own death. She came back for a week in disguise, then faked it again, but only Hound knew she was alive that time. Hound poisoned Spider, which is how he died. Lena was gone three years before I found her—" he shuddered at the unpleasant thought. "Walking down the aisle. Almost immediately, her entire family, Squadron Thirteen, Phoenix, Hound, Tiger, and Eagle, went into hiding. We hid for a year before all of us came back for a visit. She killed Jackson while we were gone. Lena got captured, escaped, tried to commit suicide, failed. We got into another battle where Eagle got hurt. She became Beta and was poisoned. I was pronounced Alpha. She nearly got exploded by Mary, who was the one that poisoned her. Now, she's recovering from Mary's people breaking in a couple days ago."

Raven's eyes were open wide as she slowly shook her head. "I don't ever want the long version."

"Oh, and we're engaged now. Would you like to see her?" He looked strained from having to conjure up so many memories at once. Raven just nodded, and Trevor twisted the knob. He pulled it open for her before following her in.

Lena was lying there trying to look at the door without lifting her head as they entered. "Raven, it's good to see you." Lena paused, seeming to remember something long since buried. "Welcome back, I suppose you're in?"

"Of course. Now, will you explain why I need to be in?"

"They are our largest enemy, and I've been intending to either join forces with them, corrupt them, or merge completely. You'll be the chip we need to integrate any plan there."

There was no smiling between the two, just a serious conversation. Trevor wasn't sure what to do, so he decided to return to his seat beside Lena.

"Why me?"

"You're smart and resourceful. You've always liked a challenge, and I know you didn't have anyone here to hold you here. I figured a new space would be a good change after growing up here with no chance to leave."

"Thank you."

"I'll speak more with you in the morning. You can sleep in bunker two. It was good to see you again. Get some rest. Goodnight."

"Goodnight, Beta."

Lena watched her leave before facing Trevor. "I'm sorry about that," she said softly.

"It's no problem. We'll need to test her and get her a new squadron."

"No, we can't."

"Why?"

"She isn't fully TNT any more. She's a mafia leader that is loyal to us. Raven will fight with us eventually, but until then, she's a high-level spy that will be elsewhere. Coming back was dangerous." Lena looked back at the door and sighed, "I shouldn't have sent her."

"She could've stayed there, but she came back. It was her choice. That's enough stress now. You do need sleep." Trevor smiled a little as she closed her eyes and almost instantly fell asleep. He decided to follow suit and fell asleep a minute later.

Chapter 35

Lena was allowed the next day to sit up, yet not to leave the bed. Trevor brought in Mary's folder before Lena had woken up and had it laid out across her lap for when she woke up. She sat up slowly, gazing down at all of the documents and pictures neatly spread before her. "You got it?" she murmured, still drowsy.

"We're leaders now. We're allowed everywhere." Trevor shrugged modestly.

Lena smiled at him, glad to feel that a lot of the pain from her ribs was gone. Her eyes then began scanning the documents as she leaned back against the bed frame. Eventually, her eyes landed on a picture, which she picked up. It depicted her mother, Aunt Maria, and Avery standing in a large backyard with beaming faces. They looked to be maybe ten in the photo. Lena stared at their smiling faces for quite some time. "My mother knew Avery when they were young."

She grabbed a pile of documents and riffled through them, looking for Mary's family tree. Lena found it and scanned the DNA test's findings quickly. She looked surprised and dropped the paper for another, enthralled in the information.

Trevor picked up the family tree and scanned the information. It showed that Avery was the niece of Mary's parents so was Mary's cousin and Lena's second cousin. There was a star marking leaders of TNT beside her grandparents' names, which then jumped to Avery's and Michael's before moving down to Lena and Trevor's. He wasn't sure who updated these folders but registered a moment of shock in the current nature, nevertheless.

Trevor looked up and saw Lena reading another paper. It was thin and stained by some long-forgotten substance, but this ratty paper held her full attention. Slowly, she looked back up. "My grandparents didn't give Mary her birthright. She wants it back."

"What do you mean?"

"Viper, my grandmother, viewed my mother as incapable of running TNT. She gave it to her niece instead of her two daughters. Avery and Michael just handed it back to the rightful line. Max should've been given the title of Alpha but turned it down, so it came to me instead. They weren't lying after all." Lena looked down at the file and began to put away the papers, leaving most of the papers unseen and pictures unviewed.

She made to stand up, but Trevor held her back. "Lena, you know your limits. What do you need?" Trevor looked serious as he stood up.

"I need to go somewhere. I have to get somewhere." Lena tried to get up again. He, yet again, held her down.

He grunted, straining to withhold her against her will. "I will get a wheelchair for you." Lena relaxed a little, knowing it was the best she was going to get. He carefully released her and left to get a wheelchair. By the time he got back, she was curling the bed sheet into a small ball in her lap.

"I got the chair."

"So, I can see." She lifted her arms, and Trevor lifted her into the chair. "I hate these things," Lena grumbled as she wheeled herself out of the room and down the hall. People moved out of her way quickly as she sped down the hall. Each looked after her as she turned down another hall. Trevor ran after her as she went, huffing as she slowed.

"Where are we going?" Trevor asked as he leaned against

the wall, unsure how he could be so out of breath so quickly.

"Here. You haven't seen this place yet, and I shouldn't have either," she murmured as she unlocked the door and wheeled herself in. Inside was a large computer system and walls covered in files. The place smelled of dust and had an electric hum to it. One wall was filled with black binders, seeming to be important; the other three were covered in manila folders that seemed less important yet were more copious. These folders looked like Mary's, yet he had only to go to his office for hers, not here.

"What is this place?" he asked, walking over to one of the walls with manila folders and pulling out one he saw with a name and code name printed on it: ~~April Washington, Maple.~~

"It's the file room. The binders are missions lead by past leaders with all the necessary information. Folders are every member that have ever been with us along with confirmed kills, history, missions, descriptions. The type of stuff that could convict every one of us. I believe the right wall is full of information about known members of other gangs," Lena said, logging onto the computer as she spoke.

"I've always wondered how are we not on the news every day? We have killed people, had car chases, all sorts of shit that should be everywhere," he pointed out, carefully returning the folder to its place on the shelf. Trevor determined on his own that the red line through the name meant she hadn't made it. He didn't need to know any more.

"Either our clean-up crew or the other gang or mafia or whatever-they're-in deal with it before police arrive. According to the law, we don't exist. I'm dead, Max died of cancer when leaving college, you're a missing person; everyone has a cover. If you ever need to reappear, we can make it happen. Police don't mess with us; there's a huge cover up with us. They hide our mess for us if they do get to something before us. Finding already dead bodies in another person's grave is already disturbing enough when that person is supposed to be buried in a different grave, let alone that making the news."

"Do we ever talk to the police?" he asked, kneeling beside her.

"Sure, we do. I've talked to them several times since being pronounced dead."

"When? Why? Wouldn't you be in prison?" He had never spoken to a police officer and couldn't imagine doing so now.

"We make deals to keep our secrets and theirs. They know we have more resources than they do. They need us and like to think it's benefitting them. It works quite well. We've hunted down about a hundred or so of their criminals over the years. Anonymous tips come from us and other gangs in the area. They think they keep us in check this way, but they don't know shit about us. We've got two people in the force right now. The chief knows and hates their guts, but uses them in more of their operations," Lena chuckled.

She began typing again, shaking her head as she scrolled through the information.

"Whatcha findin'?" he asked in a sing-song voice, choosing to ignore the information given.

"Information on my grandparents. Their folder should be up to date."

"How?"

"You're just full of questions today, aren't you? We send out lower squadrons for field work to update our files. They get extra practice, and we get information. They research the person or family and travel with an older member to check their work along the way. It's great trial and error, but we can't send out recently deceased members as everyone will recognize them. We can send them long distance though." Lena sighed; she returned once more to her work. She only managed to focus for a few more moments before a loud alarm began blaring through the entire complex.

"Fire, shit!" She jumped up, grabbing a small flash drive out of the computer as she went. "We have to go now."

Trevor pushed her back into the seat and pushed her to the door. Once they were in the hall, she stopped to lock the door, forcing Trevor to stop pushing for a moment. He continued once the door was locked, but as they passed another door, Lena yelled at him to stop.

She jumped out of the seat once again and ran into the room. Trevor yelled after her, but she didn't stop. It was blazing hot, and smoke filled the room, but still, she plunged in after a whimpering sound.

"Beta! Come back!" Trevor shouted.

"No! Someone's here. Hello? Where are you?" she called into the smoke, trying not to choke as it filled her mouth and nose.

"Here!" a small voice replied from a back corner. Lena ran back there, ducking around flaming cabinets and wardrobes around her. She saw a distant outline behind some flames and forced her way through, coughing at the smoke.

"Lena!" Trevor's voice was faint over the roaring flames as Lena lifted the girl. She was young and light enough for her to carry, but she could still imagine Katie yelling at her in that moment.

"B-Beta, you shouldn't be here," she coughed, clinging to her neck gratefully. It was one of the girls who followed her in her delirium.

"I'm not leaving you here to die."

Lena stumbled and barely missed a flaming pole as it fell

with a crash behind her. They made it to the hall, which was quickly filling with smoke. She set the girl in the wheelchair, and they began running down the hall again. Another cry came from a room as they passed, and she skidded to a halt.

Trevor caught her arm. "You can't do this."

"No, I can't leave them. Get her to the rest of them outside. I'll see you outside." Lena pushed him quickly in the direction of the door then ran into the next burning room. She heard the girl pleading with him while she plunged again into the fire.

A man could be heard in the back. Lena rushed to where she believed him to be, ripping off the bandages on her head as they were beginning to smolder. She managed to get there and pull his arm over her shoulder.

"Can you walk? I can't carry you," she yelled over the flames.

"I can try, Beta," he replied upon seeing his savior. They worked together to get him out of the room, Lena doing most of the heavy lifting, though it sent pain through her whole body. She got him into the hall and heard yet another cry. "Go, ma'am. I'll be fine."

She nodded and took off into yet another room. The flames were moving fast through the beams, not allowing Lena time to think of a source, only time to outpace the flames.

Trevor paced outside where they were all to meet in such an event. People were slowly trickling out of the quickly deteriorating building, soot and ash covering their skin. Many stood behind him, forming up with their squadrons, but many were still missing.

After another ten minutes, a large group staggered out of the building and limped to their squadrons. Lena still hadn't come out.

A loud crash came from inside the building, and some of those behind him screamed. He just stared as the right side of the building began to collapse. It seemed to be in slow motion, making the ground tremble as the remnants hit the ground. The left side didn't yet seem in danger of falling, but it wouldn't be long now.

Two more soot-blackened people pulled themselves from the left side, the last remaining door from the building. Trevor rushed forward. "Beta?"

"She was just behind us, sir. There was another person we heard cry out as we left. She went after them," the woman told him, lifting the boy's arm farther over her shoulder. Trevor took his other and helped her to deposit him with the correct squadron before she went to her own.

Trevor looked back at the building, silently cursing her protective nature. He felt a hand on his shoulder and turned to see Maxwell looking at the building. He, too, was looking into the smoke with terror.

They both heard the cough at the same time and rushed forward, just as the second groan came from the building, and the rest began to fall. Trevor tried to grab her, but it was too late. The door came crashing down. A shrill scream filled the nearly silent air. He dropped to his knees.

Max rushed past him to the burning wood. Ignoring the pain of the fire, he began heaving the chunks of wood and metal off where he saw his sister fall. Others ran forward to help. Trevor couldn't move through the rush of bodies to help until he heard the glorious cry, "We've found her! Nurse!"

He still couldn't get to her as the throng of nurses rushed forward at the cry to take her and the woman she saved from the men who uncovered them. Trevor was rebuffed time and time again by the nurses as they tried to work on Lena with their limited supplies. Eventually, he decided to go check on other members.

A young girl cried to her sister. "Our home. Marissa, what are we going to do?"

The sister saw him looking at them and gave him a pained smile. She turned back to the girl, who he now recognized as the first girl Lena had pulled from the flames.

As he looked around, he saw more scenes like that playing out across the wreckage. A man held his son, tear streaks smearing the ash on his face. A woman clutched a baby who clearly wasn't her own. Another woman stood over a body of a boy younger than Trevor.

He grabbed a metal rod and slammed it against another metal pipe now exposed on the ground. A metallic boom rang across the groups. Each fell silent, leaving only the sound of the nurses and the flames to be heard. Some sniffles could be heard, but all eyes faced him.

"We will fix this!" he yelled over everyone. "For now, we must leave. Beta and I have a place for us all. It will be tight, and we'll have to work to expand, but it can host us while we fix our home. Those of you with houses, I ask you to go there and wait for our call. Gather as many things as you can. We all leave at sundown."

Max jogged up to him. "I know what you're planning. It won't work. You don't realize how many there are."

"It has to work. It's our only option. They need somewhere to stay. They can't go to the street. Most are considered dead, missing, or don't exist in the first place," he reminded Max, hopelessly searching for support.

"I know. Alyse and I will help you. You won't be alone." Max looked defeated in the bleak surroundings but fed off Trevor's limited strength.

"Your wedding must go on as planned," Trevor told him, looking for a distraction in the grey surroundings.

"I spoke to Alyse. We'll join weddings with you. When you marry Lena is when we'll marry. She agreed with me. We can wait."

"Thank you, Max."

"No problem. Now, let's get everything in order. We don't have much time."

Chapter 36

A week had passed since they arrived, yet Lena still hadn't woken up from where she lay in her bed. Everyone in the bunkers had been moved into the other cabins now, and food delivery had been negotiated and planned between members residing in the city. Trevor and Max had agreed that cabins needed upgrading now that there were so many people, but Trevor had other priorities first.

He had hired a contractor that had previously worked with TNT, according to Avery, who agreed to help them build two more cabins, upgrade the gym, and get blueprints started for the new headquarters back in the city.

The two new cabins were to be two stories with a laundry room on the ground floor of the first and storage on the ground floor of the other. The second story was dedicated to more bunks. Both were to be the start of a second ring of cottages and were located near the new car field. Max had agreed to run things back home while Trevor ran things around camp.

Everything was well underway and allowed Trevor to sit at Lena's bedside most days. Avery and Michael returned to camp with them and helped to run things in his absence, knowing he needed to be by her side, Bianca doing the same with Maxwell back at home.

Trevor was asleep by Lena's bed when a knock came at the door. He jumped awake and walked slowly to the door. He yawned before opening it and stepping into the morning light. "Oh, hello, Mr. Flores."

"It's Kevin. Now, sir, I have the blueprints if you'd like to go over them with me," he sighed. They'd had the debate over his title every day that week, but Trevor wasn't budging.

"Of course, Mr. Flores. Follow me," Trevor said, inviting him into the house.

"Has she improved?" he asked as they walked to the small sitting room they often sat in.

"No, she'll get better though."

"I'm sure," he agreed quietly. He didn't voice that Lena's color hadn't changed in days and didn't seem to be on the verge of changing. The man needed to hear good news, not his worries.

He laid out the blueprints on the coffee table. They were rough but the best he could manage in the time crunch.

"This is all stone and metal?"

"Of course, sir. I'm working on finding some non-flammable insulation as we speak."

"Great. Now, these are the dorms on the outside? Which are the cafeteria and gyms?" he asked, pointing at various bits of the paper.

"Yes, sir, all forty-five are along the outside. Tech is this second ring here." He touched the second ring in then pointed to the middle circle. "This is the cafeteria and three gyms."

"And beneath it all?"

Mr. Flores lifted the sheet to show another page showing the basement floor. "Storm shelter, gun and weapon storage, uniform storage, and cells. All split into quarters as you requested."

"Top level?"

He turned another page. "A smaller ring with in-wall storage for folders and binders, as you said."

"Then it's all covered," Trevor told him, although the man already knew.

"Sir, the exterior design."

"I told you to go to Phoenix."

"I did, sir. I thought you would like to check off on her designs."

"Go ahead then."

"Hammered steel plating along the outside and tin roof."

"Make sure it doesn't look like a tin box."

"Of course. There will be four main doors, one to each cardinal direction, and a landing pad on top."

"Perfect. Also, car storage?"

"The cars will be parked below the dorms. Large enough for four each, double stacked in. Ramps will lead down."

"That'll be great. What's the cost?"

"A few million."

"How many?"

"Fifty-four at least."

"How long?"

"A year, sir."

"Get it done in six months and I'll double it. No cutting corners, though. I'll send people to check progress."

He gulped but nodded before practically running out the door. "It'll be done, mister. First priority."

Trevor nodded and walked back to his seat beside Lena. "This'll never happen again. I'm making sure of that." He kissed the back of her hand and waited for the normal morning visit of Katie to check Lena's vitals.

She was right on time, just like normal, and went about changing needles and water bags. "How did you sleep?"

"I slept fine."

"And your morning?"

"Another visit from Mr. Flores. The new base will be started in a couple days," he sighed, moving to the chair away from the bed so Katie could move.

"How much is this costing?"

"A lot."

"Trevor."

"Fifty-four million, doubled if he finishes in six months rather than a year."

"Trevor, you didn't." She turned to look at him, worry written across her face.

"I can't risk something like this happening again. I'll plunge us into debt first. Anyway, Avery told me not to worry about money. She said we've got plenty and more on the street. I will keep everyone safe." He fixed his eyes on Lena's pale face, not wanting to see Katie's disappointment.

"I know, but she hasn't shown any change," she told him softly.

"I don't care!" he yelled at her, on his feet in an instant. If anything, it made him a menace rather than a protector as his height over her threw his already heavy bags under his eyes into sharper contrast with his pale face as he loomed over her, painting his face into tones of shadow that Katie didn't believe could appear on his youthful face.

She jumped back in fright at his outburst and caught her breath. "I love her, too. She's always been there for me. Don't think that you're the only one in pain. If you don't remember, Sean was injured in the fire as well. He was one of those that Lena saved. I'm sacrificing time with him to help the one that saved him. Don't ruin it," she spat back at him.

"I'm so sorry, Katie. I haven't been able to control myself lately. That's no excuse. I just need her to wake up." He fell back into his chair in shame.

"We all do," she sighed, relaxing a bit with his sitting down. "I have my earpiece in if you need me."

"I know. Thank you again."

She waved and walked out. Trevor got up and returned to his normal seat to resume waiting.

Another month passed, and Trevor was having an argument with Max, who had come for a visit.

"You need to be around people. Beta wouldn't want you isolating yourself," Max threw at Trevor.

"You watch it, Gamma."

"No, that's my sister. I know you think you know what's best for her, but you don't. I do. I always have. I've always been there. When she was dead, it was the worst years of my life. I hated that I didn't have her any more. Don't say I don't know her." Max held his ground without faltering.

"I can demote you from Gamma. Don't make me do that," Trevor threatened.

"Fuck you, Trevor. You think I care more about being Gamma than I care for my sister? This is why she didn't want to make you Alpha. You may be my leader but not my friend, not when you're acting like this. Don't go near my sister until you can fix yourself." Max walked off, slamming the door to the room where Lena was still lying.

Alyse walked up and looked after him before turning to Trevor. "I don't agree with a lot of his positions about his sister, but I do agree this time. Sort yourself out before you lose your only remaining family. You underestimate how much he means to her. She'd drop you like it was nothing for her brother and you know it. She wouldn't like it, not for one moment, but she'll never let her brother go. Now, if you'll excuse me." She rolled her eyes and ran off to the door to knock.

The yard was silent as he looked after his best friend and near-brother. He felt himself crumbling. He had thought he was doing the right thing, but apparently not. Trevor decided to go for a walk to clear his mind, finding himself stumbling toward the forest. After a few minutes of walking, he was sitting beside the old waterfall.

The waterfall drowned out the sound of empty air coming from his earpiece. The last memory of this place flooded his mind, and he felt hot tears trailing down his face as well as the cold mist from the waterfall.

"A nice place to think, isn't it?" Sierra had stopped going to school like the rest of the TNT children. She was tutored by some of the adult members along with the rest of the kids. Unlike the rest of the kids, she had distanced herself, becoming more elusive. She was like the dark side of Lena. He didn't like it; it was unsettling.

"Sierra, I didn't see you," Trevor said, quickly wiping away his tears.

"No one does any more. Only Lena saw me. She cared about me. My brother didn't even notice when she sent me out of those flames. They didn't notice. You didn't either. She did; Lena always cared," Sierra told him, staring at the horizon. It was true; he hadn't. Only now did he even see the scars that distorted parts of her arm and shoulder, hardly healed, even now.

"You shouldn't be so close to the ledge, Sierra," Trevor warned, noticing her legs swinging over the edge.

"Oh, shouldn't I? Great, now you care. Lena told me stories about this place. Did you know she tried to commit suicide four times here? She only jumped once though. You saved her then. What about the other three times? You've saved her once. I think all those years of bad luck are coming to haunt her," Sierra continued, still not moving from her seat at the edge.

"Sierra, what're you saying?"

"She never told you of the pact?" She laughed to herself, scaring Trevor more than ever. "She said when that garden was gone, she would be too. It's gone now, Trevor." Sierra picked herself up and walked back toward camp, like the reaper himself.

Trevor looked back at the waterfall and felt like he was falling into its icy depths again though the ground was firm beneath his feet. It may as well be gone for how distanced his thoughts were from the Earth.

Chapter 37

Yet another month went by, and the weather began to get colder as winter drew nearer. The new cottages were finished, and progress on the new headquarters was well underway. Trevor had yet to see Lena again as Max's visit morphed into him taking their cabin with locked doors. Alyse had told him, though, that she hadn't improved. Her face was hollowing; she hadn't had proper food in months as her coma continued, based on what Alyse told him.

Sierra had only fallen into a deeper depression since their conversation and the few times that Trevor had tried to talk to her ended with her saying more phrases that gave him nightmares. "Fifty days, Trevor. Use it wisely," or "Time passes slowly on your death bed, but slower when you don't have the one you love." Those visits stopped as the countdown got lower. Her weird predictions and premonitions haunted him, nevertheless.

Most days now were spent in the gym or lying on his bed, thinking about what Sierra had said. Though he hated it, he had calculated what date Sierra had decided Lena would die on. It was her twenty-seventh birthday. If he was right, then he only had twenty-seven days left. Whenever this thought crossed his mind, he tried to quash it by saying it was just conspiracies and were dumb thoughts of a little girl. They would never go away completely.

He shook himself and hopped off the top bunk. The kid in the bottom bunk did the same. The kid, Thomas, had somewhat adopted Trevor and followed him like the others had followed

Lena in her delirium. Trevor had given up trying to get rid of the kid as having a companion was better than nothing.

"Hey, boss man."

"Yes, Tommy?"

"Can you show me how to shoot an arrow? That sounds like fun."

"After we try to see Beta."

"Okay, boss man. Can I try to talk to Gamma this time? He might let me in."

"Sure, Tommy," Trevor said dully.

This kid wouldn't give up on this. He supposed it was why he got named Racoon after everything. He was a short Asian kid with jet black hair and ever-tanned skin. Tommy had a white mother and Asian father, both of which had been killed when he was only a few weeks old. Crow had found him and practically raised him at TNT. He was 'never a bore', as Crow put it. He had placed top in trickery and traps, so got placed fairly high, Rank-Two, especially for his age. He was one that Crow had taken for her own squadron.

They arrived at the time they always did, so when Tommy knocked, they could hear Maxwell yell, "No, Alpha! You can't get in."

"It's Racoon, not Alpha!" he yelled back, matter-of-factly. Trevor slouched next to the door, leaning against the wall that used to be his.

"What do you want, Racoon?" he asked, opening the door. He caught sight of Trevor, who just nodded to him.

"Hey, Gamma. Long time no see."

"I want to see Beta," Racoon told him, bouncing on his heels with kid energy that seemed endless.

"Fine, come in, buddy." Max moved to the side to let him

pass. He appraised Trevor sadly. "It's good to see you out."

"Thanks. How is she?"

"Same as ever."

"Can I please see her?"

"No."

"Why?"

"You haven't changed. I watch to see if you're interacting; you're not."

"I miss her," Trevor told him, looking at the ground.

"I know." He softly closed the door.

Inside, Racoon went to the edge of the bed and shook his head. "You set that up wrong."

"What did we set up wrong?" Katie asked, turning away from the monitor to look at Tommy.

"That." He pointed to the drops and sauntered over. He picked himself up onto the edge of the bed and adjusted various pieces and moved the needle. He nodded to himself as he looked at her vitals, which had improved very slightly. "You're welcome. Can Trevor come in now?"

"Why should he?" His kind tone was gone, although his voice remained soft.

"Because he's going to marry her, he's your boss, he's doing better, he loves all you people, I fixed her, and you owe me," he listed, counting them off on his fingers as he went. "So, can we let him in?"

Alyse looked at Maxwell then turned back to Tommy. "Of course, you can let him in." Max started to object, but Alyse cut him off quickly. "It's been a month, Gamma. He's engaged to her, for God's sake. Don't take away what may be his last chance to see her."

"But—"

"No, Maxwell!" Alyse yelled. He backed down, and Tommy giggled.

He muttered under his breath while going to let in Trevor, "Someone knows his place now."

The two women in the room, besides Lena, busted out laughing at the remark as Max turned red. Tommy opened the door, quite proud of himself, and waved Trevor in. They all heard the scraping of rocks under Trevor's feet as he stood up. Slowly, he came to the door and glanced around before entering and sitting down beside Lena.

He whispered quietly, "I'm sorry I didn't visit. I was being delayed. It won't happen again."

Tommy walked over to Katie and tugged on her sleeve. "She can hear us, right?"

"Yeah, she can. You can go talk to her if you'd like."

Tommy walked over and clambered onto the bed to sit at Lena's feet. "Okay, Lena. It is Lena, right?" He turned to get confirmation from the group. Each nodded, so he turned back.

"Okay, sorry. It would be super embarrassing if I got your name wrong during a story. Anyway, before I make this even worse. Oh gosh, which story? Oh yeah, okay. Um, so last week Trevor and I went out fishing. It was fun, except when I hooked Trevor and not a fish. I really thought it was a fish too. I tried to reel him in and everything. I seriously thought he was about to kill me then. He has this massive hole in the back of a shirt now. He's not good at sewing. I must say that."

"Hey, I was doing my best," Trevor complained.

"Anyway," he resumed dramatically. "He's not good at sewing, so we need you to wake up and show him how to sew better. That would be helpful. I hear you're good at everything; I'd bet you're good at that too. I could show him, but where's the fun in that? You could show him then he could fix his shirt. Oh, he also promised to show me how to shoot an arrow. Probably isn't a good plan because I'm not very good with weapons, but oh well. He promised, so we're doing it. I'll come back later to tell you how it went. You should wake up before that. Story telling is much more fun when it's a dialogue and not a monologue. Anyway, we should go, so I can shoot Trev—the target."

He jumped up and started pulling on Trevor. Trevor refused to move; Alyse moved forward instead. "Why don't I show you?"

"Nope, he promised. I'd feel bad if I shot you with an arrow. Not him. It's a much better story when he's injured."

The girls laughed again. Alyse poked Trevor, saying, "You heard the kid. You owe him an archery lesson. We'll let you know if she increases again."

"Again?"

"Yeah, Tommy helped us improve her vitals a bit," Alyse informed him happily.

Thomas nodded proudly and said, rather directly, "And I expect an in-person thank you, too, none of this family thanks business. You hear that, Lena?"

Her pulse rose a little, and everyone looked amazed as he walked over and carefully touched her hand. It moved under his and he recoiled. Her eyes opened slowly. Katie rushed forward, propping her up and checking her temperature.

"Lena?" Tommy asked, looking confused.

She blinked a few times and turned to Tommy. Lena smiled weakly as he walked up. She whispered, voice hardly audible, "I guess I owe you a thank you."

Trevor's eyes were wide and glossed over. She slowly turned to him, still smiling. He beamed at her and kissed the back of her hand. "You're awake!"

"I know, right," Lena joked quietly. "I miss being awake."

"Lena." Alyse knelt at the end of the bed.

"Hey, girlie. You married yet?"

"We were waiting for you," Max said, moving to stand behind Alyse.

"Why would you go and do that?" she asked with a small cough.

"They would like to do a double wedding with us," Trevor replied softly.

"Do they now? Okay, but, for now, I want to see Tommy learn how to shoot a bow. I'd even stay in my wheelchair if I have to," Lena said, laughing a little at their worried looks.

"Really? Yes! No getting out of it this time. Trevor, Ms. Sick Lady wants boss man to teach me how to shoot. Nurse lady, you should come too. I feel like Trevor will need you too," Thomas decided loudly, turning away from the bed in excitement.

Katie nodded after a moment of hesitation. She looked at Lena with a moment of worry before going to find the wheelchair in a closet.

"How did we get here?" Lena asked, voice cracking from strain.

"We brought you here," Trevor told her solemnly.

"How long?"

"Nearly two months now," Alyse replied.

"How many people did I—"

"Nineteen, thanks to you. Two people died but none were left in the building," Trevor said, looking pained.

"Good, how are the families? Where are the twins and Sierra?"

"Twins have a class they're leading, and Sierra is likely by the waterfall."

"Can someone get them out? I want to see them."

"Of course," Alyse agreed. "I'll get them once we head outside."

Lena smiled at her in gratitude. Trevor squeezed her hand. "Can I talk to you about Sierra?"

"She told me about her theory when I was... asleep. This wasn't another attempt. I don't want to die. I told you that, Trevor. What is suicide is trying to teach Racoon how to shoot, which I very much want to see," Lena reminded them.

Tommy blushed and went to pull more on Trevor's sleeve to cover up his embarrassment. "Come on, boss man. Lena said you have to show me, and we still need bows and arrows. Please, come on," he begged.

Katie wheeled in the chair and chuckled at Tommy. Trevor shook off the boy and took the chair from Katie. He carefully lifted Lena into the chair once Katie had disconnected her; she was lighter than he remembered. Max draped a blanket over her legs.

"It's colder out there then you remember," he told her calmly.

"Take these." Katie forced a cup of water and a plate of crackers into her hands. "You drink and eat that while you watch, then you come right back. No detours and no dilly dallying. This is against my better judgement. I'm going to be there shortly."

"Yes, ma'am," Lena replied amicably. She raised the cup in cheers before downing it. Katie rolled her eyes, smiling despite herself, and went to refill her cup before they set off. She returned shortly, returning the refilled cup. "Okay, everyone. Let's go. I'm on a time crunch apparently."

Tommy laughed and ran to grab the door, excited to finally

get to leave. He and Alyse took off before everyone, Alyse agreeing to race ahead to the gym. Thomas went for their equipment while Alyse went to relieve the twins of their class.

The twins ran up with excitement just as Trevor and Lena finished a brief argument about him not allowing her to take the wheel again. Timothy came first, eyes set on Lena from the start. "You're awake!"

"Why is everyone so surprised?" she asked sarcastically, opening her arms for a hug. He laughed as he bent down to hug her, shock not yet gone from his features.

"Wait, why are you out here? You should be in bed," he pointed out, backing up. His voice had a hint of authority, though it was buried under a heap of joy.

"Because Racoon needs to learn how to shoot an arrow."

She spotted Dillon coming out of the gym, trailed by Alyse, who waved then set off toward the woods to find Sierra. Dillon had a look identical to his brother, and Lena repeated the interaction word for word. By the end of the second interaction, Tommy was back, and Katie was heading their way.

"You sure I shouldn't teach him?" Dillon asked, looking doubtfully at Trevor from his spot by Lena.

"He won't be dissuaded from me teaching him. Believe me, I've tried," Trevor sighed tiredly though a smile didn't leave his face now.

They spent the next half hour shooting arrows with Tommy before Katie told Lena she had to go lay down.

"But I miss talking," Lena complained.

"And I didn't say you couldn't talk. You just need to lay down," Katie reminded her, taking the chair into her hands.

"But Sierra never came," Lena said, looking sadly into the forest. Alyse had returned long ago and had asked around but couldn't find her.

"When she turns up, we'll get her to come by the cabin," Katie promised, already beginning to wheel her back.

Lena nodded reluctantly and yawned. The group split up, twins going back to their class, Max and Alyse going to the dining hall, and Tommy heading to the gym to return the equipment.

Katie left once she was sure Lena was secured and stable, nodding to her and Trevor. "I'll tell Sean you're awake. He'll come by in the morning."

"Thank you, Katie," Lena replied, already curled up on the bed.

Trevor sat in his seat beside her, holding her hand tightly in his. The door shut, and Lena smiled at Trevor. "I told you I would see you outside."

"You owe me so much for the last two months."

"Luckily, we have a lifetime to make it up," Lena replied, yawning again.

"Get some sleep, dear."

"All I've done is sleep," she complained, eyes already closed.

"I know."

Chapter 38

A nagging worry had come with the morning; Sierra hadn't appeared through the night as she always did. Trevor sent out search parties, hoping she had just fallen asleep in the forest. Days went by with no results. Lena remained frail, and worry creased her skin as the search for her sister lengthened from days into weeks.

Twenty-five days after the order was given, it was Lena's birthday, the last day that mattered for Sierra's prophesies. Trevor had formed a small party to celebrate in the dining hall. It was simple, with balloons and a cake. Lena had become more careful after leaving her coma.

Lena sat at the head of the table, picking at her cake while festivities continued around her. Trevor sat with her, his hand in hers, while he discussed the new base with Max.

"I already explained. Squadrons will be around the outside of the base in what we're calling dorms. Mr. Flores and I have already determined that they'll look like the old ones but with a small meeting space between the two bedrooms," Trevor explained exasperatedly, drawing an invisible map with his fingers.

"But why?" Max matched his tone.

"Because meeting around a bed is good and all, but it won't work for everyone."

"Okay, and where is the whole gang going to meet?"

"One of the gyms has a collapsible wall and Mr. Flores was clever and created a pull-out platform for a stage," Trevor explained.

A ripple of silence was going through the party-goers, causing both Lena and Trevor to stand to investigate the source. The leaders of the search teams were all walking in. Lena and Trevor left the table and moved to them. The leaders walked back outside upon seeing that they were following. The couple looked at each other before following.

Lena gasped as they looked out the doors. Sierra was lying there in the yellowed grass. Lena ran out; Trevor followed slowly, a hollow feeling forming in his chest.

"Why isn't anyone helping her?" Lena cried to the leaders.

They didn't move, and Trevor looked back at Sierra. "Lena, I think it's too late," he said gradually. Trevor waved the others back into the hall as he whispered for someone to get the brothers.

Lena held her sister in her lap, leaning over her, sobbing and rocking back and forth. "No, this shouldn't have happened. Sierra, why?"

Trevor walked the last remaining steps to kneel beside her, tears sparkling in his eyes. The doors behind him rocketed open as Max burst through, twins close behind. He moved aside to allow the brothers to take his place around their sisters. Their sobs echoed through the empty air; the laughter of moments before seemed to be from a different time.

"How did this happen?" Max asked as he sat beside Lena, making a small gesture for Trevor to return. He did so, returning to hold Lena as she sobbed over the young body.

"She believed in her theory. She didn't want to live without her sister." Trevor tried to keep it short so as to not cause them more distress. Max accepted the answer as Trevor shook his head at the member who had found her. He had moved forward as to explain, but he stopped at Trevor's silent order.

Trevor stared back down at Sierra. She seemed to him to be nearly asleep, so near in appearance to Lena that he felt his grip tighten around her. He couldn't imagine seeing her like this.

After a few minutes, Trevor stood up and moved in front of Lena. He gently picked up Sierra's body. Lena clutched at it, but Trevor gently shook his head. "Lena, let me move her. We don't want the others to see her like this. Please, just across camp."

She sniffed and nodded, standing alongside him. The rest of them stood and followed the couple to their cabin. Once there, Trevor set her on the bed that sat in the room across from theirs.

Trevor and Max, unable to look at the body any longer, met in the sitting room. Both sat slumped in the chairs, staring at nothing.

"Worst birthday ever," Max groaned, sinking ever further.

"Yeah," Trevor sighed. "The funeral needs to be as soon as possible. I can plan it if you'd like."

"That would be great." Max winced at the words but didn't try to correct the statement.

"I'll get started in the morning. I just ask that you don't leave her alone. I'll be with her at night, but I need to take care of TNT too."

"Of course, I will. Alyse and I will try to keep her mind off it. That'll be hard though. She wanted Sierra to be her maid-of-honor."

"I know; we had discussed that as well. Something I wanted to ask, though I know now isn't the right time. Will my family be allowed to attend?"

Both seemed pleased with the momentary distraction, though it couldn't last long.

"In secret, yes. Alyse's father will as well. It'll be a happy day."

"Come on. We should get Lena to lay down," Trevor suggested as their conversation ran out.

Max nodded; they both stood to go into the other room. Lena was singing quietly as she combed through Sierra's knotted hair. The twins were kneeling at the end of the bed, watching their sister. Both Max and Trevor paused at the door before moving over to them.

"Lena," Trevor whispered. "We should go lay down."

"No," Lena murmured.

"She wouldn't—" Max started.

"No one knew what she wanted!" Lena cried out in frustration and grief.

"We realize that. It doesn't change that she loved you and wouldn't want you hurt," Trevor responded, looking down at the peaceful seeming Sierra.

"She should've lived. This shouldn't have happened. She could've been happy." Lena began to cry again.

Trevor hugged her and nodded slowly. "I know. She made her own choice, though. This isn't what we wanted, but it did. It does you no good to exhaust yourself."

She nodded a little, and he led her into the other room. Her brothers let themselves out the back door. The final click of the door behind them rang through the house.

Lena fell asleep almost immediately. Trevor held her tightly to him but couldn't take his eyes off the door behind which Sierra lay. He remembered her being a tiny baby that he was hardly allowed to hold in his arms. Now the young girl was lying on a bed with ice-cold skin and empty eyes because they had stopped caring for the baby within her.

No one was going to take the news well. Trevor couldn't imagine they would. Trevor figured that everyone knew what had happened now. None of their leaders had returned to the party after the return of some somber searchers. Even if they didn't know she was dead yet, they would know by the rumors that something had happened and have their fears confirmed by the funeral.

Trevor couldn't sleep that night. He got up early to shower and returned to find Lena still sleeping, fitfully as ever. He walked over and sat on the edge of the bed and rubbed her arm lightly. Lena awoke at his touch and gave him a small smile before she sat up, remembering what had happened as her face turned sad again.

A knock at the door made them both jump. Trevor called, "Come in."

"Hello, sir." It was Mr. Flores again.

"Mr. Flores, how lovely to see you. How is the building coming?" Trevor asked, his voice bare of any gratitude.

"It's finished, sir. Oh, ma'am. I see you have woken. It's nice to see you up," he said courteously.

"Thank you, Mr. Flores." Lena didn't show any more enthusiasm than Trevor and kissed Trevor's cheek lightly before going to the bathroom.

"Payment is in order, sir."

"Then don't get snippy with me. Come," Trevor told him firmly. He turned on his earpiece and said quietly, "Gamma, get to Beta please."

"On my way," came his tired response. Trevor guessed Max hadn't gotten any more sleep than he had last night.

Trevor spoke again, unafraid of Mr. Flores hearing this time. "Hey, Leopard. Can you meet me at the treasury?"

"Of course, Alpha," came the immediate response.

Michael's voice grunted on. "What's up?"

Avery sounded exasperated, "You aren't Alpha any more, Eagle. Go back to bed."

Laughter flickered on, and Trevor snapped, "Is everyone listening to this line?"

"Calm down, Alpha," came Bianca's calm voice.

"The three of you, meet at the treasury now."

Trevor dropped his hand to his side. Mr. Flores looked confused. He ignored it and continued toward the uniform storage where they had added a treasury after it was built. "Wait out here," Trevor grumbled.

Mr. Flores stopped as Trevor entered the storage. Someone was inside as he opened the door. Trevor could see very little in the darkness. He pulled out his gun. The figure turned around and smiled at him, her teeth sparkling in the dark.

"Who are you?"

"You don't recognize me? I'm hurt." Her pouting voice sounded familiar. He knew exactly how he knew her an instant later.

He was young. He hadn't yet officially met Lena, still just a boy. He'd just found out about his adoption, a hard time in his life. Trevor was walking along a road in the park about a week before school started up.

A girl was sitting on a bench across the park, leaning back to look at the clear sky. She had a false shade of red-brown colored hair that fell down to her shoulder blades. As he neared her, he could see her nearly neon green eyes, clearly enhanced by contacts. They made her seem younger than she was, more his age rather than the couple years older that she must be.

The eyes made him pause for a moment before continuing through the park. She giggled and looked over at him. "You're not very sneaky, ya' know?"

They had spent the rest of the summer through the fall wandering the park when they had time, just talking. She never seemed to have anywhere to be and was waiting for him to arrive with his extra snacks and books, which they would sit reading. Then one day, he had come like always, and she was gone. He hadn't seen her since.

Trevor could've lived without ever seeing her again. He wasn't very pleasantly surprised, though he felt part of his mind rejoice at her reappearance. Her black hair and green eyes were a familiar memory. "Kirsty."

"You do remember then. Did you miss me?" She moved forward, ever the flirt, so she was practically hanging off him.

"Why are you here?" he asked, ignoring the question.

"For you, of course." She smiled happily, her neon eyes glinting like a snake in the low light, still enhanced by contacts.

"How did you find me?"

"You're not hard to find with the right contacts. I only had to follow that rude contractor out there."

"You have to go."

"Not without you, my love."

Trevor rolled his eyes, not removing the gun from her side where he had first aimed it. "I'm engaged. Go back to running away."

"Oh, so you are hurt. I never wanted to leave," she pouted, hearing his harsh tone.

"That was twenty years ago. Nothing happened. Get out of here," Trevor snapped at her.

"Well, that's not nice."

Trevor reached up to his earpiece again and spoke clearly.

"Leopard, I need an escort for an intruder. Please, come into the storage."

He dropped his hand as the door opened; finally, she stepped away. Avery entered instead of the expected Leopard.

"Who's—well, damn. Really, Chica? Where have you been?" Avery walked over and hugged Kirsty.

"Avery, you're looking well."

"Thank you, dear."

"Who?" Trevor looked between them, extremely confused.

"Alpha, this is my daughter. Haven't seen her around of late. Ran away when she was seven."

"How didn't I know?" Trevor asked, looking in horror at Avery. That's when it clicked why her face seemed like a recent memory; it was a near-identical face to that of her sister, Bianca.

"We don't like talking about her. She's the disgrace. We kept our tabs though. This brings me back to my point. Why the fuck are you here? You should know to keep your distance." Avery's jaw tightened as she faced her long-lost daughter; her demeanor lost the momentary joy.

"Wow. Thanks, Mom. This is the warmest welcome I've ever received. I'm back for my boyfriend." She turned back to Trevor.

"Uh, what? One, we were never a thing; two, I'm engaged; three, back off. You left, and I… moved on," Trevor hissed in disgust, not quite able to stop his mind from recalling more memories with her. He tried to cover his hesitation with another comment. "Four, we were like eight."

"You'll inform me later, Alpha. For now, I agree with him. You leave or be held captive. Your decision."

"I'll be held captive then. That sounds fun." Kirsty smiled and held her arms out for cuffs. Avery pulled some off a shelf and put them on her, beginning to walk to the door. "Oh, I want to meet this fiancé. Can I see my sister too?"

"Not if I can help it. Oh, hey, Hound," Avery said exasperatedly, closing the door. Trevor stood in the darkness and sighed before trying to remember why he had come in. Eventually, he remembered and walked back outside, handing the first portion of the money to Mr. Flores before walking away. The rest was set to be paid over time as to seem less concerning, although it was still kept under the radar for all intents and purposes. Leopard finally arrived with another member as he was walking away.

Chapter 39

The funeral went on without a hitch, yet, as the days passed after the funeral, tension began to build between Lena and Trevor. Christmas passed quickly and, before long, they were sleeping in different rooms. Even as they moved back into the newly built TNT, they lived separately. Kirsty's continued imprisonment sparking more arguments the longer she remained there.

Max had tried at one point during the intervening month to reconcile the two, yet only caused a rift between himself and his sister. Lena had insisted that Alyse and Max continue with their wedding without her and Trevor going to the altar at the same time. Eventually, they had agreed, making it possible for Lena to be in the back of a chapel, helping Alyse with her wedding dress.

Her gown had lace trim and a tulle skirt. Lace circled her waist and formed sleeves in her princess gown. Lena had already put on her own lavender knee-length dress, which also had white lace trickling down the top, though finished around the waist rather than the hem. With her blonde hair tucked into a tight bun, a single lavender ribbon fell into her face as she smiled a little at Alyse.

"Soon you'll be an official member of the family. Will you apologize to Max for me?"

"Of course. You'll apologize in two weeks when we get back though, okay?" Alyse was bubbling with excitement, making Lena giggle with her, though Alyse could tell she didn't feel the joy she should.

"We best get you out of here. We wouldn't want Max to wait

much longer, would we?" Lena murmured, busying herself with the ribbon in her hair.

"Are you sure? We could just stay for a few more minutes," she said nervously, tittering a bit.

"Yes, come on." Lena pulled her out, trying to make her smile as genuine as it should be. "You've both waited much too long."

Alyse caught sight of her father almost immediately outside of the door.

"Pumpkin, it's been so long," he groaned as she hit him full force in a 'Daddy' hug.

They talked for a minute while Lena went to grab the bouquets. She allowed them a few more moments before she handed one to Alyse. "This is yours. We really should go."

"Thank you, Beta. Oh, I'm so excited."

"Then let's get this show on the road." Lena guided them to the doors and pushed them open for herself first. The music began, and she caught sight of an awestruck Trevor as she walked down the aisle. She averted her eyes to the flowers and glided to a stop. Alyse then opened the doors with her father, and everyone stood.

Lena couldn't focus through the ceremony as she and Trevor continued to make accidental eye contact. Both would quickly move their eyes away, though it didn't stop either from seeing the pain from the other. Lena found herself twisting her engagement ring and clapping when the others clapped. She exited quickly after it had been dismissed.

Trevor tried to catch up, yet she fled out of the old chapel before he could catch her. He met her outside in the rapidly freezing snow.

"Lena, what are you doing out here? You'll freeze."

Lena looked up from the small bench she was sitting on. Finally, the tears were trailing down her face, crystalizing as they went. Trevor went to take her hand, but she shook her head slowly. "I finally figured out what Sierra actually meant by her warning. I can't stay in this relationship any longer. I'm sorry." Lena felt the tears burning against her cold skin as she took off her ring and set it on the bench. She walked away slowly, wanting him to beg her not to go, yet he didn't.

He didn't speak as he took her place on the bench, picking up the ring. Trevor watched it sparkle like one of the snowflakes as his own tears fell in the silence of winter.

Lena had decided to wait for Max and Alyse to return before telling them of what she had done and what her plan was. She sat them down to tell them just a few days after their return. Both were shocked and even a bit angry.

Alyse cried out, "What? No, Lena, you didn't."

"I couldn't stand seeing his eyes when he saw her. He loves her," Lena said sadly. She looked down at her clasped hands as she continued calmly, "I'm releasing myself from Beta, passing the rule to him. Tonight. I'll remain, but I can't give orders by his side."

Max opened and closed his mouth a few times before words came out. "Have you spoken to him?"

"There's nothing to say. I love him, and he loves her. I know him. I won't stand in the way any longer." Lena sucked in her lips to keep back her tears before standing hastily and walking out.

Max looked to his wife with clear concern. "It's her position. Why should she give it up?"

"Because it's easier to give up everything," Alyse replied quietly. She saw the pain in Lena's eyes as she spoke. It didn't limit itself to Trevor. The coma had changed her. While Trevor had grown into the role, she hadn't. She had instead been in delirium or sleeping. Lena, yet again, was doing the right thing rather than the best thing.

Lena called the meeting immediately and stood on the stage alone. Everyone filed in confused and muttering to their neighbors. Lena spoke firmly over them without the aid of a microphone, demanding their complete attention. "I know you're all confused. This will not directly affect many of you, only those who deal directly with the leaders of TNT. I am here to renounce my position as Beta."

The silence was deafening before the roar of protests. Trevor mounted the stage, scared and confused.

Lena carried on, tears running down her cheeks as she plowed on. "I can no longer fulfill your needs as a whole. I can hardly take care of myself. I will remain in TNT as nothing more than Sparrow. Please, respect this decision. Thank you."

Lena started to leave the stage, but Trevor took her arm. Lena shook her head and gently tried to remove his hand. "I'm sorry. This is all for you. Please understand. I'm sorry."

Trevor shook his head, following behind her as she tried to race away again. "Wait!"

People began to leave in stunned silence, no one sure what to say or do. Those most loyal to Lena remained behind to wait for her to return and talk among themselves. No one was more shocked than Raptor, who stood solemnly at the back, refusing to display his dismay.

Trevor managed to catch up outside the one gym that had been left untouched in preparation for the meeting. "Stop! Lena, what the hell?"

Lena slowed yet walked on, her tears still clearly falling.

"For your good." Her voice was coarse and sad as she spoke.

"This isn't for my good. I love you. I've wanted to be with you since I was sixteen. What of the last eleven years?"

"You don't love me. You love her. I see it every time you look at her, every time she's brought up. You used to look at me that same way. I love you more than I can say, so I let you go. You can be happy that way. You'd never be completely happy with me. I don't want that question mark in the back of your head every time you look at me." Lena stopped in the hall just outside the gym and rested her head there.

He went over and put his hand on her shoulder. She pushed it off with a sob as she opened the door. Trevor followed her nevertheless and watched as she went for the knives. "I never wanted this."

"Nor did I. I never even wanted to come into your life. I knew I'd ruin it. I guess I practically completed my assignment." Lena chuckled dryly as she rolled one of the knives expertly from finger to finger as though it were a coin. "If only Sierra would've lived. You would have never gone alone to that room. None of this would have ever happened."

Lena flung the knife hard across the room and hit the bullseye, even as tears continued to trail further, rolling off her chin, though she seemed not to feel them any more.

"Can we try starting over?" Trevor begged.

"Why?"

"So, I can prove myself. So, I can save us."

"Not yet. I want to know for sure Kirsty isn't a problem. I want you to try being with her."

"I can't do that. It would break you."

"There's nothing left to break." Her voice caught before she plowed on, "Maybe it'll work out. If it doesn't, we'll start over.

Not yet, though." Lena flung the other knife, and it hit the wall next to the target. She sighed and turned to look at him.

"Can we at least be friends?"

"I don't have friends. I have family. You're not family. I'm sorry."

Lena went and pulled out the knives, stored them away again, and walked away, the charms at her neck clinking as she walked. She didn't return to the meeting hall but went to the Squadron One dorm. Lena rather liked the space and went straight to one of the two bunk rooms. She was asleep before her head hit the pillow.

Trevor started dating Kirsty a week later, a few days after she was deemed capable and released from her hold. Lena avoided their presence as much as possible but couldn't always succeed. At mealtimes, they sat together, and Lena would leave early each day. Next, they would see each other in the Squadron One meeting room. They would walk in smiling, making Lena leave promptly, just leaving a letter behind with her whereabouts.

Lena also restarted writing letters about her days and memories; they began slowly accumulating as weeks went on. The first month was torture, the second was agony, but the third was the final blow.

She had moved into the dorm, but one morning began packing her things. She was nearly done with her bag when Reet came in.

"Lena, I need—" Reet began as she walked in. She stopped short before finishing. "What're you doing?"

"I'm leaving. I've held out as long as I can."

"Don't go."

"Why? Reet, tell me why I shouldn't go. I told the man I love to go to another women. I told him if it went badly that we could try again. I told him I would stay. I can't any more. They are perfect. I can't breathe here. I suffocate any time I'm near him, and he doesn't even know any more. I let him go, so he can be happy. I need out." Her voice broke on the last word, and tears started again, as they had many times through the months.

"You know he—"

"Don't tell me something that would make me stay, please. This is my home. I'm leaving. I hate it. It'll hurt more the more hope I have. I would suffocate faster. I would stay and die because I love him so much. It hurts to see him with another; it's fatal at this point. The only thing keeping me here is that I told him I'd try. He's happy, so I'm gone."

"I know that. What about your brothers?" Reet asked sympathetically.

"I'll tell them. Max is busy with Alyse anyway. The due date was scheduled for July eighth. They're busy. You're with Timothy and Dillon's doing his own thing. They'll be okay." Lena tried to smile but only managed a pained grimace.

Lena placed the last of her things in her bag and handed four letters to Reet. "After I'm gone, please."

"Where will you go?"

"Away."

"Where?"

"Gone. Dust in the wind. I'll pop up once in a while. Goodbye, Reet. Tell the others I love them, will you?"

"Of course, Lena. Don't forget you always have family here." There was a power in her voice that made Lena pause.

"I know. I won't forget." Lena walked out the door with her uniform on and her black string bag across her back, full of the few things she deemed necessary.

Lena passed a few people in the hall and didn't look at them. Dinner was about to start, and she peered in to see Trevor and Kirsty sitting happily. He glanced up, and their eyes met. Lena turned and moved along.

Footsteps followed her, but she was determined to continue without looking back. "Sparrow! You have no orders to leave!" Trevor yelled after her.

"I have no orders to stay either. Just a promise 'til death do us part. Go back to her."

"Who's her?"

"You already know."

"I want you to say her name." He was right behind her as she neared the nearest exit door.

"Kirsty, Mackenzie, Angelica. You pick. You didn't pick me, so I have no business here. Go back to her."

"I choose you."

"No, you don't. Holding her hand with laughter filling the empty space isn't picking me. Waiting for three months isn't choosing me. Do me a favor, don't invite me to your wedding." Lena walked out the door and shut the door firmly behind her.

Trevor pulled the door open again, but she had disappeared, as he had known she would.

Chapter 40

"Reet, how long have you had this?" Trevor yelled at her, holding out the unopened letter.

"Since the night she left. She wanted to be long gone," Reet said, slightly scared.

Trevor huffed frustratedly. "Two weeks?"

"She said. It wasn't my fault."

"Forget it. Go away." She left quite willingly, and he popped the seal as he had done thousands of times before.

4.2.31

My love.

You used to own me. You need to own me. You do own me.

I loved you forever. You loved me a while. We loved us briefly.

I need, needed, wanted you.

I can't, won't, never have you. I love, lust, crave having you.

I understand, know, lament why we aren't us. Don't give up on, remove, forget love.

You, of all people, deserve, need, create love. I'm sorry, upset, gone.

I'm dead, and I'm sorry for it.

-Lena

Both his and her tears dried on the page. They would live forever and die together. Trevor put his head in his lap and let the tears come freely. He knew his mistake and his regrets, but they hadn't directly hit him but someone else. He stood and dried his eyes.

A knock came at his door. "It's open." His voice was hoarse

and cracked. Kirsty opened the door. "I don't want to see you. Go away. We're over."

"What? That's sudden. Why?" She didn't seem worried at all as she moved toward him.

"Get back, Kirsty. Get out. I want you gone."

"Ma wouldn't like that. Come on, you're just upset."

"I don't give a fuck what Avery likes. I'm in charge, so get the fuck out!" His voice echoed through the room. She jumped back before running out.

Trevor went out after he was sure she was gone. He sought out Max, whom he was sure would get a letter, too.

He was sitting stunned on the bed, looking at his own letter. "Max, you got a letter?"

"Yeah, and you?"

"Yes, I did. Trade?"

Max nodded, and they traded letters.

4.2.31

My brother,

I'm sorry I left. You deserve a better little sister. You won't know where I am, and you won't like it. I can't tell you where I went. You'd find me and lead others. Good luck with your daughters. You live as you would've done. Anything you would've entrusted to me, tell your wife. I love you. I'll miss you, but you'll prosper.

-Lena

Trevor looked up at Max, whose jaw had tightened. "We need to talk to Reet," Trevor decided. He chewed on his lip and had stiffened at the lack of information.

"Agreed."

They both marched out in an awful fury. Reet had locked her door; Max pounded on it loudly.

Trevor yelled through the door. "Doe, we require you to open the door!"

"Open the door," Max intoned quickly.

They could hear her chair creak as she stood, and the lock clicked as she opened the door. "What could y'all possibly want? I don't know anything more than you do."

Trevor shook his head. "That's not true. What'd she say before she left?"

"To tell y'all she loved you. That she's dust in the wind. I don't know," she replied animatedly.

"What did she leave with?" Trevor asked quickly.

The door cracked open, so they could see a sliver of her. "Her backpack and uniform. That's it. I don't know if she left anything behind. All I know is she gave me those letters. She said she was suffocating, and that her brothers and you would be fine as you're all busy. Don't say you weren't. She tried staying for you; every second became harder. I don't blame her for leaving." Reet spoke calmly and closed the door on them as she finished. They could hear her sit in the chair again as they moved away.

Trevor threw his head back in frustration and groaned, "How was I so stupid?"

"To not see Lena suffering, or to not stop her?"

"Both. I knew I loved her. I ignored it, so I could try and change history, like a dumbass."

"I don't think you should go after her."

"What? Why?" He seemed outraged at the thought.

"She faked her death. Came back to save you by killing John. She faked her death again. You brought her back. She tried to go again but couldn't, so ran off with us only to be kidnapped by Jackson, who she then killed. Michael got paralyzed, and her mother had tried to kill her more times than any mother should.

Now she's gone again. I think she's safer on her own than she is with us."

"No, I can't."

"Let her go, Trevor," Max told him. "We can't save someone who doesn't want to be saved."

"How can you say that? You're her brother," Trevor shot at him.

"How can I say that?" he shouted, turning red. "It's because I love her, and I know her so well. I know her well enough to know when she doesn't want to be here. If I could help her, I would do so in a heartbeat. There's nothing I can do this time. We have a life too. I can't keep chasing, and she knows it. You shouldn't keep chasing either, Trevor. Give yourself a chance too." Max walked away, shaking his head.

Trevor was shaking as he walked toward her bunk room. He sat on the bed that still smelled of her and pulled at his hair in frustration. His anger got the best of him. He yelled and ripped at anything and everything around him. Finally, he pulled at a drawer, and letters fluttered down around his feet.

Trevor knelt and picked one up. These didn't have her usual seal on them; rather, they pictured a rose surrounded by carnations set in white wax. He looked at it for a while before he looked at the sheer amount of letters surrounding him. He didn't open any of them yet but piled as many as he could in his arms and walked out.

He decided to go to the one person that may know the meaning of her new seal: Katie. She was in the gym with Sean, wrestling in playful laughter. Katie noticed him first and knocked Sean onto his back again as to escape the ring. "Long time no see. Oh, what are those?"

She snagged one off the top when she realized he didn't have a free hand.

"What does the seal mean?"

"Well, it looks like a wedding bouquet, but the flowers don't seem right." Katie looked closer, struggling to make out the shaped in the white wax. She shook her head and called over to her fiancé, "I'll be right back. I need to go look at something."

She walked with Trevor following her, examining the seal as she went. Katie went straight for a rear tech room. Once there, she put it under a magnifying glass, which Trevor didn't even realize they had. As she spoke, she started to point at different portions of the seal. "So, a rose for love. These aren't carnations they are... oh wait. I know this."

"What are they?" he asked frustratedly, setting the other letters down on a nearby table.

"White mountain laurel. Highly deadly. I can see how many would see them as carnations. This detail is amazing. Did you know that white represents death and lost fortune in some cultures? It's so interesting that we use it for weddings."

"Thanks, Katie," he said dryly.

"Hey, she's still out there. She's a big girl." Katie handed him back the letter, saying softly, "She expresses emotion better than most, but she's cryptic. Once she gave me a letter when I was joining TNT with a seal that represented torture and anguish. She explained later that she meant it to represent my past and not the future. The start of a new chapter."

Katie patted his shoulder then walked out to rejoin Sean. Trevor looked back down at the letter and slumped down by the table to begin reading them all. The first one he grabbed read:

4.19.31

I don't want to know what day.

He took her ice skating during the spring. Bianca and I spent the whole day laughing about it. Correction, she laughed. I just sat there. She told me that Kirsty had left in three layers before complaining about the Texas heat. I don't think she likes her sister.

Bianca told me so many stories that I couldn't pick them apart. Bianca seems to forget sometimes how much she looks like her sister. I hate how I've begun to resent her. It bothers me that a shiver runs down my spine at the sight of her. Bianca deserves a better memory than this.

-Lena

Trevor set it down and began popping open the next.

1.29.31

The first day.

Not much happened. It feels like a bad dream. If it is, then I hope I wake up soon. Maybe it's just the coma's hallucinations again or my poor memory. I could've hallucinated Sierra's death. That'd be good. I could've done the same with the breakup a week ago. Is it bad to wish for a coma?

-Lena

Trevor sighed and looked at the next. He looked closer at the seal and saw something slightly different. The flower still had perfect edges and had a pink tinge.

5.16.31

Information you.

I mean this for only the eyes of <u>Trevor Lee Stephens.</u> Do not continue if this is not your name.

I know you got my letter. You had to know I would have an insurance policy on it. I'm glad to know you weren't rash. This isn't about us, though. It's about Raven. They had planted a spy in TNT.

I advise consulting with her. I want you to be safe. Good luck.

Love, Lena

The ink was so fresh that it had bled onto the folded page, making the words hard to read. Trevor looked up and sighed. "I'm sorry for everything."

He itched to scour TNT for her, scanning security feeds, but he knew it would be no use. She was gone again and probably for good.

Chapter 41

Time flew as if they were seconds, and soon another ten years had passed. Trevor had found a woman that he loved. Not a day passed without a thought of Lena, but her image was less distinct in his mind's eye. Her voice, on the other hand, was untainted. He remembered how he got the recording to remember her from.

Two years after she had left, an unknown number had gone through to voicemail on his phone. Later, he had looked to see that the number had left a voicemail. "H-hello, I know you probably don't want to hear from me anymore, but I wanted to give you a call, anyway. Oh gosh, I had a whole speech written out, but I can't read that. Look, I miss you, but I'm not coming home." Her nervous laugh filled the recording for a second. A recording that he would replay over and over just to hear any amount of happiness,

"I don't know if I'll ever see or hear from you again, but I wanted to tell you to not have that disappointment. You wouldn't know that part if you didn't want to hear from me. I would like to beg a favor of you. I want my brothers to know I'm safe and alive. I won't tell them anything else. I don't want to hold you any longer. I love you, Trevor. Uh, goodbye." The recording went on for another couple of seconds, where he could hear her muttering at herself. He remembered laughing the first time he heard it.

Trevor had attempted to call back, but she seemed to have called from a payphone somewhere in Washington. The recording reminded him of what he had lost and kept him humble when life seemed too good.

He was preparing to delete the recording as he had plans to propose to Hailey. Trevor had promised himself to delete it the day he would propose. He had hesitated for the last week and couldn't hold out any longer. His finger was unsteady as he deleted the message. It hurt to do, even though he hadn't seen her in ten years. He looked into the mirror across from him and straightened up his suit.

He had gotten that night off from TNT with the promise of Bianca to look after it. She had basically taken over as Beta for the last decade without the recognition. Once, he had offered her the post, but she had quickly turned it down and proceeded to take a week off. That week had proven to be the worst week, and TNT almost collapsed before Trevor made a hurried call to get her back in.

Trevor walked to his car to go pick up Hailey when the call came in. "Hello, Alpha speaking."

"Help me," her voice was strained yet fresh in his mind, yet still didn't register immediately.

"Who?"

"Trevor, please. I-I can't answer that. I need help now. Please, help me." Her voice was becoming frantic as she sped up. A scream rang out, making him stop the car.

"Lena!" The name felt odd on his lips after years without her, years trying to let her go.

"T-Trevor," her sob was muffled and quieter than before. "I'm so sorry. I shouldn't have called." Another scream.

"Lena, hold on." Trevor pulled up his private phone and dialed Bianca as fast as he could.

"Trevor, I can't. Please, I can't talk right now," Bianca huffed.

"Whatever you're doing can wait. Lena is being tortured. Track my phone call now."

"L-Lena?" Bianca stammered as he hung up.

Lena was still talking on the other phone as he went back to it. "I love you. I always have. I'm sorry." Her voice was quick and full of nothing but fear.

"Lena, what's happening?"

"H-he." She seemed to be hyperventilating.

"Who's he?"

"Spider. I can't do this. I need to go. This should've ended. Please forgive me." She was spooked as the line went out.

"No! Lena, why did you hang up?" It was as if no time had passed. All the feelings he had muffled had returned just as strong as before. He dialed Hailey quickly.

"Hello, where are you?"

"I'm not coming any more. It's over."

"Why? What's happened?"

"I can't get over her. I'm sorry. I just can't do this any more. Goodbye, I'm sorry." He hung up, crazed with worry, driving with manic energy to get back to TNT.

Bianca was in just as much panic as he was when he arrived at their normal tech center. "Did you get her brothers?"

"No, I just broke up with my almost fiancé. They weren't high on the list."

"They are now. Get them here," she ordered.

Trevor dialed Max first. The ringing was slow and made him more nervous than before. Eventually, it picked up, and laughter filled the line. "Hey, Alpha. Can I call you back?"

"Lena's being tortured."

Trevor could practically hear him freeze before he yelled, "Lena... Alyse, get the babysitter! Anya, Kyla, Elijah! Mom and

I have to go."

"Bring them. We have people to watch them. Just hurry."

"We'll be there."

He hung up, and Trevor went to dial Timmy. Reet answered, "Yes, Alpha?"

"Husband, now."

"He's in the shower. Whatcha need?"

"Get him out and get here. Lena's being tortured."

"Lena. Oh my god, Tim! Tim, get out of the fucking shower!" Trevor heard the phone hit the floor before he hung up.

Trevor called over to Bianca. "Is Dillon leading a class?"

"Gym two," she replied without breaking concentration.

Trevor ran off faster than he had in years. He was in his early forties, and although he was fit, running didn't like him any more than he liked it. Huffing, he entered the gym and beckoned to Dillon.

"Hey, man. Long time no see." He jogged over happily. He had grown a mustache and beard, both of which were neatly trimmed, and he had a knack of playing with as he did now.

"Lena. Lena is being tortured. Spider back," Trevor panted, leaning on the wall.

Dillon's eyes grew wide; he shook his head. "No, she can't be back."

"She is and we have to help her. Tell someone… to take over or dismiss your class. We've gotta go."

Dillon nodded and called to his class. "Dismissed early. Later classes postponed until further notice. Alert others."

The class gave a nod and went about cleaning up. "Let's go," Trevor sighed, standing up off the wall. They took off together and went back to Bianca. Everyone had arrived in record time. Trevor nodded to them. "Reet, I need you to watch after Max's kids. You can stay in dorm one."

"What? No, I want to see Lena too," she cried out, ignoring that she was seven months pregnant and couldn't even see her own feet. Her eyes inexorably went to Alyse for support, but all she got was a slight shake of the head from her.

"Reet. Please," Tim said softly, putting his hand on her belly. Reet's eyes went to her husband; she glared at him but agreed. Reet took Elijah's hand from Alyse and led the other female twins out of the room.

"Where is she?" Trevor asked, leaning in next to Bianca to look at a map of part of the city he didn't recognize.

"Nearby. Warehouse district. I don't know which one." Bianca seemed frustrated as her fingers just kept moving faster, small mistakes having to be corrected more often. Eventually, she threw up her arms in frustration and anger. "They scrambled the feed. It could be coming from any of the ten."

"Round up the squadrons," Trevor said quickly. "We'll send one of each ranking to each building based on where it's most likely that she'll be. We'll send the extras to patrol and go where they're needed the moment they're called."

Alyse tightened her jaw at the idea. She found it too risky but knew she'd have no support in this room. Everyone else was already nodding. Bianca was already laying out the plans to stay back, directing the gang from their earpieces. Alyse kept silent, deciding to go with the plan.

Trevor gathered everyone in gym one: the largest one available.

"Hello, TNT. We have a large problem. Sparrow has reappeared and needs help. I need everyone's full attention, so we can leave immediately. Okay…" Trevor laid out the plan quickly and clearly. All the years of leadership under his belt had done him some good, even if Bianca had done most of the leg work.

They were on the road within ten minutes and outside the warehouse within fifteen. Trevor didn't know what to expect. Lena hadn't been seen, located, or heard from significantly in ten years. He had sent people to look for her. Everyone's first task when they joined was to find her. They would be reassigned after a month. Squadrons without assignments would be sent to find her too. It was the only thing he could do with his responsibilities to TNT.

Trevor still didn't know if they had found her or not. If they had, they hadn't told him. If they hadn't found her, it left Trevor with the normal amount of disappointment.

He found himself going through how she had looked in the years previous to her disappearance and couldn't think of what she would look like now. Even as he jumped from the car, leading three squadrons at his back to the entrance of their building, his mind raced ahead, trying to figure out if he'd recognize her. Trevor pushed open the first door; Max stepped in front of him. They led as a well-oiled machine, having worked together for more than half their life now.

Lena wasn't in their building, and a muffled call came from a lesser group, a less likely building. "Squadron Six reporting a hit. People are here. Back up immediately."

Trevor jumped at the earpiece. "Squadron One on our way." He waved for them to move out of the way before the rest followed him; the squadrons at his building sprinted off to the small building where the hit was reported, careful to watch for attackers. It seemed peaceful.

He was shaking by now with anticipation. They approached the leader quickly, and the man backed up. "About twenty guards overall. Two main targets and Sparrow. You're lucky I recognized her. She doesn't look good."

Trevor nodded stiffly. "Take care of the guards outside of the main room. Let's go." He took a deep breath before running in, knives already drawn. Three people dropped in front of him before someone appeared beside him.

"Alpha, stay behind me when we confront Spider." Avery was tense and alert even as she panted.

"No, you're too old now to do this."

"You will do it, Lynx. I may no longer lead, but Spider doesn't necessarily know that. We can at least hope he doesn't know yet. You need to focus on Sparrow," she responded crisply in her old commander's tone. Trevor blinked then nodded, momentarily forgetting that he was in charge.

Avery led the force to the main room; she stood tall, even as her old bones shook from her weight. The time hadn't been kind to her after the stress of leading had been lifted, and the stress of taking care of Michael took over, a position which was not agreeing with her.

"Hello, Spider," she called.

"Tiger, it's so good to see you again. You brought toys. They're so cute," he sneered. His hair had greyed fully in the intervening years, and although he was the same age as Avery, he was wrapped in muscles.

Trevor looked around for the strong figure of Lena, her long blonde hair and bright eyes being defiant as ever. Instead, he only saw another man standing behind Spider, defending someone in the shadows. He looked closer and saw a trail of blood leading into the space the man was blocking. Trevor clenched his jaw and fists to keep himself from yelling. He knew she was there.

Spider seemed to be watching him. "So, you like my present,

do you? You must be the one my daughter was pleading to save. I hope you're worth something." John motioned at the man, who turned and grabbed Lena from the shadows.

A hush fell over the TNT members as she was pulled out. Only her screams and struggles could be heard in the room. Lena seemed to have landed something as the man stumbled back. "Get your hands off me. Run! Please, run. I'm sorry," her screams called to them all as she continued to struggle. Finally, the man succeeded in getting her to the light.

Lena's arms were ripped with muscles that had been cut and gashed to pieces. Her legs couldn't be seen beneath the fresh blood. Her hair had been roughly cut at her shoulders, yet her bright blue eyes were shining with the same fierce light. She could hardly stand as she stumbled on her feet.

Trevor couldn't stop looking at her where she refused to look his way but stared at her father instead.

"John, may I ask for something?" she called over in as casual as a voice as she could manage after her screams.

"Excuse me?" He turned to stare at her. Lena just smirked; she knew she had gotten on his nerves. Trevor was impressed by her confidence; even he saw a new puddle forming around her. Slowly, she was growing paler, but she didn't act it. She seemed all the more confident as her legs continued to tremble.

"If I'm going to die anyway, and they're going to kill you anyway, maybe we should just duel. A fair fight. Winner walks free just like old times. A knife each. What do you say, Dad?"

He appraised her before laughing, "Of course, my dear. I'm sure your brother can provide adequate weapons."

They both turned to Max, who looked confused to be put on the spot. "Hawk, please," Lena begged quietly.

Max looked heartbroken to see his sister again and in such a state. He looked to Trevor as he replied, "O-okay, um…" He moved forward, but Trevor stopped him.

"No, I will. I'm sure that'll be fine. Right, Mr. Foster?"

Lena had no choice but to look at him. He saw as her eyes briefly welled up with tears. He wiped it away quickly for her as he handed her the blade. She carefully appraised her weapon and spun it lightly, smiling despite herself.

"I missed these. Maybe I'll use them more often. TNT, stand down. Sit at ease or remain outside. I will not tolerate a disturbance," Lena called across the crowd as Trevor handed another knife to Spider at arms-length. Everyone sat at once to watch. Trevor found himself clasping hands tightly with Avery, who had a look of supreme tolerance on her face, a peace he couldn't portray on his own face.

"We must have someone to start us off. You." He pointed to one of his few guards. "You know how, then go to the other room and await your next orders," John called to his helper.

He hurried over and stood between them. "A single knife each. The ring is this room. Fight to the death. Last words."

"Once and for all. To the best," Lena said with a small bow that set her off balance, almost making her fall.

"To that," John laughed.

"Begin!" the guard yelled, running to the other room as he had been instructed.

Lena didn't move as her eyes appraised John quickly. John moved quickly forward; Lena managed to clutch his blade in her hand, cutting a deep gouge but keeping her feet under her. The crowd didn't breathe as they watched her lunge over John and run her blade over his chest. His shirt fell to shreds like a vest, and she stumbled on landing. Lena did an unintentional roll and gained her feet, only to dive again, landing on her arm, which made her cry in agony, but she didn't stop.

John and Lena danced back and forth but with such similar styles that it was no surprise they were related. Trevor had to be forcibly held down during a run. Lena was pinned to the floor, John's knife slipping ever closer to her throat. In one last burst of energy, Lena managed to force it up, and the knife flew up into his neck instead of hers. More blood splattered onto Lena as she threw her father off her, sobbing and gagging.

Lena pushed the people surging forward aside as she made her way back to her feet, tears yet again blocking her vision. No one was quite sure what to do, but Alyse stepped forward and just stood next to her, not speaking, although there was something between them that Trevor didn't understand. A few seconds later, Alyse found herself supporting Lena as she hugged her. Alyse was saying something to her, yet no one else could hear.

Lena stayed there a few moments before allowing herself to pull away. She didn't look at anyone as she limped past everyone. Trevor followed quickly behind, remaining two steps behind her.

She went straight for the nearest car and pulled open the nearest door. Lena climbed in and lay on the back seat, staring at the ceiling as she clenched a strip of her shirt in her hand. Her skin was going grey. Trevor stood there, unsure of what to do until she looked back up at him. "Did you know you're going grey?"

"That's how you start a conversation?" He didn't mention the same of her complexion.

"How else? Everything else would be boring and bring up conversations I don't want to have."

"Like what?"

"Like how I've been gone for a decade. How I was just tortured by my dad. How I'm covered in my dad's blood. How my little brothers are in their thirties and just met their father.

How I couldn't tell my brother's apart." Lena lay back again and shook her head as stars danced in her eyes. "I hoped that I would've had the courage to not call. I didn't. I don't. I'm sorry about Hailey."

"How did you know?"

"I know you. I never left. Your new recruits were so close. I felt bad watching them knock across the street. They were so disappointed," Lena chuckled quietly.

"You never – then why didn't you write? At least your brothers?"

"You read Max's letter. It was so disappointing walking past you so many times."

"Wh-when?"

"I sat next to you on the train. I was behind you on your first date with Hailey. She's so nice by the way. I was at the ring store. Never once did you see me. I should've left. I should've worked to forget you." Lena closed her eyes and tried to stop the tears, but it didn't work. Trevor shook his head as he went to the driver's seat quietly to drive them back to TNT.

"I'm glad you didn't forget me," he told her.

"As if I could. Before I left, you asked for a fresh start."

"I don't want a fresh start. I want us to continue right where we are. There's too much history to forget."

Lena nodded a little, smiling. "I agree. Go to my house. I'll be quick."

He drove there quietly, feeling the weight of her decreasing health weigh on him. He assumed the house was the same one as before. He wasn't wrong as they pulled up to the old house. Lena smiled as she got out of the car and walked across the street, waving to a neighbor that looked horrified by her. Trevor heard her call, "Sorry, Ms. Tambar."

Trevor rolled his eyes and reversed into the correct driveway. He waited a moment or so before she reappeared. "Okay, I'm good."

"What did you get?"

"I'll show you and my brothers later. First, I want to see my nieces, nephew, and new sister-in-law."

Trevor began to drive off and glanced in the back mirror; he was still in shock that she was really there. "Question."

"Answer," she replied promptly but quietly, as her color got worse still.

Trevor smirked, trying to ignore the further change as he drove faster and continued, "How do you keep getting these houses?"

"Easy, I use a lot of money and sign a contact. Also, I use a fake name. Well, someone else's name. That house is Alyse's. If they want it, they can have it. It's paid off." Lena went back to playing with her charm necklace as her eyes fell a bit lower.

Trevor did a double-take upon seeing the gleaming silver. "You still wear that?"

"Uh, yeah. I also found this and wear it." Lena held up her hand to display the engagement ring now resting on her pointer finger.

"I was going insane trying to find that."

"You wouldn't have sold it. We both know that."

"And if I did?"

"Then you're stupid. It's so pretty. I would've bought it right after anyway." Lena blinked a few more times as her eyelids fell. "I'm going to nap a little."

Trevor did a double-take at her complexion and saw how deathly pale she had become. "Lena, don't sleep."

"Why? Do you know how exhausting that fight was?"

"Stay awake 'til we get to TNT. Goose needs to look you over."

"Why not Katie or… or…" Lena fell asleep right there. Trevor gunned it back.

Chapter 42

Lena awoke in a hospital bed with two young girls sitting at the end of the bed. Both had brown hair, caramel eyes, and identical faces. Lena smiled a little. "Hello."

"You're awake!" the one on the left cried.

The other smiled. "We were hoping you'd wake up soon."

"Okay, uh. I feel like I should know you. Who are you?" Lena smiled even as her confusion showed through her words.

"I'm Anya," said the one on the right.

"I'm Kyla. We're your nieces," said the other.

"Where's your mother?" Lena couldn't believe she didn't remember their names yet could feel the names slipping again.

"She's with Elijah. Who knows where, though?" Kyla remarked somewhat irritably.

Anya rolled her eyes. "I'll go get them and Alpha. He must've wandered off." She pulled her sister away, leaving Lena alone.

Lena looked around her room and found the small remote on her bedstand. She smiled and pressed a small button on the console. A small charm started flashing. The door creaked, and she hit the button again to stop the flashing.

Alyse was being dragged in by one arm while the other held her son on her hip.

"Hey, 'sis," Lena chirped as she looked at her.

"You're awake. Anya, did you find Alpha?" Anya shook her head, and Alyse rolled her eyes. She pressed her finger to her earpiece and spoke. "Alpha, come to the ward now with the rest of the family."

Lena could hear her twice and found that an earpiece had been put in her ear while she was asleep. Alyse walked over and knelt beside the bed. "How do you feel?"

"Better if I could hold my nephew," Lena giggled, holding out her arms. Alyse rolled her eyes but smiled as she lifted Elijah onto her lap.

"Elijah, this is your Aunt Lena."

"I know. Dad talks about her." He had inherited many of the Foster features, including the brown hair and orchid-blue eyes. He had gotten his mother's nose, though, and her serious look.

"Where's Trevor?" Lena asked quietly as she continued to appraise Elijah in her lap.

"He should be on the way."

"Why was he not here?"

Alyse pursed her lips. "He had to talk to Hailey."

"Oh, okay. Am I allowed to walk yet?"

"Yeah, I'll grab you a uniform."

"Thank you, Alyse." Lena could feel the heightened distrust coming off Alyse now but didn't blame her.

"It's no problem."

"No. I mean it, Alyse. Thank you… for everything."

"Oh hush. Give me a moment."

Alyse went into the hall and grabbed a set of clothes before she took her son back and herded the girls out of the room. Lena tried to change as quickly as she could, her arms and legs protesting as they pulled on the stitches lining her entire body.

She made her way into the halls to wander as she used to. Lena had missed being there in plain sight. Unconsciously, she had walked to one of the gyms. Lena entered quietly and went to one of the weapons racks. Her fingers went over the different weapons until they closed on a bow. Lena smiled a little as she took it from the rack, arm aching already.

She notched an arrow calmly and let it fly. It flew straight to the middle. She nodded and notched another. The quiver ran out before she realized she was being watched.

Lena turned and saw a young boy quickly turning away. "What's your name?"

"I'm Fox," he replied shyly.

"Do you know how to shoot?"

He shook his head, the bowl cut of red hair on his head swishing back and forth.

"Would you like to?"

"I don't know if I should. My mom wouldn't like it." He backed up a little.

"I'm sure she wouldn't mind. I can show you. If you don't like it, you don't have to shoot another. How does that sound?" Lena replied, kneeling down.

He nervously stepped forward. Lena smiled encouragingly. He pointed to the board. "Don't we need arrows?"

Lena got back on her feet and pulled out the arrows carefully from the board. She returned quickly and helped him hold the overly large bow, kneeling by his side to help. Lena remained patient even as he dropped the first arrow, making him blush with embarrassment. "Just try again. It takes practice to get good at this."

Finally, he shot one that flew beyond a few feet and hit the outside of the target. Fox reached for another arrow, seemingly excited. He tried to position it on his own for a bit before he looked to Lena for help. She positioned it again and watched as he moved closer to take his shot. It landed closer to the center.

Someone cleared their throat by the door, and Lena

whispered, "Keep working. I'll be right back."

Fox nodded as he reached for another arrow though he couldn't lift the bow on his own. Lena walked to Trevor by the door. "Hello, Sparrow."

"Hey, Alpha. How did that go?"

"Better than I expected considering we've been dating for the last four years."

"I'm sorry you had to break-up with her."

"I didn't have to. I chose to. Now stop apologizing. Why are you out of bed?"

"Phoenix said I was allowed out. Why isn't Katie taking care of me?"

"In the hospital with her second boy. I thought you were keeping tabs?"

"Oh, so she and Sean are married?" she asked, avoiding the question.

"Yeah, a couple years ago now. Are you okay, hon?" he asked, looking concerned.

"Um, yeah I have been. Just a memory thing, I think, linked to the attack and blood loss. We're not as young as we used to be." She giggled nervously.

He chuckled a bit, and Lena looked back over at Fox. Trevor watched her face as his own became serious. Her memory had always had issues. Trauma could've made it impossibly worse. Her eyes seemed vaguer in a way he couldn't explain, but it concerned him.

"Lena, I was thinking."

"Uh-oh." Her wit wasn't gone, at least.

"Oh, shut up. I want you to be Beta again."

"Okay. I never gave you my gift." Lena grabbed at her pocket to pull out the remote again.

"What is that?" Lena handed it to him and pulled her necklace out of her shirt, holding it up next to it.

"Press the first button," she told him. He did so, and it started blinking. "Mostly for when I lose it. Saved me a couple of times."

He pressed the next one, and it started chirping. Trevor smiled. "Echolocation."

"You can signal me that way. Last one."

He clicked it, and numbers appeared. "Coordinates?"

She nodded. "It works the fastest up close, but decently far away."

"Thank you," Trevor said softly, turning off the necklace.

"We need to see Allie soon. She's got a new recruit for us." Lena looked back over to Fox again and began to walk over with Trevor trailing. It took him a moment to remember Allie, her cousin that he hadn't thought about for years.

He dropped another arrow, and Lena lifted it back up before he could. "Thank you, Sparrow."

"No problem, Fox. You keep practicing. I've been sent back to bed. I'll see you at dinner, okay?"

"Thank you, Sparrow." He smiled a little. Lena stood again to walk out. "Sparrow," he called. She turned back. "Welcome back from Squadron Eighteen."

"Thank you. I'll send my brother to find you later. He's the best archer in this place, or so he says. We should have a competition to find out. Bye, Fox."

"Bye, Sparrow."

Lena walked the halls happily with Trevor. She avoided his questions about her time away from home while Trevor did his best to answer most of the questions, though he didn't fully answer some too. Lena only truly answered one question.

"Why out of all people did you call me?"

"I... no one else would've told you. They would've waited to tell you until you were married. They would've kept me hidden again. I knew your feelings for Hailey would only be tested if you were put on the spot. Why did you break up with her?"

"She wasn't the one."

Lena didn't respond to that but kept walking in silence. Trevor asked his last question only when they were outside of her ward door. "You won't leave again, right? You've said before that you wouldn't leave. I don't want to lose you again."

"No, if I did, I don't think anyone would come after me again. I'll stay until my last breath." She walked in, and Trevor was a bit wary. He didn't like how she said 'last breath'. Lena seemed troubled as she lay down and patted the bed next to her.

Trevor smiled a little and sat down beside her. "It's been a while since it was the two of us."

"No, we were alone after the battle."

"You know what I mean." He took her hand in his. It was rougher than it had been before but just as small.

"Yeah, I know. Last time, times really, it was sad. I don't like thinking about that, though. Much too sad. I like thinking about New York. That was fun," Lena smiled a little, thinking back on the fond memory.

"I don't think I've gone on a date with you since then," he thought out loud.

Lena tried thinking back too, but her mind was foggy at best. "I can't think of one either." There was a faint memory of another date, yet she couldn't recall.

"Well, would you like to go one a date with me, Lena Foster?"

"Gosh, a second date? I'd have to think about it," she mocked quietly. "Of course."

"I think we've done this a bit out of order," Trevor laughed, thinking about their history.

"What? No, never. Going on one date, taking a three-year break, starting dating, breaking up, taking another three-year break, getting back together, getting engaged, getting unengaged, taking a ten-year break, then date two is totally normal. I think I missed something," Lena chuckled, trying to figure out what was missing before she just shrugged. "Oh well."

"Do you think Max has had a better dating history?" Trevor asked jokingly.

"Nah, he just kidnapped her, brought her to Texas, started dating, got engaged, stayed engaged forever, got married, then had three kids. That's so much more complicated." Both laughed and rolled their eyes at their mess of a life.

"I have to go, work to do. Be ready by eight. Wear something nice." He gently kissed her forehead, then stood up and went to the door. Trevor waved then went to plan their date.

Chapter 43

Lena sat blindfolded in the passenger seat of the car in her simple white dress and silver jewelry. "Do you realize how cliché this is? Also, I feel like I'm being kidnapped."

Lena heard the engine purr to a stop as Trevor spoke. "Uh, no. Okay, cliché yeah. Kidnapped? I wouldn't go that far. Just pretend you're Alyse if you wanna call it that."

Lena just chuckled and asked, "Are we there?"

"No, we're at a stoplight."

"Oh, okay. I wanted to know. What's Hailey like?" She turned her head to face him though she couldn't see him.

"Really? This is a date. You want to talk about another girl?"

"It's our second date. I know nothing about you. Anyway, I think we've passed the point of me getting jealous and dumping your ass. Come on," she whined playfully.

"Why did I agree to this?"

"Not only did you agree to this; you planned it. Now, answer my question."

"When we get there."

"Why?"

"Because we're pulling up."

"Then you can tell me."

"I knew you would say that. Wait just a moment." He got out of the car and led her to the front of the car. "Okay, you can take it off."

Lena took it off carefully and looked out at the Dallas Skyline. "It's beautiful, and I've seen it. Now, where are we going?"

"I'm hurt. I really am. This is the location."

Lena laughed and shook her head. "Back in the car you go. Here put on the blindfold." Lena got behind the wheel and waited for Trevor to put on the blindfold before she was willing to so much as move the wheel.

She drove swiftly along the coast of the lake towards the marina. It was a quiet drive with very little talk but for occasional ponderings of how near they were to the destination. After a quiet couple of minutes, Lena pulled up to their final destination.

"Okay, you can take off your blindfold. Follow me." Lena got out of the car before he had even removed the fabric from his eyes. She waved him onto the pier as she raced off toward a boat. Trevor jogged after her, looking around to see if anyone was watching them.

"Are we stealing a boat?" he whisper-shouted at her as he approached a sailboat she had jumped onto.

"God no. I own this boat. Isn't it cute?" She smiled and wandered around the deck, pulling at ropes and poles around the boat that seemed to be in no particular order to him.

He stepped onto the polished boards of the deck and spotted that over all the poles were lines of fairy lights. Trevor decided to try and find the switch for the lights while Lena worked to set sail. After a couple of minutes, he still hadn't found the switch, but Lena had gotten them into the middle of the lake by then.

"Need some help there?" she asked, watching him make his third round on the boat.

"How do you turn on the lights?"

Lena chuckled and reached around him to the center pole, where a small switch was outlined in more lights. Trevor huffed in embarrassment as the lights came on around the boat.

"Are you okay, honey?" Lena asked as he stared at the switch.

"I'm just an idiot. How did I miss that?"

Lena shook her head and went to lay down on the deck. Trevor narrowed his eyes a bit but followed suit. She turned onto her side, propping up her head with her hand. "You haven't answered my question."

"Which one?"

Her eyes bore into him as they hadn't in years, making him laugh in surprise at how he had missed it. "Yeah, okay. What do you want to know?" he asked, his tone showing his happiness.

"What was she like?"

"Oh, wow. Um, she was like a mellow you."

"So, not like me at all," she giggled, watching how uncomfortable he was talking about Hailey to her.

"Well, she was just as stubborn. She wasn't so keen on violence."

"Violence is always the answer. Didn't you know that?" she asked sarcastically.

Trevor smiled but sighed. "You know, I listened to the voicemail every day." He found he didn't have anything else to say about Hailey. Four years and it still boiled down to her similarity to Lena.

"I had planned it all out in my head, too. My speech just disappeared as I heard your voicemail," Lena said.

"What were you going to do if I answered?" He turned his eyes to hers to see her eyes looking like the midday sky.

"I have no idea. I wouldn't have hung up, but I don't know if I would've spoken. Maybe just wait for you to hang up," Lena decided.

He laid his head back on the deck again, remaining silent.

Lena moved over and rested her head on his chest as the boat rocked gently in the tide.

"Remember when we were young and carefree?"

"Carefree?" he snorted, shaking his head.

"Well, you were for a time. It was easier at the beginning, anyway."

"How so?" He lifted his head a bit, feeling the now-familiar stiffness that came with the ever-increasing stress of TNT.

"Well, we didn't have so many people hunting us. Only John. It was so much better when I believed John to be dead."

"What happened, Lena? How did you find him?"

She took a deep breath and continued to look at the sky. It was a long enough time before she started speaking that Trevor had started to believe she wasn't going to answer. "Well, it was an accident. I had told you there was a spy in TNT. Raven helped you to find them and remove them."

"She said it was dealt with."

"It was. She brought them to me. They were a spy. That's all I knew. I didn't know who for or why they were there." She shook her head a little, watching as an airplane blinked by through the light splattering of clouds. "I never would have guessed he worked for John. It took quite some coaxing to get it out of him. I didn't get anything else from him, though. He took a tablet, gone in the minute. It was hard to watch."

"I'm sure you've seen worse in your time."

"I have, yet it never gets easier. Has it for you?"

"The initial sting of death has faded, but the nightmares never go away. What happened then?"

Lena began fiddling with her hair. One of the members had fixed the cut for her during the day so it was neat, yet the short hair didn't agree with her. It was never something Lena had wanted.

"I spent the next four years trying to find him. I found Mary first. She wanted to be found, I think. We talked for a very long time before I killed her. She's the reason for so much pain. She is why Jackson knew y'all were gone, why I was poisoned and kidnapped. Hell, she even sent Kirsty after us. Mary gave me clues on John before I shot her. I think she craved death." Lena stopped, gathering herself. Trevor stopped too. Her ability to kill was horrifying. It had taken her to both of her parents, and they were only the latest.

"Once I found him, he came to meet me. We actually got along for a little while, forgot our past and pretended to be a happy family. I don't know what happened, though. One day he had a new mission for me. I turned it down. We had some small arguments over that, but nothing too bad. After one particularly bad day with him, I left. That was a year ago. I called you when he found me. He had never changed. Not really."

"I'm sorry, Lena."

"I should've known years ago. I fooled myself into believing him. A mistake I should've never made." Lena sighed again but didn't seem too upset. She just was done with the mess.

"You said that you'd visit," Trevor reminded her. His pain was raw again. Trevor wasn't about to let her stop the truth-telling now.

"I did visit. I stayed by your side the whole time."

"Lena."

"I know, Trevor… I did visit though. I came and saw Reet twice. I saw Phoenix once. That was accidental, though," Lena chuckled, rolling her eyes at the idea.

"They never told me."

"They were told not to. They're good at keeping secrets.

Especially Alyse. We didn't talk long. They told me of the boys and you. I told them about very little of my travels, just enough for them to know I was safe and somewhat happy."

"Why do you say Alyse was particularly good at keeping secrets?"

Lena hesitated for a moment before saying, "She caught me sneaking around TNT at three in the morning one day. She walked me out like she would any other member and drove me home."

Trevor didn't respond for a moment. "She knew where you lived?"

Lena nodded. She turned onto her side to talk to Trevor more directly, finally ignoring the night sky. "She knew, but she never made a house call. She sent pictures of the kids every once in a while, or one of you or Max or the twins. Alyse kept me sane."

Trevor shook his head in amazement, placing it back on the deck. "And all the while you were right where you always had been."

Lena didn't reply. Trevor felt her head back on his chest again. For a few minutes, he enjoyed the silence and knowledge of her being there.

"Lena, should we head back?" he asked gently.

She didn't stir from her position. Trevor raised himself again to look at her. A small trail of blood was coming from her nose. She was breathing yet passed out.

He pulled himself up, careful not to move her too fast. There was no use in yelling. There was no one to hear. Trevor looked around the boat to see if there was any way he could get them back to land, but there were too many ropes, too many poles.

He pulled out his phone, but it was dead. He grabbed Lena's instead. There wasn't much signal but enough to get by. He called

Max. It went to voicemail. Same with the twins and Bianca. Finally, he called Alyse. She picked up immediately.

"Hey, the kids are sleeping. Why are you calling so late? Lena, are you okay?"

"No one else is answering. Alyse, she's sick. There's blood coming out of her nose. She passed out on the boat."

"I know where that is. I'm on my way."

"We're in the middle of the lake."

"I'll be there. Elevate her head so the blood doesn't block her nose."

"Thank you."

"I'll see you soon."

Trevor heard her hang up. He did as he was told, but he couldn't shake that Alyse wasn't surprised by anything he said. She didn't become rattled but knew exactly what to do. It was a long while before he heard the rumble of a boat in the distance.

Trevor knew she could see the well-lit boat. Alyse seemed to know more than she had ever let on. It bothered him more than he cared to admit that he wasn't as trusted as her sister-in-law. These feelings were put aside, however, when Alyse pulled her speed boat alongside their boat.

"Get her over here quickly. Be careful with her head." Alyse already had a small cot set up in the boat and a pillow positioned. There was gauze sitting next to the driver's wheel.

He ignored it for the moment. Trevor moved her over with the help of Alyse, trying to keep himself from falling into the water at the same time. Once they were securely in, he looked back at the other boat. "What about this one?"

"I'll call Reet. She'll get it for me," Alyse told him, grabbing some gauze.

"Alyse, what's happening?"

"We can discuss it at home. We need to get her back."

He nodded though he didn't like her secrecy. He trusted that she'd tell him. As Alyse directed the boat back to shore, she pulled out her phone. "Reet, can you get the boat and meet me back home? Yes, he's with me. Okay, thank you. I'll see you soon."

Chapter 44

Alyse handed him a cup of coffee while Reet tended to Lena. She sat on the other side of Lena's living room, rubbing her eyes to keep awake. She had already sent a message to her husband about where she was and could devote her whole attention to Trevor.

"What's happening, Alyse?" he demanded, not drinking the coffee in his hand.

She gave a small, sad sigh. "She has a brain tumor. There's almost no history of it in her family; time hasn't been kind to her. Her grandfather had a tumor. That's what TNT records said, anyway. His formed much later, however, and was much less severe. The stress is what caused it to form; that's what the doctors said, anyway."

"She went to doctors?"

Alyse nodded and took a drink of her own coffee. "When she was gone, she had to go. She had a seizure in the middle of the mall one day. They couldn't find her in their system if that's what you're worried about. When they asked for someone to contact, she called me. The only number she could remember, I think."

"Why didn't you tell me?"

"She didn't want anyone to know. You were with Hailey; she was gone."

Trevor shook his head, brow furrowed. "Why does Reet know?"

"I couldn't take care of her on my own. My kids needed my attention too."

"Does Max know? How did you know about the boat? How

long does she have?" He stammered out, questions finally spilling from him.

"Max doesn't know. I tell him I have a job. Lena pays me from a private account. She bought the boat years ago. When we found out about the tumor, I told her that every time she went on the boat that she had to tell me. She had to keep her phone on. Answer when I call. I've gone out there so many times. I've told her to stop." Alyse seemed so tired in that moment. It was an exhaustion he had seen in her before and attributed to her children, never imagining it could be anything else.

Trevor couldn't process it very quickly. He moved to sit next to her. "So, her forgetting things is common now?"

"Yeah, it is. It's becoming more common. Hopefully, being around you will help her. She seems to be doing better. She hasn't complained of headaches so often. The medicine helps too."

"You didn't say how long."

Alyse sat in silence for a long while. She seemed older in that moment, the grey more pronounced in her hair and the wrinkles deeper in her pretty face. "The doctors said they didn't really know. It could be a year or three."

"How long ago was that?"

"Two years ago."

He seemed to flatten, curling forward onto his own lap. His arms crossed over his head. Alyse slowly put her hand on his back. She pulled him onto her lap, where she felt him crying.

"I just got her back," he moaned softly.

Alyse felt her own eyes glazing over as she rubbed his back. "I know, Trevor. It's going to be okay. She's back now. You should be with her."

He remained there for another couple of minutes before he sat up again and wiped his face. "Thank you, Alyse. I owe a lot to you."

"Don't worry about it. Now go wash up your face and propose to that girl."

Trevor's eyes widened. "Would she say yes?" he whispered.

Alyse rolled her eyes but nodded, smiling at how unconfident he was about this. He hadn't been there when Lena had forgotten all the years and went back to planning her wedding. She watched as he went into the bathroom to splash his face with water before going to Lena's bedroom, where Reet was sitting.

Lena was awake but seemed groggy. Reet spotted him first and stood up. She squeezed Lena's hand and went back over to Trevor, whispering, "She's got a massive headache. Talk softly. Not too fast either. I gave her some medicine that will help too."

"Okay, thank you, Reet. Alyse is in the living room."

He took her spot by the bed and took Lena's hand. "How do you feel, Lena?"

"Like shit, but you're here. Did Alyse explain everything to you?"

He nodded. "She did. It was hard to hear. Why didn't you tell me?"

"I was having a fun night. I didn't want to ruin it."

"You saw Reet and Alyse many more times than once or twice then."

She smiled. "I did. I couldn't exactly tell you that, though, without explaining. I suppose I got out of that all together."

"You did. Well, almost." He pulled out the ring box he had bought earlier that day. He set it on the bedstand and opened it for her. "Please say yes."

"We don't have the time to plan a wedding," she said sadly, staring at the ring.

"We can elope for all I care. I want you to be mine for all of the time I can."

"Okay," she whispered. She smiled and squeezed his hand. "I need some sleep."

"Okay, dear. I'll stay here with you."

She yawned, closing her eyes and wincing. Lena reached up and touched her head. "Oww. Aspirin, please."

"But Reet said she already gave you medicine."

Lena groaned and rolled onto her side. "I don't remember that. Trevor, it hurts."

Trevor felt conflicted. He stood and went to the door. "Reet!"

There were shuffling feet before she appeared. "What's up?"

"Can she have more aspirin or no?" he asked, looking back at Lena, who was rubbing at her head furiously.

"She's already had quite a bit as part of her medicine. I don't want to give her any more. Lena will be fine in a couple minutes. That medicine will put her back to sleep."

"I hate seeing her like this."

"You'll get used to it in time. Just sit with her, rub her hand or neck. It calms her down," Reet suggested, looking past him. He hated that he knew he would have to get used to her pain.

"Lena, you can't run missions any more," Trevor told her again, feeling frustrated.

She looked confused as she looked up from the folder. "Of course, I can. I'm just as fit as ever. It's not fair for me to just sit around here."

"Lena, you're sick. The doctor said you shouldn't be exerting yourself. This definitely qualifies. I'm not letting you go."

"I'm Beta though. You don't have that authority."

"I do though!" he shouted, slamming his hands down on the table. "I ran this for you for ten years. I know what I'm talking about. You can't do this one. You need to focus on the wedding plans. Did you take your medicine?"

She glared at him but rubbed her head. Lena knew he was right. No matter how much she wanted to ignore her condition, too much had happened in the last month. He had helped her through too many strokes, too many sleepless nights, too many lost memories, too many fits, which reverted her back to her years with Jeff or her father.

"I don't know if I took it or not. I can't remember." She put her head in her hands, leaning on the table. "Trevor, I don't want life to change. I want my old life back."

He sighed and slumped back into the chair he had occupied when he first gave her the folder. "I know. I understand. It can't be that way, though. We have to be more careful, take care of you. I don't want to lose you sooner than I have to."

"You're not losing me. I'm losing my life. I want to enjoy what I still have left though. Please, let me do something. I don't care what. I need to have something other than a wedding."

"It's not just a wedding. It's ours and in a week. After that, we can do more. I'll give you a class to teach, sales to manage, something. Right now, I need you to do that, so I can take care of TNT."

Lena agreed finally but continued to flip through the folder. "Who should we send instead, then?"

"That's why I gave it to you."

"Well, everyone I would normally send are either new parents or have a new life because I was gone for so long. I don't know what you want me to say."

Trevor moved into a nearer chair and glanced at the folder

too. It was a low-level operation to protect some local politician that a shady cop wished to protect. He had only gotten the deal yesterday.

"Well, what type of people do you want to send?"

Lena looked at the politician's record and stature. She spotted the different specs and thought for a moment before she laid out a general plan to Trevor. They discussed for a moment before he agreed and asked her to call Squadron Thirteen.

Trevor watched her leave, feeling the worry set on him again when she was out of sight. They didn't have much longer, he knew, but that didn't make him enjoy the spats about power any more enjoyable to him. Instead, he wished they would agree on those little things to have more time available to enjoy themselves. That wasn't a part of his job description, though, and wasn't a part of their personalities.

Chapter 45

Lena sat on the bench outside the courthouse with Trevor as they stared at the document in their hands. Such an innocent piece of paper that they had waited so long to receive. They were officially married.

At forty-two, they had achieved what they had believed wouldn't happen after everything in their life. Trevor had planned to frame it on a wall somewhere where they lived, but Lena didn't want to. She said that would take too long with how little time was left.

Lena looked more ashen every day, and Trevor knew she was deteriorating fast. They had spent the previous week at TNT. Bianca told Trevor to leave, said she would take care of everything so he could spend time with Lena. He had protested at first but agreed with little persuasion.

They were to leave on a trip paid for by TNT. Avery had insisted. In ten hours, they would touch down in Hawaii and spend as much time as they wanted there. A house was provided by a member that had missions to run in the meantime. He had said that he would be proud to know he had provided them something.

Lena had spent the last day checking their bags, again and again, forgetting she had already checked them. Trevor found it both worrying and yet sweet at the same time. No matter how many times she forgot, she was still the same person as always.

He offered her his hand as they walked away from the courthouse. She accepted and laced her fingers into his as they walked toward the car.

"Trevor, I don't want you to feel required to take care of TNT after I'm gone."

"Do we need to discuss it now?" he asked.

"You never want to talk about it. We need to eventually," she reminded him.

He shook his head. "Not now."

"Why not? We avoided it for this long now. I don't have much longer left at this point, anyway. You know it too." She stopped walking, halting him as well.

"Lena, we don't have to do this now, though. Come on, let's just go to the car." He tried pulling her further, but she didn't walk with him. "Bianca's waiting to take us to the airport. We need to leave."

"No, we need to talk."

"Please, let's go to the car. We can talk there. We'll be fine."

She didn't seem to agree yet walked with him to the car either way. He was correct in that they had to make it to the airport on time. Bianca was a little way down the road in one of the grey cars Lena had bought during her time away.

Trevor pulled open her door, and Lena got into the car. She was starting to get used to him doing these things for her, acting as though she were fragile. Bianca smiled back at them.

"So, it's official now?"

"As official as it can be," Lena replied, handing her the certificate.

She looked it over briefly but didn't seem entirely interested in the paper. Bianca handed it back. Trevor took it and looked it over yet again.

"Hey, Bianca. Are you sure you don't want Beta after this?" Lena asked before they began heading to the airport.

"No, I don't want to take over," Bianca assured her.

"But you could," Lena told her.

Bianca rolled her eyes and shook her head. "I'll think about it."

Lena smiled briefly then looked back to Trevor. She muttered, "Don't think I've forgotten."

He shook his head a little, clearly a bit annoyed but not altogether surprised. Trevor offered her his hand again. She accepted as they drove toward the airport.

Bianca dropped them by the TNT jet that had been approved for the flight. She wished them well and took off as her phone began ringing from yet another member calling.

Lena boarded first and chose some seats toward the back. The member piloting briefly came back to help with their luggage and to remove the stairs from the edge of the plane before shutting the door. She nodded to the couple before returning to the front. "Should be a smooth flight. Use the earpiece if you need anything."

"Will do. Thank you, Gull," Lena replied.

Trevor sat beside her and rested his head on her shoulder. "The doctor approved flying, right? You didn't lie about that."

"I'm fine to fly. I double checked with him." Lena waited until they were airborne before returning to their previous subject. "Trevor, what will you do when I die?"

"Cry."

"Please, just tell me what you're thinking," she begged, more desperate than Trevor had seen in days.

He thought for a while before he responded. "I'll look after TNT. I don't know for how long. Maybe I could go to college, online at least. I always liked tinkering as a kid. Maybe I'd be good at it."

"I think you would be. Will you try to find someone new?"

"I'm not sure. I tried with Hailey, but it wasn't the same. She wasn't you." He turned his head to bury his nose in her shirt, enjoying the smell of her perfume.

"No one will be me. Will you try anyway?" she asked again.

"I'll try."

"Can we talk about the funeral?" Lena glanced down to see that he had closed his eyes as he spoke. She liked that. She had missed that when he was serious, he would close his eyes to think better, pinching between his eyes as though it helped.

"Sure. Promise we won't discuss this again for a while?"

"Yeah, of course." Lena felt the pang of pain in her head as she realized yet again that she would be gone soon. A while may never come.

They talked about the grim details of the funeral for a while as they continued to fly west. Lena had already decided on some of the details Trevor didn't want to decide: the casket, flowers, tombstone. It seemed to him that she was only telling him out of courtesy. He didn't mind; it wasn't like they were things he wished to figure out later.

"Can we talk about something happier now?" Trevor asked, sitting up and wiping away the wetness from his eyes.

"What would you like to talk about, then?" Lena pulled her legs up to her chest and rested her head on her knees like she had done when they were younger.

"What do you want to do first when we get there?" His eyes had lit up again as he spoke, making Lena smile.

"Well, it's Hawaii. Why not swim?"

Again, they talked, though it was happier, imagining what they would do, as though their time was infinite. Lena mentioned the lava spills while Trevor went on about surfing. It was happy until Lena had another fit. She looked dazed and couldn't remember getting married or getting on the plane.

Trevor tried to coax her down, but she wouldn't have it. Eventually, he had to give her a sedative that put her to sleep while he sat over her sadly. It was supposed to be all fun and games, yet he knew the happy times would be sprinkled with times like this, times when he couldn't recognize his Lena any more.

Lena had awoken by the time they landed. She didn't remember the fit but seemed to remember everything else. Trevor tried to ignore the incident and helped them unload. They thanked Gull and took a local taxi to their temporary house.

Trevor had them unpacked quickly, and by the time they were ready to swim, the sun had already begun to sink into the horizon. Lena didn't mind, though; she went running into the waves. Her hair flowed out behind her in the misty wind. She beckoned to Trevor, who followed her more slowly into the waves.

They stayed out until their hands were wrinkled from the ocean water and their eyes were red from the salt. Neither could care less about that, though. Instead, they acted like teenagers, running and splashing in a carefree way that neither could remember doing ever before.

Epilogue

Two months they had spent in the warm air and water of Hawaii before the inevitable happened. Trevor had held her as she died. A seizure had caused her to hit her head on a counter when he was in the bathroom. She had been cooking when it happened.

He had been soaked in blood by the time the ambulance arrived. She was gone before it arrived. Trevor had to be pulled off her, kicking and screaming by the medics. Lena was flown back to Texas for the funeral she had planned before they left.

Trevor had dressed in the black suit he had been given and did as he was told at the funeral. He didn't give a speech but had something written that Alyse read for him before her own speech. Many people spoke. She had touched many lives. Many people Trevor had never met had come, speaking right alongside the rest as he allowed everyone to come into TNT that wished to, member or not.

After the service, he had sat by her gravestone for hours. It was Bianca who had come to take him home. She had fed him and made sure he kept busy. She didn't expect him to take over TNT again yet helped him do so when he was ready.

They argued a lot, yet after a year, when he had asked her on a date, she said yes. Both worked well together and could understand their differences. No one was surprised when they began dating, nor when they got engaged and married.

Often times, when they were together, Lena would appear in conversation, and neither could deny that their connection to her kept them together. Trevor wore both wedding rings, but Bianca didn't say anything. She celebrated with him on their anniversary and cried with him on his anniversary. It was a partnership that brought them to have a child.

Her name was Delphina. Bianca had insisted on it. Trevor had been more reluctant but seemed grateful for her continued insistence, though even his daughter couldn't fill the hole.

"Delphina, come downstairs!" Bianca yelled up to the second floor. The girl was sixteen now and sassier than either her parents had expected.

"Give me a moment. So impatient," Delphina muttered, pulling her long brown hair into a tight braid as she came down the stairs. "I'm not late."

"You said you'd be down here five minutes ago. Come on, we need to go," Bianca told her only daughter angrily.

"Why do we still do this? She's been gone for twenty years now. She isn't coming back," the girl whined, slouching as she walked past.

"Excuse me? Delphina Stephens, get back here," Bianca demanded. She was nearly sixty now, hair dyed to be black, though the grey roots gave it away. Her thin frame had remained, though the bones no longer had the toned muscles and smooth skin of her youth.

Delphina walked back over. She knew she shouldn't have said it. "It's just that you're his wife. Not her. She's been gone all my life, yet we still go to a birthday party every year."

Bianca gritted her teeth but couldn't deny she didn't understand it either. "She was your father's first love and wife. Anyway, this way we get to see your uncles and cousins. Don't be saying anything like that around Dad, okay?"

Delphina nodded. Her father would have yelled at her rather than just talked to her like her mother would. It wasn't something she would get away with. Her mom wasn't wrong, though; she did enjoy seeing Uncle Tim and Dillon. Uncle Maxwell would be retelling the same old stories she had already heard, but she had to admit that she would've liked her namesake. On top of everything, though, her cousins would be back for the first time from college and spill about all the new guys they had met.

She walked behind Bianca to the car. Her father was sitting in the driver's seat. Trevor looked calm, though both knew he'd be crying again soon. He only cried during the party now. It was the one time he allowed himself to grieve any more. Delphina knew he had never really gotten over her. He loved her mother, yet something seemed different with how he talked about her namesake. He seemed younger and happier during those times.

Delphina had been right about the party. It was the same as ever, with a huge feast of food for the large family. The cake was tiered and massive, while the guests were loud and seemingly happy.

Alyse greeted them at the door, hugging each as they came through. "Trevor, Max is in the kitchen finishing up the chicken if you want to join him. Oh, Bianca, how are you? I'll come see you in a moment. Wow, Delphina, you look lovely tonight. The girls are in the living room. They were waiting to talk to you."

Each thanked her and entered the overly full house. The family had grown over the years, with each brother having at least two kids, some of which were already married and had kids of their own. Delphina always felt different around them, though. Her name seemed almost taboo around her uncles during any encounter, though they seemed to be fine with calling her Delphina.

Small remnants of the old Delphina seemed tied to her. She had been bitter when she was little about not being her own person, but, eventually, she had grown out of it. It didn't matter at school, only around the family.

The daughter of Dillon was sitting on the couch with her best friend, Uncle Timothy's youngest son. They had left for college at the end of August and only just got to come home. Both spotted her and waved her over, where they all proceeded to gossip about the start of school. It was fun until speech time. It happened every year and always followed the same track.

It didn't matter, though. They all went to the kitchen and listened to the adults raise a glass to the dead woman. Trevor went last.

"Thank you all for coming. Thank you, Maxwell and Alyse, for hosting this year. It's been another long year without her. I can only imagine what it would be like without my lovely wife and daughter. I do have one last story for the night. I don't think I've told it before. It's about my daughter."

Eyes shifted to her. Delphina hated it. She didn't want to be put on the spot like this. Luckily, her father only paused a moment to offer her a smile before continuing. His smile didn't show a hint of a joke, putting her at ease as she listened.

"Before she passed away, she and I spent her last months in Hawaii. While I didn't wish to discuss her approaching death, she didn't give me the option, as was her way." A murmur of laughter went between the adults. None of the children joined in. "We talked about my future. She wanted me to move on with my life. It was then that I spoke to her about naming my daughter after her, should I have one. She yelled at me for even proposing it."

He smiled a little as he looked at his wife. She returned the smile, though seemed intrigued. Delphina realized she hadn't heard the story. Somehow, in all their years together, in their conversations of naming her, he'd never mentioned this.

"I promised her I wouldn't name my daughter after her if I were to have one. I broke that promise for my wife. I guess I moved on a lot sooner than I thought I did. Bianca, my love, I stopped wearing her ring today for you. You have been there from the beginning, and you deserve a husband that doesn't continue to grieve the past. I love you, Bianca," he told her, raising his glass across the table to her.

Delphina looked at her mother, who had a furrowed brow and went over to him. She whispered to him for a moment before he nodded. Bianca beamed and kissed him. Her uncles cheered loudly while the kids gave a mixture of giggles and blushes. Delphina smiled a little. She had never seen her father be so happy at this party.

In that moment, she felt herself relax, as though she had been ready for something to happen all her life, as though the first Delphina would walk back into their lives and steal her father. She also felt that, even if she had, Trevor wouldn't have left this time. He had finally moved on and decided to be happy with where life had brought him, even if that didn't include Lena.

CPSIA information can be obtained
at www.ICGtesting.com
Printed in the USA
LVHW041500200723
752763LV00001B/66